The Rozabal Line

By
Shawn Haigins

ISBN: 978-1-4303-2754-7

Author's Note

This book is a work of fiction. Religion, history and factual narrative have been liberally interspersed with the fictional narrative in order to give context and colour to the plot.

Wherever possible, notes have been provided at the end of the book to explain, justify, attribute or acknowledge.

My greatest thanks are to my wife, my mother and my sister. My three pillars of the divine feminine. They are my greatest source of inspiration. My wife's suggestions regarding the plot line were often brilliant and kept me going even when I was exhausted.

My sincere and grateful thanks to Mark and Angela of Angel Editing, whose inputs and suggestions were of immense help.

My thanks to Aparna Gupta, Namita Devidayal, Vivek Ahuja, and Ritu Singh whose opinions, comments and corrections were constructive, positive, and ruthlessly sincere!

Chapter One

Srinagar, Kashmir, India, 2012

The onset of winter in idyllic Kashmir meant that the days were gradually getting shorter. Even though it was only three o'clock in the afternoon, it felt like nightfall. Icy winter winds, having wafted through the numerous apple and cherry orchards of the area, sent a spicy and refreshing aromatic chill to the man's nostrils. The leather jacket and lamb's wool pullover underneath it were his only comfort as he knelt to pray at the tomb.

Father Vincent Morgan rubbed his hands together to keep warm as he took in the sight of the four glass walls, within which lay the wooden sarcophagus. The occupant of the tomb, however, resided below in an inaccessible crypt. Standing in front of a Muslim cemetery, the tomb was located within an ordinary and unassuming structure with whitewashed walls and simple wooden fixtures.

Vincent's blonde hair, blue eyes, together with his athletic build and pale skin clearly marked him out as separate and distinct from the locals. The goatee and rimless spectacles completed the slightly academic look.

The sign outside informed visitors that the Rozabal tomb in the Kanyar district of old Srinagar contained the body of a person named Yuz Asaf. Local land records acknowledged the existence of the tomb from 112 A.D. onwards[i].

The word Rozabal, derived from the Kashmiri term *Rauza-Bal*, meant "Tomb of the Prophet". According to Muslim custom, the gravestone had been placed along the north-south axis, however, a small opening revealed the true burial chamber beneath. Here one could see the sarcophagus of Yuz Asaf, which lay along the east-west axis as per Jewish custom.

Nothing was out of the ordinary here - nothing that is except for a carved imprint of a pair of feet near the sarcophagus. The feet were normal human feet - normal, barring the fact that they bore marks on them; marks that coincided with puncture wounds from a crucifixion.

1

Crucifixion had never been practised in Asia, so it was quite obvious that the resident of the tomb had undergone this ordeal in some other, distant land.

❦

Mecca, Saudi Arabia, 2012

The thousands of male pilgrims to Mecca during the Islamic month of *Dhu-al-Hijjah* were dressed identically in *Ihram* – a simple white, unhemmed cloth. It was impossible to distinguish one pilgrim from another in the white sea of humanity.

After all, this was *Hajj*, and all of Allah's followers were meant to be equal before Him. Some, however, were more equal than others.

The simple face and ordinary features did not reveal the depth of this particular pilgrim as he performed the *Tawaf* - circling the holy *Kaaba* - swiftly four times, and then another three times at an unhurried pace.

This was Ghalib's second visit to the Kaaba. A week ago he had already been through the entire routine once. After completing the *Umrah*, Ghalib had stopped to drink water from the sacred well of *Zamzam*. He had then travelled to Medina to visit the mosque of the Prophet before performing the final three acts of Hajj - journeying over five days to the hill of Arafat, throwing stones at the devil in the city of Mina, and then returning to Mecca to perform a second Tawaf around the Kaaba.

Ghalib was praying: *Bismillah ar-rahman ar-rahim.* "Allah, the most kind and the most merciful, please do not show your legendary kindness or mercy to my enemies."

He felt refreshed. Blessed. Purified.

The *Lashkar-e-Toiba*, the Army of the Pure, had been fighting a bloody Jihad in Kashmir for the restoration of an Islamic caliphate over India. The outfit was on the radar of most intelligence agencies around the world. Ghalib, however, was not even a blip on the screen.

Unknown to most intelligence agencies, the Lashkar-e-Toiba had spun off an even more elite group within itself called the *Lashkar-e-Talatashar*, the Army of Thirteen, consisting of twelve elite holy warriors who would deem it an honour and privilege to die for the cause of Allah. They were not confined to Kashmir but scattered across the world[ii].

Their leader, the thirteenth man, was their general. His name was Ghalib.

London, UK, 2012

The Department for the Study of Religions was part of the School of Oriental and African Studies, which in turn was part of the University of London. The school boasted a vast library located in the main school building just off Russell Square.

On this damp morning, faculty librarian, Barbara Poulson, was attempting to prepare the library for its first wave of students and faculty members at the opening time of 9 a.m.

Most students would start their search on the library catalogue, which indicated whether the library had the required item. From the catalogue one could find the class mark - a reference number - of the item one wanted and this could be used to find the exact location of the book.

The previous day, Professor Terry Acton had been attempting to locate a copy of the Hindu treatise, *The Bhagavad Gita*, published in 1855 by Stephen Austin. The absentminded professor had been unable to locate it and had requested Barbara's assistance. She had promised to find it before his arrival that morning.

She mechanically typed the words "Bhagavad Gita" into the library's computer catalogue. There were only two books displayed, neither of which was the one that the professor wanted. She then recalled the professor mentioning that *The Bhagavad Gita* was actually part of a broader epic, *The Mahabharata*. She quickly typed "Mahabharata" into the computer and saw two hundred and twenty-nine entries. The twelfth entry was "The Bhagavad Gita, A Colloquy Between Krishna and Arjuna on the Divine". She clicked on this hyperlink and she had it - the book by Stephen Austin, published by

Hertford in 1855. Noting the class mark - CWML 1220 - she looked it up on the location list.

Items starting with "CWML" were located on level F in the Special Collections Reading Room. The extremely efficient Barbara Poulson headed towards level F, where she started moving in reverse serial towards CWML 1220.

CWML 1224...CWML 1223...CWML 1222...CWML 1221... CWML 1219...Where was CWML 1220?

In place of the book was a perfect, square, crimson box about twelve inches in length, width and height. It had a small, white label pasted on the front that simply read "CWML 1220".

Barbara was puzzled, but she had no time in her efficient and orderly world to ponder over things for too long. She lifted the box off the shelf, placed it on the nearest reading desk and lifted off the cardboard lid to reveal the perfectly preserved head of Professor Terry Acton, neatly severed at the neck. On his forehead was a yellow Post-It that simply read "Mark 16:16".

The cool and extremely efficient Barbara Poulson grasped the edge of the desk for support before she fainted and fell to the floor.

The passage Mark 16:16 of the New Testament reads as follows:

He that believeth and is baptized shall be saved; but he that believeth not shall be damned!

<hr />

Waziristan, Pakistan-Afghanistan Border, 2012

Waziristan was no-man's land, a rocky and hilly area on the Pakistan-Afghanistan border, and a law unto itself. Even though Waziristan was officially part of Pakistan, it was actually self-administered by Waziri tribal chiefs, who were feared warriors, as well as being fiercely independent and conservative.

The presence of the lanky, olive-skinned man wearing a simple white turban, camouflage jacket and holding a walking cane in his left hand was a little out of place in this region. The man was extremely soft-spoken and gentle in his ways. His overall demeanour was that of an ascetic not a warrior. So what was he doing in this harsh land where swords and bullets did most of the talking?

He was sitting inside a cave on a beautiful Afghan rug. His few trusted followers sat around him drinking tea. He was talking to them. 'As for the World Trade Center attack, the people who were attacked and who perished in it were those controlling some of the most important positions in business and government. It wasn't a school! It wasn't someone's home. And the accepted view would be that most of the people inside were responsible for backing a terrible financial power that excels in spreading worldwide mischief!'[iii]

'Praise be to Allah!' said one of the followers excitedly.

'We merely treat others like they treat us. Those who kill our women and our innocent, we kill their women and innocent until they desist.'

'But Sheikh, we have already achieved a sensational victory. What else is left to achieve?' asked one of his followers.

'We started out by draining their wealth through costly wars in Afghanistan. We then destroyed their security through attacks on their soil. We shall now defy the only thing that is left - their faith.'

'How?' wondered the followers.

'Ah! I have a secret weapon,' said the Sheikh in his usual hushed voice.

Vatican City, 2012

Popes had ruled most of the Italian peninsula, Rome included, for over a millennium until 1870. Disputes between the Pope and Italy had been settled by Mussolini in 1929 through three Lateran Treaties, which had established the *Stato della Citta del Vaticano*, more commonly known as The State of the Vatican City. It instantly became the world's smallest state, with an area of just 0.44 square kilometres.

His Eminence Alberto Cardinal Valerio was just one among 921 other national citizens of The Holy See but was extremely important among the 183 cardinals.

5

He now sat in his office wearing his black simar with scarlet piping and scarlet sash around his waist. The bright scarlet symbolized the cardinal's willingness to die for his faith. *To die or to kill*, thought His Eminence.

He picked up the sleek Bang & Olufsen BeoCom-4 telephone that contrasted dramatically with his Morano antique desk and asked his secretary to send in his visitor.

The young woman who entered his office had delicate features and flawless skin. It was evident that she possessed a beautiful blend of European and Oriental features. Her bright eyes shone with fervent devotion and she knelt before His Eminence.

'Bless me, Father, for I have sinned. It has been a year since my last confession.'

'Go ahead, my child,' whispered His Eminence. He motioned for her to talk by waving his podgy hand. On his ring finger sat a pigeon-blood-red Burmese ruby of 10.16 carats.

Swakilki began. 'I severed the professor's head and left it in the library as a lesson to those who mock the sanctity of Christ's suffering. He deserved it for his blasphemy.'

'And are you repentant for this terrible sin?'

'Oh my God, I am heartily sorry for having offended Thee and I detest all my sins because of Thy just punishments, but most of all because they offend Thee, my God, who art all good and deserving of all my love. I firmly resolve, with the help of Thy grace, to sin no more and avoid the near occasions of sin. Amen.'

His Eminence pondered over what she had said for a few seconds before he spoke. 'May our Lord Jesus Christ absolve you; and by His authority I absolve you from every bond of excommunication…I absolve you of your sins in the name of the Father, and the Son, and the Holy Spirit. Amen. *Passio Domini nostri Jesu Christi, merita Beatae Mariae Virginis et omnium sanctorum, quidquid boni feceris vel mail sustinueris sint tibi in remissionem peccatorum, augmentum gratiae et praemium vitae aeternae.*'[iv]

Valerio made the sign of the cross and looked squarely at the young woman. Swakilki looked up at the cardinal. He was seated on a large leather sofa in the luxurious office.

'Do you reject sin so as to live in the freedom of God's children?' asked Valerio.

'I do,' replied Swakilki.

'Do you reject Satan, father of sin and prince of darkness?'

'I do.'

'Do you believe in God, the Father Almighty, creator of heaven and earth?'

'I do.'

'Do you believe in Jesus Christ, His only Son, our Lord, who was born of the Virgin Mary, was crucified, died, and was buried, rose from the dead, and is now seated at the right hand of the Father?'

'I do.'

'Do you believe in the Holy Spirit, the Holy Catholic Church, the communion of saints, the forgiveness of sins, the resurrection of the body, and life everlasting?'

'I do.'

'Then it is time to eliminate all those who make people believe otherwise…now listen carefully…'

***

Zurich, Switzerland, 2012

In 1844 Johannes Baur opened his second hotel in Zurich, right beside the lake and with an open view of the mountains. The hotel would soon become one of the most luxurious hotels of Zurich, the Baur au Lac.

Nestled within one of the deluxe suites of the Baur au Lac, with a beautiful view of Lake Zurich, sat Brother Thomas Manning. He was quite obviously a very valued regular patron. Why else would the hotel specifically stock Brunello di Montalcino, his favourite Tuscany wine?

There was a discrete knock at the door. The brother commanded in fluent German, '*Kommen Sie herein!*' and the door opened.

The visitor was a thin, spectacled man.

Mr. Egloff was the investment advisor from Bank Leu, the oldest Swiss Bank in the world. Bank Leu had started out as Leu et Compagnie in 1755 under its first chairman, Johann Jacob Leu, Master of the Purse and later Mayor of Zurich. The bank's clients had soon included European royalty such as the Empress Maria Theresia of Austria.[v]

'Herr Egloff. Under instructions from His Eminence Alberto Cardinal Valerio, I require a sum of ten million dollars to be transferred from the Oedipus trust to the Isabel Madonna trust,' said Brother Manning.

'Very well, Brother Manning,' replied the banker.

Unknown to the outside world, the strange sounding offshore trusts managed by Herr Egloff for his clients had anagrams as the beneficiaries. Brother Manning chuckled to himself.

After all, the beneficiary of the Oedipus trust was Opus Dei and the primary beneficiary of the Isabel Madonna trust was Osama-bin-Laden.

Chapter Two

Ladakh, India, 1887
Dmitriy Novikov was tired[vi]. His expedition from Srinagar through the 3500-metre-high Zoji-la Pass into Ladakh had been exhausting in spite of several men taking on the burden of luggage and equipment. The onward trek to Leh, the capital of Ladakh, and thereon to Hemis had sapped all his energy. To make matters worse, he had injured his right leg as a result of a fall from the horse that was carrying him.

Hemis was one of the most respected Buddhist monasteries in Ladakh, and their visitor was welcomed as an honoured guest. The monks quickly carried him into their simple quarters and began tending to his injury. While he was being fed a meal of apricots and walnuts washed down by hot butter tea, he met the chief Lama of the monastery.

'I know why you are here, my son,' said the Lama. 'We too honour the Christian Son of God.'

Dmitriy was dumbfounded. He had not expected such a forthright approach. 'Would it be possible for me to see the writings that talk of Issa?' he began cautiously.

The wise Lama smiled mischievously at Dmitriy and then quietly continued, 'The soul of Buddha certainly was incarnate in the great Issa who, without resorting to war, was able to share the wisdom of our beautiful religion through many parts of the world. Issa is an honoured prophet, who took birth after twenty-two earlier Buddhas. His name, his life and his deeds are noted in the texts that you refer to. But first you must rest and allow yourself to heal.'

Dmitriy's leg was throbbing with pain. The Buddhist monks applied a wide assortment of herbal remedies and packs, but they were of little help. He attempted to ignore the pain and continue his animated conversation with the Lama.

The Lama was turning his prayer wheel when he stopped and said, 'The Muslims and Buddhists do not share commonalities. The Muslims used violence and battles to convert Buddhists to Islam. This was never the case with the Christians. They could be considered honorary Buddhists! It's truly sad to see that after having absorbed such great wisdom that Issa picked up from the Buddhists, the Christians decided to forget their roots and go further and further away from Buddhism!'

Dmitriy was sweating profusely. The Lama's words seemed to be questioning years of conventional wisdom. He realized how momentous his discovery was, but he also knew the danger of exposing his knowledge to the Western world. He would be branded a traitor and a liar. His words would be considered blasphemous. He would need to proceed carefully.

Dmitriy quickly asked again whether he would be able to see the sacred writings that the Lama was referring to. The Lama looked at him and smiled. 'Patience is a Buddhist virtue, my son,' he said. 'Patience.'[vii]

⚜

Dmitriy was as patient as could be. He waited for several days to see the writings that the Lama had spoken of, the ones about Issa. It was difficult to conceal his anticipation and he had been sorely tempted to ask for the manuscripts without further delay. Today his patience had finally paid dividend. The Lama brought him a number of ancient scrolls written in Tibetan by Buddhist historians.

An interpreter was called for and began translating the scrolls while Dmitriy attempted to make copies of them.

The scrolls told the story of a boy called Issa, born in Judea. The story went on to explain that sometime during the fourteenth year of his life, the boy arrived in India to study the teachings of the Buddhists. His travels through the country took him through Sindh, the Punjab and eventually to the south, where he studied the Vedas, the ancient Hindu texts of knowledge. However, Issa was forced to leave when he began teaching those whom the Hindu Brahmins considered "untouchables" due to the rigid caste system of Hinduism.

Issa then took refuge in Buddhist monasteries and began learning the Buddhist scriptures in Pali, the language of the Buddha. Thereafter he headed home to Judea via Persia. In Persia he made himself unpopular with the Zoroastrian priests. They expelled him into the jungles, hoping that he would be eaten alive by wild animals.

He finally reached Judea at the age of twenty-nine. Having been gone for so long, no one seemed to know him. They asked, 'Who art thou, and from what country hast thou come into our own? We have never heard of thee, and do not even know thy name.'

And Issa said, 'I am an Israelite and on the very day of my birth, I saw the walls of Jerusalem, and I heard the weeping of my brothers reduced to slavery, and the moans of my sisters carried away by pagans into captivity. While yet a child, I left my father's house to go among other nations. But hearing that my brothers were enduring still greater tortures, I have returned to the land in which my parents dwelt, that I might recall to my brothers the faith of their ancestors.'

The learned men had asked Issa, 'It is claimed that you deny the laws of Moses and teach the people to desert the temple of God.'

And Issa had replied, 'We cannot demolish what has been given by our Heavenly Father and what has been destroyed by sinners. As for the Moses Laws, I have striven to re-establish them in the heart of men, and I say to you that you are in ignorance of their true meaning, for it is not vengeance, but forgiveness that they teach.'[viii]

Dmitriy was excited. Then petrified. He knew that there was no going back on his discovery. He now knew that he held in his hands one of the most stunning revelations in two millennia.

A revelation about Issa, the Arabic form of the Hebrew name *Yeshua*, also known as *Jesus*.

Chapter Three

Srinagar, Kashmir, India, 1975
The house of Rashid-bin-Isar was overflowing with joy. His wife, Nasira, had just delivered a baby boy. The proud father had announced that he would feed all the poor and homeless in the city for a week. Large vats filled with lamb *biryani*, a local spicy and aromatic rice dish, overflowed into the streets as beggars and street children flocked to Rashid's home to feast.

Rashid cradled his firstborn in his arms as he recited the Islamic prayers, *Adhan* in the right ear and *Iqaamah* in the left ear of the child, as he awaited the *Khittaan*, the ritual circumcision.

Father and son appeared on the balcony a few moments later as cheers erupted from the throngs in the street. 'I want all of you to bless my son. By the will and grace of Allah, he will be great. His name shall be *Ghalib* - which means "the Victorious One"!'

❧

Gulmarg, Kashmir, India, 1985
Ten years later, the members of the Indian Army who burst into the weekend home of Rashid-bin-Isar were convinced that he had financed the activities of those responsible for the bomb blast in the market the previous day.

He pleaded his innocence, but his cries and protestations were to no avail. His terror-stricken family watched as their beloved *Abba* was arrested on the spot.

He was quickly handcuffed and dragged away to prison, where he was punched and kicked till he could barely see, hear, talk, or walk. The next day he was found hanging in his cell; he had used his own clothes to fashion the noose around his neck.

The family had been allowed to take away his body to give him a burial. As per Islamic custom, in preparation for burial, the family was expected to wash and shroud the body. However, this step was to be omitted if the deceased had died a martyr;[ix] martyrs were to be buried in the very clothes that they had died in. Rashid-bin-Isar was going to be buried in the very clothes that he had died in because he was no less than a martyr.

The mourners carried his body to the burial ground where the Imam began reciting the funeral prayers, the *Salat-i-Janazah*. Prayers over, the men carried the body to the gravesite. Rashid's body was laid in the grave without a coffin, as per custom, on his right side, facing Mecca.

Standing by the grave was little ten-year-old Ghalib, tears streaming down his cheeks. The Imam placed his hands on Ghalib's shoulders and said, 'Son, you should not cry. You are the son of a hero. Your father's death was not in vain. You will avenge his death. Henceforth, you shall not shed tears. You shall shed blood!'

Little Ghalib was confused. How could he possibly take revenge? He was merely a ten-year-old boy.

'Come with me, my son,' said the Imam, and taking Ghalib by the hand he led him to the mosque. The next day, the Imam journeyed across the Line of Control to get to Muzaffarabad on the Pakistani side of Kashmir. Here the boy was enrolled into the *Jamaat-ud-Dawa Madrasah*, an Islamic school of learning.

The lanky, olive-skinned Imam wearing a simple white turban bid him goodbye. 'See me after you have completed your studies,' he said simply.

⟡

Muzaffarabad, Pakistan, 1986

During the next few years in Pakistan, Ghalib would go through two separate courses of study. In the *Hifz* course, he would memorize the holy Qur'an. In the *'Aalim* course he would study the Arabic language, Qur'anic interpretation, Islamic law, the sayings and deeds of the prophet Muhammad, logic and Islamic history. At the end of his study, he would be awarded the title of *'Aalim*, meaning scholar.

One day, when he was in his Islamic history class, his teacher told them about the Islamic conquests of India.

'The first was the invasion by Mohammed-bin-Qasim in the seventh century. This was followed by the eleventh-century incursions of Muhammad of Ghazni. Ghazni was followed by Mohammed Ghori, who left India to be ruled by his Turkish generals. Then came the attacks by the Mongol hordes of Chenghiz Khan. 1398 A.D. saw one of the most successful attacks under Timur,' said the teacher.[x]

Little Ghalib argued, 'But none of these people stayed in India. They were mostly interested in looting rather than ruling.'

Whack! The cane was swift on his palm.

'You must never say that again. Babar invaded India in 1526 and established Mughal rule over India for the next hundred years. In fact, it was God's will that India be ruled by Muslims. Till then, Hindus had continued to indulge in idolatry. The Muslim invasions made them realize the greatness of Islam!'

'So why do Muslims not rule over Kashmir today?' asked Ghalib.

'This is the reason that you must fight,' explained the teacher. 'It is your duty to do so. Fight a Jihad to restore Islamic rule over Kashmir and then over the whole of India!'

'Allah-o-Akbar!' shouted the teacher.

'Allah-o-Akbar!' shouted the children in unison, including little Ghalib.

Waziristan, Pakistan-Afghanistan Border, 2012

The lanky, olive-skinned Imam wearing the simple white turban who had escorted the ten-year-old was now Ghalib's controller. Everyone simply called him *Sheikh.*

He was sitting on a beautiful Afghan rug inside his cave in Waziristan, located on the Pakistan-Afghanistan border.

On his right sat Ghalib-bin-Isar, the young, thirty-something leader of the Lashkar-e-Talatashar. He was here with his army of the dirty dozen.

The host first looked at Ghalib. He then swept a glance at Ghalib's men - Boutros, Kader, Yahya, Yaqub, Faris, Fadan, Ataullah, Tau'am, Adil, Shamoon, Yehuda, and Fouad. Each of these veterans had crossed the Khyber Pass from different parts of the world and had enrolled in the Khalden camp run by Al-Qaeda as fresh recruits, and were now toughened and battle-ready.

Khalden was a mishmash of tents and rough stone buildings. It used to take in about a hundred recruits at a time. Each group consisted of Muslims from Saudi Arabia, Jordan, Yemen, Algeria, France, Germany, Sweden, Chechnya and Kashmir. Ironically, the Al-Qaeda Khalden Camp used teaching and training methods originally adopted by the American CIA to train the Mujahideen guerrillas to fight the Soviets.[xi] Even text books in Arabic, French and English on terror techniques had been made available for the recruits, courtesy of the CIA.

Each morning at Khalden, the group would be called to parade and then asked to pray. After the morning meal, they would go through endurance training followed by strength training. They would also be taught hand-to-hand combat using a variety of knives, alternative forms of garrottes and other weapons. They would learn to use small firearms, deadly assault rifles and even grenade launchers. The science of explosives and landmines was also part of their study. Representatives of Islamic terror groups, such as Hamas, Hezbollah and Islamic Jihad would regularly visit the camp in order to teach the recruits more about the practical applications of their knowledge.

The final result of the efforts at the Khalden Camp had been this elite Army of Thirteen, the *Lashkar-e-Talatashar*.

The Sheikh was happy with the output. These men would help him teach the whole world of infidels a lesson that they would not forget. 9/11 would seem like a tea party in comparison.

It was time to re-establish the supremacy of the Islamic Caliphate.

Chapter Four

Osaka, Japan, 1972

On March 9th, Pink Floyd performed live at the Festival Hall in Osaka. Among those in attendance was a pretty young woman, Aki Ogawa. She had a job in the large Daimaru store in the Shinsaibashi district of the city but was now on leave because she was eight months pregnant. The concert tickets were a present from her friends at the store.

Pink Floyd's *Dark Side of the Moon* was a big hit with the Japanese youth attending the concert. The show was reaching its finale when Aki felt her water break. Her friends rushed her to Osaka National Hospital, where the doctors performed an emergency caesarean section.

Her daughter, Swakilki, arrived six weeks short of a normal forty-week pregnancy. Luckily she weighed five pounds, was 12.6 inches tall, and had fairly well developed lungs, enabling her to survive.

On Swakilki's sixth birthday, her mother threw a party. Aki entertained the guests inside the cramped shoebox home while one of her friends took little Swakilki to the garden for some fresh air. As she cuddled the little girl in her arms, she felt the shock from the hot blast that ripped through Aki Ogawa's home.

The cause of the explosion would later be diagnosed as an accident - a gas leak.

It was indeed a gas leak; accident it was not.

Yes, Swakilki was indeed a survivor. Born without a father and alive without a mother.

Tokyo, Japan, 1987

Orphaned at the age of six, Swakilki had been transferred to the Holy Family Home, an Osaka orphanage run by kind, gentle and caring nuns. She would spend the next six years here.

She was one of the "lucky" ones to get adopted at the age of twelve by a fairly well off couple in Tokyo. What she could not have known was that the adoption would come at a price. Little Swakilki was abused and raped by her adoptive father at the age of fourteen; he said that it was their "special little secret".

Scared and confused, she ran away a year later to take up a job in an *Oppaipabu*, one of the sleazy establishments on the outskirts of Tokyo where customers were allowed to fondle the female staff to their heart's content. It was at the Oppaipabu that she met an older man, Takuya.

She shared his bed on the first night they met, and he shared with her his knowledge of *anandamides*.

<hr/>

Anandamides are naturally occurring neurotransmitters in the brain whose chemical make-up is very similar to Cannabis. The word "anandamide" is derived from the Sanskrit word *ananda*, which means bliss.

Swakilki learnt how to experience the rush of anandamides within her brain when she killed. She then learnt how to make men experience the same rush when she had sex with them.

Takuya trained her well over the next few years. First came the techniques of killing - suffocating, strangling, drowning, garrotting, poisoning, exploding, shooting, stabbing, castrating and ritual disembowelling.

Next were the techniques of seduction. Tantric sex and the Kama Sutra became her daily study rituals. Self-grooming, dressing, conversation, cuisine and wine selection were next on the menu.

The friendship between Takuya and Swakilki was one of mutual dependence. Takuya was closely linked to *Aum Shinrikyo*, a lethal religious cult. He was a member of a small group that carried out assassinations of important and influential people who were considered enemies of Aum Shinrikyo. Swakilki was an ideal recruit. She was gorgeous, sexy, ruthless and, most important, emotionally barren. The final product was sexy, seductive, sultry, silent, and sharp. Razor sharp.

Her first assignment would be Murakami-san.

Tokyo, Japan, 1990

Swakilki and Murakami-san had dined at a very expensive *Kaiseki* restaurant. Kaiseki cuisine was historically vegetarian owing to its Zen origin, though not anymore. Only the freshest seasonal ingredients were utilized, and these were cooked in a delicate style aimed at enhancing their original flavours. Each dish was exquisitely prepared and carefully presented along with elaborate garnishes of leaves and flowers.

They were now in his penthouse on the top floor of a skyscraper in the neon-filled district of Shunjuku in northwest Tokyo. They lay completely naked on the king-sized bed; she had worn him out completely. Swakilki knew some of the finest techniques in the art of pleasuring a man. Her petite frame, perfectly rounded breasts and delicate features only accentuated her oozing sex appeal.

She had just finished giving him a tantric blowjob. She had taken Murakami through several waves of near orgasm using different styles of stroking and stimulation. She knew that after coming close to orgasm a few times, most men experienced very strong and sometimes very lengthy orgasms.

The art of *tantra* had taught her that it was possible for a man to experience the feeling of orgasm without actually ejaculating.[xii] The trick was to stop the flow of semen before it reached the penis. By pressing firmly on a secret spot near the base of his penis, she was able to make him experience the feeling of orgasm without actually ejaculating. She had made Murakami experience several of these "dry" orgasms in a row. When she allowed him a final release, the actual orgasm was so intense that it was a full body tremor lasting over a minute.

It was thus no surprise to Swakilki that the ancient Indian sex treatise, the *Kama Sutra*, was still a bestseller even though its author, Vatsyayana, had written it way back in 600 A.D.

She looked at Murakami-san, who was gently snoring and sleeping like a contented baby. Quietly she lifted her pillow and brought it down upon his face. It was time for Murakami-san to sleep more deeply.

⟨❧⟩

Tokyo, Japan, 1993

Seishu Takemasa was sound asleep.

Swakilki had just given Seishu a hot, sensual mineral bath in the luxurious sunken marble tub of the Imperial Suite.

The legendary grande dame of Tokyo, the Imperial Hotel, had 1057 rooms, including sixty-four suites which were mostly reserved for statesmen, royalty and celebrities.

Seishu Takemasa was all of the above. His proximity to His Imperial Majesty Akihito, the 125th Emperor of Japan, was well known. He was also close to the political establishment, including three successive prime ministers - Tsutomu Hata, Tomiichi Murayama and Ryutaro Hashimoto. His photographs with Madonna, Oprah, Prince Charles, Bill Gates, Tom Cruise and Bill Clinton appeared regularly in the society pages.

Over the years, Swakilki had grown even more attractive. She was built like a beautiful and graceful Japanese doll. Her pale ivory skin was flawless. Her dark black hair had just a hint of auburn and cascaded down all the way to the curve of her hips. Her face was exquisite, with deep pools for eyes, an aquiline nose and delicate but full lips. She looked every inch a princess.

After giving Seishu a hot sensual mineral bath, she began to massage him. Her intention was to tune him inward while deepening his awareness. Her knowledge of tantra allowed her to focus on all the seven *chakras*, the nerve centres, starting from the base of his spine, to his genitals, onward to his belly, upward to his heart, further on to his throat, northward to his forehead - the proverbial third eye - and finally to the top of his head. Her pampering ministrations had turned him into soft clay that she could mould in any way that she wanted.

Her present focus was on his G-spot and his prostate gland. These were purportedly the access points for *Kundalini* energy, which was supposed to lead to enlightenment.

As she massaged him, he began experiencing a deep emotional release. Tears ran down his cheeks. He was laughing. Then crying. It was wave after wave of immense pleasure. He looked up at her gentle smiling face to express his gratitude for her incredible skills.

He barely noticed the flash of the extremely sharp razor as it gently slit his throat.

❧

Osaka, Japan, 1995

On March 20th, 1995, during the morning rush hour, ten members belonging to the Aum Shinrikyo cult boarded five trains at different stations. At a predetermined time, they punctured bags of sarin gas. Twelve people died and thousands were incapacitated.

The Japanese police thought that the attack had been perpetrated by ten members of the gang. It had actually been twelve.

Osaka, Japan's third largest city with a population of 2.5 million, was the economic powerhouse of the Kansai region. Higashi-Osaka, or East Osaka, was a residential suburb and its industrial district produced electric appliances, machinery, clothing fibre, and paper. It had also produced Swakilki and Takuya.

Takuya had been born in 1955, the same year as Asahara Shoko, the notorious founder of the Aum Shinrikyo sect. Like Asahara, he had failed the entrance exam at Tokyo University and had turned to studying acupuncture. Both Asahara and Takuya had joined *Agonshu*, a new religion that stressed liberation from "*bad karma*" via meditation. Asahara had visited India in 1986 and upon his return to Japan claimed to have attained enlightenment in the Himalayas. He had named his new group Aum Shinrikyo.[xiii]

In *Aum*, a believer could eliminate bad karma by enduring various sufferings. As a result, members of the cult were free to justify the abuse of other members.

As Asahara's cult grew, so did his power and wealth. All new entrants had to sever ties with their families and contribute their wealth to the cult. Aum Shinrikyo became infamous for bloody initiations, involuntary donations, threats and extortion. Takuya was the brains and muscle behind many of these activities, although purely for commercial motivations.

As Asahara became crazier, he felt the need to convince the world that an apocalypse was about to happen and that he was the world's only salvation. In 1994 he ordered clouds of sarin gas to be released in the Kita-Fukashi district of Matsumoto. This was soon followed by the horrible train attack.

Asahara was eventually found hiding in a secret room in the village of Kamikuishiki. He had in his possession a huge amount of cash and gold bars. Many of his followers were also found - comatose, under the influence of pentobarbital, an anaesthetic. Asahara and 104 followers were indicted.

Two were not.

Unlike the others, Swakilki and Takuya had been with Asahara for commercial reasons alone. They had no emotional or spiritual ties to Asahara or to Aum Shinrikyo, and they were now free to do as they pleased.

Tel-Aviv, Israel, 1995
On November 4th, 1995, Yitzhak Rabin, the Prime Minister of Israel, was assassinated by Yigal Amir, a right-wing activist. The popularly accepted version of the killing was that the assassin had felt betrayed by Rabin's signing of the Oslo Accord, which prompted him to take Rabin's life.[xiv]

No one knew of the two other international conspirators who had taken the Thai Airways flight 643 from Tokyo to Bangkok and the connecting El Al flight 84 from Bangkok to Tel Aviv.

Madrid, Spain, 1988

Lopez Tomas, President of the Spanish Constitutional Court, was in his office at Madrid Autonomous University when a gunman rushed into his office and shot him at point-blank range.

The commonly accepted view was that the Basque separatist group, E.T.A., was behind his murder.

The camera slinging Asian couple that had arrived in Frankfurt on Lufthansa's flight 711 from Tokyo had not bothered to shoot any photographs in Germany. Instead, they had taken the connecting Spanair flight 2582 to Madrid the very same day.

There had been much more to shoot in Madrid.

Dushanbe, Tajikistan, 2001

On October 27th, Otakhon Khairollayev, a journalist of repute from Tajikistan, was shot dead at point-blank range. The same day a Japanese woman had entered the capital, Dushanbe, wearing an Afghan burqa.

Asuncion, Paraguay, 2002

On June 27th, Luis Santa Cruz, the finance minister of Paraguay, was gunned down in his car. He had been a likely candidate for President.

A Japanese woman had been visiting all the tourist spots, including Asuncion for a week around the same time.

Athens, Greece, 2005

On June 16th, David Roberts, a British military attaché in Athens was shot dead by gunmen on motorcycles who belonged to N17, the Marxist revolutionary organization. A newly married honeymooning couple from Japan had been on a cruise of the Greek islands at that time.

Manila, Philippines, 2007

On February 26th, Filemon Montinola, an upcoming left-leaning politician in the Philippines, was assassinated.

A young Japanese woman visited the Minor Basilica of the Immaculate Conception, more commonly known as the Manila Cathedral in order to light a candle the next day.

Belgrade, Serbia, 2010

On May 9th, Draginja Djindjic, the foreign minister of Serbia, was shot twice in the chest at 11:28 a.m. inside a government building. His assassin, Vojislav Jovanović, had fired the bullets from another building in the area. The same building had been visited by a Japanese woman that morning.

Yes, business was good for Swakilki and Takuya. They could now work entirely for themselves, given the fact that Asahara and Aum Shinrikyo were history. It also seemed that no one was really looking for them.

Actually, someone was looking for them.

His name was Alberto Valerio.

Vatican City, 2012

Alberto Valerio was busy reading a dissertation by the renowned scholar Professor Terry Acton, head of the Department for the Study of Religions, at the University of London. The good doctor had built up a cogent case to prove that Jesus Christ had not died on the cross at all.

Cardinal Alberto Valerio took a sip of his Valpolicella, and continued reading:

If the vested interests of the temple Jews had wanted to kill Jesus, they had the power to do so by stoning him to death without taking any permission from Rome. Why did this not happen?

Instead, Jesus was punished by the Romans under Roman law and then crucified - a punishment meted out to enemies of the Roman Empire. Why punish a man under Roman law if he had no political agenda and only a religious one?

Under Roman law, he would have first been flogged, causing a significant loss of blood. In this weakened state, his arms would have been fastened by thongs or nails to a solid wooden beam placed across his shoulders and neck. He would then have been made to walk to the final place of crucifixion while continuing to bear the weight of this beam.

At the place of crucifixion, the horizontal beam would have been attached to a vertical one, with the victim still hanging. Thus suspended, the victim would have been able to survive for a couple of days provided that his feet remained fixed to the cross. His feet remaining fixed would have enabled him to keep breathing by reducing the pressure on his chest.

Eventually the victim would have died from exhaustion, thirst or blood poisoning caused by the nails. The victim's protracted agony could have been brought to an end by breaking his knees, causing the entire pressure to shift to the victim's chest, resulting in immediate asphyxiation. Thus, contrary to popular opinion, the breaking of the knees was not malicious - in fact, it was an act of mercy. Jesus' knees were never broken, yet he died within a few hours on the cross. Why?

During his suspension from the cross, Jesus said that he was thirsty. Popular opinion tells us that he was sadistically offered a sponge soaked in vinegar instead of one soaked in water. It is worthwhile to note that vinegar was used to revive exhausted slaves on ships. In fact, the vinegar should have revived him temporarily. Instead he spoke his final words and died immediately upon inhaling the vinegar fumes. Why did it have the opposite effect on him?

There is one possible explanation. The sponge may not have contained vinegar. Instead it may have contained a compound of belladonna and opium. This would have made Jesus pass out completely, only making it appear that he was dead. This would have prevented the guards from carrying out the final act of breaking his knees, thus leading to actual death from asphyxiation.

Roman law specifically prohibited bodies of crucified victims being given back to the family. Bodies were meant to remain on the cross to decay or to be consumed by birds of prey. Why did Pontius Pilate, the Roman governor of Judea, decide to ignore Roman law and allow Jesus' body to be handed over for burial to Joseph of Arimathea?[xv]

Cardinal Alberto Valerio smiled a contented smile as he took another measured sip of his delightful Valpolicella. It was time to send another heretic to burn in hell!

Cardinal Alberto Valerio was a jovial, rotund and gregarious individual. His smiling eyes, his pink face and his Buddha-belly gave him the demeanour and appearance of a jolly Santa Claus. The position that he occupied, however, was sombre and serious. He was head of the *Archivio Segreto Vaticano*, the Secret Archives of the Vatican.

The Vatican Secret Archives were the central repository for all documents that had been accumulated by the Roman Catholic Church over many ages. The Archives, containing thirty miles of bookshelves, had been closed to outsiders by Pope Paul V in the seventeenth century and they had remained closed till the nineteenth century.

Alberto Valerio had been born in 1941 in Turin. Ordained in 1964, he had soon been offered his first appointment in the Roman Curia and had rapidly risen through various positions in the Sacred Congregation for Seminaries and Universities till he had eventually become its undersecretary in 1981.

After taking some time off to pursue a doctorate in theology from the Catholic University of Leuven in Belgium, he had returned to the Vatican to become Secretary for the *Congregazione per le Chiese Orientali*, the Congregation for the Oriental Churches, at which time he had travelled extensively within Japan. He had held several positions within the Curia till he was given charge of the Archivio Segreto Vaticano, a position that he relished immensely.

What was common knowledge was his membership in the Priestly Society of the Holy Cross, an association of the clergy who were completely supportive of Opus Dei and its activities; his Eminence Alberto Cardinal Valerio was one of them. What was not common knowledge was Valerio's membership of the *Crux Decussata Permuta.*[xvi]

He picked up the Bang & Olufsen telephone on his antique Morano desk and began to dial. +81…3…

After a few rings a female voice answered at the other end. His Eminence began '*Ohaya gozaimasu…*' in fluent Japanese. 'I have an assignment for you. Can you meet me in London sometime in the next two days?'

'*Hai, wakarimasu,*' said Swakilki respectfully. 'Where shall I meet you?'

'The Dorchester. We'll meet in my suite.'

'*Domo arigato gozaimasu.*'

'God bless you, my child.'

Swakilki looked across the table at Takuya as she put the phone down.

She remembered the Sisters of Charity of St. Vincent de Paul who had taken such good care of her during her six years at the Holy Family orphanage in Osaka. She also remembered the jovial Santa Claus who had brought candy for all the kids in the orphanage in 1983. She had always thought of him as Santa Clause ever since; his real name of course had been Alberto Valerio.

He had taken special interest in her due to his personal friendship with Swakilki's late mother. After her adoption she had continued to receive postcards from him for the next two years, but she had lost contact with him after she ran away from her abusive adoptive father. He had somehow managed to track her down several years later. She had confessed her plight to him, revealing the most intimate details of her life. He had then said to her, 'I absolve you from your sins in the name of the Father, and of the Son, and of the Holy Spirit.'

Swakilki could only remember how relieved she had been to unburden herself to him. Henceforth she would no longer kill for Aum Shinrikyo.

Only for Christ.

<hr />

London, UK, 2012
Virgin Atlantic's flight 901 from Tokyo's Narita airport took off on the dot at 11 a.m. and landed at London Heathrow a few minutes before the scheduled arrival time of 3:30 p.m. local time. On board in Virgin's Upper Class cabin was a Japanese couple who had spent the entire twelve-and-a-half-hour flight sleeping soundly.[xvii]

They had not asked for any reading material, nor did they turn on the personal entertainment screens. When the elaborate dinner consisting of shrimp with fish roe, zucchini in miso paste, egg yolk crabmeat rolls, buckwheat noodles and green tea, began to be served, they continued to sleep. They were certainly the freshest passengers to emerge from the Airbus aircraft in London.

Just another camera-slinging Japanese tourist couple, the immigration officer thought of Mr. and Mrs. Yamamoto while cursorily checking their passports. The landing cards that they had filled in on the flight indicated that they were staying for a week at the Grosvenor House Hotel on Park Lane. He stamped their passports matter-of-factly and waved them through.

They had no checked-in luggage, only onboard strollers, so they did not need to wait at the conveyor belts that were being crowded by hundreds of bleary-eyed passengers. Instead, they passed through the green channel at Heathrow's Terminal Three and walked straight through the arrival area to the taxi departure point without raising any suspicion. There were four London cabs waiting and they got into the first one in line.

'Where to, guv?' asked the cheerful cabbie.

'The London Hilton on Park Lane, please,' came the reply. Not the Grosvenor House.

At the reception desk of the London Hilton, the uninterested blonde required their passports and a credit card. Mr. Hiro Ogawa was happy to give her two passports, one belonging to him and one to his wife, along with a Visa card.

Upon reaching their room on the Executive Floor, Swakilki took off her curly wig and Takuya removed his clear-glass spectacles and his neat little moustache. They got out of their casual travelling clothes and showered vigorously before putting on fresh formals. They then took the elevator from the club floor to the lobby and walked out of the hotel onto Park Lane, turned right, and walked from the Hilton at 22 Park Lane, to 54 Park Lane, which housed The Dorchester Hotel, just a few blocks away.

Once there they were to receive their formal assignment from His Eminence Alberto Cardinal Valerio.

Chapter Five

New York City, U.S.A., 1969

On July 20th, the first television transmission from the moon was viewed by 600 million people around the world. Matthew Morgan sat riveted on a well-worn sofa and watched Neil Armstrong become the first man to walk on the moon. Also watching the incredible spectacle was his wife Julia, along with their three-week-old baby boy, Vincent Matthew Morgan.

Another important event had taken place a year before Neil Armstrong's arrival on the moon and little Vincent's arrival on Earth. Terence Cardinal Cooke had become the archbishop of New York. On the day of Cooke's installation, Martin Luther King Jr. was assassinated, leading to bloody riots in many American cities.[xviii]

Cooke's tenure as archbishop would be difficult. Between 1967 and 1983 the number of diocesan priests in New York would decline by around thirty percent, infant baptisms would fall by around forty percent, and church weddings would decline by around fifty percent. It seemed that Catholicism was quickly going out of fashion in New York.

In the midst of this turmoil within the archdiocese of New York, the Morgans, who were extremely religious, hoped that their son would eventually make them proud by entering Saint Joseph's Seminary.

Vincent's demeanour, even as a child, was one of piety and the priesthood seemed preordained.

Thus it was preordained by God and ordained by his parents that Vincent would become one of the rapidly shrinking minority groups - that of diocesan priests.

⁕

New York City, U.S.A., 1979

Vincent Morgan at the age of ten was just another kid. He was playing with Kate, the neighbour's daughter, in the backyard. They were on a swing that his father, Matthew, had rigged to a sturdy branch of a strong tree in the yard. Vincent had already had a go at sitting on the swing and being pushed by Kate, it was now her turn to sit and be pushed.

Boys will be boys. A mischievous glow was on Vincent's face as he began pushing the swing for Kate. As the momentum increased, he found that he could send her higher and higher into the air with less and less effort. The resultant effect was a look of panic on Kate's innocent face.

Pushing was certainly more fun than being pushed.

Then the inevitable happened. The final push was too strong and Kate lost her balance. Poor little Kate fell to the ground and grazed her knee. Vincent's mother, Julia, and his aunt, Martha, ran out to apply an anti-bacterial ointment for the little girl, who was lying on the ground with tears streaming down her rosy cheeks.

Vincent was standing next to her, feeling apologetic and offering his hand to help her up.

While holding out his hand, he was repeating the words, *'Talitha Koum. Talitha Koum. Talitha Koum.'*

The Biblical passage of Mark 5:41 reads as follows:

He came to the synagogue ruler's house, and he saw an uproar, weeping, and great wailing. When he had entered in, he said to them, 'Why do you make an uproar and weep? The child is not dead, but is asleep.'

They ridiculed him. But he, having put them all out, took the father of the child, her mother, and those who were with him, and went in where the child was lying. Taking the child by the hand, he said to her, 'Talitha koum!' which means, 'Girl, I tell you, get up!' Immediately the girl rose up and walked, for she was twelve years old.[xix]

New York City, U.S.A. 1989
Four years of high school, four years of college and four years of theology later, Vincent Matthew Morgan would be called to ordination by the archbishop at St. Patrick's Cathedral.

Construction of St. Patrick's Cathedral, located on 50th Street and 5th Avenue in the heart of Manhattan, had been completed in 1879. However, it was only in 1989 that the cathedral received a new amplification system as well as modernized lighting. Due to this technology upgrade, Father Vincent Morgan's ordination to the Roman Catholic priesthood was seen and heard clearly by all who were present.

Present among the crowd were two very proud parents, Julia and Matthew Morgan as well as a bored but dutifully present aunt, Martha Morgan.

His Eminence John Cardinal O'Connor, the Archbishop, had imposed his hands on Vincent's head and had repeated the words from Psalm 110:4 'Thou art a priest forever after the order of Melchizedek!'

This marked the beginning of Vincent's new life as a diocesan priest in the Church of Our Lady of Sorrows in White Plains, New York. His duties included celebrating Mass on Sundays and other days, hearing confessions, anointing the sick, baptizing newborns, marrying the marriageable and burying the dead.

Besides his church duties, Vincent also began teaching history to a class of catholic boys at the nearby Archbishop Stepinac High School.

***

White Plains, New York, U.S.A., 1990
The school's oldest fixture was a grizzly old janitor, Ted Callaghan. On Vincent's first day at school, Ted had cornered him in the schoolyard. 'Father, can I ask you some questions regarding some serious matters that have been bothering me?' asked Ted slyly.

Without waiting for an answer, Ted plodded on, 'You see, the Bible's Leviticus 15:19-24 tells me that I am allowed no contact with a woman while she is in her period of menstrual uncleanliness. Problem is, how do I tell? I have tried asking, but most women take offence!'

Vincent chuckled.

Ted, blowing an ugly puff of acrid smoke from a cheap cigar, continued with his "serious" issues. 'Also, Father, Exodus 21:7 allows me to sell my daughter into slavery. What do you think would be a fair price?'

Vincent was getting the idea.

Pretty much oblivious to Vincent's reactions, Ted went on, 'Leviticus 25:44 also says that I may possess slaves, both male and female, provided that they're from neighbouring countries. Do you think this applies to both Mexicans and Canadians?'

By now Vincent was laughing uncontrollably. Ted paused for effect and then continued, 'I have a neighbour who insists on working on the Sabbath. Exodus 35:2 clearly states that he should be put to death. Am I morally obliged to kill him?'[xx]

Ted reached the climax of his joke and guffawed loudly as he delivered his punch line while dramatically brandishing the now dead cigar stub in his hand. Vincent couldn't help doubling up with laughter. From that day onwards, Ted and Vincent were firm friends.

White Plains, New York, U.S.A., 2006

They would remain pals for the next sixteen years that Vincent remained ensconced in his uneventful little world. However, things were about to change.

'So when we think of Abraham Lincoln as the 16th President of the United States, we often forget that he worked on a riverboat, ran a store, thought about becoming a blacksmith and studied law. We tend to forget that he was unsuccessful in many of his pursuits. He lost several law cases, lost the effort to become the Republican Party's vice presidential nominee, and lost again when he ran against Stephen Douglas for the U.S. Senate. The important thing to remember is that he didn't let these defeats stop him. He ran for President in 1860 and won,' concluded Vincent.[xxi]

The boys were impatiently waiting to get up. The bell announcing lunch break had sounded a full thirty seconds earlier, but Vincent's concluding remarks had overrun. He hastily picked up his books and headed to the staff lounge, where stale coffee awaited him.

The coffee was a small price to pay for a job that he now loved. There was nothing more refreshing than opening up young minds. Moreover, he was passionate about his subject. This passion allowed him to transport his young audience into times bygone with flair. It was no wonder that Vincent had become one of the most admired teachers at Stepinac High.

Vincent had been able to settle down in Westchester quite easily. His parishioners at the church were decent people and his flock continued to grow along with his own stature within the diocese. His casual and comfortable style had immediately put people at ease within the first months of his arrival.

After one of his Sunday sermons, one of the middle-aged male attendees had come up to him and had congratulated him for a "short and sweet sermon, so unlike the long and boring ones delivered by his predecessor". Vincent had quickly retorted that a sermon was meant to be like a woman's skirt, long enough to cover the essentials and short enough to keep one interested! The word had soon got around that the new boy was actually quite a lot of fun, in spite of being celibate!

The coffee that greeted him was stale but hot at least. He had just settled down in one of the armchairs in the lounge and opened his newspaper when janitor-of-the-year Ted Callaghan walked in.

'Phone for you, Vincent,' he said.

Vincent looked up and asked, 'Who's calling?'

'Dunno. Probably some chick that you blessed with holy water,' chuckled Ted.

Vincent ignored the sarcasm and got up to take the call at the phone located near the lounge entrance. He picked up the receiver and spoke, 'Hello?'

'Is that Mr. Vincent Morgan?' asked the female voice at the other end.

'Yes, it is. Who's calling?'

'I'm Dr. Joan Silver from Lenox Hill Hospital. I'm afraid I have some bad news for you.'

Vincent was immediately alert. He knew that something was seriously wrong. He pressed on, 'Please do go on.'

'Mr. Morgan, this morning at around 8 a.m., a car accident took place. Your father died on the spot I'm afraid. Your mother suffered head wounds but by the time she arrived here, it was too late. She was dead on arrival.'

Father Vincent Matthew Morgan let go of the receiver and knelt down to pray, but he was unable to; all he could do was weep.

***

Queens, New York, U.S.A., 2006

In 1852, a city law forbade burials within Manhattan. Manhattanites could be born in Manhattan, could study or work in Manhattan, could get married in Manhattan, could die in Manhattan, but they could not get buried in Manhattan.[xxii]

The rain made the burial a rather messy affair. Both Matthew and Julia Morgan were to be buried in St. John Cemetery in Queens County, where they would join Vincent's paternal grandparents, who had also been buried there.

The presence of Vincent's aunt, Martha, was of great comfort to him. Martha was the significantly younger sister of Vincent's father, Matthew, and had been more of a friend than an aunt to Vincent.

Martha Morgan had remained a spinster. At the age of thirty-two, she had given up a career in interior design so that she could pursue her study of *Iyengar Yoga* in India. Her travels in India and Nepal had lasted for three whole years and she had grown fond of the subcontinent. This had been followed by a few years in England, where she had become a practitioner of past-life healing, working in the Spiritualist Association of Great Britain.

She had returned rather reluctantly to New York to set up her own yoga academy. Her tryst with India had opened up her mind to philosophy, religion, meditation and spirituality; this fact made her seem eccentric to most men.

She now stood next to Vincent, trying to be the best comfort possible in his grief.

Vincent stood silently in prayer with folded hands, ignoring the rain pouring down his face as his friend and colleague, Father Thomas Manning, read from Psalm 23:4, 'Yea, though I walk through the valley of the shadow of death, I will fear no evil for Thou art with me.'

Vincent's eyes were closed in prayer-induced stupor. Everyone was holding umbrellas and trying as best as possible to stay dry. The light showers were becoming ugly and there were occasional lightening flashes in the skies above the cemetery. The coffins were being lowered into the ground. Vincent's eyes were tightly shut. He was merely following the words being recited by Father Thomas.

'Daughters of Jerusalem, stop weeping for me! On the contrary, weep for yourselves and for your children!' Vincent's snapped out of his trance and opened his eyes wide. These words were totally out of place for a funeral.

The words were not from Father Thomas. His Bible was closed and his lips were not moving. The prayer was already over. Who had said that?

Flash! He felt a camera flash bulb go off inside his head. '*Eloi Eloi Lema Sabachthani?*' Vincent was in a daze. Was he hearing things? Was he going mad?

Flash! Jerusalem. Why was he holding a wooden cross? *Flash!* Wailing women. 'Impale him! Impale him!' *Flash!* Blood. '*Eloi Eloi Lema Sabachthani?*' The scenes were flashing through Vincent's head at a dizzying pace, much like a silent movie reel.

Vincent stood pale and frozen. He then bent over while standing and drew both his arms close to his right shoulder. He resembled a man carrying a heavy wooden object on his right shoulder. Simon! Alexander! Rufus! What were these names? Vincent fell awkwardly to the ground.

Sympathetic friends assumed that grief had overtaken the young man and attempted to help him up and comfort him.

Vincent passed out.

The Biblical passage of Mark 15:34 of the New Testament reads as follows:

And at the ninth hour, Jesus shouted in a loud voice, 'Eloi Eloi Lema Sabachthani?' which is translated as 'My God, my God, for what have you forsaken me?'

❦

Vincent woke up in a brightly lit room of the Queens Hospital Center. He first saw the anxious face of Father Thomas Manning. He then saw a nurse standing with his Aunt Martha. Next he saw the white light fixture on the ceiling.

An intravenous line was attached to his arm. Patches were attached to his torso to monitor his heart rate, blood pressure and lung function.

Vincent was mumbling incoherently. Father Thomas put his ear close to Vincent's face to understand what he was trying to say. He was uttering sporadic words. '...impressed...service...passer-by... Simon...Cyrene...country...the   father...Alexander...Rufus...lift... torture...stake...'

Father Thomas immediately recognized the Biblical passage which spoke of Jesus' journey through the streets of Jerusalem on his way to Golgotha to be crucified. Since Jesus had become physically too weak after all the physical trauma that he had endured, the Romans had ordered a man called Simon to help him bear the burden of the cross.

The passage that Vincent seemed to be muttering was:

Also, they impressed into service a passer-by, a certain Simon of Cyrene, coming from the country, the father of Alexander and Rufus, that he should lift up his torture stake.

Why was Vincent sputtering these words? 'Relax, Vincent. You have been subjected to trauma, shock and exhaustion. You need rest. You collapsed at the cemetery and we had to bring you here to recuperate,' began Father Thomas.

Vincent couldn't care less. His shoulder was hurting. His arms were aching. He could hear screams and jeers. He was sweating. He was walking on blood! He was carrying a cross!

Aunt Martha was lying down on the sofa in the hospital room when Vincent stirred. The doctor had prescribed Dalmane shots to ensure that he slept calmly. It was around eleven o'clock in the morning.

'Good morning, sweetheart,' said Aunt Martha as she sat up on the sofa. Even though she had been up all night, Martha still looked fresh. The years of yoga and meditation had obviously helped her; she certainly did not look to be in her mid-forties. Her youthful skin, auburn hair, pert nose and her well-toned 34-24-34 figure ensured that she did not look a day over thirty-five.

Vincent responded. 'Hi Nana. What's happened to me? Am I sick?' Martha was relieved to hear Vincent calling her by the name that Matthew's entire family had called her by - Nana. It obviously meant that Vincent was recovering. Martha got up from the sofa and walked to the side of the bed.

'You had a shock during the funeral, Vincent. You passed out. Poor baby, you've been in and out of consciousness for the past two days. We couldn't feed you through your mouth so we had to nourish you intravenously.'

Vincent thought back to the funeral and said, 'Nana, where's Father Thomas? I need to speak to him.'

Martha replied. 'He was here last night, baby. He left rather late. I think he'll come back to see you around lunchtime. What did you need to ask him?'

'Nana, I think I'm going crazy. At the funeral, before I fainted, I thought I saw visions. They were so real that it was scary. I was even more scared because I thought I saw myself in some of the pictures that flashed before my eyes,' said Vincent.

Martha held Vincent's hand as she said, 'Vincent, sometimes when we confront shocks in our lives, they tend to electrify portions of our brain that we normally don't use. This can sometimes bring older memories to the forefront, memories that have been long suppressed.'

'This wasn't an older memory, Nana. I have never been to Jerusalem, yet I could see it in vivid detail. This wasn't a memory. It was something else...I just can't explain it. The scary bit is that I saw myself carrying the cross of Jesus!'

Martha looked straight into Vincent's eyes and asked, 'It could be your imagination...As a priest you have read virtually everything there is to learn about Jesus. Some of those stored facts could trigger visualizations. Possible, isn't it?'

'You're absolutely right, Nana. It's the shock that's causing hallucinations. It's nothing for us to really worry about,' said Vincent, just about convincing himself.

Martha rang the bell at Vincent's side so that the nurse could sponge him and arrange for some breakfast. Though she didn't comment any further, she couldn't but help remember Vincent as a small boy standing next to the sweet little Kate, mumbling something in another language that only she had been able to understand.

'*Talitha Koum. Talitha Koum. Talitha Koum.*'

<hr />

New York City, U.S.A., 2012

It had now been six years since his parents' death. Martha Morgan and Vincent Morgan were sitting together in the trendy York Avenue studio of Martha's yoga academy. Since Vincent had been discharged from hospital six years ago, Martha had succeeded in convincing him that he needed to recharge himself by practising *Pranayama*, the ancient yogic science of breathing.[xxiii]

Since the passing of his parents, Vincent had made it a point to visit Aunt Martha each week. He looked forward to these visits because she was a lot of fun. Moreover, she was the only real family that he had left.

Aunt and nephew were sitting with legs crossed facing one another. The classic yogic position called *padmasan* was not as easy as Nana had made it out to be. The right foot had to be under the left knee, and the left foot was to be kept under the right knee. Easier said than done!

'Breathing is life. But how much do we notice it? For example, do you observe or notice that you use only one nostril at a time to breathe?' said Martha to her student. Vincent was sceptical.

Martha quickly continued, 'At any given moment, only the right or left nostril will be breathing for you. Did you know that the active nostril changes approximately each ninety minutes during the twenty-four-hour day? It's only for a short period that both nostrils breathe together. The ancient Indian yogis knew all this and much more. They discovered and explored the intimate relationship between one's breath and one's mind. They knew that when the mind is agitated, breathing almost certainly gets disturbed. They also knew that if one's breath were held too long, the mind would have a tendency to get disturbed. Since the yogis were fundamentally attempting to control the mind, they figured that controlling the breath could possibly regulate the mind,' she concluded.

She had succeeded in holding his interest. Slowly but surely, Vincent Morgan began to learn how to breathe and relax.

Not for long.

Central Park covers 843 acres or around six percent of Manhattan. The park stretches from Central Park South 59th Street in the south, to 110th Street at the northern end, and from 5th Avenue on the east side, to 8th Avenue on the west side.

As a child, Vincent had loved visiting the Central Park Zoo. In later adult years, he had enjoyed attending performances at the park's Delacorte Theatre and indulging in the occasional culinary treat at the park's most famous restaurant, Tavern on the Green.

Martha's regimen of yoga and meditation was working wonders for him and he was feeling energetic as he headed for a quiet spot in the park's Reservoir. The Reservoir is located in the heart of Central Park. It is quite a distance away from any of the bordering streets and is one of the most tranquil areas within the park. It was here that Vincent found a bench to try out the *Vipassana* techniques that Martha had been teaching him for the past few months.[xxiv]

In Pali, the original language of Buddhism, Vipassana meant "insight". It was also more commonly used to describe one of India's most ancient meditation techniques, which had been rediscovered by the Buddha.

Vincent sat down on the bench and then drew up his legs so that he could assume the padmasan position that Nana had taught him. He then closed his eyes and began to focus on his breathing. Inhale. Exhale. As he settled into a relaxed state of mind there was a familiar flash! The same damn flash from the funeral six years ago!

Damn! Vincent thought. *I thought that the craziness was over and done with!*

Blood. *Flash!* Wounded soldiers...bandages. *Flash!* A blood-red cross with equal arms. *Flash!* A Bassano portrait...an elegant lady. *Flash!* A stately house...reception rooms on the ground and first floors. *Flash!* Number 18. *Flash!* London streets. *Flash!* Iron fencing ...an "S" logo. *Flash!* Indian antiques. *Flash!* Parties, food, musicians, soldiers. *Flash!* An old LaSalle ambulance. *Flash!* Buckingham Palace. *Flash! Bell...Grave...*so soon?

What was that? Vincent opened his eyes in mortal fear. Why was this happening to him? *Bell...Grave...so soon?* What in heaven's name did that mean? Was he to die? Was this a premonition? And why was he seeing images of London streets and stately homes? Vincent Morgan was convinced more than ever that he was going mad.

He got up and started running wildly. Luckily he was on the periphery of the reservoir of Central Park, which was mainly used by joggers.

No one found it odd to see him running. They thought that he was running to exercise himself. How could they possibly know that he was running from himself?

◆━═❀═━◆

'Help me, Nana. I'm going stark, raving mad. Either that, or I'm possessed. Do you think that I should call Father Thomas Manning for an exorcism? What is wrong with me? Why am I seeing strange things and hearing strange words?' Vincent was on the verge of hysteria.

Nana realized that she needed to calm him down. 'Relax, sweetheart. It isn't uncommon to have recollections of events, things, people or places that are hidden in our brains. In fact, it isn't strange to remember past lives either. Unfortunately, you're a Catholic priest... how on earth can I possibly discuss past life issues with you when you have closed your mind to such possibilities?'

Vincent's eyes widened. 'You think that I could be having past-life recollections? But surely that's nonsense, Nana. The Bible says that it is appointed unto men to die once, and after death comes the judgment.'

'Listen, Vincent, I know that I will always be the eccentric, esoteric, Eastern philosophy-espousing crazy aunt to you, but isn't it possible that what you have learnt so far is not the whole truth? Isn't it possible that there are things that you are yet to learn?' asked Martha rather innocently.

'Sure, Nana, but I can't question my faith. My faith is all that I have.'

Martha said, 'Okay. Let me try to help you see things my way. We all know the bit from the Bible about the blind man...you know, the bit when Jesus' disciples asked him: "Rabbi, who has sinned, this man or his parents, that he should be born blind?" Tell me, Vincent, why would the disciples have asked this question if there was no belief in a past life? Huh?'

Vincent remained silent in thought.

Martha continued, 'You probably do remember the passage where Jesus says: "I tell you the truth, no one can see the kingdom of God unless he is born again."' Tell me, sweetheart, how is it possible to be born again unless you have more than one life?'

Vincent was ready with arguments of his own.

'Nana, the fact that the disciples asked Jesus about the reasons for the blind man's condition only means that reincarnation as a concept was alive in his era. It does not mean that Jesus believed in it. Also, when Jesus talked about being born again he was referring to spiritual awakening, not birth in the literal sense.'[xxv]

Martha was just as determined to have her way. She countered defiantly, 'So what else do you think can explain your strange visions and flashes?'

Vincent was quiet. He really didn't have a logical answer.

'May I suggest something? Sometimes, a past-life memory can be triggered by a place or an object. Is there something that you can recall from your recent flashes?'

'The only thing that I can recall seeing in today's visions is Buckingham Palace. I've never been there...but I've seen it on postcards. Let me think...what else? At Mom and Dad's funeral, I remember seeing flashes of Jerusalem - at least I think it was Jerusalem. The rest of the stuff that I saw can't really be pinned down to a definite place.'

Martha quickly cut in. 'I think it's time that you and your aunt had a vacation in London. What do you say, Vincent?' She winked at him, a large grin on her face.

'I thought I was the crazy one! Are you out of your mind, Nana? I don't believe in this past life nonsense. In any case, I can't afford it; I'm a priest, remember? We don't really earn all that much!'

'Oh shut up, Vincent! Your Nana has made some serious money from her Eastern mumbo-jumbo. I'm paying. So you damn well get your holy ass on that blessed flight, Father Vincent Morgan!'

Chapter Six

Harare, Zimbabwe, 1965

Terry Acton was born on November 11th, the very day that Ian Smith, Prime Minister of Rhodesia, made a unilateral declaration of independence for the country.

Terry's father had moved to Rhodesia from England upon being offered a position at the De Beers Mining Company. He had married the daughter of his British supervisor a year after moving and had decided to make Rhodesia his home. Terry had been born two years later.

Unfortunately, Rhodesia was in turmoil. The government of Prime Minister Ian Smith was a white minority running an apartheid regime. The country was in civil war with the rebels being led by Robert Mugabe, who eventually seized power in 1980.

Mugabe's regime was one of corruption, sleaze, torture, and dictatorship.[xxvi] The Actons were forced to leave the country and return to England in 1991.

London, UK, 1991

Terry's parents ended up losing their lifesavings when they fled Zimbabwe. Circumstances made them poor East Enders, living in the working-class borough of Hackney.

The economy was in recession and Terry's father was lucky to get a blue-collar factory job at Lesney's. Lesney's factory was located in Hackney Wick, and produced *Matchbox* toys such as miniature cars and trucks. Lesney's was the main employer in the area; in fact, it was pretty much the only employer in the area.[xxvii]

Senior Acton had not taken the knocks well. He became an obnoxious, red-nosed drunk who excelled at beating his wife often and his kids occasionally, depending upon the alcohol level in his bloodstream. Little Terry was a frail and frightened little boy who suffered from asthma, a chronic respiratory condition that weakened him further.

Terry's mother was an angel from heaven who somehow managed to lock away her emotional and physical scars to produce the finest Yorkshire pudding, rhubarb crumble and shepherd's pie in England for her son. Terry loved returning home from school to his mother, but he hated his father coming home.

He was relieved when his father shot himself when the Lesney's factory, one of the last few remaining businesses in Hackney, shut up shop and made him redundant.

Knocks in his early years would make Terry even more determined to succeed at school and eventually in life. The Rhodes Scholarship to Oxford two years later was his ticket to his future.

He silently thanked Cecil John Rhodes for having instituted the Rhodes Scholarships.

Cecil John Rhodes, the founder of the state of Rhodesia, which eventually became Zimbabwe, had made his millions by shrewdly investing in the diamond mines of southern Africa. In 1880, he had created the De Beers Mining Company, which would eventually bring him great power, fortune and recognition.[xxviii]

In 1877, Rhodes would contend that: 'We British are the finest race in the world; and that the more of the world we inhabit, the better it is for the human race.'

Rhodes would die young at the age of just forty-nine. In his last will and testament, he would leave his fabulous wealth to create a secret society; one that would allow Britain to rule over the entire world. It was projected by Rhodes that by 1920 there would be around 2000 to 3000 men in their prime scattered all over the globe, each having been mathematically selected to achieve the goals set out by Rhodes.

Rhodes had confided to a close friend that it was necessary to create 'a society copied...from the Jesuits...a secret society, organized like Loyola's, supported by the accumulated wealth of those whose aspiration is to do something…a scheme to take the government of the whole world!'

The Rhodes Scholarships, which would become very famous, would merely be a tool to recruit the most promising and bright future leaders - in whichever arena they chose to work - politics, business, government, banking, finance, arts, science, medicine, technology or social work.

The 42nd President of the United States, Bill Clinton, would be a Rhodes Scholar. His administration alone would have more than twenty other Rhodes Scholars.

In 1993, one of the new recruits into Rhodes' secret society was Terry Acton. He was one of the youngest and brightest members of this elite group, accepted into Oxford to pursue an undergraduate degree in Psychology. Two years into his Oxford degree, he was offered the opportunity of a lifetime - a chance to obtain an advanced degree in Clinical Psychology at Yale. Terry grabbed it with both hands.

❦

New Haven, Connecticut, U.S.A., 1993

Terry's Rhodes Scholarship had opened a new door, not only to Yale, but also to Yale's secret society - The Order of Skull & Bones.[xxix]

The previous year, he had climbed to the tower of Weir Hall overlooking the Bones courtyard and had heard blood-curdling cries from within the structure as fifteen newcomers had been put through their initiation.

Terry's moment arrived on "tap night" when fifteen seniors led by Stephen Elliot had arrived outside his room and pounded on the door. When he had opened his door, Stephen had slammed Terry's shoulder and shouted 'Skull and Bones: Do you accept?'

Bewildered, Terry had mumbled, 'Accept.'

He had been handed a message wrapped with a black ribbon and sealed in black wax with the skull-and-crossbones emblem and the number 322. The message mentioned a time and a place for Terry to appear on initiation night.

On initiation night, he was taken by Stephen Elliot to a special room which had a question written on its walls: *"Wer war der thor, wer weiser, bettler oder kaiser? Ob arm, ob reich, im tode gleich."*

Translated, the German sentence meant: "Who was the fool, who the wise man, beggar or king? Whether poor or rich, all's the same in death."

The origins of that particular riddle were very old indeed. They could be traced back to 1776.

In 1776, the Bavarian Illuminati had come into being at the University of Ingolstadt in Germany. The Latin word *Illuminati* meant 'the enlightened ones'.[xxx]

These were people for whom the illuminating light came, not from an authoritative source such as the Church, but from elevated spiritual consciousness. The secret society would have elaborate initiation rituals. The initiate would be shown a skeleton, at the feet of which would be a crown and sword. The initiate would then be asked whether the skeleton was that of a king, nobleman or beggar. Unable to answer, the initiate would be told that it was unimportant...the only thing of importance was the character of being a man.

At the end of the day, all humans were merely Skull & Bones.

Terry Acton had realized that he had a "spiritual gift" after the death of his wife, Susan.

Terry and Susan had been university sweethearts at Yale. She had been working as a waitress in Romano's, the pizza hangout for Yallies and he had tried the most ridiculous pick-up lines on her each day till she had agreed to go out with him. They got married during his final year at Yale. Stephen Elliot, who had initiated Terry into Skull & Bones, had been his best man.

They had been honeymooning in the Pocono Mountains when his car had swerved off a wet road. Terry survived, but Susan did not.

Terry's life came to a standstill. He mourned the loss of Susan. He mourned the loss of the children that they had planned but never had.

America was no longer attractive. It reminded him too much of Susan, so Terry took the first available flight back to London. He did not bother to inform anyone of his decision, except for his close friend and confidant Stephen Elliot.

London, UK, 1996

Lonely and miserable in London, Terry was left with no alternative but to fill the vacuum. He began to fill it with a bottle of Bell's whisky each day.

He realized that he needed discipline in life. Therefore, he disciplined himself into walking into the Star Tavern pub at 11:30 a.m. sharp each morning.

Terry was sitting at his usual table in the Star Tavern when a young lady walked into the pub and started walking to each table and hurriedly asking the men, 'Excuse me. Is your name Terry?' After several failed attempts she finally reached Terry's table.

'Excuse me. Is your name Terry?' she enquired. Terry continued to stare at the glass in his hand and nodded his assent without looking up.

'I have a message for you from Susan,' she said.

Terry's hand dropped the glass and the whisky and ice spilled on the table. 'Who the fuck are you?' he demanded in a sudden fit of rage.

'Please listen to me. I'm not a crank. I know that Susan's dead. I work next door at the Spiritualist Association. I'm a psychic medium,' she pleaded.

'Fuck you! You sick, perverted bitch! Bugger off.'

Terry was furious. The mere mention of Susan had opened up raw, unhealed wounds.

The woman was equally determined and stood her ground. 'Listen, you pathetic drunk, I have no inclination to carry on a conversation with you. I do, however, suggest that you let Sabrina and Jonathan go to summer camp.'

With those words, the woman did an about-turn and stormed out of the pub.

Terry's jaw dropped and his throat went dry. Since the day that Susan and Terry had started planning for children they had zeroed in on two names, Sabrina and Jonathan, for their yet-to-be-born children. Susan used to joke that she would pack the children off to camp each summer so as to get some respite from motherhood, much to the consternation of Terry, who could not bear the thought of his kids ever being away from him.

No one else had ever shared this private conversation between husband and wife.

The Spiritualist Association of Great Britain, or the SAGB, sat inside a charming Victorian building in southwest London. The ninety-two-year lease had been purchased by the association in 1955 for the unbelievably low price of £24,500.[xxxi]

The building housed several independent rooms that were bare except for two chairs facing one another in each room. One of these would be used by the visitor, and the other would be occupied by any of the several psychic mediums who worked there. Each room had a glass skylight to allow energy to flow in and out of the room.

The SAGB offered one-on-one sittings with psychics for spiritual healing, psychic workshops as well as regression sessions.

Terry Acton had come to the SAGB looking for the woman who had approached him in the pub. He was unable to recall her name. Actually, he was quite sure that he had not even given her a chance to introduce herself.

Luckily the SAGB lobby had a bulletin board with the names and photos of all the psychic mediums working there and he had recognized her picture on it. The photo was obviously one of her at a younger age, but it was unmistakably her. Martha Morgan.

He had gone up to the reception and hesitated. The elderly receptionist had looked up and said 'Yes? May I help you, sir?'

'Yeah. I uh…was wondering whether Martha Morgan would be available for a psychic session today?' he had asked.

'You're in luck. She is presently in a session that should be over in around fifteen minutes. Shall I book you for a sitting? The cost of a thirty-minute private appointment is thirty pounds,' the receptionist had added helpfully. Terry had thought about it only for a moment and had then quickly shelled out the thirty pounds for the sitting with Martha.

'Could you please wait in room number six? She'll be with you shortly.'

Terry had never imagined that he would be at the SAGB waiting for a psychic sitting. This was so unlike him. In a short while, Martha had walked in.

He had not known that this one sitting would change his life forever.

⟨❖⟩

He expected her to be mad at him for the way that he had behaved at the pub. Instead, she was gentle, warm, friendly and genuinely concerned for him. By being so nice, she ended up making him feel even more guilty about his obnoxious attitude at the pub.

'Please do not feel any guilt,' she said to him. 'It's important to let go of your guilt. Life puts us in situations so that we can learn from them. Once we have learned, it's time to throw away the guilt and move on,' she said.

She continued. 'Everyone is endowed with psychic gifts. These gifts could be empathy, prophecy, cognition or vision. Each of us has some of these in lesser or greater quantities. They are the various ways in which psychic perception is possible. As you open yourself to these offerings, spiritual energy becomes your teacher and you become more acutely aware of your sixth sense.'

She then lowered her voice and said, 'During the past few weeks, I have been feeling the presence of a spirit which is not completely at peace. A few days ago, when I was meditating, I heard a female voice telling me that her name was Susan and that I needed to give a message to her husband, Terry, who was at the pub just next door,' she said.

Martha paused to look into Terry's eyes for disbelief - she found none.

'She wanted me to tell you that she is happy. She is in a place where she is in the midst of happiness and love. She wants you to understand that our lives on this earth are merely illusions. Each life is nothing but a change of clothes. Bodies die and decay, but what remains unchanged is the soul; that is eternal,' she concluded.

Terry's eyes had turned moist. He started feeling the healing touch of a soothing balm on his tired and aching spirit. Her gentle voice was comforting him, like a mother's lullaby.

Martha continued, 'She knew that you would not believe me and that's why she gave me the children's names. She said that you have a clean and pure heart and that you can easily help others by looking inside yourself and discovering your spiritual self.'

Martha only stopped when she saw Terry looking up at the skylight in the room, sobbing and laughing alternately, as he felt the warmth of Susan's spirit enveloping him.

Being a student of psychology, Terry had some basic understanding of the past-life therapy that had been pioneered by Dr. Brian Weiss; however, he was quite unprepared for the regression that Martha put him through a few days later.

In 1980, Dr. Brian Weiss, head of the Department of Psychiatry, Mount Sinai Medical Center, in Miami Beach, had started the treatment of a patient, Catherine. Catherine had been a twenty-seven-year-old woman, completely overwhelmed by depressive moods, anxieties and phobias. Weiss had used hypnosis to help bring to the surface forgotten or repressed incidents, traumas and memories from her infancy and childhood.

Catherine had ended up not only remembering incidents from her childhood, but also successfully providing detailed descriptions from several of her eighty-six previous lives.

Catherine's phobias had eventually been eliminated because the process of recollecting her past lives had made her realize the reason for these phobias in her present life. Past-life therapy had now become a medical term.[xxxii]

Martha wanted to heal Terry's wounds by using it on him.

Martha said, 'Past-life therapy is a great way to heal old wounds or to understand the cause of certain ailments or developments in our present lives. For you to be able to heal anyone else, Terry, it is first necessary to heal yourself. I am going to try to make you understand how the entire process works by making you the subject. Fine?' Terry had nodded his assent.

'Okay, let's just start by getting you comfortable, physically comfortable. Settle back into your chair and begin to relax...that's right...just...relax.' The voice was soothing but firm.

Terry actually began to let go and concentrate on Martha's voice: 'Look up now, and observe the skylight. You can see a little green dot on the skylight. A green dot is simply what it is. Its shape is round and its colour is green. The shape and colour are really quite irrelevant. All that I want you to do is to completely focus your concentration on that spot for a while as you continue to listen to my voice.'[xxxiii]

Martha continued, 'A peaceful, easy feeling is settling over you like a comfortable quilt. Relax. Allow yourself to drift. As you focus on the dot, something will begin to happen. The dot may move. It may change shape. It may change colour. As you notice these transformations, you will also begin to feel changes within yourself. Your eyes are tired. They're fed up of focusing on the dot. Your eyes and your eyelids want to close. That's fine.'

She continued with the same soothing voice, 'Now drift deeper with every breath that you take. Feel your body getting heavier and sinking further. You're comfortable and relaxed, but you're heavy and sinking. Deeper. Deeper. Okay. Now I want you to allow your mind to drift back in time...drift back to this morning...drift back to last night ...drift back to university...to your high-school days...drift back to your infancy...drift back beyond your infancy...that's right.' Martha now began to probe with gentle questions.

'Where are you now?'

'I'm on a farm somewhere in northern India.'

'Who are you?'

'I'm a landlord. I own lots of land in the area.'

'So you're a farmer?'

'No. I only own the land. I then rent it out to landless farmers who till the land and share the produce.'

'Where do you live?'

'I have a palatial house which is on the banks of a beautiful river. It has a very nice outdoor veranda where I sit and smoke a *hookah*.'

'What is a hookah?'

'It's a big copper pipe. My servants fill it with tobacco, saffron, cardamom, hot coals and water. I sit and smoke it all day long while gazing at the river.'

'Do you have many servants?'

'Yes. One's importance is determined by the number of servants that one has and the head of cattle one owns.'

'Are you married?'

'Yes. My wife is very beautiful. We got married when we were children.'

'So you fell in love with her?'

'No. Our marriage was arranged by our families. I had to marry her because my father insisted. I was lucky that I eventually fell in love with her. I would do anything for her. I worship her...I am hopelessly devoted to her.'

'Do you have children?'

'Three. A daughter and two sons.'

'Do you love them?'

'Yes, but I had to give my daughter away in marriage when she was just thirteen.'

'Why?'

'Because child marriage is the norm. I love her and want her to be happy - but she's just a child! She misses me terribly.'

'What about your sons? Do you love them?'

'Yes. But the eldest one is always reckless. I get very angry with him. I always have to beat him to knock some sense into his head.'

'How does that make him feel?'

'I think that he detests me.'

'How old are you?'

'I am quite old. I do not exactly know my age because no one noted the exact date or time when I was born. Unfortunately, I am quite ill.'

'Why?'

'The tobacco has given me a terrible cough. It never goes. And I am hopelessly addicted to the hookah. I cannot stop smoking.'

'Do you think this could be the reason for your asthma and breathing disorders in your present life?'

'Yes. Probably.'

'Why are you addicted?'

'I have been under a great deal of pressure. My youngest son is a teacher and has written a book questioning the caste system of the Hindu religion. Many Brahmins and priests have turned against him.'

'What is this "caste" that you talk about?'

'Hindus believe that your position in society is determined by birth. Many people are treated unfairly due to this. Untouchability is a direct consequence of this system.'

'You must be very proud of your son for having written about the problem.'

'No. I dissuaded him from doing it. Why rake up controversies? Let sleeping dogs lie. He is very upset with me.'

'Do you see any familiar faces from your present life?'

'Yes.'

'Who?'

'My mother. She is my wife in my previous life.'

'Anyone else?'

'My father. He is my eldest son in my previous life - the one whom I beat.'

'Any other faces that look familiar?'

'Susan. My wife in my present life.'

'Where is she?'

'She is my daughter in my previous life - I arranged to have her married off to someone when she was just thirteen!'

'What can you learn from all this?'

'My mother gave me intense love in my present life. It was because I had intensely loved her when she was my wife in my previous life. She was merely returning the favour.'

'And?'

'I used to take out my anger on my eldest son in a previous life by beating him. He became my father in my present life to teach me how dreadful it feels to be on the receiving end of a parent's anger.'

'Anything else?'

'I ensured that my daughter was parted from me at an early age as a result of her early child marriage. She became my wife, Susan, in my present lifetime. She taught me the intense sorrow and despair of separation by dieing young.'

'Anything that your younger son taught you? You know, the one who wrote about the evils of caste discrimination.'

'One can never let sleeping dogs alone.'

London, UK, 2012

Professor Terry Acton had an annoying habit of looking cute when he was unkempt. His hair was finger-combed and his face had a permanently unshaven look. His jeans and sweater had certainly seen better days. Strangely enough, all of this only enhanced his appeal to the opposite sex. There was pain in his eyes and this seemed to make him more attractive to women.

The previous sixteen years since that fateful day of his session with Martha had produced positive healing for Terry.

Terry had decided to use his background in psychology and combine it with past-life therapy and a comparative study of religion at the Spiritualist Association. Terry had first started out by being a spiritual medium. He had then mastered the art of hypnosis. He had then moved on to regression when Martha had moved back to the States to start her yoga academy.

After his first few sessions with Martha, Terry had begun attending lectures on spirituality at the Department for the Study of Religions at the University of London. His teachers had awakened Terry's interest in religion and spirituality. This had eventually led to a prestigious teaching assignment at the university.

This day in 2012, Terry was delivering a lecture on Hinduism and its twin pillars of reincarnation and Karma.

'It's impossible to place a date on the origin of Hinduism, but even way back in 4000 B.C., it was being practised in the Indus Valley. Hinduism is the third largest religion in the world with approximately 940 million followers,' started Terry.[xxxiv]

Without consulting any notes, he continued. 'Hinduism is similar to many world religions. For example, the Holy Trinity exists in Hinduism. The trinity is that of *Brahma*, the creator; *Vishnu*, the preserver; and *Shiva*, the destroyer. The Trinity is also repeated in the divine Hindu mother goddess, with *Lakshmi, Saraswati* and *Kali* being three manifestations of the supreme feminine force. Hindu mythology has an abundance of gods. This is quite similar to the ancient Greek and Roman philosophies. However, unlike the Greeks or Romans, Hindus hold the view that all their gods are merely different manifestations of the same supreme god. Thus, Hinduism is monotheistic, not polytheistic.

'Hinduism talks of *Brahman* or the one supreme and divine entity. The fundamental belief is that every living thing has a soul which is connected to a greater being, Brahman. Hindus believe that they have eternal life due to their fundamental belief in reincarnation.'

Terry noticed a student in the front looking sceptical. He paused and asked, 'Any questions?'

The sceptical one raised her hand and said, 'Professor Acton, in your book you have said that the word "reincarnation" is derived from the word "carnate" which translates into "flesh". Therefore, "incarnate" means entering flesh and hence reincarnate means re-entering flesh. You say that the soul enters the body at birth and leaves the body upon death, and that this is a continuous cycle. Why? What is the purpose of such a cycle?'

Terry smiled at the lengthy question and replied, 'With each life, the soul learns something more until the soul reaches the stage of *Mukti* or complete enlightenment. This is the goal that all Hindus must work towards. At the stage of Mukti, which happens after many lifetimes, the soul is reunited with Brahman. Now, you may ask, what determines when and where a soul is reborn?

'This brings us to the theory of Karma. Karma literally means "deed", and as a theory it outlines the cause and effect nature of life. Karma is not to be confused with fate. Man has free will and creates his destiny based upon his actions. The most dramatic illustration of Karma is found in the Hindu epic, the *Mahabharata*. The Hindu concept of Karma was also adopted by other religions such as Buddhism.[xxxv]

'The theory of Karma is not really crazy when one thinks about it. Almost all religions have at some point of time in their histories believed in reincarnation - including Christianity. References to reincarnation in the New Testament were deleted only in the fourth century when Christianity became the official religion of the Roman Empire. It was sometime in the year 553 A.D. that the second Council of Constantinople declared reincarnation as heresy. These decisions were intended to increase the power of the Church by making people believe that their salvation depended solely on the Church.'[xxxvi]

Chapter Seven

North-eastern Tibet, 1935
'Tah-shi de-leh. Khe-rahng ku-su de-bo yin-peh?' asked the leader of the search party. Little Tenzin Gyatso looked up innocently and replied, *'La yin. Ngah sug-po de-bo yin.'*[xxxvii]

Dalai Lamas were manifestations of Buddha who chose to take rebirth in order to serve other human beings. The thirteenth Dalai Lama had died in 1933. The Tibetan Government had not only to appoint a successor but also to search for and discover the reincarnation of the thirteenth Dalai Lama.[xxxviii]

In 1935, the Regent of Tibet travelled to a sacred lake near Lhasa. The regent looked into the waters and saw a vision of a monastery with a jade green and gilded roof and a house with turquoise tiles.

Soon, search parties were sent out to all parts of Tibet to search for a place that resembled the vision. One of the search parties went east to the Tibetan village of Amdo, where they found a house with turquoise tiles sitting dwarfed by the hilltop Karma monastery. The monastery had a jade green and gilded roof.

The leader of the search went into the house and found the child, Tenzin Gyatso, playing inside. He had been born to his parents on July 6th, 1935.

'Hello. How are you?' asked the leader of the search party to little Tenzin Gyatso in Tibetan.

Tenzin looked up innocently and replied, 'I am fine.' Then the little boy immediately and authoritatively demanded the rosary that the leader of the search was wearing.

It was a rosary that had belonged to the thirteenth Dalai Lama.

Born to a peasant family, His Holiness Tenzin Gyatso was recognized at the age of two, in accordance with Tibetan tradition, as the reincarnation of his predecessor the thirteenth Dalai Lama.

The tradition of wise elders seeking out the reincarnation of their spiritual leaders had continued through the ages. In fact a similar search had been carried out in Bethlehem in 7 B.C. by three wise men.

Bethlehem, Judea, 7 B.C.

A triple conjunction of Jupiter and Saturn in a given year was very rare indeed. This conjunction in which the two planets seemed to almost touch one another occurred on May 29th, October 3rd and finally on December 5th in the year 7 B.C.[xxxix]

The three Buddhist wise men observing this astronomical miracle were convinced. A reincarnation had indeed arrived on Earth and it was finally time to meet Him. They would then need to convince themselves that He was indeed the one that they were looking for. They would then embark on the task of preparing Him for His mission in this life.

They needed to visit Jerusalem.

Jerusalem, Judea, 5 B.C.

King Herod was livid; Judea was impossible to rule.

To add fuel to the fire, there were these three strangers who claimed that they had seen Jupiter and Saturn kiss each other in the heavens and thought that it was some idiotic celestial signal. Damn them!

They now wanted to find a two-year-old boy who was supposedly an incarnate of some spiritual leader or the other. Damn them!

He hated the fact that he was a friend and ally of the Roman Empire. He hated being looked down upon by the Jews because of his Arab mother. At times he even hated Octavian and Mark Antony for putting him in charge of Judea in the first place, even though he had wanted so desperately to be king. Damn them all![xl]

And then it struck him!

Kill all the two-year-olds that he could find. At least it would give him something to do. Damn them all!

'Kill him,' said Herod.

Cairo, Egypt, 5 B.C.

'Kill him,' said the governor of Cairo. He had heard that the little boy had entered the temple of Bastet, the lion goddess, and that the idols had just crumbled to the ground before him. He was quite certainly evil.

After Herod's decision to kill all two-year-olds, the boy's parents had realized that the only way to save his life was to flee from Bethlehem to Egypt. They had made their way from Bethlehem to Rafah, on to Al-Arish, further on to Farama and then on to Tel Basta.[xli]

This was the city of the lion goddess Bastet.

When the child had entered the temple of the lion goddess, the ground had shaken and the idols of the temple had crumbled in submission before him.

They had then proceeded to old Cairo where they took refuge in a cave. When the governor of the region had heard the stories of crumbling idols in Tel Basta, he started planning the boy's murder and this prompted the family's departure to Maadi.

They went on board a sailboat that took them to Deir Al-Garnous. From here the family moved on to Gabal Al-Kaf and rested in a cave before heading towards Qussqam, home to the Al-Moharraq monastery.

This was one among many monasteries in Egypt that would play a role in the boy's education.

***

Egypt, 4 A.D.

The little boy who had fled with his parents from Judea did not know that he owed his education to developments that had taken place two hundred years earlier.

A mystical revolution had happened among the Jews of Egypt and Palestine about two centuries before. In Egypt, these mystics called themselves "Therapeuts" and their spiritual counterparts in Palestine called themselves "Nazarenes" and "Essenes".

The Therapeuts, Nazarenes and Essenes had remarkable similarities to Buddhists. For example, they were vegetarians; they abstained from wine; they chose to remain celibate; they lived monastic lives in caves; they opposed animal sacrifice; they considered poverty to be a virtue; they worked towards attaining knowledge through fasting and extended periods of silence; they wore simple white robes; and they initiated novices through baptism in water.

The origins of ritual immersion in water were Indian. Two millennia later, one would still be able to see millions of Hindus practising this ancient rite each day on the banks of their sacred Ganges.[xlii]

The boy's teachers were experts. Many of them had extraordinary powers such as those of levitation, clairvoyance, teleportation and healing. The fruits of their labours were similar to the results achieved by exponents of yoga in ancient India.

The boy was made to study various ancient texts. Many of the teachings in those texts had arrived in Egypt because of a brutal murder that had taken place in 265 B.C.

⟪⟫

Kalinga, North-East India, 265 B.C.

'Murderer! Killer of innocents! You are the devil incarnate!' the crazy old woman cried while sobbing uncontrollably. She was old and haggard; dried tears caked her face and her hair was strewn across her features like that of a witch. In her lap was the body of a young boy, probably her grandson, who had been killed by Emperor Ashoka's army.

Ashoka had killed 100,000 people in a massive show of strength when he had invaded and overrun the neighbouring kingdom of Kalinga in eastern India.[xliii]

War over, Ashoka had ventured out into the city. Corpses littered the streets. Once happy homes lay completely destroyed. *What have I done?* thought Ashoka. This was far too high a price to pay for victory. Enough of war, his future conquests would be those of love and peace.

The great king had converted to Buddhism and had decided to spread its message of peace, compassion, non-violence and love to each and every person in his kingdom, and even beyond.

Among the recipients of Ashoka's missionaries of love and peace would be King Ptolemy II Philadelphus of Egypt.

Egypt, 258 B.C.

Ptolemy II Philadelphus sat on the throne. Next to him was his wife, and his sister. In fact, his wife was his sister.

He was listening to some missionaries who had been sent by the Indian King Ashoka to spread the word of some man who called himself the Buddha.[xliv]

They called themselves *Thera*-vada monks. Curiously, Egypt would soon become home to a set of monks with a name that was suspiciously similar - these would be known as the *Thera*-peutae. These were the famous reclusive monks of Egypt, devoted to poverty, celibacy, good deeds and compassion; everything that the Buddha, who was also known as Muni Sakya, stood for.

Ptolemy II could not have possibly known that 500 years later, the great Egyptian port of Alexandria would have its own Muni Sakya - Ammonius Saccas.

Alexandria, Egypt, 240 A.D.

Ammonius Saccas was dying. After many years of study and meditation, he had opened his school of philosophy in Alexandria. The school lived on but he was fading. History would record his name as Ammonius Saccas. His name was derived, in fact, from Muni Sakya, the Buddha's commonly accepted name.

His most famous pupil would be Origen, one of the earliest fathers of the Christian Church. Origen's writings on reincarnation would be considered heresy by the Church three centuries later.

Ammonius Saccas was a follower of Pythagoras. Pythagoreans were philosophers, mathematicians and geometricians. They were famous for their belief in the transmigration of souls. They would perform purification rituals and would follow ascetic, dietary and moral rules, which would allow their souls to improve their ranking.

Of course, Ammonius Saccas could not possibly have considered the fact that Pythagoras had derived a great deal of his knowledge from a sage who had lived in 800 B.C.

India, 800 B.C.

Baudhayana, the great Indian sage, was sitting in the forest attempting to figure out the right dimensions for the holy fire. The fire would burn inside a specially constructed square altar. Into this fire would be poured milk, curds, honey, clarified butter, flowers, grain, and holy water as offerings to the gods. He was attempting to figure out the resultant effect on the area of the altar as a result of changes in the dimensions of the square. His mind was calm, but one could almost hear the humming of the machinery inside his head. Yes! He had it. He wrote carefully, "The rope which is stretched along the length of the diagonal of a rectangle produces an area which the vertical and horizontal sides make together."[xlv]

Around 250 years later, a mathematician and philosopher from the Greek island of Samos, would further revise the theory propounded by Baudhayana. He would write the Pythagorean Theorum as: "The square of the hypotenuse equals the sum of the squares of the sides."[xlvi]

Five hundred years later, a Gnostic school in Aegea would be solely focused on teaching the Pythagorean theories. A branch of the Essenes, the Koinobi, would teach the philosophy of Pythagoras in Egypt. A Gnostic college in Ephesus would be flourishing where the principles and secrets of Buddhism, Zoroastrianism, and the Chaldean system would be taught along with Platonic philosophy. While in Alexandria, the Therapeutae would spend lifetimes in meditation and contemplation, the Essenes and Nazarenes would be perpetuating many of these schools of thought back home in Palestine.

By the time the boy who had fled Judea was ready for school, Gnosis, or ancient wisdom of self-knowledge, would be flourishing in Gnostic groups and mystery schools all over Egypt. The boy would be able receive his education in some of the best Gnostic schools of the time. It wouldn't matter whether they followed Pythagorean, Chaldean, Platonic, Essene, Therapeut, or Nazarene teachings or anything else. The fundamental knowledge would be derived from the same source: Buddhism.[xlvii]

It would remain buried thereafter till 1947.

Qumran, Israel, 1947

'Stupid goat!' muttered Muhammed. The damn goat had wandered inside the cave and Muhammed picked up a stone to pelt it in order to bring the dumb animal running out. This stone was about to make him famous.

In 1947, a young shepherd by the name of Muhammed edh-Dhib threw a stone into a cave in an effort to coax a wandering goat out of it. His stone flew inside and ended up striking a ceramic vessel. This vessel was just one among many earthen clay jars that contained ancient scrolls that would later come to be known as the "Dead Sea Scrolls". Subsequent efforts by the local Bedouin and archaeologists would recover 900 documents during the period of 1947 to 1956. Based upon carbon dating, it would soon be established that the scrolls had been written between the first century B.C. and the second century A.D.[xlviii]

The scrolls were quite obviously from the library of a Jewish sect and may have been hidden away during the Jewish-Roman war in 66 A.D. It is believed that this sect was that of the Essenes.

Christian theologians were quite perplexed to discover that most of the Beatitudes in the Sermon on the Mount, which were attributed to Jesus, were already present in the Dead Sea Scrolls, many of which had been written several years before Jesus lived.[xlix]

This seemed to indicate that much of the knowledge imparted by Jesus to his disciples had emerged from earlier works of the Essenes;

who themselves had derived significant spiritual wisdom from Buddhism.

It was this spiritual wisdom that would be reflected in the Gnostic gospels discovered in Egypt in 1945.

Nag Hammadi, Egypt, 1945
'*Shukran li-l-láh*! Thanks be to Allah!' cried Muhammad as he saw the jars that were buried in the ground.

His brother Khalifa-Ali watched curiously. '*Tawakkaltu 'ala-l-lláh*! But what if this contains an evil genie that pops out and destroys us?' he asked.

It was a hot December day in Upper Egypt. The two peasants, Muhammad and Khalifa-Ali, had been digging for fertilizer and had stumbled upon an old but large earthenware jar. They were hoping to find hidden treasure but were scared that the jar may contain an evil genie!

'*In shá' Alláh*, it will be all right!' said Muhammad and eagerly opened the jar, only to be disappointed as well as relieved. He was disappointed that the jar did not contain treasure, and relieved that it did not contain a genie.

The jar contained around a dozen old papyrus books bound in golden brown leather. They had been placed there hundreds of years before.

The fifty-two sacred texts contained in the jars were the long-lost Gnostic texts that had been written several hundred years previously in the earliest days of Christianity.[1]

The Gospel of Mary Magdalene. The Gospel of Thomas. The Gospel of Judas. The Gospel of Philip. Gospels that would be shut out by the Church fathers.

In the same way that they had tried to shut out Dmitriy Novikov.

Paris, France, 1899
Dmitriy Novikov just couldn't believe it! He was finally being accepted into the *Societé d'Histoire Diplomatique*, the most exclusive and famous association of celebrated historians, writers, and diplomats. He could not believe that he was here among them all; he was both proud and relieved.

He couldn't help thinking back a dozen years to 1887 when he had discovered the ancient Issa manuscripts in Ladakh.

After his discovery, his intention had been to immediately publish the manuscripts. The archbishop had tried desperately to dissuade Dmitriy from doing so. Dmitriy had then gone to Italy to seek the opinion of a high-ranking cardinal, who had been equally and vehemently opposed to any such publication.

Dmitriy had, however, remained steadfast, and had succeeded in getting a French publisher for his book, *Les années secrètes de Jésus*, meaning "The Secret Years of Jesus", which had eventually rolled off the press in 1896.

After publication, Dmitriy had made a trip to Moscow, where he had immediately been arrested by the Tsar's government for literary activity that was 'dangerous to the state and to society'. He had remained exiled, without trial, for the next several years.

His book had stirred a hornet's nest of criticism. The renowned German expert, Max Müller, had led the critics who protested against any notion that Buddhism had influenced Christianity.

Some critics had argued that Dmitriy Novikov had never visited the Hemis monastery in Ladakh and that the Issa manuscripts were a figment of his imagination.

Dmitriy Novikov had become a pariah and an untouchable. For a pariah to be accommodated into the Societé d'Histoire Diplomatique just a few years later was a rare honour indeed. Probably the Societé knew something that Max Müller didn't.

Possibly, they had read the works of Hippolytus.

Rome, Italy, 225 A.D.

Hippolytus, a Greek-speaking Roman Christian, wrote that: "Buddhists were in contact with the Thomas Christians in southern India...who philosophise among the Brahmins, who live a self-sufficient life, abstaining from eating living creatures and all cooked food...they say that God is light...God is discourse."[li]

Trade routes between the Greco-Roman world and the Far East were flourishing during the age of Gnosticism and Buddhist missionaries had been active in Alexandria for several generations after Ashoka had first sent his emissaries to Ptolemy II.

The Thomas Christians of ancient India were named after Thomas Didymus, one of the twelve apostles of Christ. He was speared to death in around 72 A.D. No, he wasn't killed in Palestine or Egypt. He was killed near Mylapore, in southern India.

Before reaching the south, he had visited King Gondophares, whose kingdom lay in the northwest regions of India. He even wrote about it in his *Acta Thomae, The Acts of Judas Thomas.*[lii]

Historians and Church authorities alike had dismissed the very existence of any King called Gondophares. There was no record of any such king having ruled northwest India around that time.

By 1854 all of them would have to eat their words.

Calcutta, India, 1854

Sir Alexander Cunningham, the first Director of the Archaeological Survey of India, would report that *Gondophares* could no longer be dismissed as fictitious.

Cunningham would report that since the commencement of a British presence in Afghanistan, more than 30,000 coins had been discovered. Some of these coins had been minted by the Parthian king, Gondophares, who was now miraculously transformed from myth to reality.[liii]

Suddenly the *Acta Thomae*, or *The Acts of Judas Thomas* was no longer a work of fiction and necessarily had to be moved from the fiction to the non-fiction shelves.

In which case, one would also have to believe the rest of the book, right up to 72 A.D.

⟡

Mylapore, South India, 72 A.D.

Thomas Didymus was praying in the woods outside his hermitage when a hunter, who belonged to the Govi clan, carefully aimed his poisoned dart and hit him. The wound was critical and St. Thomas died on December 21st, 72 A.D.[liv]

Thomas had arrived in Cranganore, just thirty-eight kilometres away from Cochin, India in 52 A.D. He had begun preaching the gospel to inhabitants of the Malabar Coast and had soon established seven churches in the region.

Some time before his arrival in India, he had been at the court of King Andrappa of Turkey. The court had been celebrating the wedding of the king's daughter. Besides the wedding, there was another celebration in King Andrappa's court.

The apostle, Thomas, according to his own words in the *Acta Thomae*, had been able to meet and reunite with his master, Jesus, who was also present at the wedding,[lv] looking quite well and surprisingly relaxed after his crucifixion!

Chapter Eight

Balakote, Line of Control, India-Pakistan Border, 2012

Balakote, a remote village on the India-Pakistan border, was literally sitting on the fence. It was neither here nor there. The river, Jallas Nullah, flowed through the middle[lvi], hence the village lay half in Pakistan and half in India. It was here that Ghalib was celebrating, having just returned from his meeting with the Sheikh.

He had first checked the animal's eyes and ears to ensure that it was healthy. After all, only a healthy animal could be considered suitable for sacrifice. He had then given it water to drink and had pointed the animal towards Mecca.

He had then chanted, '*Bismillāh, i-rahman, i-rahīm* - in the name of Allah, most gracious, most merciful. *Sibhana man halalaka lil dabh* - praise be upon he who has made you suitable for slaughter.' He had slaughtered the lamb using the Halaal method - by cutting the animal's neck arteries with a single swipe of a non-serrated blade. He had then watched the blood drain from the beast. As per law, he had refused to touch the animal until it had died.

It was Eid ul-Adha and the animal sacrifice was part of the festival. It was the tenth day of Dhul Hijja as per the Islamic Calendar and seventy days after the end of Ramadan.

Ghalib-bin-Isar, leader of the Lashkar-e-Talatashar, sat in the centre with his army sitting around him in a semicircle. In the centre, the lamb was being roasted over a roaring fire, and another smaller fire was being used to bake naan bread.

Ghalib was overcome with emotion. He looked around at his team; these were his fiercest, most loyal companions. They would die for him willingly. He needed to show them that he not only loved them, but that he also respected them. He stood up and took off the *Pathan*-suit that he was wearing and tied a coarse cotton cloth towel around himself. He then filled the iron tub meant for the utensils with warm water. He called his comrades one by one and began washing their feet and then patting them dry with the towel. Boutros was reluctant, but Ghalib insisted.

Duly washed, they sat down and were served the lamb. Ghalib took the hot naan and, breaking it into pieces, lovingly served it to his men.

He then spoke to Yehuda. 'In Srinagar, there is a Japanese woman looking for me. You will go, find her, and tell her that you will deliver me to her.'

The *kahwa* tea was boiling in the samovar. He poured it into a large bowl and passed it around. His young men would leave for each of their destinations within a few days.

He knew that his time had come.

Jerusalem, Judea, 27 A.D.

Knowing that his time had come, Jesus asked that the Passover feast be organized. Before supper, Jesus got up from the table, took off his outer garment and tied a towel around himself. He then poured water into a basin and one by one washed his disciples' feet; he then wiped them dry with the towel. Simon Peter hesitated but Jesus insisted. He soon finished washing everyone's feet, put on his clothes and sat down at the table with his disciples.

While eating, Jesus remarked that he would be betrayed by one of the men around the table. Judas asked Jesus whether he was alluding to him.

'You have said it,' replied Jesus.

During the meal, Jesus broke the bread into pieces and offered them to his disciples while saying, 'Take this and eat; this is my body.'

He then took a cup of wine and gave it to his disciples saying, 'Drink from it, all of you. For this is my blood, the blood of the covenant, shed for many for the forgiveness of sins.'

Balakote, Line of Control, Indo-Pak Border, 2012

Because the river, Jallas Nullah, flows through the centre of Balakote, either side of the landscape is dotted with rocky hills.

Ghalib-bin-Isar needed to explain the reasons and motivations behind his intended actions to his men as well as to the extended army. He stood atop one of the hillocks closest to the river and began to speak.

'Being poor does not mean that God does not love you. Thousands of rich Americans died in the Twin Towers on 9/11 by the will of Allah. He protected you! Not them!' he said as his army looked up at him in awe.

He continued, 'The families of those who died in New York mourned. They said, "Had we known the evil that America does all around the world, we would never have supported our government." Let me tell you, that Allah will protect these people who have now understood our cause. God will protect and comfort these mourners.'

He carried on in the same casual tone. 'The Americans say that we Muslims do not like their way of life and that we wish to destroy their free society. I ask you, why do we attack America and not Sweden? Sweden is as free as America. The difference lies in America's arrogance. Doesn't America know that it is the meek that shall inherit the Earth?'

The mood was jubilant and his team was getting charged up. Ghalib raised his voice a little. '*Bismillāh, i-rahman, i-rahīm*, in the name of Allah, do we not fast in the holy month of Ramadan and savour the delicious taste of food and water after the fast is over? That is the way that I want you to hunger and thirst for the word and the will of Allah! The hungrier and thirstier you are, the more worthy you are in the eyes of God!

'Our brothers and sisters in Palestine, Lebanon, Kashmir and Chechnya have been murdered, looted and raped. Yet we have not done the same to the infidels who perpetrate these ghastly crimes. Instead, the will of Allah showered terror and fire on the perpetrators almost automatically. We are Muslims. We are merciful even in the most trying of circumstances!' thundered Ghalib.

His words were met by chants of '*Allah-o-Akbar*'.

Ghalib's voice softened. 'All that God asks of us is to have our conscience clear. Our hearts should remain clean and pure. Only this can ensure that we are victorious. *A'uzu billahi minashaitanir rajim!*'

'The Qur'an[lvii] tells us in Chapter 4, Verse 90: "Thus, if they let you be, and do not make war on you, and offer you peace, God does not allow you to harm them". Don't you think that Muslims all over the world would prefer peace over war? Islam is a religion of peace and the peacemakers are beloved of Allah! Unfortunately, the infidels do not want peace!' shouted Ghalib.

Ghalib's voice was now choked with emotion. He continued, 'The Noble Qur'an 49:13 says that, "the most honoured of you in the sight of Allah is the most righteous of you". For years we have been persecuted and have continued to remain righteous. This is why we are beloved of Allah! Our friends who led the attacks on 9/11 willingly allowed themselves to be martyred for the cause of righteousness.'

He then drew to his conclusion. 'Do not worry if the world calls Ghalib a terrorist or if my enemies hurl insults at you. As long as you do Allah's will, you shall have his reward. Keep this in mind when we execute our plan,' he said as he stood on the hill and looked at his followers with pure, raw emotion.

❦

Sea of Galilee, Capernaum, 30 A.D.
He stood on the hill and looked at his followers with pure, raw emotion as he delivered to them a sermon on the mount.[lviii]

High on a mountain, towards the north end of the Sea of Galilee, near Capernaum, Jesus spoke to his disciples and to a large gathering of followers.

'Blessed are the poor in spirit, for theirs is the kingdom of heaven. Blessed are they who mourn, for they will be comforted. Blessed are the meek, for they will inherit the land. Blessed are they who hunger and thirst for righteousness, for they will be satisfied. Blessed are the merciful, for they will be shown mercy. Blessed are the clean of heart, for they will see God. Blessed are the peacemakers, for they will be called children of God. Blessed are they who are persecuted for the sake of righteousness, for theirs is the kingdom of heaven. Blessed are you when they insult you and persecute you and utter every kind of evil falsely against you because of me. Rejoice and be glad, for your reward will be great in heaven.'

❦

Balakote, Line of Control, Indo-Pak Border, 2012
Ghalib lay on the exquisite *Shahtoosh* shawl that was carefully laid out over the mattress inside his tent. In one corner sat a rosewater jar that had been sprinkled with *Jannat-ul-Firdaus*, literally, the perfume of heaven.

Resting her head on his shoulder was his wife - his one and only wife, Mariyam. She had borne him a beautiful daughter, Zahira.

Unlike many Muslim men, Ghalib was devoted to a single wife. While the Qur'an sanctioned polygamy, Ghalib's view was that the Surah An-Nisa of the Qur'an actually said, "Marry other women of your choice, two or three, or four, but if you fear that you shall not be able to deal justly with them, then only one…"

Ghalib had decided on only one. She was the most exquisite creature that had ever lived, and he was hopelessly devoted to her. He lovingly ran his fingers through her silky reddish-brown hair as she nestled her head on his shoulder.

Suddenly she got up to retrieve a small phial that she had prepared during the day. It was an intense, warm, and fragrant musk that she had extracted from the fibrous spindle-like needles of the Nalada plants that grew in the area.

'This is just a small token of my love,' she said to Ghalib as she opened the phial and poured it over his feet. She then applied the perfume to his feet and then lowered her head over them. Her soft hair trailed along his soles and produced exquisite sensations throughout his entire body. She then began kissing his feet and gently licking his toes. She playfully sucked on a few of his toes while her hair continued to caress his skin. She guided him to her already wet and warm core and once he was fully inside, she kissed him passionately.

Gar bar-ru-e-zamin ast; hamin ast, hamin ast, hamin asto. The Persian couplet, uttered by the Mughal Emperor Jehangir to describe

72

the beauty of Kashmir, meaning, "If there is a paradise on earth, it is here, it is here, it is here!"[lix]

Ghalib remained in paradise with the wonderful scent of Nalada wafting through his tent.

Bethany, Israel, 27 A.D.

The Latin name *Nardostachys Jatamansi*[lx] was derived from the Sanskrit word *'Nalada'*. This tough and hardy herb grew in the Himalayan foothills. The fibrous spindles of the plant grew underground and were rich in oil. This oil would be made into a dry rhizome oil extract called Nardin. This was the source of Nard.

Six days before the Passover, Jesus had arrived at Bethany, where Mary Magdalene took about a pint of pure Nard, an expensive perfume; she poured it on Jesus' feet and wiped his feet with her hair. The house was filled with the aromatic fragrance of the perfume.

Chapter Nine

New York, U.S.A., 2012
British Airways flight BA 0178 left John F. Kennedy airport at 9:15 a.m. and was scheduled to reach Heathrow at 9 p.m. GMT. Occupying two seats in the second row of World Traveller Class with 351 other passengers and 39,900 pounds of luggage on the 747-400 were Martha and Vincent Morgan.

The customary drinks and salted peanuts had arrived and aunt and nephew were getting into the mood of the trip. 'Vincent, you must write down whatever you saw in your visions. Very often we tend to forget things like that,' said Martha.

Vincent replied, 'Actually Nana, I've already done that. In fact, I have my notes of the images that I saw during Mom and Dad's funeral as well as what I saw when I had those crazy flashes in Central Park.'

Vincent got up, opened the overhead luggage bin and pulled out his duffel bag. Unzipping it, he quickly found his leather-bound notebook. Taking it out, he zipped up the bag and returned it to the overhead storage before sitting back down. Opening it, he turned to a page that had been tabbed with a yellow Post-it. He gave the notebook to Martha. There were several notations on the page:

"St. John Cemetery: Daughters of Jerusalem. *Eloi Eloi Lema Sabachthani?* Jerusalem. Wooden cross. Blood. Wailing women. Impale him. Simon. Alexander. Rufus."

There followed a couple of entries for 1996 in White Plains. The notations were rather cryptic. These entries were followed by:

"Central Park: Blood. Wounded soldiers. Bandages. Greek cross. Red. Bassano Portrait. Stately house. Number 18. London street. Iron fencing with an "S" logo. Indian antiques. Parties. Food. Musicians. 1940s La Salle ambulance. Buckingham Palace. Bell. Grave. So soon?"

'Excuse me, ma'am. Would you prefer the chicken casserole or the sliced roast beef?' enquired the flight attendant.

'Neither. I've pre-ordered a vegetarian meal,' said Martha.

The stewardess referred to a list and immediately pulled out an appropriate tray from her cart. Stir-fry vegetables with basmati rice, pasta salad, and fresh fruit yoghurt for Ms. Martha Morgan.

Vincent tucked into a meal of sliced roast beef with scalloped cheesy potatoes and green beans, garden salad with ranch dressing, and blueberry cheesecake; not bad for airline food. For a while at least, they forgot about the notebook and its contents.

London, UK, 2012

The ridiculous name, Airways Hotel, belonged to a nineteenth-century period home that was located just a stone's throw away from Buckingham Palace. It had now been converted into a forty-room bed and breakfast priced at around £45 per night. It was just one of the many little family-run places that one saw in the oddest parts of London. They all looked identical to one another - in fact, without the signboards outside, one wouldn't be able to tell one Victorian townhouse-hotel with its pillars and white facade from another.

This is where Martha and Vincent checked in upon arriving in London. Vincent had decided that he would rather be near Buckingham Palace in order to be able to experience the area a little better. They had boarded the Piccadilly Line from Heathrow to Hammersmith and had then taken the District Line to Victoria Station, which was just a short walk away from the hotel.

The front desk was supervised by a middle-aged matron. She was the proverbial English landlady with rosy cheeks, wide matronly hips and checkered apron. She quickly rattled off the deal to Vincent, 'Your bedrooms have independent bathrooms. Both rooms have a telly, hairdryer, fridge and tea-coffee maker. Direct dial in your room gets billed to your account. The tariff includes traditional English breakfast served downstairs in the morning between eight and nine o'clock. VAT included. Any questions, luv?'

The traditional English breakfast the next morning was essentially a full-blown frontal cholesterol attack. Besides toast, marmalade, fruit, and porridge was the fry-up which included sausages, bacon, kippers, black pudding, fried eggs, mushrooms, tomatoes, baked beans, and hash browns. Vincent couldn't believe the amount of grease that the English consumed each morning, until Martha told him that not all English people ate like that everyday. While Martha attempted to rid herself of her jet lag, Vincent settled for some tea and toast. He then quickly made his way to Buckingham Palace.

During the journey from New York to London, Vincent had succeeded in convincing himself that his trip to London was going to turn out to be a waste of time - this talk about past-life experiences was humbug nonsense.

He now headed along St. George's Drive till he reached Warwick Square where he turned left and started walking down Belgrave Road. When he reached the intersection with Buckingham Palace road, he turned right and kept walking until he reached Buckingham Gate. The walk had taken him less than thirty minutes. It was only when he reached Buckingham Palace that it struck him.

He hadn't asked for directions. He hadn't referred to a map. He hadn't visited London ever in his life. And yet he had walked effortlessly from his hotel to the palace as if he had lived there his entire life!

<hr />

Buckingham House had originally been built in 1703 as the private residence of the Duke of Buckingham. In 1762, the house had been purchased by George III to be used as one among many homes belonging to the royals. George IV had subsequently engaged the services of architect John Nash, who had redesigned Buckingham House with a marble arch as its entrance; this would later be relocated to Hyde Park. In 1837, Queen Victoria had made Buckingham House her principal residence in London, and Buckingham House had now officially become Buckingham Palace.[lxi]

The Household Troops had guarded the monarchy since 1660, their foot guards attired in the familiar uniforms of red tunics and bearskins. In summer, the main attraction for tourists continued to be the changing of the guard, which happened in the forecourt of the palace at 11:30 each morning. The forty-five-minute, minutely choreographed ceremony involved the new guard marching to the palace from Wellington Barracks accompanied by a band and taking over duty from the old guard.

It was only around 10:30 in the morning and the forecourt was quiet at this hour except for a few enthusiastic tourists. Vincent just stood and surveyed the façade of the palace, attempting to see whether it stirred any latent memories inside him. Nothing. So it was a false alarm after all. A complete waste of time, as expected.

After thirty minutes of wandering about, Vincent decided to make his way back to the hotel to check on Martha. He walked along Buckingham Palace Road and turned right in to Eccleston Street. He kept walking till he reached a lovely Victorian residential quarter. For some uncanny reason, Vincent walked further towards it. He was now found himself in Belgrave Square.

Bell...Grave...so soon? It struck him like a thunderbolt! It was one word - *Belgrave*, not two - bell and grave. Belgrave was the word that was hitting his brain cells during his memory flashes in Central Park. If the past-life theory held true, and if Vincent had lived in this area before, he would have passed Buckingham Palace often enough. His primary recollection would be of Belgrave Square, but he would also have a fleeting memory of the Buckingham Palace environment. Yes, that made sense.

Vincent looked around the square. The grand white-stuccoed townhouses with their uniform pillared façades gave him a sense of déjà vu. He felt a chill run down his spine. He trembled; this was eerie. All the terraced houses had the same Victorian "period feel" to them. The house that he had mentally seen in his visions in Central Park was very much like these homes.

He quickly consulted his notebook. Number 18. Could that mean a house number? He kept walking along the side of the square that he had entered until about halfway along he saw number 18. It had a sign outside which read "The Royal College of Psychiatrists". This couldn't be what he had seen - a psychiatric college? No. He had clearly seen a residential house, not a college. Vincent was about to do an about turn when he noticed the "S" logo design that had been delicately incorporated into the iron railings running along the boundary.

It was the same sort of "S" design on the ironwork that he had seen in his flashes. He was feeling faint with excitement and anticipation. He felt the sweat running down his back. He felt compelled to go in and find out more about this place.

In the reception area there was a help desk for visitors, and a lounge with some comfortable chairs arranged around a low-level coffee table. He noticed a few glossy brochures on the coffee table and he casually picked up one. It was about the Royal College of Psychiatry. He quickly leafed through the sections on the college's courses, career options for students, publications, college events, faculty, and fees and finally reached the college history and college campus section. It read:

> *The district of London known today as Belgravia was developed in the 1820s. Previously it was called the Five Fields and was a rural area between London, as it was then, and the village of Knightsbridge.*
>
> *In the early nineteenth century the landowners, the Grosvenor family, began developing the area. The name "Belgrave" comes from their property of that name in either Cheshire or Leicestershire.*
>
> *The square is ten acres in size. Belgrave Square was laid out in 1826. The corners of the square are on the points of the compass and number 18 is part of the southwest terrace line, the last to be completed.*
>
> *The development was a success from the start, probably helped by George IV's decision to convert nearby Buckingham House into a palace for his residence. Later Queen Victoria rented number 36 for her mother and this was considered to be a royal seal of approval for the square.*
>
> *Many of the tenants were members of the aristocracy and people of political importance. The first tenant of number 18 was Sir Ralph Howard, who was himself MP for Wicklow, with extensive property in Ireland...*

The next tenant was Clementine, Lady Sossoon. She too had overseas connections; her husband's family, the Sossoons, came originally from Baghdad and India. She lived here from 1929 until 1942 and kept open house for the troops during the Second World War. She is said to have had parties here for soldiers during the war; also, part of the property was used as a Red Cross supply depot during this war. Lady Clementine left in 1942 but retained the tenancy until she died, aged over ninety, in 1955.

Number 18 was taken over by the Institute of Metals in 1956 and the College came in 1974.[lxii]

Vincent quickly consulted his notes from Central Park:

"Central Park 1997: Blood. Wounded soldiers. Bandages. Greek cross. Red. Bassano Portrait. Stately house. Number 18. London street. Iron fencing with an "S" logo. Indian antiques. Parties. Food. Musicians. 1940s La Salle ambulance. Buckingham Palace. Bell. Grave. So soon?"

Well, this place was very close to Buckingham Palace. It was in Belgrave Square. It certainly was a stately house with all the elements of Victorian architecture. It did bear the number 18. The "S" was definitely a part of its grillwork. Coincidence? Imagination?

Then it struck him! Bell...Grave...so soon. *Sossoon!* The house in Belgrave Square had been occupied by Lady *Sossoon*. It wasn't "*so soon*". It was *Sossoon!* That also explained the "S" in the iron grills! Vincent was now sweating profusely.

He went over the bit about Lady Sossoon again:

"The next tenant was Clementine, Lady Sossoon...kept open house for the troops during the Second World War...said to have had parties here for soldiers during the war...also part of the property was used as a Red Cross supply depot during this war."

'What is wrong with you, Vincent?' he said to himself irritably. 'Don't you realize that every cross is not a cross of Jesus? An equal armed cross is not only a Greek cross, it's also the symbol of the International Red Cross!'

Vincent stepped outside the house at 18, Belgrave Square. His cell phone had run out of power. Looking around, he located a bright red phone booth and managed to get through to Martha. Before she could get a word in, Vincent said, 'Listen, Nana. I need to talk to you very urgently. There's a pub quite close by. I saw it this morning while getting here. It's called the Star Tavern, I think. It's on the mews adjoining Belgrave Square. Can you meet me there ASAP?' Vincent then quickly made his way to the rendezvous.

The pub was located at the end of the secluded cobbled mews that were just off Belgrave Square. The pub had probably been built sometime in the early part of the nineteenth century to meet the food and drink needs of the domestics who served in the aristocratic homes of Belgravia. The mews, obviously, were for the horse stables as well as accommodation for coachmen. Of course, in the present day, the mews housed neither stables nor servants' quarters, merely millionaires' homes.

The pub was furnished with comfortable benches and scrubbed pine tables and Vincent also noticed a friendly room upstairs, which seemed to be a dining area. Vincent sat down and ordered himself a Fuller's London Pride and waited for Martha.

The table next to his was occupied by a dashing young man. Terry Acton had just finished his morning sessions with his patients at the Spiritualist Association and had wandered over to the pub for a relaxed lunch of fish and chips washed down with a pint of Chiswick Bitter.

About fifteen minutes later, Martha walked in. Vincent waved to her to let her know where he was seated. Martha walked over, took off her coat, folded it over the back of the chair and sat down. 'So Vincent, what's this about?' she began.

'Martha, is that you?' came the incredulous voice from the next table. Martha looked sideways at the occupant of the table next to theirs and saw the smiling face of Terry Acton. It took a few seconds for it to sink in.

'Martha, sweetheart! It's great to see you after so many years! You're looking great. Where on earth have you been?' asked Terry.

'It's been almost ten years since we went to *Igatpuri*, isn't it?' said Martha jokingly. Terry and Martha had visited India around the same time after their regression sessions in London but for different reasons. While Martha had been interested in brushing up on advanced yoga techniques, Terry had been enrolled in the *Bharatiya Vidya Bhavan* - a university of ancient sciences in Mumbai, which taught astrology and a few other occult sciences. During their Indian sojourns, both had independently decided to enrol for a course in Vipassana meditation at Igatpuri, a sprawling but serene Buddhist meditation centre located five hours away from Mumbai.[lxiii]

Igatpuri had certainly not been for the faint hearted. The school had required them to sign a solemn oath that they would not leave mid-course, the course itself being twelve days long. Each day, they would meditate for about ten hours on average and would live the life of Buddhist monks. They would maintain perfect silence and would be allowed the luxury of talking only on the twelfth day of the course.

Terry and Martha had, by pure chance, been allotted sleeping quarters that were next to each other. Unfortunately, they could not talk to one another at all for the full eleven days. On the twelfth day, when they had been given permission to talk, talk they certainly did; starved as they were of conversation for the previous 264 hours! They had driven back to Mumbai together after the course and had then continued to remain in touch while they pursued different vocations in India. Six months later, Martha had left India to return home to New York, whereas Terry had returned to London to the Spiritualist Association and his university research. They had lost contact completely thereafter. It was truly a wonderful surprise for both to meet like this, by sheer luck.

Martha continued, 'By the way, Vincent, this is one of my closest friends, Professor Terry Acton.'

'Nice to meet you, Professor,' said Vincent. 'I am Father Vincent Morgan. I have heard a lot about you from my aunt, who always talks about you very fondly.'

After a few pleasantries, Terry asked, 'Martha, I always thought that you were going to settle down in India permanently. What happened?'

81

Martha replied, 'I moved back to New York within a couple of years. I now teach yoga at my own centre in Manhattan. How about you?'

Terry responded. 'I owe my life to you, Martha. Without you, I could never have overcome the grief of losing Susan. My advanced degree in psychology from Yale would have been worthless if it weren't for your introduction to the Spiritualist Association. Today, I not only practise my art at the Spiritual Association here in Belgrave Square, but I also use it as the basis of psychiatric therapy. I also devote time to research in the fields of spirituality and religion. To that extent, I'm more theoretical than you.'

Vincent couldn't hold himself back. 'Mediums? Please don't think I'm being rude, but what exactly do you people do, Nana?'

Martha hesitated. She had deliberately kept her Spiritualist Association connections concealed from Vincent precisely because of his possible opposition. She then reluctantly spoke up. 'Well, as you know, the concept of reincarnation tells us that when we die, we shed our mortal bodies but the soul lives on. This soul generally finds another body and another life from which it can continue to learn. Once a soul has completely learned everything that there is to learn about life, it reunites with the Supreme Being in a state of Nirvana or bliss. In between the various lives that it takes rebirth in, the soul also takes rest. It is possible to tap into this spiritual energy through a spiritual medium and contact one's lost loved ones who may no longer be present in flesh but certainly are in spirit.'

Terry suddenly spoke up. 'I never believed in this stuff till I lost my wife some years ago. Your aunt, Martha, helped me reach out to her. Now I help people reach out to their loved ones. Besides being spiritual mediums, your aunt and I are also certified regression therapists, so we can help people who want to know more about their previous lives so that it can help them understand and deal with their present lives a little better.'

Vincent had many questions to ask. He was reluctant to ask them all for fear of seeming rude. Martha cut short his mental debate by telling Terry, 'Vincent obviously doesn't believe in reincarnation since he's a priest in the Roman Catholic Church.'

'Ah. Then I had better be careful about what I say,' said Terry light-heartedly, 'I wouldn't want to get into a theological debate with the clergy!'

Quite unexpectedly, Vincent turned to Terry and said, 'Please help me. Maybe God has guided me to you by providence! I want to know more.'

Vincent, Martha, and Terry were sitting in St. James' park, probably the most beautiful park in London. The tourists and locals were out in full force, strolling through the park, feeding the ducks, watching the pelicans, viewing Buckingham Palace from the bridge, supervising their kids in the playground, or enjoying refreshments in the park's café.

The three of them had eaten a quick lunch at the pub and had then walked over to the park so that they could discuss the issues surrounding the concept of reincarnation and regression. Martha had attempted to fill Terry in on the broad details of what Vincent had been going through since the death of his parents six years earlier, as well as the flashes and visions that he had been experiencing.

Terry took over. 'Listen to me, Vincent. Even if the entire idea of reincarnation is anathema to Catholicism, it doesn't mean that you can't believe in it. There are indeed many Christians who believe that reincarnation is not incompatible with Christianity. Consider this: Homosexuality is not approved by the Roman Catholic Church, but does it mean that there aren't any gays who continue to be Roman Catholic, culturally at least?'

Terry continued. 'The Roman Catholic Church tried Galileo in 1633 and held that his view of the planets revolving around the sun were rubbish. Can you be certain that the present view on reincarnation will not change at some time in the future? There are several non-canonical texts in the Nag Hammadi finds, the Dead Sea Scrolls, as well as the Gnostic gospels, that do, in fact, support reincarnation.'

Vincent listened to Terry patiently and then spoke. 'The fact is that for the first time in my life, I find some parts of myself in conflict with my faith.'

Martha suddenly cut in. 'Can I suggest something? You are obviously familiar with the concept of *Gnosis*, or personally experienced knowledge. Reincarnation as a theory can be debated endlessly. Instead, if you were to experience some part of the theory yourself, maybe through a regression session, your ability to accept or reject a certain point of view may become much easier.'

⟨✦⟩

Vincent was in his hotel room, semi-reclining on the bed, with several pillows propping him up. Terry had pulled up a chair next to him and had sat down. Martha was downstairs in the hotel lounge.

'Okay, I'm going to try to take you into a state of deep relaxation. I want you make yourself comfortable, settle back and relax...if you find that any limb or muscle is uncomfortable, just move it into the most comfortable position and then relax it.'

Vincent settled in and Terry continued. 'I now want you to focus on your breathing. Feel your breath going in...and out...in...and out ...imagine that with every exhalation you are breathing out all your toxins, your stress, your worries and your fears. With every inhalation, you are breathing in life-giving energy. Now visualize a beautiful light ...it is just above you...it's entering your body and healing you...all that's important to you is my voice...a peaceful easy feeling is settling over you like a wonderfully soft blanket...I will now count backwards from five down to one. You will feel yourself floating into a deeper and deeper trance with each number. Five...four...three...two...one.'

Vincent seemed to be semi-comatose so Terry went on. 'Now visualize that you are walking down a flight of stairs...with every step you take, you go deeper and deeper into a relaxed state...at the bottom of the stairs is a peaceful, tranquil oasis filled with energy, happiness, love, peace, joy, contentment...your mind is now so relaxed that it can allow itself to open up and remember almost everything.'

Terry paused before saying, 'Now think back to a childhood memory...it could be anything...something nice and happy...just be a neutral observer of the memory...it doesn't matter if your mind wanders a little...just experience the sensation of the memory...I will now count backwards from five down to one and you will become a child once again...Five...four...three...two...one.'

'Where are you?'

'I'm in the backyard of my parents' home in New York. There's a slight chill, but it isn't cold...it's probably autumn.'

'What are you wearing?'

'It's a baseball jacket and cap - New York Yankees. My father and I both love the Yankees.'

'Who are you with?'

'My dad and I are playing catch in the backyard. My mom is barbecuing hot dogs in the corner. I love the smell of the hot dogs. She puts on extra mustard, relish, ketchup, chopped onions and sauerkraut for me!'

'Are you enjoying yourself?'

'Oh I love the days that my dad doesn't have to go to work. We play catch and my mom barbecues. I love every minute of it. My parents are the most wonderful parents in the world. They take me to the movies, to the zoo and buy me cotton candy.'

'Okay, just enjoy the love and warmth that you are experiencing. Just relish the memory, savour it. I now want you to float above it a little and when I count backwards from five, I want you to go back deeper beyond the womb...think you can go deeper? Okay...five...four...three...two...one...where are you now?'

'It's a lovely Victorian house. It's definitely London. But the street is a mess. There's tension all around...I think there's a war going on.'

'Are you fighting in a war?'

'No. I'm a doctor. I make trips back and forth between the supply depots and the hospitals. The hospitals are overflowing with wounded soldiers and civilians. The Germans have been bombing London incessantly. I also drive the ambulance.'

'Really? What sort of an ambulance is it?'

'It's a sturdy 1940s Chevy…it's been modified…I think it's a La Salle. It's seen a great deal of action. The front fender is badly bent, but we have no time to fix it.'

'So why are you in this Victorian home?'

'Oh, it's a Red Cross supply depot. The house belongs to a wealthy Jewish lady who has allowed part of it to be used by the Red Cross. She is very kind and generous. She often hosts parties for the soldiers. I have attended one of them. Music and some food, whatever is possible, what with the war rationing.'

'Do you know her personally?'

'I have met her many times. She is very elegant. Her portrait photograph is in the lounge downstairs, done by a famous artist, Bassano, I think. The lounge opens into a beautiful square. The front door and grills have the family crest emblazoned on them…'S', I think.'

'Do you remember her name?'

'Sossoon, I think.'

'Sure?'

'Yes. Sossoon. The house is on Belgrave Square. I have to pick up my supplies from there. I often go past Buckingham Palace to the hospitals where I unload the stuff. Their family is quite famous. They made their wealth in Baghdad and then India.'

<hr />

Sossoon Ben Saleh had been born in 1745 and around thirty years later had been appointed Sheikh of Baghdad. Since the lion's share of Baghdad's earnings was derived from Jewish business, the Governor of Baghdad used to always appoint a Jewish finance minister or Sheikh.

In 1821, a new anti-Semitic Governor of Baghdad had ended up causing the departure of many Jewish families, including the Sossoons, who would eventually settle down in the Indian port of Mumbai, or Bombay, as it was then known.

Sheikh Sossoon's son, Matthew, was born in 1791. Matthew would acquire British citizenship and set up Matthew Sossoon & Co. in

Bombay, one of the most profitable firms exporting Indian opium to China.

Down the ages, his son, Jonathan Sossoon, would move to London to set up J.D. Sossoon & Co., which would soon own interests in shipping, real estate and banking, Jonathan would die in 1885 leaving behind a widow, Clementine, Lady Sossoon, who would continue living at 18, Belgrave Square, in London.

Alexander Bassano (1829-1913) was one of the most famous photographers of the time. He had the opportunity to turn out photographic portraits of some of the most aristocratic and beautiful women of the time.

Among these had been Clementine, Lady Sossoon.

***

'Okay. Forget the Red Cross and Sossoons. Is there anyone important in your life? Parents? Brothers? Sisters? Wife? Kids? Lover?' asked Terry. Vincent was still lying peacefully on the bed in his hotel room.

'My parents aren't alive. I have no wife or kids. The only one that I have is Clementine. She has everything - wealth and power. But she will soon die.'

'You must love her very much?'

'She is everything to me in an otherwise dreary world. Unfortunately she has cancer. It's a matter of time...she will soon die.'

'Do you remember what she looks like?'

'She's beautiful, and graceful, and delicate. But she is withering away. The hospitals are overloaded and medicines are a problem. I'm trying really hard to look after her as best as I can.'

'Can you see anyone who is from your present life?'

'Clementine - she's Nana in my present life.'

Vincent was still in a deep hypnotic state. Terry gently probed, 'So why do you think she is here with you again in this life?'

Vincent paused and then replied, 'She seems to be taking care of me, nurturing me, much the same way that I took care of her in our previous lives.'

'Can you see anyone else you recognize?' asked Terry.

'My parents.'

'Present life or past life parents?'

'My present life ones. They were strangers who were simply crossing the street and I was in a hurry to get some wounded soldiers to the hospital. My ambulance knocked them down!'

'What are you doing?'

'Not much I can do. They are dead. There is a young boy standing at the edge of the road. He's crying! I think he's their son. Oh God! What have I done?'

'Relax, Vincent. What do you think you can learn from what you have done?'

'I caused someone to lose their parents by my carelessness…my parents were lost by me in exactly the same circumstances!'

'Vincent, I now want you to once again hover above the memories. I will again count backwards from five, and I want you to go deeper, beyond the lifetime that you have just recounted…much further…five …four…three…two…one…and what do you see? Where are you now?'

'In Ireland, I think. They have no food.'

'Why? Who are they?'

'There is a famine. The Catholic farmers are starving. I am the tax collector. I have betrayed them all. I collect taxes from them that they just cannot pay, even if they were to sell themselves!'

'Anyone familiar?'

'Yes, I think so.'

'You think so?'

'Yes. I have a friend. Thomas Manning. I don't think it's him… No…it may be his father or grandfather.'

'Who is he?'

'I have betrayed his family. Will he betray me?'

Terry realized that he was not getting much out of Vincent, so he quickly shifted gears. 'Let's go deeper, Vincent…five…four…three… two…one…where are you?'

'A farm in rural India, a palatial house which is on the banks of a beautiful river.'

'Who are you?'

'I'm the son of a landlord. I am a teacher. I have just written a book.'

'Do you love your father?'

'Yes...No...I don't know. He is taking the side of the village elders. He does not want me to tamper with the traditions and caste equations of the village. I feel very let down.'

Terry was feeling the sweat building up on his forehead as he asked the next question.

'Do you see anyone familiar?'

'Yes. It's you! You! Terry! You are my father! I hate you! You sided with them!'

'Anything to learn?'

'For you. Not me.'

'What?'

'You prevented the truth from emerging. You blocked my path. You will make amends in another life, maybe this one. You will go to any lengths to ensure that the truth emerges.'

Terry digested this information and decided that it was time to move on. 'Vincent, hover above the memories again...I will again count backwards from five...go deeper...much further...five...four... three...two...one...and what do you see?'

'*Abwûn d'bwaschmâja nethkâdasch schmach têtê malkuthach nehwê tzevjânach aikâna d'bwaschmâja af b'arha.*'

'Which language are you speaking in? Is this your native tongue?'

'*Hawvlân lachma d'sûnkanân jaomâna waschboklân chaubên aikâna daf chnân schvoken l'chaijabên wela tachlân l'nesjuna ela patzân min bischa metol dilachie malkutha wahaila wateschbuchta l'ahlâm almîn.* [lxiv]'

'Vincent, I cannot understand what you are saying. I want you to float above the scene and see it as an impartial observer...I need you to tell me what it is that you see.'

'I am in Yerushalem. I am here on a visit to the great city.'

'Where have you come from?'

'Cyrene. It's in North Africa.'

'What are you doing? Can you see who is around you?'

'The streets are filled with people. The rough stones that line the street have blood on them. There is lots of shouting. I can see Roman soldiers everywhere.'

'What does Jerusalem look like?'

'Yerushalem? It is the most magnificent city. It is the biggest city between Alexandria and Damascus, with almost 80,000 people living here. Almost 250,000 visitors are here right now because of the Passover!'[lxv]

'Is it very crowded?'

'The pilgrims share the roads with teams of ox who are hauling huge blocks of limestone. Large-scale construction work is going on. As you approach the city, on the left side is a massive wall around 150 feet high. It's not the temple - it's just the platform of the temple! To my right is the upper city where the Jewish priests live in splendour.'

'So the city is being rebuilt?'

'Herod is a great builder. He has built forts, palaces, cities and an artificial harbour. He has rebuilt all the existing meandering streets on a paved grid and has created a palace that is surrounded by a moat and boasts of wondrous water gardens. He wants to outdo King Solomon.'

'How?'

'Tradition forbids enlarging the temple beyond Solomon's original size. Herod has added this gigantic thirty-five-acre platform, on which the temple sits. Some of the stones weigh more than fifty tonnes each.'

'Can you describe the temple?'

'The temple mount has seven entrances, but the main entry is from a stairway on the south side. At the foot of the stairs are shops selling sacrificial animals. There are also baths for ritual purification.'

'What do you do at the temple?'

'Sacrifice. A lamb for Passover, a bull for Yom Kippur, two doves for a child's birth.'

'So, one buys the animals and sacrifices them?'

'Yes, but to buy animals, one has to first change Roman Denarii for Shekels.'

'What are Shekels?'

'Shekels are temple currency. The coins have no portraits on them. They do not contradict Jewish law.'

'What is the temple like?'

'There are thousands of priests and scholars. There is smoke from the pyres as well as the screaming of terrified beasts that are about to be sacrificed. The abattoir smells terrible and there is blood all over.'

'How did you come to Jerusalem?'

'Caravan. Goods come in caravans from Samaria, Syria, Egypt, Nabatea, Arabia and Persia. Yerushalem is very cosmopolitan. Greek, Aramaic and Hebrew are spoken here.'

'Are the Romans in charge of the city?'

'Yes, but they do not really control things. In one of the corners of the Temple is the Antonia, the great Roman garrison that houses about three thousand soldiers. Many do not like what Herod has done by virtually demolishing the old temple. He has more or less built a Roman temple. People seem to hate being under Roman rule.'

'Which religions are under Roman rule?'

'Most of the temple elite consists of the Sadducees and the Pharisees. The Zealots are rather militant in nature whereas the Essenes live in monastic groups outside the city. There is a lot of tension among these groups.'

'What is causing the crowds on the streets?'

'I know...I saw it myself. Caiphas, the high priest of the Sanhedrin has asked Pontius Pilate to crucify this man who is bleeding. People are lining up in the streets to see him. He is being made to carry his crossbeam to Golgotha. The crowds are shouting Barabbas! We want Barabbas!'

'Anything else?'

'Εβραίος! βοηθήστε αυτό το κάθαρμα να φέρει το σταυρό του!'[lxvi]

'Vincent, you are again slipping into a language that I cannot understand. What did you just say?'

'Greek! They are calling me a Jew in a contemptuous way and asking me to help him with the cross.'

'Who is telling you this?'

'The Roman soldiers coming down the Mount of Olives.'

'What are you doing?'

'I am lifting up the crossbeam for him. I can see the man's face and body. He has been beaten savagely. He can hardly be recognized.

He is stooping even though I am now taking the entire load of the crossbeam. He is trying to say something to me.'

'What?'

'*Nayim Mayod Simon. Toda. Hashem Yaazor!*'

'You're again speaking in an alien language. I need you to float above the scene so that you can be a neutral observer. Now, what is he saying?'

'Nice to meet you, Simon. Thank you. God shall help. Hebrew. How in heaven's name does he know my name?'

'What else can you see around you?'

'The Jewish leaders. They seem to be very excited. They are hurling insults at him. Some women are crying. He is saying to them, "Daughters of Jerusalem, stop weeping for me. On the contrary, weep for yourselves and for your children! In the days ahead the childless woman will be considered lucky. When the end-time comes, men and women will be calling on mountains and the hills to cover them. If they do this when the tree is green, what will they not do when it is dry?"'

'What else can you see or hear?'

'*Eloi Eloi Lema Sabachthani?*'

'What are you saying, Vincent? What does that mean?' asked Terry.

Vincent continued animatedly. 'I have seen his agony as the hammers pound nails through his body. It's excruciatingly painful when the crossbeam is hoisted by ropes up the vertical post. They have placed two criminals on either side of him.'

Vincent had been in a hypnotic state for close to an hour. Terry was sweating profusely and his pulse was racing. Could this be real? A person in this life having seen Jesus upfront and alive in a previous life?

'"My God, my God, why hast thou forsaken me?" is what he is saying. They have put a sign over his head.'

'What does the sign read?'

'*Iésous o Nazóraios o Basileus tón Ioudaión.*'

'What is that?'

'Greek. Jesus the Nazarene, King of the Jews.'

'What else can you see?'

'The soldiers are dividing his clothes among themselves. The crowd is taunting him. They say that he saved others but could not save himself.'

'Is he replying to them?'

'Τους συγχωρήστε τον πατέρα επειδή δεν ξέρουν τι κάνουν.'

'What's that?'

'Forgive them, Father, for they know not what they do.'

'What else does he say?'

'Σας υπόσχομαι ότι σήμερα θα είστε στον παράδεισο με με.'

'Okay. To whom is he saying that and what does it mean?'

'He is talking to one of the criminals. He is promising him that he will take him to paradise. Two men are sharing a private joke near the cross. One man is commenting that the crucified king of Jews is calling for Elijah. The other fellow is saying, "Let's stay and see if Elijah helps him down!"'

'Anything else?'

'He's thirsty. They aren't giving him water. They are putting something that looks like vinegar. Is it vinegar? I can't quite make it out. No wait, it's a combination of a couple of things that they are putting on the sponge at the end of a long stick. They are now putting it to his lips. He's groaning. Wait! He's saying something..."Father, I commit my spirit to your hands. It is finished." He seems to have passed out.'

'Is he dead?'

'I can't be sure. He has definitely fainted. He surely looks dead. The centurion seems nervous. "Surely that good man was a son of God," he is saying. The crowd that has been standing around is now beating their chests with their fists. They are going away.'

'So everyone is leaving?'

'Since it's the day of preparation for the Passover, the temple clergy doesn't seem to want the bodies to stay on the crosses over the Sabbath. They've sent representatives to Pilate to ask that the legs of the crucified men be broken so as to bring death quickly. This will allow for their bodies to be removed in good time.'

'Are they breaking the legs?'

'They have broken the legs of the two criminals but they are checking to see whether Jesus is dead. One of the soldiers is raising his spear and thrusting it into Jesus' side...blood and water! He must be alive for blood to spurt like that! They seem to think he's dead. No point breaking the legs of a dead man, they are saying.'

'Where are you?'

'I am standing a little distance away. Near me are his mother and Mary Magdalene. I'm going closer to the cross. I want to see his condition. What's that smell? It isn't vinegar. It's some sort of opium ...opium and belladonna? I can't be sure.'

'What time is it?'

'It's evening. I'm hanging around to see what happens. There's this rich fellow called Joseph of Arimathea. He's been to Pilate and has obtained permission to take down the body and bury it. I wonder whether he realizes that the man could be alive?'

'Who is this Joseph?'

'Well, the people here say that he's a secret follower of Jesus. He's also very rich and can have his way with Pilate. Pilate was apparently quite surprised that Jesus died so quickly. I wonder whether he knows anything?'

'What's happening now?'

'They're carrying the body to a tomb that Joseph had hewn from a rock close to Golgotha. It's quite surprising that Pilate has allowed them to bury the body...Roman law does not allow for burial of crucified men. Joseph and another man, Nicodemus, are taking the body down. They have brought a long linen winding cloth and about a hundred pounds of crushed myrrh and aloe vera.'

<hr />

Pittsburgh, U.S.A., 2004

The scientists of the University of Pittsburgh had finally made the breakthrough in 2004. They had proved that an extract from the leaves of aloe vera could preserve organ function in rats that had lost massive amounts of blood. Indications were that aloe vera could possibly end up being the ideal treatment for battle wounds because the extract could help buy time until blood became available.[lxvii]

Accelerated loss of blood was quite difficult to replenish rapidly and this often led to organ failures. Aloe vera could step in at such times.

Dr. Mitchell Fink, the author of the Pittsburgh study, had formally indicated that the study had revealed that when the human body lost large quantities of blood, it would go into haemorrhage shock because blood would get diverted from the rest of the body to critical organs such as the heart, brain and liver. This would cause a drop in blood pressure.

The University of Pittsburgh team had found that the juice of aloe vera leaves actually reduced the force required by blood to flow through blood vessels, thus increasing the chances of survival. Some of these properties had been known to Indian sages since 1400 B.C.

❧

North India, 1400 B.C.

The great sage, Vyasa, was writing *Ayurveda* - the 'science of life'- by combining relevant medical texts from various ancient Indian books of wisdom. The sage was presently engrossed in the properties of a herb called heerabol. Heerabol was a herb that had a long history of therapeutic use in Ayurveda; it was routinely used to treat inflammations and infections.

The uses of heerabol were later introduced by Ayurveda into the Chinese and Tibetan medicinal systems during the seventh century. The *Gyu-zhi, The Four Tantras*, was one of the first Indian medical texts to be translated into Tibetan. As a result, in Tibetan and Chinese medicine, heerabol began being used in the treatment of impact injuries, wounds, incisions, and bone pain.

Subsequent research by the Memorial Sloan-Kettering Cancer Centre, would find that heerabol had anti-inflammatory and antipyretic properties when used on mice. According to the Memorial Sloan-Kettering Cancer Centre, a constituent of heerabol was a potent inhibitor of certain cancers.[lxviii]

The scientific name for heerabol is *Commiphora Molmol*. It is also known by its more common name, myrrh.

"Joseph and another man, Nicodemus, are taking the body down. They have brought a long linen winding-cloth and about a hundred pounds of crushed myrrh and aloe vera."

<hr />

London, UK, 2012

Vincent was still in his hotel room, semi-reclined on the bed. The pillows propping him up were damp from his perspiration. Terry continued to remain frozen on the chair next to the bed, and Martha was still downstairs in the hotel lounge.

The regression session had been going on for over an hour, and even though Terry was overwhelmed with the richness of detail that Vincent was able to recall, he realized that he needed to terminate the session and continue it another day, for the sake of his own health as well as for Vincent's well-being.

Terry began the process of bringing Vincent back into the present. 'Vincent, it's time for you to return to waking consciousness. I will now start counting upwards from one to ten. Let each incremental number awaken you more. By the time that I reach ten, you will open your eyes and will be fully awake, remembering everything that you saw... one... two... three... you're awakening... four... five... six... you're feeling good...seven...eight...you're nearly awake now... nine...ten...you can now open your eyes. You are now fully awake and are fully in control of your body and mind.'

Vincent's eyes adjusted themselves to the dimly lit room. It had become dark outside and the light that had been filtering in through the window when they had started the session was no longer available. Terry reached out to the bedside lamp and switched it on.

'So, how do you feel?' asked Terry.

Vincent's words came gushing out. 'Awesome. Terry, I am truly blessed to have been able to see the Lord. I had only read about the cross-bearer Simon, but I'd never ever imagined that I could have been that person in a previous life. I am truly blessed. Thank you for helping me experience this.'

Terry thought for a moment and then, lowering his voice, he said 'Vincent, I must tell you that I am as excited as you are. I have never been through a more nail-biting regression therapy session than the one that I just put you through. It's natural that you will want to share this experience with others. My advice is that you should be selective in choosing the people you share this information with. You should be prepared that many will think of you as a lunatic if you tell them what you just experienced.'

'Thanks for the advice…tell you what, let's go someplace where we can have a drink and I can share this with Nana!' said Vincent, excitedly kicking his feet off the bed and picking up his jacket that lay folded on the armchair in the corner.

Terry stopped him. From his jacket pocket he took out a folded envelope and handed it over to Vincent. On the face of the envelope were two words, *"Bom Jesus"*.

Vincent was confused. 'What is this?' he asked.

Terry replied, 'I have spent that last few years studying virtually every religions. Inside this envelope is a document that will have dramatic consequences for the world. I do not expect you to understand it. Just keep it safe and promise me that you will research it further in the event that your regression experiences point you in a certain direction. Having held back the truth in a previous life, I need to ensure that the truth prevails in this lifetime! I can't let sleeping dogs alone, my friend!'

❧

Even though Martha was curious about the outcome of the regression, she suppressed her eagerness. The three of them headed to the White Horse.

The White Horse, located at Parsons Green, was probably London's best pub, precisely because most Londoners did not know about it. The pub's cellar man, Mark Dorber, was internationally acknowledged as one of the best craftsmen in the storage and serving of English casked beer. The pub's menu was wide, but their hot favourites were bangers and mash, red bean soup and goats' cheese salad. The pub was one of Terry's regular haunts.[lxix]

Having settled in and ordered their drinks and food, Martha finally spoke. 'Well, Vincent, how did it go?'

Vincent recounted what he had seen during the hour-long session that Terry had put him through. Martha was wide-eyed with amazement as he attempted to recall each detail between gulps of Gales Trafalgar, a deep amber beer.

Vincent couldn't help pondering over the fact that Jewish burial customs had not changed in almost 3500 years and that Jewish burial simply involved washing the body and burying it. Embalming the body with herbs was never involved.[lxx]

So why were crushed myrrh and aloe vera being used on Jesus after he was taken down from the cross? And why was the soured-wine-vinegar sponge smelling of opium and belladonna? Why was Pontius Pilate willing to give the body of Jesus to Joseph, even though Roman law did not allow those sentenced to crucifixion to be given a burial?

There were just too many questions and not enough answers. *I have to discuss this with someone who can possibly help me reconcile what I have just seen with my faith*, thought Vincent as he helped himself to another succulent sausage with creamy mashed potatoes as he thought of his friend, Brother Thomas Manning.

Thomas Manning and Vincent had attended St. Joseph's seminary together and had been ordained to the priesthood at the same time. When Vincent's parents had died, it was Thomas who had taken care of all the funeral arrangements. He had continued to visit Vincent each day in the hospital while he was recovering. Yes, Thomas was just the person to give him direction and advice. But hadn't he seen Thomas Manning in Ireland in a previous life? Was he doing the right thing? Yes, he was sure he could trust Thomas.

As they were getting up they saw a petite Japanese woman sitting along with a Japanese man at a table by the window. She was sipping red wine and speaking rather softly, despite the din of the noisy customers. Vincent couldn't help thinking, *What a delightful creature!*

He did not notice her fixed gaze on Terry while they were inside the restaurant. He also did not notice her following Terry as he headed over to the university to pick up some reference material from the library later in the evening.

Most important, he did not notice his aunt, Martha, staring intently at the young Japanese woman.

Chapter Ten

Ireland, 1864

The Great Famine of Ireland had been caused by the failure of a single crop, the potato, which was the staple diet of Irish peasantry. Even though Catholic peasants were able to grow enough potatoes, most of their crop had to be sold off in order to pay the exorbitant land rents that were demanded by protestant minority landowners.[lxxi]

One of the poor Catholic families that fell victim to the Great Famine was the illustrious Ó Mainnín clan, descendants of Mainnín, a great chieftain of Connacht.

They were left with no alternative but to emigrate to America in 1864 because of the damn potato!

The Catholics who left Ireland and arrived in America never forgot the hunger that they had experienced and clung to their faith with fervent devotion. They also clung to their hatred of the protestant minority which had caused their hunger in the first place.

Middle Village, New York, U.S.A., 1968

One could not escape death in Middle Village. It was a neighbourhood in west central Queens that had grown precisely because of the cemetery business.

Middle Village had begun as a cluster of English families and had derived its name because of its central position between Williamsburgh and the Jamaica Turnpike. In 1879, St. John's Cemetery had been established just east of 80th Street by the Roman Catholic Church. The hamlet's economic progress had soon become inextricably linked to death.[lxxii]

Ninety years later, Thomas Manning had been born to parents who lived in a simple nondescript house along Metropolitan and 69th Street. Thomas' father worked for *The Ridgewood Times*, the local newspaper, which had been around since 1908. The name "Manning" was simply the English equivalent of the Gaelic Ó Mainnín.

In 1853, the bishop of New York had observed that there were many Catholics who were without a church in the Middle Village area. He commenced the construction of St. Margaret's Church and school in 1860. Thomas Manning would be baptized here in 1968.

The church and school would become the centre of Thomas Manning's early years growing up as a child in Middle Village. His favourite teacher, who taught the students science, economics and mathematics, made sure that he inculcated the right values among his wards. His favourite lessons and teachings were taken from a book of 999 sayings or maxims.

The book of 999 maxims, entitled *The Way* had been written by Josemaría Escrivá, the Spanish priest who had founded Opus Dei.

Yes, Thomas Manning was a very good student.

<hr/>

Einsiedeln, Switzerland, 1988
In fact, Thomas Manning was an excellent good student.

After preaching for several years at St. Catherine in Virginia, Manning had settled down in Switzerland in the Benedictine abbey of Einsiedeln some years later. Even now, the book of 999 maxims continued to remain by his bedside. His affiliation to the Priestly Society of the Holy Cross continued to be strong - much like the foundations of Einsiedeln. Father Thomas Manning had morphed into Brother Thomas Manning.

Einsiedeln traced its origins back to 835 A.D. when Meinrad, a Benedictine monk had withdrawn as a hermit into the Dark Forest. Many more hermits had followed him. Around a century later, Eberhard, a priest from Strasbourg, had assembled the hermits into a monastic community and had founded the Benedictine monastery of Einsiedeln.[lxxiii]

Einsiedeln would eventually become extremely important for Swiss Catholicism and also an international pilgrimage site. Einsiedeln would spur the creation of monastic foundations in North and South America, some of which would go on to become significantly bigger than Einsiedeln itself.

In fact, it was one of these American foundations that had found Thomas Manning and arranged for him to meet Cardinal Alberto Valerio in Italy. Valerio had discreetly spoken to the master of Einsiedeln and had ensured that the Oedipus trust had its way in recruiting the right man for the job.

When Manning had first arrived in Einsiedeln, it had taken him a while to become acquainted with daily monastic of prayer and work. This had been followed by a novitiate year during which he had been introduced to the Rule of St. Benedict, monastic spirituality, prayer, and community life. He had then taken vows for three years.

During these three years, he had been required to either study philosophy and theology or "work in his craft".

Brother Manning had chosen to apply his knowledge of mathematics and economics to better managing the finances of the monastery. Unknown to the other brothers of Einsiedeln, he was also managing several secret numbered accounts in Zurich for his mentor, Cardinal Alberto Valerio.

It was indeed true that it was no longer sufficient to slip into a monk's habit and sing *Gloria Patri*. The skills required by Brother Manning were altogether of a different order of magnitude.

London, England, 2012
Vincent was sitting in the pathetically small lobby of the Airways Hotel reading a newspaper.

In the UK, the commonly accepted joke was that *The Times* was read by the people who ran the country; *The Mirror* was read by people who thought they ran the country; *The Guardian* was read by the people who only thought about running the country; *The Mail* was read by the wives of the people who ran the country; *The Daily Telegraph* was read by the people who thought that the country needed to be run by another country; *The Express* by those who were convinced that, indeed, it was; and *The Sun* was read by people who couldn't care less who ran the country as long as the naked girl on page three had big tits.[lxxiv]

Vincent, however, was blissfully unaware of the big tits on page three. He was staring at the photograph of his new friend, Terry Acton, on page one.

The news story that followed was filled with gruesome details of the discovery of the severed head of Professor Terry Acton in the library of the School of Oriental and African Studies. It quoted a visibly shaken librarian, Barbara Poulson, saying that she, "could not believe that any human being could do this to another". Obviously Ms. Poulson was not up-to-date with global crime.

The story quoted a detective chief superintendent saying that a note had been found along with the severed head and that it had been decided to keep the contents of the note confidential to avoid public misconceptions about the nature of the crime. He went on to say that efforts were ongoing to locate the rest of the body and to track down the perpetrators as soon as possible.

Vincent was trembling. Why was God doing this to him? Why bring Terry into his life? Why open up secrets of a previous life? And who would want to kill Terry?

Vincent continued sitting in the lobby of the Airways Hotel, not bothered that the furniture and décor had seen better days. He continued staring at Terry's photograph until he made up his mind.

He got up, walked over to the front desk and asked the middle-aged matron behind the desk to lend him the phone. He pulled out his AT&T USA Direct calling card from his wallet and dialled the local access number in London - 0800 89 0011. The electronic English voice that answered prompted him to enter the area code and the seven-digit number in the United States. He entered 718 777 2840 for the number in Queens, New York. He was then prompted to enter his international calling card number, which he quickly did. He heard the single, long and straightforward ring tone that was so different to the local English hyphenated one. After four rings, Thomas Manning answered the phone.

'Hello?'

'Tom! I'm glad I caught you in New York. I wasn't sure whether I'd find you there or in Switzerland.'

'Vince, where are you? It's been ages.'

'I'm in London.'

There was a pause at the other end. After a moment, Thomas asked, 'Why are you in London?'

'Well, why not? Listen, Tom, I have to tell you something…I'm wondering whether it's such a great idea to have this conversation over a phone, but I don't know when I'll get a chance to meet you…'

'Vince, is something wrong? Has something happened?'

'Before I can say anything else, I need your promise to keep this conversation confidential.'

'Sure, but what exactly is the matter? You're beginning to worry me.'

'Okay, here goes…as you know, I had been having strange visions after the passing away of my parents. I needed to explore these strange visions. Don't ask why…but that's why I arrived here.'

'I don't understand, Vince. Why this phone call?'

'Tom. Yesterday I met a person by sheer chance, Terry Acton, a professor of spirituality and religion. He helped me explain some of the confusion surrounding the odd flashes that were going off in my head.'

The pause at the other end was much longer.

'Tom, are you still there?' asked Vincent.

'Yes, Vince. Sorry, my mind had wandered off elsewhere. You were talking about this professor.'

'Precisely. We spent an entire day together and he was killed the very same night!'

'What? How did that happen?'

'I have no idea. Tom, I'm really scared. Could God be punishing him for having opened up my past lives?'

'Whoa! Hold it right there. What past lives?'

'It's a long story.'

'Go ahead…I'm all ears,' said Thomas Manning as he pressed the automatic recording button that was built into the phone.

⟡

New York City, U.S.A., 2012
Thomas Manning picked up the phone and dialled the number in Vatican City.

The Bang & Olufsen phone buzzed gently. His Eminence answered it on the first ring. He pressed the button on the SV-100 scrambler that was attached to the line; one couldn't be too careful nowadays.

When the voice answered, Thomas quickly spoke in Latin, '*Salve! Quomodo vales?*'

The voice answered, '*EGO sum teres. Operor vos postulo ut sermo secretum?*'

Thomas replied in hushed tones, '*etiam Vincent Morgan postulo futurus vigilo.*'

The voice was concerned. '*Quare?*'

Thomas began explaining the situation to His Eminence. 'Is orator volo...we have a problem...'.

His Eminence was on alert.

'Terry Acton may have spoken with someone before his death,' continued Thomas.

His Eminence was getting angry and he spoke sharply, 'Who?'

'Father Vincent Morgan. Apparently they spent the entire day together before Acton was killed.'

His Eminence was turning crimson red, the colour of his faith, but he controlled his rage.

'Do you think that he knows about Terry Acton's research? Is he Illuminati?' asked His Eminence.

'I don't think he knows as yet. And no, I don't think that Vincent is Illuminati. Terry Acton was definitely Illuminati, but I don't think Vincent is a secret follower. Terry Acton's connections to the Illuminati only happened because of his Rhodes and his Skull & Bones connections,' explained Thomas Manning.

Valerio cut in. 'Thomas, let me be specific. Do you think that Acton would have shared the *Bom Jesus* records?'

Thomas Manning was quiet for a moment. He then replied, 'It's very likely, given the fact that Vincent believes that saw Jesus Christ in a previous life.'

'Blasphemy!' shouted His Eminence.

'True. But he genuinely believes it. I have the recording of the conversation I had with him over the phone. I am quite sure that Terry Acton also believed it. It's quite possible that they discussed the Bom Jesus papers,' replied Thomas.

'Then there's only one solution. I will meet you in Zurich to decide the final steps to rid ourselves of this Illuminati menace!' shouted the loyal member of the *Crux Decussata Permuta*.

Virgin Atlantic's flight VS 900 from London Heathrow to Tokyo's Narita airport took off at 1 p.m. in the afternoon. The camera-slinging Japanese tourist couple, Mr. and Mrs. Yamamoto, were in Virgin's Upper Class cabin having received their professional fees for the library job from their mentor at the Dorchester Hotel. He had checked out the same day and left for Vatican City.

Mr. Yamamoto did not know that Mrs. Yamamoto had received a fresh assignment involving her "husband".

Unknown to them, another flight from Rome was taking off fifty-five minutes after their departure. Swiss International Airlines flight LX 333 was on its way to Zurich. Since the airline did not have a first-class section on this flight, His Eminence Alberto Cardinal Valerio had no option but to settle for business class.

The previous evening, Brother Thomas Manning had boarded American Airlines flight 64 at JFK Airport. He had arrived in Zurich at 7:05 a.m. the next morning, a full nine hours before His Eminence. He had proceeded to Einsiedeln only to return to Zurich on a forty-seven-minute train ride leaving Einsiedeln for Zurich at 3 p.m. Swiss time, with a single change at Wädenswil.

Mr. and Mrs. Yamamoto arrived in Tokyo twelve hours after their departure from London. Takuya was tired and decided to soak himself in the bathtub while Swakilki decided to dutifully unpack for both of them.

Swakilki thought about the specific instructions that she had received from His Eminence. Future activities were going to be extremely delicate. Duets were out; solo performances were required. Takuya was a liability.

She needed to calm herself. Where the hell was the marijuana? She steadied herself and walked over to the steamed-up bathroom and opened the medicine cabinet. She rolled herself a spliff using the cannabis stored in the innocent-looking vitamin jar. With trembling hands she lit it and inhaled long and hard. As she inhaled, she felt the easing of the tension and the onset of mild euphoria.

She was fine. She was beautiful. She didn't need Takuya. He needed her. The enemy had to be killed. She turned around and saw that he had fallen asleep in the tub and was snoring gently.

She took out the hairdryer from her travel kit and plugged it in. She then flipped on its switch and released it casually into the tub. She then watched with a blank expression as the electric current raced through Takuya's body. As his breath escaped him, she regained hers.

Zurich, Switzerland, 2012

The two men sat together at His Eminence's favourite place, Sprüngli's café on Paradeplatz. His Eminence had ordered hot chocolate for both of them.

As they sipped the rich brew, they discussed the latest complication, and two decisions were taken over two rounds of hot chocolate.

Let Swakilki handle the pest, Vincent Morgan. Let Brother Thomas Manning represent the Oedipus trust to negotiate a settlement with the Isabel Madonna trust.

Chapter Eleven

London, England, 2012

The Church of the Holy Ghost at 36, Nightingale Square, had its convent chapel dedicated in 1890. The present church building had opened seven years later in 1897.

Vincent and Martha were among the several students, colleagues, friends and family, who sat inside the church attending the special memorial Mass for Professor Terry Acton. Vincent still found it hard to believe that someone could brutally murder a simple and harmless man for no apparent reason. The manner of his death seemed to indicate something far deeper.

Martha was thoroughly shaken. The depth of her loss could be seen in her moist eyes that would well up every few minutes.

They sat quietly listening to the sermon. 'The faith that Jesus had in God, allowed him to look at death in a detached way. In fact, he seemed to approach the whole issue in a rather relaxed way. Death was simply a door that led to a far better existence,' the pastor was saying.

Memorial Mass over, Vincent and Martha stepped out from the cool, dark interiors of the church into a sunny afternoon. Vincent tried consoling Martha.

'Why should you be sad? You are one of the most ardent believers of life after death. Terry has simply moved on. He's probably with his wife right now. C'mon, Nana, be brave,' said Vincent.

Vincent continued, 'Terry gave me a document after our regression. He specifically asked me to follow up on the regression because it might prove a theory of his. Nana, I am going to need your help.'

'Vincent, I am in no condition to help anyone. I can barely manage myself,' snapped Martha.

Vincent shot back, 'Listen, I know this is difficult for you, but if you are Terry's friend, then you will do what he would have wanted you to do…you owe it to Terry.'

Vincent and Martha took the stairs to the third floor of the SAGB, which was used for healing therapies such as Reiki, spiritual healing and regression, and borrowed a room. Martha was still loved and remembered by the administrative staff and they were happy to oblige.

'Okay, get yourself comfortable, physically comfortable. Settle back and relax...that's right...just...relax,' started Martha. 'Look up and observe the skylight. You can see a little green dot on the skylight ...completely focus your concentration on that spot for a while as you continue to listen...a peaceful easy feeling is settling over you...your eyes want to close. That's fine. You want to go deeper and relax. Your eyelids are heavy...your eyes will close on their own just to rest themselves...I will now count backwards from five down to one. You will feel yourself floating into a deeper and deeper trance with each number. Five...four...three...two...one. Okay, Vincent, where are you?'

'I think I'm in France.'

'What is happening?'

'There are public executions going on. I'm in the crowd, but in front of me is the Place de la Revolution. There is a guillotine in the centre.'

'What sort of guillotine is it?'

'It has two large upright posts joined by a beam at the top. It sits on top of a platform that is reached by two dozen steps. The whole machine is blood red. There is a huge blade that has a weight on it. This blade runs in grooves that have been greased with tallow.'[lxxv]

'Are people being killed?'

'The reign of terror has already killed thirty thousand people. In this month only over a thousand people have been beheaded.'

'Are you in the middle of the French Revolution?'

'I think so. It's 1794.'

'Who are you?'

'I am Jean-Paul Pelletier. I'm watching the public spectacle. Right now they are about to execute a young woman called Charlotte Lavoisier.'

'Why?'

'She has been condemned by trial for stabbing and wounding me, Jean-Paul Pelletier, a great leader of the revolution.'[lxxvi]

'Is she waiting for the blade to fall?'

'*Non, elle a juste arrivé dans le tumbrel normal...elle demande à Sanson, le bourreau, voir la guillotine. Elle est courageuse!*'

'Stop there, Vincent. Float above the scene. I need you to repeat what you just said in English, not French.'

'She has just arrived in the usual tumbrel...she has got off...she's asking Sanson, the executioner, to be allowed to take a closer look at the guillotine...she hasn't seen one before and is curious to see how it works...my, she is brave!'

'What's happening now?'

'She is being strapped to the bascule and the bascule is being hinged horizontally to bring her head into the lunette.'

'Go on.'

'Sanson is pulling the cord...the blade is released...the head is off! It is rolling into the bloody oil cloth in the wicker basket in front of the guillotine!'

'Okay, Vincent, I need you to go deeper into your previous lives. I'm going to count backwards from five, and when I finish counting you will be in an even older life...five...four...three...two...one... where are you now?'

'I am in Tawantinsuyu.'

'Where is that?'

'South America. I am a respected warrior under the command of Sapa Inca Pachacuti.'

'Are you an Inca warrior?'

'Yes. Sapa Inca Pachacuti has vastly expanded and created the Tahuantinsuyu. He is the head and he has four provincial governments Chinchasuyu, Antisuyu, Contisuyu and Collasuyu. These are located at the four corners of his vast empire. At the centre is Cuzco, the capital.'[lxxvii]

'Are you in Cuzco?'

'No. Sapa Inca Pachacuti has built a huge retreat in Machu Picchu. I protect his family there.'

'What is Machu Picchu like?'

'Oh, it is the most beautiful place on earth. It is located on a high mountain ridge, very high up in the clouds. It has a huge palace and several temples. About 750 people can stay in Machu Picchu at a given time. The mountain ranges in the background of Machu Picchu resemble an Inca looking up at the sky...the tallest one, Huayna Picchu, is the Inca's nose.'

'What else can you tell me about Machu Picchu?'

'We Incas believe that the solid foundation of the earth must never be cut, so we have had to build this entire place from loose rocks and boulders that did not have to be cut at all! Many of our buildings have no mortar...it is our extreme precision in cutting that allows this to be done.'

'What do you see around you?'

'Temples for Apo, the god of the mountains, for Apocatequil, the god of lightning, for Chasca, the goddess of dawn, for Chasca Coyllur, the goddess of flowers, for Mama Coca, the goddess of health, for Coniraya, the moon god, for Ekkeko, the god of wealth, for Illapa, the god of thunder, for Kon, the god of rain and for many, many others...'

'Is the king a just person? Does he treat you well?'

'*No ladrón, no mentiroso, no ocioso. Tal como estimes a otro, otros también te estimarán.*'

'What language is that, Vincent? Sounds like Spanish.'

'*Quechua.* It is the language that we speak here.'

'So what did you just say?'

'The king is a just man. His motto is, "Do not steal, do not lie, don't be lazy". He also believes that just as you love others, they will love you.'

'What is your role?'

'I am the bodyguard for Mama Anawarkhi.'

'Who is that?'

'She is the wife of Sapa Inca Pachacuti.'

'What do you have to do?'

'I am supposed to protect her. Instead I am going to kill her. She is plotting against the Sapa Inca.'

'Vincent, I need you to go even deeper…I'm once again going to count backwards five…four…three…two…one…where are you now?'

'我是在中國。我是在宮殿裡面。'

'I take it that you're somewhere in Asia?'

'我有很多痛苦。我是在極度痛苦。痛苦是可怕的。'

'Vincent, I need you to distance yourself from the scene. Can you pull away slightly so that you can tell me in English?'

'I am in China. I am in a palace. I have a lot of pain. I am in agony. The pain is terrible.'

'What has happened to you?'

'The empress, Wu Zhao is the evil power on the throne. She had my limbs shattered and then had me placed in a large wine urn to die a slow death in agony!'

'Why would someone be so cruel?'

'I was an advisor to Emperor Gaozong while he lived. I advised him to be wary of Wu Zhao, the emperor's chief concubine. After the death of Emperor Gaozong, Wu Zhao has seized the throne and wants to eliminate me.'[lxxviii]

'Has she succeeded?'

'我認為不如此'

'Sorry?'

'I do not think so. Even though I am a cripple for life, I was saved by one of the other concubines, Xiao. I am lucky.'

'Can you tell the time period - which year is this?'

'I think it is 689 A.D.'

'So where are you? Why are you still in the palace?'

'The kind concubine Xiao has arranged for me to be transported to my ancestral village. Hopefully, I will be able to live the rest of my life there without being detected by Wu Zhao's spies.'

'Vincent, much deeper now…I'm once again going to count backwards - five…four…three…two…one…where are you now?'

'I am in Yerushalem. I'm outside the tomb into which Joseph and Nicodemus have taken Jesus.'

'Who else is there?'

'Mary Magdalene and his mother followed. I was behind them. But it's close to sundown and the women have returned home for the Sabbath.'

'What are you doing?'

'I am now waiting outside the tomb. Temple guards have been sent here to secure the tomb. The Pharisees are worried that the followers of Jesus may try to steal Jesus' body and then claim that he has risen from the dead. They are placing their own guards.'

'Now what?'

'I am hiding behind some bushes. I don't know why I am unable to tear myself away from here. Night has fallen. In the middle of the night, there was a visitor. He looked like an angel because of his white robes...I think he was an Essene monk. He rolled away the stone. The guards collapsed with terror.'

'And?'

'The Sabbath is over, and the two Marys have come here to roll away the stone to the tomb, but they are rather surprised to see it open. They are going inside. I'm following at a discreet distance.'

'What do you see?'

'There are two men in white robes. They look like Essenes. They are saying that Jesus is alive, not dead! They are asking the women to go and tell the disciples this news.'

'And do they?'

'They are running out. I'm waiting here to see what happens.'

'Anyone there?'

'The two Essenes are still there. The third person is not recognizable; he has come out of the bushes. Someone's coming...'

'Who?'

'His disciples; Peter and John. Both are looking around inside... no, wait, they are coming out. They seem bewildered. They are returning to the city. Ah. Here comes Mary.'

'Which Mary?'

'Mary Magdalene.'

'What is she doing?'

'She's looking inside the tomb. She seems very nervous. She's staring at the two Essenes inside the tomb. She now sees the third man in the bushes. Is it the gardener? No. It's Jesus! Mary is talking to him.'

'Can you hear what they are saying to each other?'

'Not really. I think he is asking her to go and tell his disciples. She is walking away. Jesus is also walking away, but not with her.'

'What are you doing?'

'I am following Jesus.'

'Where is he going?'

'He is following two of his disciples who are on their way to Emmaus. He is catching up with them. He is now walking alongside them and is talking to them. They do not realize that it's him.'

'What is he saying?'

'He is telling them that prophets must necessarily go through suffering. They have reached Emmaus. They have reached the house and are having dinner. Jesus is picking up a piece of bread, giving thanks and breaking it into pieces before giving it to them. Finally! They have finally realized that it's Jesus!'

'Okay. What are they doing now?'

'The two disciples are heading back to Yerushalem and are meeting the apostles and some others in a secret place. They are telling the others of their experience. Ah! Jesus has arrived here also.'

'They must all be happy?'

'They are scared. They think that he's a ghost. Jesus is telling them not to doubt him. He's pulling his robe to one side to show them his wounds. They seem reassured but not quite certain. He's asking them for food. They've given him some broiled fish. He's eating it. Now they seem to understand that he's real.'[lxxix]

'Go on.'

'Jesus is leaving. I'm still here with the apostles. Oh, it seems that Thomas wasn't here. Here he comes now.'

'What are they saying?'

'The apostles are telling Thomas about Jesus being alive. He doesn't believe them. He's telling them that unless he sees and feels the scars for himself, he cannot believe.'

'Who are you with?'

'I've decided to remain here just in case Jesus comes back. The apostles are meeting here regularly.'

'Ah, today both Thomas and Jesus are here. Jesus is calling out to Thomas and asking him to touch his wounds. Now Thomas seems to believe that this is Jesus in the flesh. Jesus is calling him a "*doubting Thomas*" because he only believes when he sees everything for himself.'

'Now what's happening?'

'I'm following Jesus to Lake Galilee. Peter, Thomas, Nathaniel, James and John are here. They are fishing through the night with no luck. Jesus is waiting for them on the beach. He's asking them whether they have any fish. They're telling him that they have not caught anything at all. Jesus is telling them to cast their nets to the right because he knows that there are some fish there. They are trying. They catch a huge load of 153 fish! Jesus has started a charcoal fire and is making breakfast for them. He's asking Peter some questions.'

'And?'

'He's walking away with Peter. John's following. I'm behind them.'

'Where are they going?'

'To a mountain in Galilee. Jesus has arranged a meeting there with all his apostles.'

'What is happening at this meeting?'

'Jesus is telling them to go to different parts of the world in order to recruit disciples in every nation. They are kneeling down as he speaks. They are now getting up and he's leading them to the outskirts of Bethany. He's blessing them. He's walking away towards Bethany ...the town of Martha, Lazarus and Mary Magdalene.'

Chapter Twelve

The term *Shinto* was simply a combination of two words - *Shin* meaning God, and *Tao* meaning path. Shinto was thus nothing else but the Path to God. *Shin* was the Chinese symbol for God and was pronounced as "Kami" by the Japanese. To that extent, Shinto was also *Way of the Kami*.[lxxx]

Kami were generally seen as divine spirits that were still caught in the cycle of birth, death and rebirth. The Meiji restoration had resulted in Shinto becoming the state religion of Japan. State Shinto, however, had ended with the Second World War. To many, it appeared that the divine spirits, or Kami, had been unsuccessful in creating a *Kamikaze*, divine wind, to repel the foreign attacks. Shortly after the end of the war, the Emperor had renounced his status as a living god.

In modern Japan, however, Shinto continued to flourish minus the divine status of the royal family. Shinto shrines continued to assist ordinary people in maintaining relationships with the spirits of their ancestors and Kami.

When Swakilki had been born, her mother, Aki Ogawa, had got Swakilki's name added to the list kept at the Sumiyoshi Jinja, one of the oldest Shinto shrines in Osaka, and had her declared Ujiko, a named child. It was a way of making sure that the divine Kami protected Swakilki during this lifetime and beyond.

Swakilki was now at Sumiyoshi Jinja. Even though she was a Catholic, Shinto belief and rituals had remained with her and she desperately wanted comforting. She had just killed the only man that she had ever come close to loving. She was now well and truly alone, except for the divine Kami.

After electrocuting Takuya, she had spent the next six hours meticulously cleaning the apartment till she had removed all traces of herself. She had then packed all her belongings, loaded his body into the trunk of her Toyota Sprinter and had driven out of Tokyo along the Toumei Express Motorway to Nagoya. She had then transferred to the Meishin Express Motorway to Osaka. Soon she was driving towards Kansai International Airport. She had stopped for a brief moment on the three-kilometre bridge connecting the mainland to the artificial island airport in order to throw the body into Osaka Bay.

She had then checked into a room at Osaka's Hyatt Regency Hotel where she had placed a "Do Not Disturb" sign on the door and had slept for the next seven hours. It was when she woke up and saw the emptiness of her bed that she realized how much she missed him already.

Swakilki now walked through the torii, the double column gate of the Sumiyoshi Jinja, and crossed over the beautiful bright red staircase bridge within the complex. Swakilki stopped at the water fountain to wash her hands and mouth, a "purification" expected before entering a shrine. She needed to find Yoshihama Shiokawa.

Yoshihama was a Shinto priest who had become quite famous in the area. His claim to fame was his combination of Shinto principles with Reiki, the ancient Japanese art of spiritual healing; Something that Swakilki desperately needed.

<hr/>

Reiki was an alternative therapy developed during the latter half of the nineteenth century by Mikao Usui in Japan. The word *Reiki* was a combination of two Japanese words - *Rei* implying the cosmos and *Ki* for energy. It was, therefore, the energy of the cosmos.

Practitioners such as Yoshihama Shiokawa believed that they could direct Reiki energy through their palms into specific parts of the patient's body. Most important, Yoshihama had combined Reiki with Shinto and Buddhist principles in order to handle mental healing along with physical healing. He believed that he could treat even deeply ingrained issues such as addiction, anxiety, and depressive tendencies by getting "visions" of incidents in the present and past lives of his patients as he energized them.

Yoshihama asked Swakilki to lie down and relax. Once she was relaxed, he began to apply his hands to various areas. Reiki energy would enter Swakilki through her seventh chakras. Her body would absorb Reiki energy to heal itself, and unwanted energy would be dissipated.[lxxxi]

Swakilki began to feel varying sensations, hot flushes, cold waves, and pressure. The Reiki energy was flowing. Her energy deficiencies were being filled, her energy meridians were being repaired and opened, blocks of stale energy were being slowly melted away.

His hands stopped in the air over her pelvic region. He was certain. This girl had definitely faced sexual trauma in her life; probably child abuse, but he didn't make any comment.

His palms were feeling warm. Too much heat. An explosion? What sort of explosion? Why was he seeing a cardinal in scarlet robes?

Yoshihama was gradually moving his palms over Swakilki's head and was moving down towards her shoulders. He stopped at the base of her neck. 'You have a severe energy blockage here,' he said as a vision flashed before him. In the vision he saw a young woman's head being chopped off by a guillotine in eighteenth-century Paris. In his vision, Yoshihama did not see the faces of Charlotte Lavoisier or Sanson. The faces were different. The young woman's face was that of Swakilki! And, unknown to Yoshihama, the executioner's face was that of Professor Terry Acton.

He moved his palms further down to her stomach. It was definitely tight and constricted. She had something to hide. Guilt? She had killed. Who? Another vision. An electric chair at Sing Sing prison in New York in 1890. The woman is killed by the flick of a switch that sends 2450 volts of electricity through her. The switch was flicked by the state executioner whose face Yoshihama could not recognize. Actually, the face was of Takuya, recently electrocuted himself.

Another vision. An Inca palace in Machu Picchu. Mama Anawarkhi, the wife of the king, Sapa Inca Pachacuti, is being strangled by her bodyguard. Bodyguard's face was not known to Yoshihama. The face was actually that of Vincent Morgan.

Yoshihama moved his palms along her arms and onwards to her hands. The hands had evil energy flows. Murder? Was this a killer that he was healing? In his vision, Swakilki morphed into Empress Wu Zhao, the evil power on the Chinese throne, shattering the limbs of Vincent Morgan as revenge for having killed Mama Anawarkhi.

She then morphed back into Swakilki as she killed again and again and again.

Chapter Thirteen

Medina, Saudi Arabia, 632 A.D.

All the wives of Prophet Muhammad took care of him during his illness. Lady Ayesha was always by his side. She would only withdraw when his daughter, Lady Fatima, came to visit him.

After a short illness, Prophet Muhammad died at around twelve noon on Monday, 8th June, 632 A.D. in the city of Medina at the age of sixty-three.[lxxxii]

The Qur'an had been revealed to him by the angel Gabriel over an extended period of time before his death. The Prophet, in turn, had dictated the revelations to his secretaries.

One of the passages (4:155-159) that was among the several others dictated by the Prophet read:

They said in boast 'We killed Jesus the son of Mary the Apostle of Allah.' But they killed him not nor crucified him. But so it was made to appear to them. And those who differ therein are full of doubt with no knowledge but only conjecture to follow. For sure they killed him not![lxxxiii]

Could the Prophet possibly have heard of Irenaeus of Lyons?

Lyons, France, 185 A.D.

The intriguing paragraph written by Irenaeus in Book II, Chapter 22, of his treatise, *Against Heresies* reads as follows:

On completing His thirtieth year He suffered, being in fact still a young man, and who had by no means attained to advanced age...from the fortieth and fiftieth year a man begins to decline towards old age, which our Lord possessed while He still fulfilled the office of a Teacher, even as the Gospel and all the elders testify.[lxxxiv]

In this rather strange paragraph, Irenaeus was telling his readers that Jesus was very much alive and teaching at the age of fifty, even though he was no longer the youthful man that he had been at the time of his crucifixion at around the age of thirty.

Was it possible that Irenaeus had read an Indian book of history called the *Bhavishya Mahapurana* that spoke of a meeting that had happened in 115 A.D.?

North India, 115 A.D.

The man sitting on the mountain had a peaceful and tranquil expression. Peace and love seemed to radiate from within him. King Shalivahana was enraptured by this man's serenity.

Shalivahana was a brave and effective ruler. He had vanquished the attacking hordes of Chinese, Parthians, Scythians and Bactrians. One day, Shalivahana went into the Himalayas. There, in the Land of the Hun, the powerful king saw a man sitting on a mountain who seemed to promise auspiciousness. His skin was fair and he wore white garments.

The king asked the holy man who he was. The other replied, 'I am called a son of God, born of a virgin, minister of the non-believers, relentless in the search of the truth.'

The king then asked him: 'What is your religion?'

The other replied, 'O great King, I come from a foreign country, where there is no longer truth and where evil knows no bounds. In the land of the non-believers, I appeared as the Messiah. O King, lend your ear to the religion that I brought unto the non-believers. Through justice, truth, meditation and unity of spirit, man will find his way to Issa in the centre of light. God, as firm as the sun, will finally unite the spirit of all wandering beings in himself. Thus, O King, the blissful image of Issa, the giver of happiness, will remain forever in the heart; it is for this that I am called Issa-Masih.'[lxxxv]

The Hindus had eighteen historical books called the *Puranas*. The ninth book was the *Bhavishya Mahapurana*. Unlike the Gospels, which could not be accurately dated, the *Bhavishya Mahapurana*'s date of origin was clearly known. It was authored by the poet Sutta in the year 115 A.D.

The historical passage on King Shalivahana and the holy man was from the *Bhavishya Mahapurana*.

Could the *Bhavishya Mahapurana* have possibly influenced Hazrat Mirza Ghulam Ahmad?

⟡

Qadian, India, 1835

Hazrat Mirza Ghulam Ahmad was born in the year 1835 in a small town called Qadian in India. He became famous in the Islamic world and before his death in 1908 he published a book titled *Masih Hindustan Mein*[lxxxvi]. He later went on to found the Ahmaddiya sect of Muslims. In his book he wrote:

> *Let it be noted that though Christians believe that Jesus, after his arrest through the betrayal by Judas Iscariot, and crucifixion, and resurrection, went to heaven, yet, from the Holy Bible, it appears that this belief of theirs is altogether wrong...*
>
> *The truth rather is that as Jesus was a true prophet...he knew that God...would save him from an accursed death...he would not die on the cross, nor would he give up the ghost on the accursed wood; on the contrary, like the prophet Jonah, he would only pass through a state of swoon.*
>
> *Jesus, coming out of the bowels of the earth, went to his tribes who lived in the eastern countries, Kashmir and Tibet, etc. - the ten tribes of the Israelites who, 721 years before Jesus, had been taken prisoner from Samaria by Shalmaneser, King of Assur, and had been taken away by him. Ultimately, these tribes came to India and settled in various parts of that country.*
>
> *Jesus, at all events, must have made this journey; for the divine object underlying his advent was that he should meet the*

121

lost Jews who had settled in different parts of India; the reason being that these in fact were the lost sheep of Israel.

Of course, Hazrat Mirza had not heard of the Bnei Menashe, who would come into prominence several years later.

❦

Israel, 2005

The report filed at the BBC World News desk in early April was crisp and concise:

An Indian tribe called the Bnei Menashe have always claimed that they are one of the ten lost tribes of Israel. Now, one of Israel's chief rabbis has recognized this Indian tribe as the lost descendants of ancient Israelites.

Lalrin Sailo, convenor of the Singlung-Israel Association, an organization representing the Jews of India, said: "We have always said we are descendants of Menashe (son of Joseph) so it is great to hear that our claims have been authenticated."

According to the community, the Bnei Menashe are one of the lost ten tribes of Israel who were exiled when the Assyrians invaded the northern kingdom of Israel in the eighth century BC. The community's oral tradition is that the tribe travelled through Persia, Afghanistan, Tibet, China and on to India.[lxxxvii]

The report spoke about the journey made by the lost tribes of the eighth century BC, but failed to mention the journey that St. Thomas had made to India in 52 A.D.

❦

India, 52 A.D.

Acta Thomae, The Acts of Judas Thomas, was written in several languages, including Syriac, Greek, Latin, Armenian and Ethiopic. According to the book, after the crucifixion, the apostles had met in order to allocate the various countries of the world among themselves. The Middle East and India had fallen into the lot picked by St. Thomas.

The book went on to say that a merchant by the name of Habban arrived in Jerusalem searching for a carpenter needed by the Indian king Gondophares. Jesus apparently met Habban, introduced himself as Jesus the Carpenter, and sold his 'slave', Thomas, to Habban for twenty pieces of silver.

Habban enquired of Thomas whether Jesus was his master. Thomas quite naturally answered, 'Yes, he is my Lord.' It was then that Habban told Thomas, 'He has sold you to me.'

Jesus had taken the twenty pieces of silver from Habban and had given them to Thomas, who then left on Habban's boat. The sea route to India took them via the port of Sandruk Mahosa, and they eventually reached the kingdom of Gondophares in India.

Thomas then proceeded southwards to Kerala. In Kodungallur, several families of Kerala were converted to the Christian faith. After establishing several churches, Thomas moved on to the east coast of India and had eventually been martyred near Mylapore.

The St. Thomas Christians would continue to flourish in Kerala after Thomas' death.

This position would remain unaltered till 1498.

———————

Calicut, India, 1498

It was May 20th, 1498. The fleet of three ships that had left Lisbon around a year earlier, the *São Gabriel*, the *São Rafael*, and the *São Miguel* had succeeded in going around the Cape of Good Hope and had arrived in Calicut on the west coast of India.[lxxxviii]

Vasco da Gama had arrived on Indian shores. Over the next 450 years, the Portuguese influence over their Indian colonies would be brutal, ruthless and extremely profitable.

The 170 expedition members had arrived in India assuming that they would need to preach Christianity to the "faithless" natives. They were shocked to see that there were already an estimated two million

Christians spread across the land, and that they had 1500 churches under the jurisdiction of a single Metropolitan of the East Syrian Church.[lxxxix]

The St. Thomas Christians were considered high caste members of society along Hindu caste lines. Their churches were modelled along the lines of Hindu temples. The East Syrian Church of the St. Thomas Christians was Hindu in culture, Christian in religion and Syro-Oriental in worship.

This was not very palatable to the visitors from Portugal. Portugal was Roman Catholic and everything outside the Roman Catholic Church was considered heretic. In order to bring the Indian Christians under his control, Pope Paul IV would declare Goa an archdiocese in 1557.

This was easier said than done. It was not possible to change hundreds of years of worship, culture, practices and customs that had evolved locally.

A possible solution was to bring the Inquisition to India.

The Goa Inquisition would be formally inaugurated in 1560, and by the time it would end around 1774, it would have succeeded in torturing and executing thousands.

The first inquisitors were Aleixo Dias Falcão and Francisco, who took the first formal action of banning Hindus from practising their religion. Any contravention was made punishable by death. In 1599, the Saint Thomas Christians were forcibly converted by the inquisitors to Roman Catholicism. This also implied severe restrictions on their Syriac and Aramaic customs. Again, violations were punishable by death. Condemned Hindus were tortured and burned at the stake.[xc]

The Inquisition gained momentum and went on to ban Indian musical instruments, the *dhoti* - the Indian loincloth favoured by men, and the chewing of betel leaves - a traditional Indian habit. Hundreds of Hindu temples were either destroyed or forcibly converted into Christian churches. Thousands of Hindu texts were burned with a view to ensuring the supremacy of Roman Catholic texts.[xci]

It was amidst this turmoil that Alphonso de Castro arrived in Goa in 1767, towards the end of the Inquisition.

⟨⟩

Goa, India, 1767

Alphonso de Castro arrived in Goa ostensibly to give further impetus to the Inquisition. Unfortunately, he was a bad choice for the task. He was more of a scholar than a religious fanatic and was more likely to be found studying the Hindu foundations of Goa's churches than burning heretics at the stake.

This obviously created a problem. The chief inquisitor wanted that he be sent back to Lisbon, but this could not be done because of the excellent rapport that Castro's father enjoyed with King Joseph I.

The next best solution was to give him a project that could keep him busy and, more importantly, out of the way. He was asked to make an exhaustive list of ancient texts that had been found in the homes, temples, churches, mosques and synagogues of the Hindus, the Thomas Christians, the Muslims and the Sephardic Jews. Any text that did not suit the sensibilities of the Roman Catholic Church would eventually have to be destroyed.

It was while going through an old set of manuscripts discovered in the bowels of the Church of Bom Jesus that Castro would find a document that would change his life forever.

The Church of Bom Jesus contained the tomb of the Spanish missionary Saint Francis Xavier, who had begun his mission in Goa in 1542. This, however, was not its principle claim to fame. History recorded that this church had been constructed in 1559. Actually, it had existed well before 1559. Not as a church, but as a mosque.[xcii]

Within one of the pillars that had been discarded in favour of non-Islamic stonework was a cavity. The cavity contained a bundle of documents that had been written in Urdu. These documents had been found by a Hindu worker, Lakshman Powale, at the site where the mosque was being torn down to make way for the church.

Unaware of the significance of the documents, Lakshman had carried them to his home in the city of Damao, where they had continued to sit unattended for many years. He had passed the bundle on to his son, Ravindra Powale, who had buried them under his house for fear of the Portuguese Inquisition. When Ravindra died at the ripe old age of eighty-four in 1702, his house was forfeited by the Portuguese administration to facilitate the construction of quarters for visiting missionaries.

The houses in the area had been acquired in 1705 but construction had been stopped for lack of funds. Construction had recommenced almost forty-three years later in 1748. It was while the ground was being broken for a new foundation that the old bundle of papers was discovered.

It had immediately been transferred to the archives of the Portuguese viceroy where it had continued to sit until it was taken up for cataloguing by Alphonso de Castro nineteen years later.

The bundle contained eleven texts, of which ten were earmarked for destruction. The eleventh was never catalogued by Castro. It was called the *Tarikh-Issa-Massih*.[xciii]

For fear of his own life, Alphonso de Castro decided that it would be better for him to leave the document in India prior to his departure for Lisbon in 1770. He was, however, determined to store the document in a place where it would be preserved so that it may be discovered by future generations.

He first set out for a trip to the northern parts of India, including Kashmir. Upon his return a few months later, he visited the Church of Bom Jesus and knelt down to pray before the perfectly preserved body of Saint Francis Xavier, just before boarding the ship that would take him back to Portugal.

Agradeça-o Deus para dar me a força poupar este livro, he thought to himself as he prayed fervently.[xciv]

Chapter Fourteen

London, UK, 2012

Vincent was reading the document that had been entrusted to him by Terry. It was a photocopy of an English translation of the *Tarikh-i-Kashmir*, a history of Kashmir, written by a person called Mullah Nadri in 1421.[xcv]

...Raja Akh came to the throne. He ruled for sixty years. Thereafter, his son, Gopananda, took over the government and ruled the country under the name of Gopadatta. During his reign, many temples were built.

On top of Mount Solomon the dome of the temple had cracked. Gopadatta deputed one of his ministers, named Sulaiman, who had come from Persia, to repair it. The Hindus objected that the minister was an infidel.

During this time Yuz Asaf, having come from the Holy Land to this holy valley proclaimed his prophethood. He devoted himself, day and night, in prayers to God, and having attained the heights of piety and virtue, declared himself to be a messenger of God for the people of Kashmir. He invited people to his religion.

Because the people of the valley had faith in this Prophet, Raja Gopadatta referred the objection of Hindus to him for a decision. It was because of this Prophet's orders that Sulaiman was able to complete the repairs of the dome.

Further, on one of the stones of the stairs Sulaiman inscribed: "In these times Yuz Asaf proclaimed his prophethood," and on the other stone of the stairs he also inscribed that Yuz Asaf was Yusu, Prophet of the Children of Israel.

I have seen in a book of Hindus that this prophet was really Jesus, the Spirit of God, on whom be peace and salutations and had also assumed the name of Yuz Asaf. The real knowledge is with God. He spent his life in this valley. After his death he was laid to rest in Mohalla Anzmarah. It is also said that lights of prophethood used to emanate from the tomb of this Prophet. Raja Gopadatta died after having ruled for sixty years and two months.

Vincent came to the end of the page. Turning it over, he found another photocopied document. It was called the *Tarikh-Issa-Massih* and had originally been written in Urdu sometime around the eleventh century. The tedious passage read much like the sixteen verses of Matthew in the Bible, outlining the royal lineage of Jesus:

Abraham was the father of Isaac, and it was Isaac who fathered Jacob. In turn, Jacob's son was Judas. The children of Judas and his wife, Thamar, were Phares and Zara. Phares would have a child; Esrom and Esrom would have a child, Aram. Aram's offspring was Aminadab who sired Naasson. Naasson would become the father of Salmon. Soon, Salmon had a child with Rachab by the name of Booz. Booz would go on to father Obed with Ruth. Obed would produce Jesse. Jesse was the immediate predecessor of David, the great king.

The great king David married the woman who had been a previous wife of Urias and fathered the great Solomon. Solomon's offspring was Roboam, who fathered Abia. Abia's child was Asa. Asa's son was Josaphat, who sired Joram. Joram fathered Ozias, whose lineage would be continued by Joatham. Joatham's son was Achaz, and his grandson was Ezekias, and his great-grandson was Ezekias. Ezekias continued the dynasty with Manasses, who fathered Amon who, in turn, produced Josias. Josias had a son by the name of Jechonias around the time that they were carried off in captivity to Babylon. It was in Babylon that Jechonias had a son, Salathiel.

Salathiel continued the unbroken line with his son Zorobabel, who fathered Abiud. Eliakim was the son of Abiud. Eliakim produced a child by the name of Azor. Azor's progeny was Sadoc. Sadoc's offspring was Achim. Achim produced

Eliud, who fathered Eleazar. Matthan was his son. It was Matthan who sired Jacob. Jacob, of course, was the father of Joseph, the husband of Mary, of whom was born Issa...

The Bible, of course, would have stopped right here. This document, however, went further:

Jacob, of course, was the father of Joseph, the husband of Mary, of whom was born Issa, who married Mary Magdala. Issa and Mary had a child by the name of Sara, who was born to them in India but was later sent to Gaul with her mother. Issa remained in India, where he married a woman from the Sakya clan on the persistence of King Gopadatta and had a son, Benissa. Benissa had a son, Yushua, who fathered Akkub. Akkub's son was Jashub. Abihud was the son of Jashub. Jashub's grandson was Elnaam. Elnaam sired Harsha, who sired Jabal, who sired Shalman. Shalman's son Zabbud converted to Islam. Zabbud fathered Abdul, who sired Haaroon. His child was Hamza. Omar was Hamza's son and he produced Rashid. Rashid's offspring was Khaleel.

Vincent's mind was in a panic. His head was reeling with this information overload. He needed to assimilate what he had just read. At the bottom of the page was written in Portuguese:

Satis est, Domine, Satis est, os dois anjos ditos. Mastrilli sem dúvida fêz a mais melhor cama de prata. Mas para guardar com cuidado um segredo dos mortos. O copo do ouro de Ignatius' é melhor do que uma cabeça de prata. A cidade é ficada situada entre o' norte 15°48' e 14°53'54 e entre 74°20' e 73°40' para o leste.

Translated into English, it meant:

'It is enough, O Lord, it is enough, the two angels said. Mastrilli without doubt made the best silver bed. But to

carefully guard a secret of the dead. Ignatius' gold cup is better than a silver head. The city is located between 15°48' and 14°53'54' north and between 74°20' and 73°40' east.'

Chapter Fifteen

Moscow, Russia, 2012

The Federalnaya Sluzhba Bezopasnosti is an unfortunate choice of name, even when abbreviated to FSB. Particularly when one considers the fact that its brand equity was much greater when it used to be called the Komitet Gosudarstvennoy Bezopasnosti, or the KGB.[xcvi]

Lavrenty Edmundovich Bakatin was sitting in his office, halfway through his customary bottle of vodka, when the phone rang. He picked it up and listened for a few seconds. He then said abruptly, 'I'll meet you at St. Louis on the Malaya Lubianka,' and hung up.

Quickly putting on his overcoat, he headed downstairs to Lubyanka Square, which was where the FSB's headquarters, and his office, were located. Just in front of the drab FSB building stood the Church of St. Louis.

It was November, and the average daily temperature in Moscow ranged from 24°F to 32°F. The heavy woollens made Bakatin look even fatter than he actually was. He made his way inside the church and sat down clumsily on the last pew.

Throughout the Glasnost era of Gorbachev, millions of dollars had been funnelled by the Vatican into Moscow using the good offices of Bakatin. This had been necessary in order to ensure that Poland be released from the Warsaw Pact.

The provider of those funds came and sat down next to Bakatin. Brother Thomas Manning looked closely at Bakatin, then sniffed. 'Have you been drinking the stuff or swimming in it?' he remarked as he smelled the vodka.

'*Vali otsyuda!*' grunted Bakatin to Thomas.

Thomas grinned. 'Fuck you too, old man!' The two men had a great equation that had been strengthened over the years by the continuous flow of cash.

Thomas Manning prided himself on being greater than any freedom fighter. His backdoor collaboration with Bakatin and Moscow had resulted in the independence of predominantly Catholic Hungary,

Czechoslovakia, and Ukraine from Russia as well as the independence of Slovenia and Croatia from Yugoslavia.

Luckily, the entire American security establishment had been ultra-conservative from the Reagan years onwards. They had been quite happy to encourage Manning's efforts, even fund them. In the post-Glasnost era, Bakatin had become Manning's conduit to the Sheikh.

'So. Are they willing to deal?' asked Manning.

'*Pacheemu ti takoy galuboy*?' asked Bakatin. Thomas was getting fed-up with the insults. Bakatin was asking him why he looked so gay!

'*Perestan' mne jabat' mozgi svojimi voprosami!*' Manning said. 'Stop fucking my brain with your stupid questions!'

Manning continued, 'It's vital that we get access to him, either in Kashmir or anywhere else. If that means purchasing equipment for the Sheikh from the Pakistanis or North Koreans, so be it.'

Bakatin looked at him through glazed eyes. He then turned serious and said, 'The Sheikh wants it all. The reactor, the raw material, delivery systems, the drawings - and the cash. In return he will give him to you.'

He then held Manning's face in his gloved hands and planted two stinging Russian vodka-breathed kisses on his cheeks before he got up and left.

Thomas thanked his lucky stars for having preached for some years at St. Catherine of Siena in Virginia. Otherwise he would never have met Bakatin through the FBI.

❦

The Fox News anchor was saying, 'There's now disturbing information regarding the FBI operative being held for espionage on behalf of the Russians. Apparently his activities, which were supposed to help the Russians, also succeeded in helping Osama-bin-Laden...'[xcvii]

The report continued, 'He sold the Russians a highly classified and secret piece of American technology, and by all accounts it seems that the Russians, in turn, may have passed on the technology to bin Laden's Al-Qaeda terrorist network.'

The FBI agent in question had been born in 1957 in Chicago. After attending Southern Illinois University, he had joined the Chicago police and then moved on to the FBI's counter-intelligence wing. After fifteen years of selling secrets for a gross remuneration of $2.1 million, he had finally been arrested in his Virginia home. Throughout his years of treachery, he had continued to attend Mass daily and was a regular parishioner of St. Catherine of Siena, a church in a Virginia suburb. One of the regular preachers at St. Catherine of Siena was a priest called Thomas Manning.

This priest would then be introduced to Bakatin.

<hr>

Bakatin would receive millions of dollars from accounts in Switzerland operated by Brother Thomas Manning.

The Pacific News of May 2001 would write:

> *Rivers of money, much of it provided by Bill Casey's CIA, poured into Warsaw and Moscow, and the Vatican found ready support from the U.S. because the security establishment...was packed with conservative Catholics. The Vatican's political work with Moscow paid off handsomely with the independence of Catholic-dominant Hungary, Czechoslovakia, Ukraine, and later, from Moscow's nominal ally Yugoslavia, of Slovenia and Croatia.*
>
> *Intelligence experts and congressional committees are puzzling over what motivated the FBI agent to spy for Moscow over the past fifteen years. Money seems to offer no clues because he lived in an ascetic style. The search for a motive is complicated by the fact that his colleagues say that he was fiercely anti-communist and a devout member of Opus Dei, an ultra conservative Catholic organization. He was a regular parishioner of St. Catherine of Siena Church, in a Virginia suburb of the capital. It may seem paradoxical that he would spy for the Soviet Union, a moral adversary and indeed a Satanic force in the eyes of Opus Dei. During Gorbachev's*

glasnost era, however, there is evidence of behind-the-scenes collaboration between the Vatican and Moscow. In particular, Vatican Secretary of State Cardinal Agostino Casaroli, a powerful Opus Dei supporter, pursued a policy of reaching out to Moscow with the aim of gaining Poland's release from the Warsaw Pact.

The entire process of securing the independence of Poland had made one man very powerful; His Eminence Alberto Cardinal Valerio.

Alberto Cardinal Valerio had earned his doctorate in theology from the Catholic University of Leuven in Belgium.

Kahuta, Pakistan, 2012

Someone else had also earned a doctorate from the Catholic University of Leuven around the same time. Not in Theology but in metallurgy. His name was Dr. Dawood Omar, one of the team members of Dr. Abdul Qadeer Khan, the father of the Pakistani nuclear bomb.[xcviii] Dr. A. Q. Khan and Dr. Dawood Omar had attended the University of Leuven at the same time as Alberto Cardinal Valerio.

Dr. Dawood Omar looked at the photographs of his nuclear facilities longingly, the way that a parent looks at his child with love. The Khan Nuclear Research Laboratories in Kahuta had been nurtured by him in 1976. Twenty-five years later, they had succeeded in closing the nuclear gap with India. Omar had every reason to be proud, even though he was now old and A. Q. Khan was now under house arrest.[xcix]

Omar had received his engineering degree from the University of Karachi before moving on to Germany and Belgium, where he had finally earned his doctorate in physics from the Catholic University of Leuven, in 1972…at the same time as someone called Alberto Valerio, later to become His Eminence Alberto Cardinal Valerio; who was now on his way to Pyongyang.

Pyongyang, North Korea, 2012

International intelligence agencies had begun to observe regular flights between Pakistan and North Korea, accelerating at the beginning of nineties when there were about nine flights per month. These flights reportedly followed the visit of high-level North Korean officials to Pakistan. Dawood Omar had made thirteen visits to North Korea, beginning in the 1990s.

This particular flight, however, was not clandestine.

North Korea's official carrier, Air Koryo, flew into Pyongyang on two days of the week only - Tuesdays and Thursdays. Both flights were from one origin, Beijing.

Air Koryo's flight JS 152 from Beijing to Pyongyang had taken off 11:30 a.m. and had arrived in Pyongyang at 2:00 p.m. On board was His Eminence Alberto Cardinal Valerio, who travelling under an alias. His visa to the Democratic People's Republic of Korea had been organized through FBI channels. For all intents and purposes, he was merely a consultant to the World Health Organization. He was met at the airport by a member of the Ministry of Public Health. At customs, he was asked to hand over his mobile phone, for which he was issued a receipt. He would be allowed to take it back upon his departure.

He was quickly whisked away to the Yanggakdo Hotel along with his car, driver, ministry representative and official interpreter.

Another flight had arrived in Pyongyang the same day that Albert Verrecchia had. Its lone Pakistani occupant had visited Pyongyang several times before as part of the delegations led by Dr. A. Q. Khan. His name was Dr. Dawood Omar.

He did not have a visa. He didn't need one. He had valuable technology to sell; not only to Iran, Libya and North Korea, but also to Al-Qaeda. The bill would be paid by His Eminence Alberto Cardinal Valerio from the Oedipus trust.

<hr />

Two trains ran between Moscow and Pyongyang - Beijing via Shenyang, and Ussuriysk in the Russian Far East. The route via the

Russian Far East was actually the shortest but least used by foreign tourists. It was precisely for this reason that Lavrenty Edmundovich Bakatin was on it, along with the Sheikh.

Bakatin had drunk vodka throughout the entire journey. His friend, the Sheikh, had prayed to Allah throughout entire the journey.

The Washington Quarterly would report that:

> *The most disturbing aspect of the international nuclear smuggling network headed by Dr. Abdul Qadeer Khan, widely viewed as the father of Pakistan's nuclear weapons, is how poorly the nuclear non-proliferation regime fared in exposing and stopping the network's operation. Despite a wide range of hints and leads, the United States and its allies failed to thwart this network throughout the 1980s and 1990s as it sold the equipment and expertise needed to produce nuclear weapons to major U.S. enemies, including Iran, Libya, and North Korea.[c]*
>
> *U.S. intelligence had at least partially penetrated the network's operations, leading to many revelations and ultimately, the dramatic seizure of uranium-enrichment gas-centrifuge components bound for Libya's secret nuclear weapons program aboard the German-owned ship BBC China. Libya's subsequent renunciation of nuclear weapons led to further discoveries about the network's operations and the arrest of many of its key players, including Khan himself. Suspicions remain that members of the network may have helped Al-Qaeda obtain nuclear secrets.*

The University of Leuven had spawned an interesting partnership between the Oedipus trust and the Isabel Madonna trust.

Waziristan, Pakistan-Afghanistan Border, 2012
The Sheikh's master, the ultimate beneficiary of the Isabel Madonna trust, was performing *Salah*, his daily prayer, for the fifth time that day. He had already completed his *Wudu*, the ritual ablution, during which he had washed his hands, teeth, face, nose, arms, hair, ears and feet, three times in specific order. He had started his *Salah* with the *Niyyah*, or the intention to pray, by reciting the first Surah of the Qur'an. He had then bowed, recited something, stood upright again, then reached his prayer mat and sat on his legs. He had placed his hands and face on the mat and had then sat up, repeating this action once more before standing up and running through the entire sequence or *raka'ah*. He was now nearing the end of his prayers by looking right and left, saying, 'Peace be unto you, and on you be peace.'[ci]

Prayers duly completed, he sat down on his rug and stared into the eyes of the Sheikh, who was present along with Bakatin. He asked, 'So what do the crusaders of the cross demand?'

'They want him…you know, our man. In return they have paid for and have arranged for the nuclear weapon. Besides, they have transferred ten million dollars from their Oedipus account to our Isabel Madonna account.'

'What if I do not give him to them? What if I decide to use him for some greater calling?'

'We promised them that we would give him up,' said the Sheikh, shifting his weight uneasily on the prayer rug.

'Have Christians kept their promise to Muslims that we should now honour a promise made by a Muslim to a Christian?' asked the Sheikh's master.

Bakatin was surprisingly sober; he could not drink in the presence of the Sheikh's master. In his newfound sobriety he said, 'Muslims have always been kind and gracious. I know that you are no less than the great Saladin!'

Flattery always worked. Bakatin's sobriety helped.

Jerusalem, 1192

Saladin, or Salah al-Din Yusuf, had recaptured Jerusalem for the Muslims in 1187. When his army had entered Jerusalem, his soldiers were strictly prohibited from killing civilians, looting or plundering. Saladin's victory came as a shock to the pope, Gregory VIII, who had commissioned Richard the Lionheart to mount the Third Crusade to recapture the holy city.

Richard marched on Jerusalem in 1192. Unfortunately his fever got in the way. His men were dying of hunger and thirst, so he appealed to Saladin to provide him with food and water. Saladin duly obliged. Being a devout Muslim, it was his duty to help the needy. He sent frozen snow and fresh fruit to Richard in abundance.[cii]

Richard was eventually unable to recapture Jerusalem and finally sued for a truce with Saladin. Saladin agreed to let Christian pilgrims visit the holy city without being troubled in any way by his Muslim brothers.

Neither Richard nor Saladin was too happy with the uneasy agreement, but both realized that it was in their respective interests to work together.

An alliance between Christianity and Islam.

Vatican City, 2012

'Wearing traditional papal robes, the 265th pontiff, appeared Tuesday on a Vatican balcony as tens of thousands gathered in St. Peter's Square to listen to him deliver his Easter address,' said CNN.[ciii]

Sitting along with the other cardinals was His Eminence Alberto Cardinal Valerio. That morning he had been reading an article that had been culled from the *Arab News*. The author was someone called Amir Taheri who had written:

> *At the start of the last century there were just six more or less independent Muslim states. By the year 2000 that number had grown to 53. When John Paul II became pope, Islam was*

no longer a neighbouring civilization of Europe but a significant and growing presence within the continent.[civ]

It was the next paragraph that had held Valerio's attention:

The history of the past three to four decades is one of intense competition between Islam and Christianity, especially the Catholic version, for converts. In 1980, John Paul II ordered a review of relations with Islam. This was based on the idea of a grand alliance between the Catholic Church and Islam. In Western Europe, the heartland of Catholicism, the pope saw Islam as an ally on such issues as homosexual "marriages", abortion, euthanasia, human cloning, and the status of women. John Paul II pursued his quest for alliance with Islam in 1986 by becoming the first pope to visit a Muslim country. During that visit to Morocco he had this to say: "We believe in the same God, the one and the only God, who created the world and brought its creatures to perfection".

Valerio had smiled a smile of quiet satisfaction and had made up his mind that on critical issues, it was advisable to work alongside the enemy. They had done it for thousands of years in the *Crux Decussata Permuta*.

Chapter Sixteen

Pipavav, Gujarat, India, 2011

Port Pipavav, located in the Saurashtra region of the state of Gujarat in western India, was one of the smaller ports, certainly much smaller than Mumbai, which handled the bulk of India's cargo flows. Phase I of Pipavav Port had resulted in three dry cargo berths and one liquid cargo berth. The three dry cargo berths had been constructed as a single length jetty of 725 metres, employing equipment capable of handling containers as well as bulk cargo.[cv]

The cargo ship that was docked at Pipavav was a standard 65,000 dwt. Panamax vessel, one that represented the largest acceptable size to transit the Panama Canal - a length of 275 metres, and a width of 32 metres. It bore the name *M/V Namgung*, a North Korean registration.

It was unloading a rather nondescript container. The container held an important piece of cargo that needed to be cleared through customs with minimum fuss. This was precisely the reason that the cargo had been sent to the port of Pipavav and not to Mumbai.

The certificate of origin indicated that the "construction jig" inside the container was from China and was headed to Himachal Pradesh in northern India. This was not entirely true. It had actually travelled from Pakistan to China, onwards to North Korea and then to Pipavav. At each stage, some critical components had been added.

From here, it would be loaded onto a massive truck that would eventually transport it by road to its final destination. The recipient was shown on the bill of lading as a company called "Fireworks India (Pvt) Ltd."

The "construction jig" was very similar to the thirteen-kiloton uranium gun-type device that had been used in Hiroshima. It consisted of four simple elements. First, there was a uranium target. Second, there was a rail on which this uranium target sat mounted at one end. Third was the gun that would shoot a "uranium bullet" and was mounted on the other end of the rail. And fourth was the uranium bullet itself.[cvi]

Neither the target nor the bullet contained adequate uranium-235 to start a chain reaction. However, critical mass and a nuclear reaction could be started if these two elements were slammed together with sufficient force. After all, uranium-235 was radioactive. This meant that it was emitting neutrons spontaneously. If sufficient uranium-235 could be held together, each of the released neutrons could strike a uranium atom, releasing another pair of neutrons, thus setting off the chain reaction that could cause the massive detonation needed.

The sort that Nostradamus had written about in 1547.

Salon, France, 1547

Michel de Nostredame was working on over one thousand different prophecies. Some years earlier, he had met some Franciscan monks while travelling through Italy. Nostradamus had thrown himself down on his knees and had reverentially clutched at the habit of one of the monks, Felice Peretti. When the monks had asked him why he was showing such reverence for an ordinary monk, Nostradamus had replied, 'I must yield myself and bow before his Holiness.'[cvii]

The ordinary monk of lowly birth, Felice Peretti, would become Pope Sixtus V nineteen years after the death of Nostradamus.

Nostradamus' quatrains would speak of three powerful and tyrannical leaders, called "anti-Christs", who would each lead their nations and people into terrible bloodshed.

Nostradamus would write about the first, Napoleon:

An Emperor shall be born near Italy, who shall cost the empire dear...from a simple soldier he will rise to the empire... a great troop shall come through Russia...the exhausted ones will die in the white territory...the captive prince, conquered, is sent to Elba.

Nostradamus would then write about his second anti-Christ, Hitler:

Out of the deepest part of the west of Europe, from poor people a young child shall be born, who with his tongue shall seduce many people...he shall raise up a hatred that had long been dormant...the child of Germany observes no law...the greater part of the battlefield will be against Hister.

Nostradamus would go on to write about a third, one yet to come:

Out of the country of Greater Arabia shall be born a strong master of Mohammed...he will be the terror of mankind...never more horror...by fire he will destroy their city, a cold and cruel heart, blood will pour, mercy to none.

Nostradamus could not have imagined how devastatingly accurate his predictions would be.

Paris, France, 2011
Ataullah al-Liby read the note in his pathetic little flat in the Banlieus, the poorest section of suburban Paris, home to the highest concentration of Muslim immigrants. In 2006, Paris had burned as disenchanted Muslim youths had gone on a rampage. The French Intifada[cviii], as it would come to be known, had been masterminded by the young Ataullah.

He now looked closely at the note that he had received from Ghalib.

January 21st, 2012.

La Triple Frontera, TBA, South America, 2011
The almost inaccessible jungle and hilly terrain nestled between Brazil, Argentina, and Paraguay was known as the TBA, the Tri-Border Area, or La Triple Frontera.[cix]

Terror groups such as the Hezbollah, al-Gama'a al-Islamiyya, Islamic Jihad, Al-Qaeda, Hamas, and the Lebanese drug mafia had been sending their recruits to this region for many years precisely because it was inaccessible and out of reach for most government authorities.

The kingpin of the TBA was Boutros Ahmad. He had been positioned here by Ghalib. He had masterminded the attack on the Israeli embassy in Buenos Aires in 1992 as well as the attack on the Jewish Community Centre in 1994.

He now read the message from Ghalib. Finally, some serious action. February 21st, 2012.

Xinjiang, China, 2011
The East Turkestan Islamic Movement had been seeking independence for the Chinese province of Xinjiang since the 1990s. The group was radically Islamist but extremely popular among the Uighur population of Xinjiang.[cx]

Even countries that had originally held the view that the East Turkestan Islamic Movement was a genuine independence movement had been left speechless when it had come to light that 1000 Uighur men had undergone training by Al-Qaeda in Afghanistan.

The group had raked up an impressive score - 200 attacks with 162 dead and more than 440 injured. Faris Kadeer enjoyed his work.

He looked at the note from Ghalib - wonderful! *Bek esil boldi!*[cxi] March 21st, 2012.

London, UK, 2011

Fouad al-Noor was reading the note in his cramped studio in Wembley. Next to him sat a cup of steaming hot tea and a plate of mutton kebabs.

He had just finished his prayers when the note arrived. It had been delivered by the old gatekeeper of the Wembley mosque on Ealing Road.

Fouad had been waiting impatiently. Good. The date was final. April 21st, 2012.

Kuala Lumpur, Malaysia, 2011

Tau'am Zin Hassan read the note. The strategist behind Darul Islam had spent many months waiting to see his dream fulfilled, setting up the Daulah Islamiah Nusantara, or the Islamic Caliphate of Indonesia, Malaysia and Southern Philippines.[cxii]

The note was one more step in that direction. May 21st, 2012.

Katra, Jammu & Kashmir, India, 2011

Five point four million devotees would pay homage to the divine Goddess in 2003. An average of 14,794 visits each day of the year. A pilgrimage to the holy shrine of Vaishno Devi was considered to be one of the holiest pilgrimages by one billion Hindus in the world. So why was Bin Fadan, one of the key operatives of the Jaish-e-Mohammed,[cxiii] in this Hindu pilgrimage town? He read the note from Ghalib:

Longitude: 74°57'00'. Latitude: 32°59'00'.
Phase of Moon: 0.274
Planet, Longitude, Latitude, Right Asc., Declination
Sun, 29 Sgr 31'38', - 0°00'03', 17:57:56, -23°26'09'
Moon, 08 Ari 00'14', 3°24'56', 00:23:59, 6°18'43'

Moon's Node, 25 Sco 35'58', 0°00'00', 15:33:04, -19°09'27'
Apogee, 29 Tau 47'12', - 0°22'58', 03:50:44, 19°43'42'
Mercury, 14 Sgr 00'41', 0°27'53', 16:50:52, -22°01'02'
Venus, 06 Sgr 00'19', 1°07'28', 16:17:19, -20°11'56'
Mars, 26 Cap 03'52', - 1°09'54', 19:53:11, -22°04'38'
Jupiter, 08 Gem 57'20'R, - 0°44'40', 04:29:29, 21°03'14'
Saturn, 08 Sco 37'09', 2°18'24', 14:27:59, -12°11'14'
Uranus, 04 Ari 38'16', - 0°42'47', 00:18:09, 1°11'18'
Neptune, 00 Psc 48'11', - 0°36'39', 22:12:18, -11°45'30'
Pluto, 08 Cap 55'59', 3°20'47', 18:37:56, -19°47'46'
Chiron, 05 Psc 36'53', 5°16'39', 22:21:54, - 4°32'17'
Quaoar, 23 Sgr 58'46', 7°32'28', 17:35:11, -15°45'55'
Sedna, 22 Tau 52'08'R, -12°02'07', 03:34:04, 6°49'24'
Sgr A*/GalCtr, 27 Sgr 01'52', - 5°36'34', 17:46:29, -29°00'38[cxiv]

An astrologer was immediately summoned; someone who could interpret the planetary positions. 'Can you tell me what this means?' asked Bin Fadan.

Pandit Ramgopal Prasad Sharma was just another ordinary visitor to Katra on a pilgrimage to the divine mother, but he always carried his *Panchaang*, the Indian ephemeris, wherever he went. After all, planetary positions were the tools of his trade.

He looked in his *Panchaang* and said, 'These are planetary positions on a given date at a particular location. Judging from my ephemeris, I would say that these positions would be attained in Katra on June 21st, 2012.'

Bin Fadan smiled at Pandit Ramgopal Prasad Sharma.

❦

Baghdad, Iraq, 2011
Kader al-Zarqawi had been born on December 11th, 1976, in Zarqa, Jordan. In fact his name, "al-Zarqawi", literally meant "the man from Zarqa". The man from Zarqa was now the man from Baghdad. He was the most dreaded and feared Islamic terrorist in Iraq and the American

government was offering a reward of US$ 50 million for his capture.[cxv]

Sitting inside a decrepit old house located close to the Al-Noor Hospital in the Al-Sho'la neighbourhood in Baghdad, virtually under the very noses of the American forces, Kader al-Zarqawi calmly read the handwritten note in Arabic that had come directly from Ghalib.

Good. He cursed, *'Ebn el metanaka!'*[cxvi]

'Those American sons of bitches will now realize what it means to be blown,' he exclaimed, thinking about July 21st, 2012.

New York, U.S.A., 2011

Shamoon Idris sat inside the Masjid Abu Bakr on Foster Avenue in Brooklyn. Around him were other members of the Islamic Jehad Council.[cxvii]

Looking at Shamoon, one could not tell that he was a terrorist. His faded jeans, his Armani glasses and the clean-shaven smiling face were not things that one associated with a fundamentalist.

Shamoon was patiently discussing the note that he had received from Ghalib. It had a date mentioned.

August 21st, 2012.

Jakarta, Indonesia, 2011

Jemaah Islamiyah was a militant Islamic terrorist outfit with a one-point agenda: the establishment of a fundamentalist Islamic caliphate in Indonesia, Singapore, Brunei, Malaysia, Thailand and the Philippines. The Jemaah Islamiyah had carried out the Bali bombing in which suicide squads had murdered 202 people in a busy nightclub.

Yaqub Islamuddin, the intellectual director of the Jemaah Islamiyah, sat inside his jail cell, which he had occupied for the past few months, reading his Qur'an.[cxviii] Among the correspondence that he was allowed to receive was a single note from Ghalib.

It contained a verse from the holy book. "Their Lord gives them good news: mercy and approval from Him, and gardens where they rejoice in everlasting bliss." Yaqub Islamuddin knew the verse.

Chapter 9, Verse 21.

9/21.

September 21st.

❦

Sydney, Australia, 2011

Muslims in Australia had a long history. Adil Afrose's ancestors had come to Australia in the form of Afghan camel drivers in the 1800s.[cxix] They had played an important role in the exploration of Australia's endless dry terrains by carrying people and telegraph poles to points that could only be reached by camel. But had they been appreciated?

The white man didn't give a rat's ass about them. Adil surveyed the beautiful Lakemba Mosque where he prayed each day. Today he was praying that God would give him strength to do Allah's will as per the note from Ghalib.

October 21st, 2012.

❦

Grozny, Chechnya, Russia, 2011

Gorozny's four administrative districts included Leninsky, Zavodskoy, Staropromyslovsky, and Oktyabrsky. While Staropromyslovsky was the main oil-drilling area, it was Oktyabrsky that housed the industries and the economy, including the mafia. It was here that Dzhokar Raduev sat inside a luxuriously appointed house, blissfully unperturbed by the $10 million reward on his head.[cxx]

Dzhokar Raduev was not merely a Chechen warlord. No. He was also a shrewd politician, a dangerous terrorist and, above all, Chechnya's most adored national hero. In his early youth, Raduev had changed his name; his new name had become Yahya Abdullah, much more in keeping with his Islamic roots.

In 1992, when Boris Yeltsin had sent his troops into Chechnya, Yahya had hijacked an Aeroflot aircraft traveling from Mineralnye Vody in Russia to Ankara in Turkey. He had threatened to blow up the flight unless Yeltsin lifted the state of emergency.

Yahya had then travelled to Afghanistan, and had developed and strengthened his bonds with the Al-Qaeda. Thereafter, he had moved back to Chechnya to carry on the struggle.

He read the note from Ghalib. A smile of satisfaction spread over his face.

November 21st, 2012.

❦

Bakhtaran, Iran, 2011

The truck had done its fair share of travel. From the port at Pipavav, it had headed to Jammu, where the consignment marked for the recipient, Fireworks (India) Pvt. Ltd., had been "officially" unloaded, even though the "construction jig" had remained on board.

The truck had then been stripped of all its accessories and had been repainted a dirty military green. The cargo container had been covered with a khaki canvass and the licence plates had been changed to a series used by the Indian Army. A military pass had been glued on the top left-hand corner of the windscreen.

The truck had proceeded in its new indentity along the inter-state Punjab-Kashmir border westwards and had stopped short of the town of Rajouri on the Indian side. From here *Azad Kashmir* or POK, *Pakistan Occupied Kashmir*, was just a stone's throw away. The truck waited at a quiet point along the Line of Control, the line dividing Kashmir into POK and Indian Kashmir. It was awaiting a signal from across the border.

Even though the Indians had constructed over 734 kilometres of fencing along the Line of Control, significant portions of the border remained unfenced. This suited the Pakistan-trained militant outfits perfectly because it enabled them to send armed groups of terrorists across the border at will.

At sharp 11:00 p.m. on observing five quick flashes of light, the truck's engine was restarted and it began the crossing. The road was non-existent and it required considerable skill to negotiate the dirt track. At 11:27 p.m., the truck was firmly in Pakistani territory, and a few hours later it was in Mirpur.

A team of ten truck detailers from Rawalpindi awaited the vehicle in Mirpur. Over the next twenty-four hours, the truck would be repainted with floral designs, bright colours, and Urdu poetry. The canvas top would give way to a hardwood body with carved motifs. This would be further enhanced by little mirrors, reflectors, ornamental brass fittings and jingling bells and chains.[cxxi]

Truck art had become a very critical part of Pakistani folk art and this particular team specialized in what was referred to as "disco painting" in which almost every square inch of surface area would be covered with decoration in the form of images or ornaments. Newly decorated, the truck would become part of the landscape and would not be noticed. The new licence plates read "KAE 5675". The number was from a Karachi number series.

The truck now moved northwards to Muzaffarabad and from there westwards to Mansehra. From Mansehra it headed in a gentle south-westerly direction towards Peshawar in the North-West Frontier Province of Pakistan where it waited to cross the famous Khyber Pass.

The Khyber Pass between Afghanistan and Pakistan's North-West Frontier Province was probably the most evocative border crossing in the world. The border, the Durand Line, had been frozen by the English in 1893 and had ended up dividing the ethnic Pashtuns into two resulting in the ongoing Pashtunistan Issue, which had pretty much determined relations between Pakistan and Afghanistan throughout history.[cxxii]

The tribal areas of Pakistan continued to be mostly outside federal control, thus creating an entirely porous Pak-Afghan border, and a smuggler's delight.

The truck's papers indicated that it was carrying construction equipment that was needed for upgrading the Kabul highway. An armed guard from the Khyber Agency had been generously tipped to accompany the truck to Torkham on the border. Stamped out of

Pakistan, the truck reached the small border post on the Afghan side and then proceeded to the main immigration post a further 500 metres ahead. The customs officers had already been taken care of. No checks.

The truck proceeded into Afghanistan and into the town of Jalalabad. From Jalalabad it took the road to Kabul and on to Chaghcharan. From Chaghcharan it progressed further towards Herat.

At one point of time in history, Herat used to be at the crossroads of civilizations. Its north-south axis was part of the old silk route, whereas its east-west axis was the gateway to Europe. Afghanistan's border with Iran continued to remain mostly on paper and maps. The ground realities were rather different along the 900-kilometre border. The long stretches of desert sands did not lend themselves well to being policed.

At Herat, the truck underwent another cosmetic surgery. The images were removed. The garish colours were painted over with dull shades of grey. The Urdu poems were replaced by Persian proverbs of religious hue. The new licence plates were yellow and bore the letters "THR 77708".

No one gave a second glance to the truck as it crossed the border from Afghanistan into Iran. It was simply a truck carrying a miniscule part of the materials needed for a $38 million road project.

Having reached Iranian territory, the truck headed southwards to Zahedan, from where it started a westward sweep through Kerman, Yazd, Esfahan, and Arak until it reached Bakhtaran, which lay just across the Iran-Iraq border from Baghdad.

The driver was tired, but he forced himself to be alert. He was yet to cross Iraq and Syria before he reached his final destination.

Ghalib decided to take a short nap. His friend, El-Azhar would take over the watch while he slept. He needed to be prepared for the final act on December 21st, 2012.

Eleven other events would precede it, one each month. And each event would wreak havoc.

Ghalib would have the last laugh. The world had been waiting for this day since 500 B.C.

Guatemala, 500 B.C.

The royal astrologer was looking up at the heavens from his observatory, which formed part of the temple honouring Kukulcan.

He was looking rather worried. He had determined the exact end of the great cycle of the Long Count Maya calendar, a 26,000-year planetary cycle. The date would have massive repercussions. It would coincide with the geomagnetic reversal of the poles of the Earth, having last occurred 780,000 years ago! The date was definite; an extremely close conjunction of the winter solstice sun with the crossing point of the galactic equator and the ecliptic path of the sun. More commonly known to Maya civilization as the Sacred Tree.[cxxiii]

December 21st, 2012.

Langley, Virginia, U.S.A., 2011

The compass had sixteen points, and it symbolized the search for information from all over the world. This information had to be brought back and centralized at one place where it would be stored, catalogued and analysed. The compass rested on a shield - a shield that was meant to defend America. This was the familiar crest that welcomed visitors to the Central Intelligence Agency's headquarters in Langley.

Hidden within the miles of corridors was a small office that housed the SAS, or the Special Activities Staff. A division of the Directorate of Operations, the SAS handled covert paramilitary exercises which the American Government did not wish to be publicly associated with. Members on missions explicitly avoided carrying anything on their person that could even remotely link them to the United States Government.

The division had less than few hundred personnel, most of them former operators of Delta Force and Navy SEAL teams, although, on occasion, they were known to employ civilians for paramilitary activities. The division used RQ-1 Predator drones equipped with high-resolution cameras and AGM-114 Hellfire antitank missiles as part of their wide arsenal. The division was known to be a major part of the U.S.'s unconventional war in Afghanistan and Iraq.[cxxiv]

The real strategic advantage of the SAS was *ADA*, or *Agility, Deniability and Adaptability*. More often than not, SAS agents would operate individually and all alone, undercover, and that too in inhospitable areas behind enemy lines. They would carry out all types of assignments including counter-intelligence, espionage, handling hostage situations, deliberate sabotage, and targeted assassinations.

One of the SAS's most prized agents was simply known by the agency nickname of "CIA Trois". He was of Arab-Algerian stock and a devout Muslim. His area of operation was Afghanistan, Pakistan and Kashmir and since he was equally familiar with all three regions, he had the nickname "Trois" or "Three".

Stephen Elliot, head of the SAS, was one of the brightest stars within the agency. He had been recruited into the intelligence service during his final year at Yale, the same year when he had "tapped" Terry Acton for the Skull & Bones membership.

Elliot was here at the headquarters deciphering the encrypted message that had reached him from CIA Trois. It simply read:

N 45:50 E 6:52 S 11:00 W 66:00 N 31:00 E 112:00 N 51:07 E 1:19 N 3:09 E 101:41 N 32:59 E 74:57 N 33:20 E 44:30 N 44:98 W 110:45 S 06:09 E 106.49 S 33:00 E 146:00 N 43.2 E 45.45 N 31:34 E 34:51.

It ended with: *Q 17:16*

The N, S, E and W were obviously North, South, East and West. Trois had provided locations. The Langley computers quickly looked up the coordinates and spat out the results.

N 45:50 E 6:52 – Rhone Alps, France
S 11:00 W 66:00 – Riberalta, Bolivia
N 31:00 E 112:00 – Hubei, China
N 51:07 E 1:19 – Dover, England
N 3:09 E 101:41 – Kuala Lumpur, Malaysia
N 32:59 E 74:57 – Katra, Jammu, India
N 33:20 E 44:30 – Baghdad, Iraq
N 44:98 W 110:45 – Wyoming, USA

S 06:09 E 106.49 – Jakarta, Indonesia
S 33:00 E 146:00 – New South Wales, Australia
N 43.2 E 45.45 – Grozny, Chechnya, Russia
N 31:34 E 34:51 – Tel Megiddo, Israel.
But Q 17:16? Elliot pulled out of his desk an English pocket Qur'an and looked up Chapter 17, Verse 16. It read:

And when We wish to destroy a town, We send Our commandment to the people of it who lead easy lives, but they transgress therein; thus the word proves true against it, so We destroy it with utter destruction.

Elliot was confused. He knew about the first eleven locations, but how had Megiddo entered this plan? He needed to discuss this with the President alone.

Megiddo, Israel, 2012
A hill near the modern settlement of Tel Megiddo was made up of twenty-six layers of ruins of ancient cities. Megiddo was also famous for another reason. The New Testament's Book of Revelation had prophesied that the final military showdown of the world would happen in Megiddo.

Soon, the word "Megiddo" had become synonymous with the end of the world. In fact, the word "Armageddon" was derived from the name "Megiddo".

Ghalib's truck was on its way there. Ghalib asked El-Azhar for his Thuraya satellite phone and began dialling a number in Pakistan +92 51...

Chapter Seventeen

Mumbai, India, 2012

Swakilki had followed Vincent from London to Mumbai via Delhi. Indian Airlines flight IC-887 had ferried her from New Delhi to Mumbai within one hour and fifty-five minutes. The Mercedes-Benz S350L sent by the Taj Mahal Hotel to receive her at the airport quickly wove its way through the notorious traffic snarls and deposited her at the waterfront paradise of the luxury hotel.

George Bernard Shaw had commented that after staying at the Taj Mahal Hotel, he had no longer felt the need to visit the original Taj Mahal in Agra. Swakilki was staying in the Heritage Wing, where individually themed high-ceilinged suites made one imagine an era when personalities like Somerset Maugham and Duke Ellington had rested their heads on soft pillows in the city's best hotel.

The discovery of the Bom Jesus document given by Terry to Vincent had resulted in endless discussions with Martha. They had finally decided that they needed to distinguish facts from fiction. The only way to do this was through a visit to India.

Upon their arrival in Mumbai, Martha and Vincent had taken a cab to the Taj Mahal Hotel. They had been put up in the business-like Tower Wing of the hotel. They did not observe the young Japanese woman who checked into the adjoining luxurious Heritage Wing. The Taj Mahal Hotel had something else that was unique to a luxury hotel. Besides the usual "house doctor" for medical emergencies, it also boasted a "house astrologer" for far more urgent counselling from the heavens. Vincent had decided to take an appointment.

Vincent had noticed the bit about the "house astrologer" while leafing through the hotel's extensive services directory. Even though he was sceptical about the occult, his last experience with the world beyond in London had opened up his mind to newer concepts.

He dropped in at the hotel's reception to book an appointment with Pandit Ramgopal Prasad Sharma, the world-renowned astrologer who practised his art and science from the hallowed portals of the Taj every alternate week. The receptionist was happy to give Vincent an appointment for 3 p.m.

Pandit Ramgopal Prasad Sharma turned out to be a wise old man of eighty-one years who spoke wonderful English, not the crazy half-naked fakir that Vincent had imagined.

'You see, Mr. Morgan, my childhood and growing-up years were spent in the picturesque fields of Hoshiarpur in Punjab. Surrounded by the splendour of the ethereal beauty of nature, I became fascinated and hooked on the basic concept of destiny. This led me to the question: is everything preordained in life? It was this question that led me to the study of the occult, Hindu astrology and philosophy,' explained Pandit Ramgopal Prasad Sharma as he poured two cups of lemon tea, one for Vincent and one for himself.[cxxv]

Pandit Ramgopal Prasad Sharma's father had been a professor of science and mathematics but had remained perpetually absorbed in subjects like astrology, palmistry, mysticism, and spiritualism. With twenty-four-hour access to his father's texts and scrolls, Ramgopal had read, re-read, absorbed and understood them with a voracious appetite. He had become so curious about the metaphysical that he began to delve deeper and deeper into the subject. Very soon there was a perpetual line of waiting visitors at his father's. People had begun to believe his uncannily accurate predictions. This had led to more enthusiasm and deeper research, eventually resulting in Ramgopal becoming one of the most sought-after astrologers in India and abroad.

'Now, I take it that you do not have a *janam-kundli*, in which case I will need to make one for you.'

'What is that?' asked Vincent.

Pandit Ramgopal explained patiently. 'A *janam-kundli* is a birth chart. It indicates the planetary positions when you were born. I will need your date, time and location of birth.'

Vincent supplied him with the relevant data. July 1st, 1969. 7:15 a.m. New York City.

The Pandit referred to a musty old tome from which he derived the latitude and longitude of New York City. Latitude 40°29'40'N to 45°0'42'N and longitude 71°47'25'W to 79°45'54'W.

Master craftsman that he was, he then started filling in the planetary positions in Vincent's birth chart. Chart duly completed, he looked at it carefully as if he were admiring a work of art.

'I will tell you a few things about your past. Please tell me whether I am right or wrong. This will ensure that the chart that I have before me is indeed accurate.'

Vincent meekly nodded his assent.

'You are an only child. No brothers or sisters.'

'Yes.'

'Your parents are dead. They died around the same time. Rather violently and suddenly. An accident?'

'Yes.'

'You are not married.'

'Yes.'

'Even though you are not married, you love children. You work with children in your career.'

'Yes.'

'You are deeply religious. In fact, your work is spiritual in nature.'

'Yes.'

'That's fine then,' said Pandit Ramgopal rather matter-of-factly as if all his accurate readings about Vincent's past meant nothing.

He then became very serious. 'The ascendant of your horoscope is Pisces with the moon in Pisces,' he said.[cxxvi]

'Huh?' said Vincent.

Pandit Ramgopal carried on, 'What it means is that in this life you are now at the end of your multiple cycles of birth, death and rebirth. This is your final lifetime before you merge with the divine. This is a wonderful horoscope. I am honoured to read it.'

'What does that mean?' asked Vincent.

Pandit Ramgopal replied. 'It means that you have been through several lifetimes in which you have learned various things. In this final lifetime, you will have learned whatever there is to learn. After this, you will not need rebirth. We Hindus call it *moksha*.'

'What else can you tell me?'

'There are three supreme forces in your life. You will need to recognize them before you can attain *moksha*.'

'How?'

'There is a holy crusader. His *Rahu* is in his sixth house and his *Ketu* is in his twelfth house. This makes him very holy, very religious. Unfortunately, his ascendant is a combination of Saturn and Mars. This makes him violent and bloody. You need to neutralize him.'

'What do you mean by "Rahu" and "Ketu"?' asked Vincent.

Pandit Ramgopal answered, 'In Hindu mythology, *Rahu* is the snake that swallows the sun or the moon, thus causing an eclipse. From the astronomical point of view, *Rahu* and *Ketu* denote the point of intersection of the sun and the moon as they move. To that extent, they are the north and south lunar nodes, hence eclipses are bound to occur at these points.'

'How do I neutralize this person?'

'By using a second person. This person has what is called a *Paap-Katri Yog* or a *Vish-Kanya Yog*. The force is probably feminine. Her moon is afflicted and surrounded by malevolent planets such as Saturn, Mars as well as *Rahu-Ketu*. This makes her almost maniacal, even though her outward appearance would be grace, charm and beauty personified. She will not hesitate to kill again and again.'

'What should I do?' asked Vincent, a chill creeping down his spine.

'Make two negatives into a positive,' retorted Ramgopal triumphantly. 'Let them cancel each other out!' he commanded as he thumped the table in front of him.

<hr />

Martha and Vincent were sitting in the Sea Lounge, one of the favourite tearooms in the Taj. They had just returned to the hotel after a hectic day of sightseeing and were enjoying the restaurant's specialty, Viennoise coffee.

Vincent had been rather shaken by the predictions of Pandit Ramgopal Prasad Sharma, and it had taken him a day to recover. In the morning, Martha had suggested that they spend the day seeing a little more of the city.

Vincent had told their guide that he wanted to see St. Thomas' Cathedral first, and that's exactly where they had headed. In the heart of the business district of Mumbai, St. Thomas' Cathedral stood like a quiet oasis in the midst of chaos. The cathedral had been built as the city's first Anglican church in 1718 with a view to improving the "moral standards" of the growing British settlement.

And then it struck Vincent. Wasn't St. Thomas one of the first apostles to come to India? He made up his mind quickly. He needed to go to the southern parts of India in order to understand the context of the Bom Jesus documents.

As they were getting up they saw a petite Japanese woman sitting alone by a window table. She was sipping Camomile tea and staring out into the ocean. Vincent couldn't help thinking, once again, what a delightful creature! Where had he seen her before? She looked familiar, but he shrugged it off.

His aunt Martha didn't.

<hr />

Cochin, Kerala, India, 2012
Vincent had decided to opt for a package tour that would take him to all the relevant spots on the St. Thomas circuit. He would proceed from Mumbai to Cochin on his own by air, while Martha would spend the next few days researching some documents at the David Sassoon Library.

Vincent's tour guide was a young Keralite by the name of Kurien. Kurien did not wait for formalities and plunged into his prepared material.

'St. Thomas visited Kerala in 52 A.D. At that time, Kerala was famous in ancient trade for spices, sandalwood, pepper, cardamom, and cinnamon and used to routinely trade with the Greeks, the Romans, and the Arabs. These trade centres in Kerala were headed by Jews. Gold coins from Rome and Greece of the period 27 B.C. to 80 A.D. have been found in ancient port cities of Kerala.'[cxxvii]

Kurien continued. '*The Acts of Judas Thomas*, a Syrian manuscript about the voyage of St. Thomas to India, and the travelogue of Thomas

Canae from Syria, who established Syrian Christianity in 372 A.D. in Kerala, describe Malabar Christians living along the Kerala coastline. When the Portuguese arrived in India in 1498, they found 143 Christian churches already established in Kerala!'

Kurien pointed out that St. Thomas had established six prayer centres in Kerala and that all of them were Jewish. Obviously, it had been much easier for St. Thomas to preach to the Jews than to the gentiles.

By the time Vincent returned to Mumbai, he was convinced that St. Thomas had indeed visited India. He now had many questions racing around inside his head.

Was it possible that Jesus had also visited India along with St. Thomas? If so, was a bloodline of Jesus still surviving in India? Could Terry Acton's Bom Jesus document lead them further? What about Mary Magdalene and the Holy Grail - weren't they supposed to have travelled to France? Could Jesus have survived his crucifixion?

He needed to discuss these matters with Martha, who was still in Mumbai, before proceeding any further.

Mumbai, India, 2012

Martha was sitting inside the David Sassoon Library. Located in the city's Kala Ghoda district, the library housed over 40,000 books, many of them extremely rare.

Martha's research had led her to a rare Persian work entitled *Negaris-Tan-i-Kashmir*. Also in front of them was a book by Andreas Faber Kaiser entitled *Jesus Died in Kashmir*.[cxxviii] In the latter, there was an interesting passage wherein the author related a conversation that he had had with Mr. Basharat Saleem, a man claiming to be a descendant of Jesus:

> *He [Bashrat Saleem] told me that to his knowledge the only written source on this subject of Jesus' marriage was the Negaris-Tan-i-Kashmir, an old Persian book that had been translated into Urdu. That [book] relates that King*

Shalivahana [the same king as met and conversed with Jesus in the mountains] told Jesus that he needed a woman to take care of him and offered him a choice of fifty....Jesus had replied that he did not need anyone and that no one was obliged to work for him, but the king persisted until Jesus agreed...the woman's name was Marjan, and that the same book says that she bore Jesus' children.

Martha recalled that Vincent's regression sessions with Terry and her had seemed to indicate that Jesus had survived the crucifixion. Martha remembered something else. In 1780 Karl Friedrich Bahrdt[cxxix] had suggested that Jesus had quite deliberately enacted his death on the cross using drugs that were arranged by the physician Luke. He had done this in order to ensure that his followers would reject the possibility of his being a political messiah and instead would embrace the more desirable alternative of his being a spiritual messiah. According to Bahrdt, Jesus had been resuscitated by Joseph of Arimathea, one of his secret disciples, who was a member of the Essenes, just like Jesus!

Next, Martha poured over the photocopies that she had made of the research done by Karl Venturini.[cxxx] Venturini had suggested that Jesus' fellow members of the secret society had heard groaning from inside the tomb where Jesus had been placed after his crucifixion. They had succeeded in scaring away the guards and had eventually rescued Jesus.

A story seemed to be emerging. A scholarly paper by Heinrich Paulus seemed to show that Jesus had merely fallen into a temporary coma and was revived without any external help in the tomb.

Martha was yet to read the *Nathanamavali*, a book on the Nath yogis of India.

In western India, there existed an extremely austere band of wandering ascetics in white robes. They are known as the Nath yogis. The Nath yogis hailed from a line of historical gurus and among several others was one called Issa Nath. A book on the history of the Nath yogis, called *Nathanamavali*[cxxxi] stated the following:

> *Issa Nath came to India at the age of fourteen. After this he returned to his own country and began preaching. Soon after, his brutish and materialistic countrymen conspired against him and had him crucified. After crucifixion, or perhaps even before it, Issa Nath entered samadhi by means of yoga.*

Samadhi, according to the proponents of yoga, was the final stage of yoga. Samadhi literally meant to "bring together". It was the bringing together of the conscious mind and the divine.

> *Seeing him thus, the Jews presumed he was dead, and buried him in a tomb. When Issa Nath's guru arrived, he took the body of Issa Nath from the tomb, woke him from his samadhi, and later led him to the sacred land of the Aryans. Issa Nath then established an ashram in the lower regions of the Himalayas.*

Martha recalled Vincent's words when he was under the trance of regression, "I am hiding behind some bushes. I don't know why I am unable to tear myself away from here. Night has fallen. In the middle of the night, there was a visitor. He looked like an angel because of his white robes...I think he was an Essene monk. He rolled away the stone. The guards collapsed with terror. The Sabbath is over, and the two Marys have come here to roll away the stone to the tomb, but they are rather surprised to see it open. They are going inside. I'm following at a discreet distance. There are two men in white robes. They look like Essenes. They are saying that Jesus is alive, not dead!'

Not completely satisfied with the progress that she had made with her research on behalf of Vincent, Martha decided to look up Holger Kersten, the leading authority on the subject of Jesus in India.

In 1983, the book *Jesus Lived in India* had created a mild storm when it had expanded the scope of Russian traveller Nicholas Notovich's experiences in Ladakh. Kersten had set out on the path ten years previously when he had first come across the theory that Jesus had lived in India.

Kersten had found that the Persian scholar F. Mohammed's historical work *Jami-ut-tuwarik*, which spoke of Jesus' visit to Nisibis, Turkey, by royal invitation, had been ignored by Western theology. Kersten discovered that in Turkey, as well as Persia, there were stories of a great saviour by the name of *Yuz Asaf*, "Leader of the Healed", who shared several similarities with Jesus in terms of character, lessons and life incidents.

Kersten also drew from the *Apocrypha,* which were texts written by the Apostles but were not officially accepted by the Roman Catholic Church. *The Apocryphal Acta Thomae*, or *The Acts of Judas Thomas,* spoke of the several meetings that had taken place between Jesus and Thomas on several occasions after Christ's crucifixion. *The Acts* further spoke of Christ specifically sending Thomas to preach in India.

Holger Kersten had found that stone inscriptions at Fatehpur Sikri, near the Taj Mahal, included "Agrapha" or sayings of Christ that were completely absent in the Bible. Their grammar resembled the Apocryphal gospel of Thomas.

Kersten had cited this fact to drive home the point that texts deleted by the Church contained extremely important information about Jesus and his life and that this information, while having been ruthlessly deleted by the Church, had not been deleted on the Indian stone inscriptions.

Martha decided that she needed to trace the *Tarikh-Issa-Massih* that had been photocopied by Terry Acton and given to Vincent. In the published *Tarikh-Issa-Massih* that she found in the library, the final paragraph said:

Issa and Mary had a child by the name of Sara, who was born to them in India, but was later sent to Gaul with her mother. Issa remained in India, where he married a woman from the Sakya clan on the persistence of King Gopadatta, and had a son, Benissa. Benissa had a son, Yushua, who fathered Akkub. Akkub's son was Jashub. Abihud was the son of Jashub. Jashub's grandson was Elnaam. Elnaam sired Harsha, who sired Jabal, who sired Shalman. Shalman's son Zabbud embraced Islam. Zabbud fathered Abdul, who sired Haaroon. His child was Hamza. Omar was Hamza's son and he produced Rashid. Rashid's offspring was Khaleel.

The problem, of course, was that even if one considered the sixteen generations after Jesus that were specifically mentioned in the book, and considering a forty-year lifespan of each generation, the book only had information for around 640 years after Jesus. Where was the lineage after Khaleel?

Martha was now pretty sure that some sort of cover-up was going on. She needed to see the original Urdu work and not the translated version. The library had the original Urdu version, but it was a third edition, published in 1862.

The lucky break was that having lived in India for many years, Martha understood Urdu perfectly.

***

She started reading in Urdu...'*Issa aur Mary ke beti paida hui jiska janam Hindustan mein huaa. Baad mein maa aur beti ko...*' She began by reading each line, first in Urdu, and then translating it to English:

Issa and Mary had a child by the name of Sara, who was born to them in India, but was later sent to Gaul with her mother. Issa remained in India, where he married a woman from the Sakya clan on the persistence of King Gopadatta, and had a son, Benissa. Benissa had a son, Yushua, who fathered

Akkub. Akkub's son was Jashub. Abihud was the son of Jashub. Jashub's grandson was Elnaam. Elnaam sired Harsha, who sired Jabal, who sired Shalman. Shalman's son Zabbud embraced Islam.

Zabbud's son was Abdul, and Abdul's son was Haaroon. Haaroon's son was Hamza and Hamza's son was Omar. Rashid's father was Omar and Khaleel's father was Rashid. Rashid had two more children, a son and a daughter. The boy's name was Muhammad and the girl was named Sultana. Muhammad died before his marriage, but Sultana produced a son. The name of her son was Salim. Salim had a son called Ikram. Ikram got married to Raziya and they had a daughter called Bano. Bano produced a son called Ali. Ali had a son, Ghulam, and Ghulam also had a son, Mustafa. Mustafa's son's name was Humayun. Humayun's son's name was Abbas. Abbas had a son called Faiz. Faiz had a son called Javed. Javed had a son, Gulzar. Gulzar had a daughter. The daughter's name was Nasreen. Nasreen had a son called Akbar. Akbar produced a son called Yusuf. Yusuf's son's name was Mansoor. Mansoor's son's name was Zain. Zain had a son, Faisal. Faisal produced a daughter called Sharmeen. Sharmeen had a son called Ibrahim. Ibrahim's son's name was Alam. Alam's son's name was Mehdi. Mehdi had a son called Bismillah. Bismillah had a son called Hassan. Hassan had a son called Shabbir.

Martha remained speechless. Here was a passage that took the lineage almost twenty-five generations further! How could this have been mistakenly omitted from the English translation?

She thought to herself, *Max Muller is admired all over the world for his translation of many historic Sanskrit works. Unfortunately, his motives are rarely discussed. It was Max Muller who wrote that, "India has been conquered once, but India must be conquered again... the ancient religion is doomed and if Christianity does not step in, whose fault will it be?"*

Martha was clear. English scholars were reluctant to expose any historical Indian works that seemed to portray Indian culture or religion as being older or more advanced than Western Christian thought. Any work that showed Jesus or Christianity as having learned from India, from Buddhism or from Hinduism would have made the work of Christian missionaries extremely difficult. Indians would have questioned why they needed to convert to Christianity if Christian thought in itself had been derived from ancient Buddhist or Hindu wisdom.

So the omissions in the English translations were deliberate? thought Martha to herself. 'There is only one way to tell,' she replied to herself out loud equally quickly, 'We must take up the challenge in the Bom Jesus document that Terry gave Vincent.'

Time to visit Goa. Had Vincent arrived in Mumbai yet?

There were many ways of getting from Mumbai to Goa. The boring way was to take a forty-five-minute flight. The exhausting way was to board an overnight bus. The economical way was by the super-fast Konkan Railways express train that got there in seven hours. The dignified way was called the Deccan Odyssey.

Aboard India's answer to Europe's Orient Express and South Africa's Blue Train, were Vincent and Martha. During his visit to Cochin, Vincent had befriended a senior superintendent of India's Western Railways. The two tickets on this super-luxury train were a heavily discounted gift from him.

The Deccan Odyssey was a dark blue train trimmed with gilded stripes. The decadent coaches were named after well-known forts, palaces and monuments of India, names that would become familiar on the leisurely journey from Mumbai to Goa. The journey would also give the duo some time to review all their research.

The Deccan Odyssey travelled at a leisurely sixty miles per hour as it snaked its way through the western peninsula of India, stopping along the way at small towns and beaches.

It was delightful to be awakened in the morning by hot coffee and toast brought by a personal valet, to be served whisky-and-soda by white-gloved bearers in the evenings and to be offered cocoa and biscuits before falling asleep each night.

On the third day they had arrived at Sindhudurg, which was famous for its Hindu temples. It was also famous for the Fort of Sindhudurg, which had taken 6000 workers three years of round-the-clock work to complete. The massive structure sat on forty-eight acres of land, a breathtaking goliath sitting in the water and surrounded by a pristine rocky coastline.

As aunt and nephew digested the beauty of their surroundings, Vincent spoke. During the train journey, he had been reading a novel called *Guardian of the Dawn* by Richard Zimler,[cxxxii] which Martha had managed to procure from the library.

'Nana, do you know that the author of this book was recently interviewed in India? Do you know what he said?'[cxxxiii]

'What?' asked Martha.

'He said that the Portuguese exported the Inquisition to Goa in the sixteenth century, and that many Indian Hindus were tortured and burnt at the stake for continuing to practise their religion. Muslim Indians were generally murdered right away or made to flee Goan territory.'

Vincent continued. 'Historians consider the Goa Inquisition to have been the most merciless and cruel ever executed. It was a machinery of death. A large number of Hindus was first converted and then persecuted from 1560 all the way to 1812! Over that period of 252 years, any man, woman, or child living in Goa could be arrested and tortured for simply whispering a prayer or keeping a small idol at home. Many Hindus, and some former Jews as well, languished in special inquisitional prisons, some for four, five, or six years at a time.'

Vincent looked at Martha for reactions. None.

He continued, 'The author was horrified to learn about this, of course. He was quite shocked that his friends in Portugal knew nothing about it. The Portuguese tended to think of Goa as the glorious capital of the spice trade, and they believed, erroneously, that people of different ethnic backgrounds lived there in tolerance and tranquillity, but they knew nothing about the terror that the Portuguese had wrought on India. They knew nothing of how their fundamentalist religious leaders made so many suffer.'

'But Islam also spread itself by the sword, Vincent. Why only accuse Christianity?' asked Martha.

'Yes. My point exactly. Both Christianity and Islam are religions of peace; however, their mass following today is partly due to blood that was shed over many years of history. On the other hand, we do not see Buddhism or Hinduism having gone to war for spreading their faith even though modern-day Hindu nationalists have been responsible for anti-minority riots.'

'So where exactly are we going with this conversation?' enquired Martha.

'Well, the aggressive competition between Islam and Christianity for converts could possibly have been handled better if they had cooperated rather than fought with each other.'

⟨✦⟩

'It now seems entirely probable to me that Jesus, having survived the crucifixion as seen by me in my past-life regressions, could have decided to come here to India to rediscover the ancient knowledge that he had been educated with,' commented Vincent as he put away his clothes into the suitcase in preparation for their arrival in Goa.

'So?' asked Martha.

'What if his children continue to live here? Wouldn't it be ironic if they were Muslim? After all, Islam came into India rather violently through Muslim invasions from the eighth century onwards.'

'Be that as it may, what is your point, Vincent?' asked an exasperated Martha.

'Well, any such offspring having a bloodline of Jesus and following Islam as a faith today would be a problem for Christians and Muslims alike.'

'Why?'

'First of all, the Church would not want to acknowledge that there is a bloodline at all…it destroys the fundamental belief that Jesus died on the cross in order to bear the burden of human sin. It means that there was no death, no resurrection, and no divine status. Also, to tell the world that Christ's own bloodline renounced the faith of Christ, would be to acknowledge that Islam has won the battle with Christianity!'

'Point taken. But why would such a descendant be a problem for Islam?' wondered Martha.

'According to the Qur'an, there is only a single religion that is acceptable to God, and that is one in which there is complete submission to God's will. To that extent, Muslims believe that Islam was also the religion of earlier prophets such as Abraham, Moses and Jesus, because they also submitted themselves completely to the will and obedience of God. Islam not only recognizes officially the bona fides of all earlier prophets, but also of any future prophets that may come.'[cxxxiv]

'So?'

'Wouldn't such a person be a threat to the power structure of Islam, if such a person were to claim prophethood?'

<hr />

Goa, India, 2012

Goa, located along the Konkan coastline of India that runs along its western edge, was India's party capital. Flights arrived in the state's capital, Panjim, but its business and commerce was in a town called Vasco, named after the famous explorer Vasco da Gama. The Portuguese traders who had landed here in the sixteenth century had succeeded in colonizing Goa, and it had remained a colony of Portugal till it was annexed by an independent India in 1961.

At every bend along the Goa coastline were picturesque coves and bays, each unique in its beauty. Along the sun-washed coast were delightful little sleepy villages with whitewashed churches and uniformly quaint houses with red-tiled roofs. The lush green and verdant miles of coconut and palm trees were breathtakingly beautiful, irrespective of the season. It was precisely because of this Hawaii-like experience at a fraction of the cost that many foreign tourists who visited Goa were reluctant to return home.

Rents in Goa varied from one area to the next, but Vincent's railway friend had succeeded in getting them a very rustic but functional cottage near Anjuna Beach for about a hundred dollars for the week. It had two small bedrooms, a bathroom, a kitchen, a living room and a delightful sit-out for relaxing evenings.

Anjuna Beach was more commonly called "the freak capital of the world". It was quite notorious for its trance and rave parties as well as the abundance of hippies. Surrounded by dense coconut groves, it was the most happening place on Wednesdays when the "flea market mania" would take over. The market was always a wonderful cauldron of flavours, colours, smells and textures.

Luckily, their cottage was not in the heart of the trance circuit but nearer the sleepy hamlet. This location offered them best of both worlds - proximity to civilization as well as the tranquillity of the quiet cove.

As their taxi, which had definitely seen better days, rattled towards their new home, it was overtaken by a fast motorbike.

Under the jacket and helmet was a pretty young Japanese woman, who sped off very quickly.

She had been staring at Martha.

Chapter Eighteen

Vatican City, 2012

His Eminence was reading the verses from the *Book of Revelation* in the Holy Bible.[cxxxv] His mind was focused on the seven angels mentioned in the book:

The first angel sounded, and there followed hail and fire mingled with blood, and they were cast upon the earth.

One-third of the trees were burnt, and all green grass was burnt.

And the second angel sounded, and a great mountain burning with fire was cast into the sea.

One-third of the sea became blood. One-third of life in the sea died.

And the third angel sounded, and there fell a great star from the heavens, burning as if it were a lamp. It fell upon one-third of the rivers, which became undrinkable and killed many.

And a fourth angel sounded, and one-third of the sun, moon and stars was darkened so that one-third of the day became dark.

And the fifth angel sounded, and a star fell from heaven unto the earth and to him was given the key of a bottomless pit. And he opened the bottomless pit; and there arose a smoke like that of a great furnace and the atmosphere became black.

Out of the smoke came locusts upon the earth and unto them was given the power to hurt men that did not have the seal of God upon their foreheads.

And the sixth angel sounded, and was asked to let loose two hundred thousand horsemen to kill one-third of humanity.

And the seventh angel sounded; and there were great voices in heaven, saying, 'The kingdoms of this world have become the kingdoms of our Lord, and of his Christ, and he shall reign for ever and ever.'

Chamonix, French Alps, France, 2012

Chamonix, in Haute-Savoie, offered some of the most stunning views of Mont Blanc. When Savoy had become part of France in 1860, this region had become French, bordering Switzerland to the north and Italy to the east.[cxxxvi] It was here that Mont Blanc, the roof of Europe, reached its highest point of 4,807 meters.

No one took any notice of Ataullah al-Liby boarding the cable car for the Aiguille du Midi. The first part of the journey, a nine-minute trip to the Plan des Aiguilles located at a height of 2,263 metres was not too bad. The second part of the cable car trip to the Aiguille du Midi station at 3,781 metres was a little nerve-wracking; Ataullah hated heights.

Reaching his destination, Ataullah was around a hundred metres from the peak of Mont Blanc and had a commanding view of the Aiguilles of Chamonix and Vallée Blanche, the largest glacier in Europe.

It was here that he would conveniently slip away into the darkness. His ski jacket had been specially fitted with high-powered Semtex. He quickly took it off.

The delayed blast on January 21st, 2012 would send a wall of hail and fire ripping through Chamonix, killing 332 people. Assignment completed, Attaullah headed for Chamonix Airport from where his flight to Geneva would eventually link him to his rendezvous in Frederick County in America.

And the first angel sounded, and there followed hail and fire mingled with blood, and they were cast upon the earth...

Riberalta, Bolivia, 2012

The epicentre of the blast was twenty-five kilometres from Riberalta, 850 kilometres northeast of Bolivia's capital, La Paz.

No one could have spotted the crude IED, the Improvised Explosive Device, fashioned from potassium perchlorate, aluminium powder and sulphur that had been left under the dense cover of the Amazon forest by Boutros Ahmad. The intense heat applied by a welding torch was enough to set off the highly unstable mixture.[cxxxvii]

The fire on February 21st, 2012 would destroy over 448,000 acres of tropical forest besides killing 113 people.

Job done, Boutros drove to Gen Buech Airport to catch his Lloyd Aéreo Boliviano flight that would get him to his meeting in Frederick County.

One-third of the trees, and all green grass was burnt.

❦

Hubei Province, China, 2012

The Three Gorges Dam spanned the Yangtze River at Sandouping, Yichang, and Hubei.

Construction of the largest hydroelectric dam in the world, more than five times the size of the Hoover Dam, had begun in 1993. The dam had become fully operational in 2009.

The reservoir had begun filling on June 1st, 2003 and now held 39.3 billion cubic metres of water. The twenty-six power generators had a combined generating capacity of 18.2 GW.[cxxxviii]

The Three Gorges Dam was strong enough to resist terrorist attacks - China had enough manpower and equipment to guard the important parts, such as the dam, power plants and the lock of the Three Gorges.

What could not be guarded was the cargo aboard the ships that went through the massive ship lift. The ship lift at the Three Gorges Dam had been designed to lift ships of up to 3,000 tonnes displacement through a vertical distance of 113 metres. The size of the basin through which ships would ascend or descend was a massive 120 x 18 x 3.5 metres. Each ship would take around thirty minutes to go up or down.

The 3000-tonne ship *Daiyang* had done this route several times before. No one could have guessed the presence of ammonium nitrate in the diesel. The technical grade ammonium nitrate granules mixed with diesel were extremely porous, resulting in better fuel absorption and thus significantly higher reactivity.[cxxxix]

The ship's crew was aware of their cargo. They were all Uighurs who were ready to die for their leader, Faris Kadeer. The sudden heat application created a reaction.

$2NH4NO3 \rightarrow 4H2O + 2N2 + O2$.

The combination with the diesel resulted in a detonation rate of around 3000 feet per second. The dam was strong enough to resist the explosion, but the lift and locks were not.

39.3 billion cubic metres of water began to flow on March 21st, 2012 as the manmade mountain; the Three Gorges Dam was cast into the frothy sea. The death toll was over a thousand people.

Faris was not there. He was on an Air China flight to London. From there he would board a flight headed for Baltimore-Washington International Airport. This would get him to his appointment in Frederick County on time.

And the second angel sounded, and a great mountain burning with fire was cast into the sea...

<hr>

English Channel, Dover, 2012

The accident happened around 1.3 kilometres north of the Dover coast on April 21st, 2012. It resulted in a hole measuring fifteen metres by four metres in the side of the Panama-registered tanker, the *Gulf Princess*. The tanker had been carrying 300,000 tonnes of oil from the Middle East to Dover when the English fishing boat had collided with it.

It was one of the worst oil spills in history. More than 239,000 metric tonnes of oil poured into the English Channel. The next two months would be hell - putting out oil fires, bringing all shipping through the channel to a virtual halt and pulling out thousands of dead fish from the ocean.

Subsequent enquiries would reveal that the English fishing boat that had caused the collision, the *Wilson Flyer*, had been sold for £16,005 by its previous owner in East Sussex through a broker,

Powertech Marine, to a wealthy boat enthusiast just a week previously. The money had been transferred electronically to the seller from an account in Guernsey belonging to the Isabel Madonna trust.

Fouad al-Noor had done his job well. He had personally trained his men to do the job of steering the fishing boat into the hull of the tanker.

Fouad was now on a British Midland's flight headed for the United States. His diary indicated an appointment in Frederick County.

One-third of the sea became blood. One-third of life in the sea died.

Kuala Lumpur, Malaysia, 2012

The Petronas Towers in Kuala Lumpur used to be the world's tallest buildings till they were toppled by the Taipei 101 in 2003.

The twin towers had one very striking feature - a sky bridge between the two towers on the 41st and 42nd floors. The bridge lay 170 metres off the ground. The sky bridge was strategically located on the podium floor because visitors wanting to travel to higher floors necessarily had to change elevators on that floor.[cxl]

The bridge was open to all visitors but the 1400 passes that were rationed out each day were only available on a first-come first-served basis.

Tau'am Zin Hassan and his men from the Darul Islam had managed to secure over thirty passes that day. Each one of them went up to the bridge and placed a small strip of what looked like modelling clay into the grooves that formed the design element of the supporting pillars.

The modelling clay was actually C-4, a deadly military plastic explosive containing RDX. Each little strip had a small NEC credit-card sized cell phone hanging from it.

Once all the strips were in place, the thirty visitors congregated together at Kuala Lumpur International Airport. All thirty of them pressed the speed dial keys on their phones that had been pre-set on the letter "A". Each cell phone was calling its partner phone inside the Petronas sky bridge.

As each mini phone rang inside the bridge, a small electrical current was sent to the speakers of each. However, none of the thirty phones inside the sky bridge rang. The phone wires that connected the speakers had been disconnected and then reconnected instead to small transistors that could be turned on by a mild electrical current. Each transistor, in turn, activated a detonator.[cxli]

At exactly 5:03 p.m. on May 21st, 2012 the sky bridge of the Petronas Towers exploded in a ball of fire. The inferno eventually came crashing down to earth.

There were over a hundred visitors on the bridge when it exploded. It came crashing down on fifty-four onlookers.

Tau'am did not wait to see the press coverage. He was on a Singapore Airlines flight that would take him to the west coast of the United States.

From Los Angeles, he would take a United flight to reach his destination at Frederick County.

And the third angel sounded, and there fell a great star from the heavens, burning as if it were a lamp.

<hr/>

Katra, Jammu & Kashmir, India, 2012
Five point four million devotees paid homage to the goddess in 2003. An average of 14,794 visits each day of the year. A pilgrimage to the holy shrine of Vaishno Devi was considered to be one of the holiest pilgrimages by one billion Hindus in the world. The holy cave of the divine goddess was situated at an altitude of 5200 feet. The pilgrims had to trek around twelve kilometres uphill from the base camp at Katra in order to reach the shrine.[cxlii]

A virtual sea of humanity would make the trek during the holiest period of the year, *Navratri*, or the festival of nine nights. The nine days were divided into three sets of three days each. Each set of three days would be used to worship three different manifestations of the supreme feminine mother.

On the first three days, the supreme feminine would be worshipped as the nurturer and the provider of spiritual and material wealth, *Lakshmi*. The next three days would be spent worshipping the divine feminine as *Saraswati*, the goddess of wisdom. Finally, the divine mother would be worshipped as the force of destruction, *Kali*.

A Shiva temple was located about fifteen kilometres away from Katra. A spring ran from the rocks in a wooded grove and flowed into a holy rivulet that eventually merged with the Chenab River.

The truck-mounted water tank was one among hundreds that supplied drinking water to pilgrims. This one, however, was different. Instead of water, it contained a deadly cocktail consisting of cyanide, arsenic, mercury, parathion, sodium fluoroacetate, cadmium, sarin, sulphur mustard and dieldrin.

The innocent accident was perfectly targeted - at the mouth of the river. It resulted in the immediate death of the driver. Kali was about to manifest her awesome powers of destruction that day on June 21st, 2012.

More than 500 killed and over 2000 lying sick or critical in various hospitals due to poisoned river water.

Bin Fadan was neither sick nor dead. He was headed for the Indira Gandhi International Airport in New Delhi from where he would catch a KLM flight through Amsterdam to New York. He would then drive to Frederick County in an Avis rental car.

...it fell upon one-third of the rivers, which became undrinkable and killed many.

❦

Baghdad, Iraq, 2012
Camp War Eagle, initially used by the 1st Squadron, 2nd Cavalry Regiment, was located in the Tisa Nissan District of Baghdad.

Conditions at Camp War Eagle had improved dramatically over the years of occupation by American forces. Air conditioners and generators hummed all over the place. A spanking new basketball court stood in the centre of the camp. Payphones allowed the men to be in direct touch with their families. New barracks were continuously being erected to accommodate additional men.[cxliii]

Unfortunately, these things did not help keep the men safe. Almost all the residents of the camp had already had a close encounter with an incoming explosive. Thousands of soldiers had been injured in the sixty-acre camp, most when they were walking towards the mess room. Luckily there had been no fatalities; not till today anyway.

They could not have visualized Kader al-Zarqawi's men launching rocket-propelled grenades and improvised explosive devices at Bayji, Daura and Basra in simultaneous and coordinated attacks.

At the same time, multiple cargo containers at various ports including Al Faw, Khawr Al Amaya, Mina Al Bakr, Umm Qasr, and Al Basraha exploded. Four of these ships contained flammable liquids. Two of the flaming boats contained resins and coatings including isocyanates, nitriles, and epoxy resins. Winds began carrying thick black smoke and releasing toxic chemicals and metals into the air.

The soldiers used to joke that the appropriate epitaph for anyone having served at the camp would be: *'And when he gets to heaven, To Saint Peter he will tell, "Just another soldier reporting, sir, I've done my time in hell"!'*

Two hundred and thirty soldiers reported to Saint Peter on July 21st, 2012. The 1191 civilians who died had no one to report to. They could only blame Kader al-Zarqawi, who had already left Baghdad by road and was about to board a flight out of Istanbul along with some friends who were meeting him there. He had been told not to be late for the conference in Frederick County.

And a fourth angel sounded, and one-third of the sun, moon and stars was darkened so that one-third of the day became dark.

Wyoming, U.S.A., 2012

Shamoon Idris was dressed as a garbage collector. In front of him was a large dustbin that could be rolled forward on a set of wheels. A close observer would have noticed that he was not collecting any garbage. The dustbin remained tightly shut.

Some minutes later, Shamoon rolled the dustbin onto a boat as it sped into the centre of Yellowstone Lake. Having reached the pre-determined point, Shamoon donned a diving suit and threw the dustbin overboard. Instead of floating, the dustbin submerged itself and came to rest on the lakebed.

Scientific studies of volcanic activity at Yellowstone National Park had shown the existence of a massive volcanic bulge at the bottom of the lake.[cxliv] Shamoon needed to ensure that the dustbin was correctly positioned on the hump and detonated before currents could move it elsewhere. Accuracy was the key.

The powerful bomb that exploded as it rested upon this hump, ruptured the bulge on the bottom of Yellowstone Lake and set in motion a chain reaction explosion that ruptured the underground magma chamber.

As the magma chamber ruptured, the ground shook as portions of the park imploded into the caldera underneath and then exploded in a massive eruption of lava, embers, dust and soot.

August 21st, 2012.

One thousand seven hundred and twelve dead and countless injured. Shamoon wasn't around. He had already reached Bozeman, Montana, from where he would travel to Hagerstown Regional Airport. He needed to be in Frederick County on time.

And the fifth angel sounded, and a star fell from heaven unto the earth and to him was given the key of a bottomless pit. And he opened the bottomless pit; and there arose a smoke like that of a great furnace and the atmosphere became black.

❧❧❧

Jakarta, Indonesia, 2012

The Bung Karno Stadium, one of the world's largest, had been built in 1962. The stadium had a registered capacity of 100,000, but at times the audience could swell to over 120,000. Named after Sukarno, Indonesia's first President, the stadium was undergoing a huge renovation exercise to host the next Asia Cup. The Football Association of Indonesia, in the meantime, had reintroduced a national cup competition featuring seventy-four clubs within the country. The first match of the series was on September 21st, 2012.^{cxlv}

Unfortunately, half the stadium was under renovation and the fans who turned up for the match that day were herded together like cattle into the remaining usable half of the stadium. There was an air of excitement in the usable half of the stadium.

The cement mixers lay silently in the area of the stadium under renovation. As half time was announced, the crowds started moving towards the toilets, when the mixers were turned on.

The anthrax spores were transported by aerosol delivery through a special spraying device built into the mixers.^{cxlvi} As the spraying continued, Bacillus anthracis was inhaled into the lungs of thousands of spectators in the stadium. Hundreds would die over the next few days.

The contracting firm providing the mixers was a small outfit called Bermis Bakti PT. Mohammed Yusif, the owner of the contracting firm, held 100% of the equity shares of his company; however, all his equipment had been procured on leases. The leases for the equipment were held by Samba, the Saudi-American Bank. The future cash flows from the leases had been discounted and securitized. The securities had been sold to a small investment trust in the British Virgin Islands called the Isabel Madonna investment trust.

Yaqub Islamuddin was on a Garuda flight, musing, *It is quite amazing the things one can plan when one has time inside prison. But it's nice to be out. This conference in Frederick County will do me good.*

...and out of the smoke came locusts upon the earth...

New South Wales, Australia, 2012
The plains of New South Wales were quiet and meditative. The vast fields of wheat and cotton stretched endlessly and the population density was extremely low.

The quiet was about to be broken by a deafening buzzing. An isolated swamp created by the previous year's rains had been well cultivated by Adil Afrose.

As he detonated a bomb in the centre of the swamp, the grasshoppers formed swarms that would travel more than 500 kilometres searching for food.

Weeks later, the Australian Plague Locust Commission would report that a single swarm of just one square kilometre had contained over fifty million locusts and had consumed eleven tonnes of vegetation every twenty-four hours. Tens of millions of dollars in damage had been done to crops, pastures, orchards, gardens, and sports fields in a single day.[cxlvii]

October 21st, 2012.

Adil was also flying, like the locusts. He was on a Qantas flight. Destination - Frederick County.

...and unto the locusts was given the power to hurt men that did not have the seal of God upon their foreheads.

⬤━❧⳹⳼⳺⳻⳽❧━⬤

Grozny, Chechnya, Russia, 2012

Yahya was in Argun Mosque coordinating efforts centrally. Soon, from 2000 mosques across Chechnya, a battle cry would be heard: '*Miyarsh Noxchi Che*! Long Live Free Chechnya!'

Coinciding with the war cry, hundreds of Chechen rebels mounted their horses and charged upon the Russian base near Vedeno in the south of Chechnya led by Yahya Abdullah. A hundred and twelve soldiers were killed. This was just the beginning.

The Vnukovo Airlines flight bound for Moscow from Grozny was completely full on November 21st, 2012. The plane, a Tupolev 154, took off at 8:40 a.m. from Grozny and was scheduled to land in Moscow three hours later. That was when Yahya and his two men took over the aircraft and diverted it to Istanbul. In Istanbul, they were joined by another colleague who had arrived by road from Baghdad. They were provided passage to Prince Mohammed-bin-Abdel Aziz airport in Medina, Saudi Arabia.

When the flight arrived in Saudi Arabia, the four men held the 128 passengers hostage till a getaway vehicle was provided. As they sped away, they remote-triggered the device that had been stored in the overhead onboard luggage rack of one the seats. Ninety-three dead, thirty-five injured.

The getaway vehicle took them to Kuwait, where they separated. Yahya switched identities and took an Emirates flight to the United States. He had done his job well. He deserved some rest in Frederick County.

And the sixth angel sounded, and was asked to let loose two hundred thousand horsemen to kill one-third of humanity.

Waziristan, Pakistan-Afghanistan Border, 2012
The Sheikh's master, the beneficiary of the Isabel Madonna Trust, was busy recording a videotape. He was seated on his rug, wearing his trademark camouflage jacket. The tape would be released to the world on December 21st, in the midst of universal turmoil. The Sheikh watched his master as he recorded his statement.

Praise be to Allah, who created the creation for his worshipers and commanded them to be just and permitted the wronged one to retaliate against the oppressor in kind. To proceed...peace be upon he who follows the guidance.

What has already transpired is merely a forerunner. The destruction of the Vallée Blanche glacier in France, the burning down of millions of dollars worth of natural resources in Bolivia, the destruction and devastation caused to the Three Gorges Dam in China, the massive oil spills in the English Channel, the blast at the Petronas Towers in Malaysia, the poisoning of river waters in India, the dramatic explosions of oil assets in Iraq, the volcanic eruptions in Wyoming, the anthrax attack in Jakarta, the plague of locusts in Australia, and the hijacking and blowing up of a Russian passenger plane that was headed out of Chechnya followed by war...these were mere appetizers. If you think that these events were hell, you have not yet seen the wrath of God. The main course is yet to come.

I say to all of you, accept the will of Allah and prevent your destruction. Give Muslims their rights, their lands, their oil, and their political power, otherwise we shall continue to rain fire and chaos upon you. Your security is in your own hands. And every state that doesn't play with our security has automatically guaranteed its own security. And Allah is our Guardian and Helper, while you have no Guardian or Helper. All peace be upon he who follows the Guidance.

Be on your guard, for Armageddon is finally here.

Click. The Sheikh, who was behind the video camera shut it off and pulled out the tape. He efficiently sealed it in a 3M Scotch cushioned envelope so that it could be delivered to Al-Jazeera Television at the appropriate time.

The Sheikh was wondering how he would meet his end of the deal. Commitments made within the *Crux Decussata Permuta* were not to be taken lightly. It was these commitments that had ensured the spread and growth of the two largest religions of the world, Christianity and Islam.

He knew that his master did not think in the same way.

Chapter Nineteen

Goa, India, 2012

Vincent and Martha had instantly fallen in love with Goa. The place was filled with famous churches, including the Se Cathedral, the Church of St. Anne at Talaulim Ilhas, the ruins of the Church of St. Augustine, the Reis Magos church built on the banks of the Mandovi river, the Basilica of Bom Jesus, the St. Cajetan Church, the Church of St. Paul, the Church of Mary Immaculate Conception, and the Church of St. Francis of Assissi.

Vincent was pained to note that Goa's magnificent temples of Christianity were pretty much a legacy of ruthless Portuguese colonization. Christianity had been forced upon the local population with religious zeal by the Portuguese, particularly during the Inquisition. This had meant a massive effort to destroy Hindu temples, and this had continued till the end of the Inquisition in 1812. Unfortunately, many of Goa's churches had been built on sites of former temples. The confiscated temple lands had been forcibly handed over to the Church.

Not surprising, thought Vincent. After all, Pope Leo X had said to King Manoel of Portugal in 1515, "Receive this warlike sword in your always victorious and warlike hands...use your force, strength, and power against the fury of the infidels!"[cxlviii]

The first step that the two had decided was to attempt to decipher the document handed over by Terry to Vincent. The document said:

It is enough, O Lord, it is enough, the two angels said.
Mastrilli without doubt made the best silver bed.
But to carefully guard a secret of the dead.
Ignatius' gold cup is better than a silver head.
The city is located between 15°48' and 14°53'54' north and
between 74°20' and 73°40' east.

The problem lay in the latitude and longitude provided. It covered almost the whole of Goa. Hence this could mean almost any church in Goa. Then it struck Vincent!

The envelope in which Terry had handed over the documents to him had the words "Bom Jesus" scrawled on it by Terry. Furthermore, the Church of Bom Jesus contained the tomb of the Spanish missionary, Saint Francis Xavier. It was claimed that the body remained in a permanent state of preservation within a silver casket constructed by Mastrilli.

They needed to get to the Basilica of Bom Jesus immediately.

It was past nine at night when Vincent and Martha arrived at the Basilica. The church was located in old Goa, which had been largely abandoned after the fall of Portuguese rule. All that remained were a few churches, a monastery and a convent.

In the quiet of the night, they made their way inside the church. In the dim candlelight they collectively gasped at the beauty of the gilded altar, the extravagant frescoes and the intricate inlay work.

To the south of the church stood an airtight glass coffin ensconced in a silver casket designed and executed by a Florentine craftsman of the seventeenth century. The embalmed body of Saint Francis Xavier lay within. Under the casket was a pair of angels holding a message, "*Satis est, Domine, Satis est.*" Translated, it meant, "It is enough, O Lord, it is enough!"

They needed to look beneath the casket.

'Are you looking for this old parchment?' the voice resonated. They froze.

It was a nun. Her feet shuffled along the marble floor as she walked towards them. 'You are searching for the documents hidden here by Alphonso de Castro, aren't you? Here, I have them,' she said as she threw the document in Vincent's face.

It was only when she was right beside him that he noticed the Japanese face and felt the cool hardness of the metal nub of a 9mm pistol pressed into his ribs.

Martha had remained completely helpless as Swakilki had led Vincent out of the church and into a waiting car. She had been very clear, 'One false move and I'll kill him.'

After a few minutes of remaining frozen, Martha thought to herself that this woman obviously knew what they were after. She had a copy of it in advance. There was only one person who knew why Vincent and Martha were in Goa. Thomas Manning. This was a bigger conspiracy than they can handle. The local police would be of little help in this. Who could she turn to?

'For heaven's sake! What is it that can save Vincent?' muttered Martha under her breath.

Then she recalled her conversation with Terry Acton a couple of days before his death. While it had been a well-known fact that Terry was researching various religions and was deeply involved in past-life therapy, what was not generally known was that his research was being sponsored by the Illuminati. Terry had been convinced that modern-day Christianity, as taught by the Roman Catholic Church, was far removed from the Gnostic spirituality of Christ. The Illuminati believed that power emanated from self-knowledge and at most times, they were at odds with the Church and they found Terry's research path breaking.

Terry had revealed to Martha that his Rhodes scholarship and Skull & Bones connection had led him to the Illuminati; after all, the origin of Skull & Bones itself lay in the Bavarian Illuminati. And the contact point for all of this was Terry's close friend from his Yale days - Stephen Elliot.

Martha remembered him because Stephen had visited Terry in London several times after the death of Terry's wife, Susan. In fact, Stephen had asked Martha out for dinner once when he was on a visit to London.

She needed to get in touch with Elliot.

It was as she was racing towards the church door that she saw the document that the nun had flung in Vincent's face before abducting him. It was lazily stretched out on the cool marble floor, not in the least bit concerned about the chaos that it had just caused.

⋘═══⋙

New Delhi, India, 2012

RAW. The name sounded earthy and rough. That's because it was. RAW stood for Research and Analysis Wing and was India's premier intelligence agency, which had over 12,000 agents operating around the world. The chief of RAW held the rather demeaning title of "Secretary (R)" in the Cabinet Secretariat, which was part of the Indian Prime Minister's office.

RAW's primary responsibility was that of gathering external intelligence. This role was complementary to that of its cousin, the Intelligence Bureau, which was responsible for gathering and analysing internal intelligence. The two organizations were meant to jointly report to the National Security Council, headed by the Prime Minister.[cxlix]

Secretary (R), General Prithviraj Singh, was pondering over the tip-off that he had received from his old friend in the SAS, Stephen Elliot.

Prithviraj was among the old-guard elitists within the security apparatus of India. Educated at Eton, with a Ph.D. in mathematics from Yale, the white-moustached, bow-tie wearing, Montecristo-smoking veteran was a gentleman in every sense of the word, except for his intellect, which was razor sharp.

As a Yallie, he had excelled in Game Theory. He had delighted himself by not answering exam questions - he would instead write detailed and well-reasoned explanations on why there were inherent flaws in the framing of the questions. His intellectual arrogance had been a source of lively debate on the Yale campus.

He stared at his friend from Mossad, Zvi Yatom. Yatom had been involved in some of the Israeli intelligence agency's most successful operations. In 1981 he had spearheaded the destruction of Iraq's Osirak nuclear reactor. Some years later, Yatom had masterminded the assassination of Abu Jihad, Yasser Arafat's most loyal aide within the

Fatah party.[cl] Zvi had flown down to New Delhi from Tel Aviv to assist Prithviraj in figuring out where exactly the bomb could be headed.

Prithviraj was now wondering how he should brief the Prime Minister. A priest kidnapped in Goa by an international assassin on behalf of a group called the Crux Decussata Permuta, a group that had already succeeded in bumping off an English professor! A nuclear device smuggled into India, a land of 3.28 million square kilometres and a population of 1.02 billion people, with no clear indication of where it was headed! It was like looking for a needle in a haystack!

He paused outside the Prime Minister's office door and then knocked twice. 'Enter!' came the voice from within. The general sighed, opened the door and walked in along with Zvi.

The octogenarian Prime Minister smiled at them, his trademark smile, one that had won him the last election. Behind the smile was a Machiavellian streak that would turn foe into friend, defeat into victory and opposition into dust.

'So what was so urgent, General Sahib?' asked the Prime Minister, using the respectful Indian suffix as he motioned both men to sit.

'Sir, we have reliable information from our American friends that the Lashkar-e-Toiba or a sub-group within the Lashkar has managed to procure a nuclear device, roughly of the capacity used at Hiroshima. The Pakistani and Korean connection seems quite evident. The reason for the urgency is that this device, according to American intelligence, is already in Indian territory. Unfortunately, we have no indication of whether it is still in Indian territory or whether it is headed to some other destination such as Israel.'

Brief. Concise. Matter-of-fact.

'What are our options?' asked the octogenarian.

Zvi spoke up. 'It seems that this could be the work of Ghalib, sir. It is likely to be the twelfth attack in a series of attacks that have been happening each month this year, including the attack that you had to cope with in Katra. The key question is, who facilitated such a nuclear transaction with the Pakistanis? Our sources indicate, incredibly, the involvement of a fringe Christian group called the *Crux Decussata Permuta* that are using the nuclear deal as barter for something else.'

'What could that be?' asked the PM.

'There is one person who could have helped us answer that question. Professor Terry Acton, who obviously knew enough to get taken out himself. According to Stephen Elliot, Terry's research was shared with a priest, Vincent Morgan. Unfortunately, he was kidnapped last night in Goa. Efforts are on to locate him, although that's easier said than done. I need your clearance to deploy one of our four Rapid Action Divisions in order to help me trace him,' replied Prithviraj.

'You have it,' came the immediate response, 'but keep this matter under wraps, gentlemen.'

'We shall be as quiet as the dew!' retorted Prithviraj, taking a leaf out of Emily Dickinson's poem as he noisily slammed shut the PM's office door on his way out along with Zvi.

Chapter Twenty

Mari, Indo-Pakistan Border, 1898
The British Army was building a watchtower on a hill called Pindi Point when they noticed the old monument.

If they had simply asked the locals, they would have been informed that it was a tomb called *Mai Mari da Asthan*. The tomb was in Jewish east-west orientation. The tomb obviously could not be Muslim, for then it would have been placed on a north-south axis. It could not be Hindu, since Hindus cremated their dead.

Translated, the name *Mai Mari da Asthan* meant, "The Final Resting Place of Mary". It was because of the tomb that the place had derived its name, Mari.[cli] It was believed that when Jesus was on his way from Turkey to Kashmir, his mother, who was around seventy years old by that time, had died in Mari and had been buried there.

This tomb, however, was not in dispute, unlike another in Kashmir.

***

Kashmir, 1774 A.D.
The dispute pertained to an old tomb located in Kashmir. The decree was finally issued by the High Court of Kashmir, under the seal and hand of the Grand Mufti.

The Seal of the Justice of Islam, Mulla Fazil, 1194 A.H. In this High Court of Justice, in the Department of Learning and Piety of the Kingdom.

Present: Rehman Khan, son of Amir Khan, submits that: the kings, the nobles, the ministers and the multitude come from all directions of the kingdom to pay their homage and offerings in cash and kind at the lofty and the holy shrine of Yuz Asaf, the Prophet, may God bless him.

Claims: That he is the only and absolute claimant, entitled to receive the offerings and utilize these, and none else has any right whatsoever on these offerings.

Prays: That a writ of injunction be granted to all those who interfere and others be restrained from interfering with his rights.

Verdict: Now this court, after obtaining evidence, concludes as under: It has been established that during the reign of Raja Gopadatta, who built many temples and got repaired especially the Throne of Solomon on the hill of Solomon, Yuz Asaf came to the valley. Prince by descent, he was pious and saintly and had given up earthly pursuits. He spent all his time in prayers and meditation. The people of Kashmir, having become idolaters after the great flood of Noah, the God Almighty sent Yuz Asaf as a Prophet to the people of Kashmir. He proclaimed oneness of God till he passed away. Yuz Asaf was buried at Kanyar on the banks of the lake, and the shrine is known as Rozabal.

Orders: Since the shrine is visited by the devotees, both high and common, and since the applicant, Rahman Khan, is the hereditary custodian of the shrine, it is ordered that he be entitled to receive the offerings made at the shrine as before, and no one else shall have any right to such offerings. Given under our hand, 11ᵗʰ Jamad-ud-sani, 1184 A.H.

The Throne of Solomon, referred to in the judgment, was more commonly known as the *Takhat Sulaiman* and had been repaired in 78 A.D.

Kashmir, 78 A.D.

The *Takhat Sulaiman*, the Throne of Solomon, was a magnificent temple located at the peak of a hill near the Dal Lake. There were four inscriptions on the structure.

The first of these inscriptions was, "The mason of this pillar is Bihishti Zargar, Year fifty and four". The second inscription was, "Khwaja Rukun, son of Murjan erected this pillar". The third inscription was, "At this time Yuz Asaf proclaimed his prophethood. Year fifty and four".[clii]

And finally, the fourth inscription proclaimed, "He is Jesus, Prophet of the Children of Israel".

The same Yuz Asaf mentioned by Shaikh Sadiq in his writings.

Khorasan, Iran, 962 A.D.

Shaikh Sadiq was dying. During his global travels, he had written several books, including *Ikmal-ud-Din*, in which he wrote of the travels of Yuz Asaf:

> *Then Yuz Asaf, after roaming about in many cities, reached that country which is called Kashmir. He travelled in it far and wide and stayed there and spent his remaining life there, until death overtook him, and he left the earthly body and was elevated towards the Light.*

Shaikh Sadiq also wrote about some of the parables that Yuz Asaf taught:

> *When a sower goes to sow and sows, some seeds fall by the wayside, and the birds pick up the seed. Some fall upon stray land, and when they reach the stony foundation they wither away. Some fall among thorns and grow not. But the seed that falls on the good land grows and brings forth fruit.*

Strikingly similar to the "sower" parable of Jesus.

The one who had been punished "instead" of Barabbas.

Srinagar, Kashmir, 2012

Barabbas was the name of the charming houseboat on the bank of the Dal Lake in Srinagar. It had a delightful cedar-panelled bedroom, with many conveniences of a luxury hotel. This particular boat had fine furniture, warm Kashmiri carpets, and modern bathroom fittings. It was moored at a location where one had a view of the beautiful lotus gardens of Kashmir. It had a balcony in the front, a lounge, dining room, pantry and three bedrooms with attached bathrooms.

Srinagar's thousand-odd houseboats were permanently moored in the Dal and Nagin lakes as well as in the River Jhelum. All houseboats in Srinagar, regardless of category, had highly personalized service. Not only was there always a butler for every boat, but also the manager and his family were never far away.

The owner of this particular boat was none other than Ghalib. He never stayed here - he was mostly away travelling; the boat was mostly used by his trusted aide and friend, Yehuda Moinuddin.

Yehuda was also the Junior Assistant Director of Archives, Archaeology, Research and Museums for Kashmir.

The owner had twelve "children".

In Urdu, the number twelve was called *barah* and the word for father was *abba*.

This particular owner, Ghalib-bin-Isar, was affectionately called *Barabba,* Father of Twelve.

Who else had twelve disciples?

<hr />

Jerusalem, 27 A.D.

Very early in the morning, the chief priests, including Caiaphas, with the elders, the teachers of the law and the whole Sanhedrin, reached a decision. They bound Jesus, led him away and handed him over to Pilate. 'Are you the king of the Jews?' asked Pilate.

'Yes, it is as you say,' Jesus replied.

The chief priests accused him of many things. So again Pilate asked him, 'Aren't you going to answer? See how many things they are accusing you of.' But Jesus still made no reply, and Pilate was amazed. Now it was the custom at the Feast to release a prisoner whom the people requested. The crowd came up and asked Pilate to do for them what he usually did.

'Do you want me to release to you the king of the Jews?' asked Pilate, knowing it was out of envy that the chief priests had handed Jesus over to him.

And the crowd shouted, 'Release Barabbas!'

The father of twelve.

Langley, Virginia, U.S.A., 2012

Stephen Elliot was here at headquarters in the middle of the night reading the information that had been sent to him by his mole, CIA Trois, several weeks earlier.

Boutros Ahmad is the point man for South America. He was definitely involved in the Bolivia affair. Boutros is the Arabic form of the name Peter.

Kader Al-Zarqawi is the head of the Iraq operations. 'Kader' means 'the strong one' in Arabic. This is similar to the name Andrew, which also means 'the strong man'.

Yahya Abdullah is the kingpin of the Chechnya operations. His original name was Dzhokar Raduev. Yahya is the Arabic form of the name John.

Yaqub Islamuddin is the brains behind Jemaah Islamiyah and the Jakarta operation. Yaqub is the Arabic form of Jacob from which the name James is derived.

Shamoon Idris, key operative of the Islamic Jehad Council in North America. Shamoon is the Arabic form of Simon.

Faris Kadeer is the chief of the East Turkestan Islamic Movement and the coordinator of the Chinese sector. Faris means 'horseman' in Arabic, which is similar to the name Philip, which in Greek, means 'Friend of horses'.

Bin Fadan is one of the key operatives of the Jaish-e-Mohammed's terrorist activities within India. Bin Fadan means 'son of the plough', which is equivalent to the name Bartholomew, derived from the Aramain equivalent 'Bar Tolmay' meaning 'son of the plough'.

Ataullah al-Liby is the kingpin of the French Intifada. Ataullah means 'gift of God' in Arabic. This is similar to the name Matthew which is derived from the Hebrew name Mattiyahu, meaning 'gift of God'.

Tau'am Zin Hassan, key operative of the Darul Islam in Malaysia. Tau'am means 'twin' in Arabic. This is similar to the name Thomas, which is the Greek form of the Aramaic name Te'oma, which also means 'twin'.

Adil Afrose is chief commander of the Australia operation. Adil means 'one who acts justly' in Arabic. Similar to James, who was often called 'James the Just'.

Yehuda Moinuddin, most trusted aide of Ghalib. Involved in all operations of the group. Yehuda is the Arabic form of the Hebrew name Judah.

Fouad al-Noor is head of the group's activities in the UK. Fouad literally means 'heart' in Arabic. The name Thaddaeus is derived from the Aramaic word for 'heart'.

Ghalib-bin-Isar is leader of the Lashkar-e-Talatashar, the Army of Thirteen. The name 'Ghalib' in Arabic means 'Conqueror'. In Arabic, the word 'bin' is used to mean 'son of'. So, Ghalib-bin-Isar would translate into 'a conqueror of the lineage of Isar'.

The name 'Isar' can be traced back to 'Isar-el', the eastern Kabbalists' sun God, from which the name Israel was derived.[cliii]

The person providing this information to Elliot was one of these thirteen people. His code name, CIA Trois, was an anagram for another word.

Iscariot.

Yehuda Moinuddin, assistant and most trusted aide and friend to Ghalib, Junior Assistant Director of Archives, Archaeology, Research and Museums for Kashmir, was Elliot's mole.

Yehuda was the Arabic form of the Hebrew name Judah, the Greek form of which was Judas.

Judas Iscariot.

Jerusalem, 27 A.D.

Then went one of the twelve, who was called Judas Iscariot, to the chief priests. And said to them: 'What will you give me, and I will deliver him unto you?' But they appointed him thirty pieces of silver.

Chapter Twenty-One

Mathura, North India, 3127 B.C.
The moon was in the constellation of Aldebaran and it was the eighth lunar day of the dark fortnight in 3127 B.C.[cliv]
The blessed virgin, Devaki, was about to deliver a baby boy; Krishna was to be his name. His birth had been heralded by the astral formation of a *Rohini Nakshatra*, a most auspicious astrological sequence.

His father, Vasudeva, was a carpenter. Unfortunately, a wise Brahmin had predicted to King Kansa, the ruler of Mathura, that a son born to Devaki would destroy him. Kansa ordered the death of all male babies born on the day of Krishna's birth to prevent the prophecy from coming true. Luckily for Krishna, his father was pre-warned and fled with the child to Gokul where he could be brought up safely.

Hinduism has long worshipped the holy trinity of Brahma - the creator; Vishnu - the preserver; and Shiva - the destroyer. Krishna, it was believed, was the second entity in this trinity. Much like the second entity in the trinity of the Father, the Son and the Holy Ghost. The name Krishna is sometimes also spelt "Christna".

The entire story of Krishna was written in a Hindu epic of 100,000 verses before 500 B.C.

Five hundred years before Christ.

Sixty-six years after the Buddha.

Kapilavastu, Indo-Nepal Border, 566 B.C.
Deep sleep produces strange dreams. Maya, the queen of Kapilavastu, had a dream that her soon-to-be-born son, Siddhartha Gautama, was entering his virgin mother's womb on a white elephant on a full moon night in July.[clv]

Soon after his birth, Siddhartha was examined by a group of Brahmins who predicted that the boy would be a great king, or a Buddha, an Enlightened One.

At the age of twenty-nine, he would leave his home and spend the next six years meditating in the jungles.

As he meditated under a tree, he would visualize thousands of his previous lives. He would realize that all beings were subject to rebirth. Good actions led to good rebirths and bad actions led to bad rebirths. The place and nature of a rebirth was governed by one's deeds, or Karma.

On December 8th, at the age of thirty-five, he would find enlightenment after forty-nine days of penance in the wilderness. This was in spite of the devil tempting and taunting him repeatedly.

The Buddha probably knew that the devil would try the same tricks around six centuries later with someone else who would be fasting for forty days and forty nights in the Judean desert.

❦

Judean Desert, 26 A.D.

Jesus was led by the Spirit into the desert to be tempted by the devil. After fasting for forty days and forty nights, he was hungry.

The tempter came to him and said, 'If you are the Son of God, tell these stones to become bread.'

He answered, 'It is written: Man does not live on bread alone, but on every word that comes from the mouth of God.'

Of course, in 1000 B.C. there was no devil.

❦

Persia, 1000 B.C.

There was no devil; only good deeds and bad deeds.

He was born to a virgin. He received his calling at the age of thirty. The whole world rejoiced at his birth. He was baptized in a river. He astounded wise men with his wisdom.[clvi]

He wandered about with his followers. He went into the wilderness where he was tempted by the evil one. He cast out demons. He restored the sight of a blind man. He revealed the mysteries of heaven, hell, judgement and salvation. He and his followers celebrated a sacred meal together.

No. It wasn't Jesus. His name was Zarathustra. The prophet of the Zoroastrian faith, whose deeds were written of almost 1000 years before Jesus. Zarathustra was a thousand years too late.

⬥

Syria, 2000 B.C.

Tammuz would rise from his cave each morning, travel across the sky by day and return to his cave at night. He was a shepherd and healer. Tammuz soon died and descended into the lower world.

However, his loving wife, Inanna, could not accept his death. She went in search of Tammuz. During Inanna's absence from earth, nature froze. When God heard the pleas of humans, Inanna was allowed to leave the netherworld along with Tammuz. The mourned death and happy resurrection of Tammuz occurred every year thereafter. It corresponded with the cycle of nature; life died in autumn and was reborn in spring.

On what date had the virgin Myrrha given birth to little Tammuz? December the 25th.[clvii] Tammuz was also a thousand years too late.

⬥

Egypt, 3000 B.C.

Horus was born to the virgin, Isis, on December 25th in a manger.[clviii] His birth was announced by a star in the east. At the age of twelve, Horus taught in the temple and was baptized in the Eridanus by Anup, who was later beheaded.

Horus performed many miracles, included walking on water. He had twelve disciples; and Horus was crucified on a tree amongst thieves. After his death, he was buried in a tomb from where he was resurrected and ascended into heaven. He raised a man from the dead. The man was called El-Azar-Os.

Later, the Bible would also speak of a man raised from the dead - his name would be Lazarus.

Bethany, Judea, 27 A.D.

Now there was a certain man sick, named Lazarus of Bethania, of the town of Mary and of Martha, her sister. Jesus therefore came and found that he had been four days already in the grave.

And he asked, 'Where have you laid him?'

They said to him, 'Lord, come and see.'

Jesus then went to the sepulchre. It was a cave; and a stone was laid over it. Jesus said, 'Take away the stone.'

And Jesus, lifting up his eyes, said, 'Father, I give Thee thanks that Thou hast heard me.'

Was it a ritual? Similar to another one in which Jesus would rise from the dead on a day which would then be celebrated as Easter Sunday?

Possibly. After all, Easter Sunday had been celebrated from 600 B.C. onwards, almost 600 years before the resurrection.

Persia, 600 B.C.

Mithras, the sun god was born on December 25th. He was a wandering teacher and had twelve disciples. He performed many miracles. He was also called the good shepherd. His sacred day was Sunday. He sacrificed the pleasures of life. Intense purity was demanded of his followers, who were baptized in blood. They usually had a communion supper of bread and wine.clix

When he died, he was buried in a tomb. After a few days, he was resurrected. Mithras' resurrection was then celebrated each year. The date on which his resurrection was celebrated was Easter Sunday, a date that would later be associated with Jesus of Nazareth.

Judea, 23 A.D.

Was he really *Jesus of Nazareth*? Or was he *Jesus the Nazarene*?

In fact, after his return to Judea many years later, Jesus would be fit for initiation into the fold of the *Nazars* because of his previously strong educational background. Admission into the fold of the Nazars would make him a Nazarene.

As a young disciple, he would be called a *Chrestos* during his probation and when he completed his probationary period, he would be anointed with oil and given the title of *Christos*, meaning "the anointed one".[clx]

The word "Nazar" itself was actually a derivative of the word "Nazir", which meant "separate" in the Aramaic language. Nazirites were Jews who had taken special vows of dedication under the rules of which they would abstain for a specific period from alcohol, cutting hair or approaching corpses.

The end of the oath required immersion in water; like the baptism of Jesus?

Jordan River, Judea, 26 A.D.

In those days John the Baptist appeared, preaching in the desert of Judea. At that time Jerusalem, all Judea, and the whole region around Jordan were going out to him and were being baptized by him in Jordan River as they acknowledged their sins.[clxi]

He said, 'I am baptizing you with water, for repentance, but the one who is coming after me is mightier than I. I am not worthy to carry his sandals.'

Thousands were being baptized in the river.

The same scene would be repeated in 2001.

Allahabad, North India, 2001

The thirty million people knew that this Kumbh Mela was special. This year the planets had come into a position that was very auspicious, occurring after 144 years.[clxii] A dip in the Ganges during the month-long festival would cleanse the human soul of all sins and enable escape from the cycle of rebirth.

The Kumbh Mela had been taking place every three years for thousands of years. A similar event had been seen in Jordan in 26 A.D. because the origins of ritual immersion in water were fundamentally Indian.

Unlike the ritual of sacred marriage - *Hieros Gamos.*

━━━━━━━━━

Bethany, Judea, 27 A.D.

She was making Jesus go through an ancient fertility ritual called *Hieros Gamos*, or "the sacred marriage".

In 1993, a book entitled *The Woman With The Alabaster Jar* by Margaret Starbird would suggest that the anointing of Jesus was carried out by Mary Magdalene as part of a sacred marriage ritual. Starbird would say:

> *Jesus had a secret dynastic marriage with Mary of Bethany. She was a daughter of the tribe of Benjamin, whose ancestral heritage was the land surrounding the Holy City of David, the city Jerusalem. A dynastic marriage between Jesus and a royal daughter of the Benjamites would have been perceived as a source of healing to the people of Israel.*
>
> *Perhaps the earliest verbal references attaching the epithet Magdala to Mary of Bethany's name had nothing to do with an obscure town in Galilee in Hebrew, the epithet Magdala literally means tower or elevated, great, magnificent...This meaning has particular relevance if the Mary so named was in fact the wife of the Messiah. It would have been the Hebrew equivalent of calling her Mary the Great.*
>
> *In older sacred marriage rituals, a woman who represented the goddess and the land was wedded to the king. Their union symbolized many things, depending on the time and place such a ritual was practised, including the blessing of ongoing fertility, the rejuvenation of the land and the community soul,*

201

and the connection between humans and the Divine. Some of these old ceremonies included a ritualistic slaying of the king, either symbolically or literally, after he was married to the priestess-goddess. In the symbolic slayings, he would then rise again in a mystical resurrection echoing the cycles of death and rebirth evident in nature.[clxiii]

The million-dollar question: if the anointing of Jesus was part of the sacred fertility ritual, could the crucifixion and resurrection also have been part of this same ritual?

So, was Jesus the bridegroom?

Cana, Galilee, 23 A.D.

'They have no wine,' said Mary to Jesus.

And on the third day there was a marriage in Cana of Galilee; and the mother of Jesus was there. And both Jesus and his disciples were called to the marriage.

And when they wanted wine, Mary, the mother of Jesus said to him, 'They have no wine.'

Mary immediately ordered the servants to do whatever Jesus instructed. And Jesus told them to fill the pots with water up to the brim. He then asked them to draw wine from them and to serve the governor of the feast.

The servants served the wine. When the ruler of the feast tasted the water that had been made into wine, the governor called the bridegroom and said to him that most people served the good wine first and the lower grade wine later. The bridegroom, on the other hand, had done the reverse.

His mother, Mary, had clearly been in charge. She was the hostess without doubt.

And the bridegroom had been Jesus.[clxiv]

Bethany, Israel, 27 A.D.

Christ loved her more than all the disciples and used to kiss her often on the mouth.

According to the Gnostic Gospel of Philip, Mary Magdalene was the companion of the Saviour. But Christ loved her more than all the disciples and used to kiss her often on the mouth. The rest of the disciples were offended by it and expressed disapproval.

They asked, 'Why do you love her more than all of us?'

The Saviour answered and said to them, 'Why do I not love you like her: When a blind man and one who sees are both together in darkness, they are no different from one another. When the light comes then he who sees will see the light, and he who is blind will remain in darkness...'[clxv]

Mary anointed Jesus twice with Nard. She once anointed his head. Another time she anointed his feet, later wiping them with her long hair. Nard was a fragrant ointment more commonly called Spikenard and was part of a sacred marriage ritual practised by Hebrew, Sumerian and Egyptian priestesses who were also trained in music, healing, magic, chants, dance and herbal medicine. In the Old Testament's Song of Solomon, this act of anointing was carried out as an element of the marriage ceremony.

Lynn Picknett, a researcher of religious mysteries, would later write:

In their time was a sublimely pagan rite that involved a woman anointing a chosen man both on the head and feet – and also on the genitals – for a very special destiny. This was the anointing of the sacred king, in which the priestess singled out the chosen man and anointed him, before bestowing his destiny upon him in a sexual rite known as the Hieros Gamos.

Mary Magdalene was effectively royalty from the tribe of Benjamin, and since Jesus was from the royal family of David, their marriage would have been a powerful dynastic alliance. It now became clear why Jesus was called the "King of the Jews". His was not merely a spiritual title but also a temporal and political one.[clxvi]

Eleven years earlier, *Holy Blood, Holy Grail*, a book by Henry Lincoln, Michael Baigent, and Richard Leigh, had come up with the theory that Mary Magdalene's womb was, in fact, the Holy Grail which eventually carried the child of Jesus Christ.

In his book *King Jesus*, Robert Graves had suggested way back in 1946 that Jesus' ancestry and marriage would have been kept hidden from virtually all except a few in order to protect the bloodline.

So this was a temporal and earthly king. A good man, a great man who did good deeds, but simply a man nonetheless. How could he be made divine? Fast forward to 337 A.D.

Constantinople, 337 A.D.

Emperor Constantine lay on his deathbed. He had decided to be baptized into the Christian faith before his death. After all, in 312 A.D., he had been able to defeat his rival for the imperial throne, Maxentius, only through Christian support.[clxvii]

During his lifetime, he had been sympathetic to the Christian cause but had essentially remained a sun worshipper. In fact, Constantine had ordered the judiciary to observe its weekly holiday on Sunday, which was the "venerable day of the sun". Christians, on the other hand, had continued to have their weekly rest on the Jewish Sabbath - Saturday. The Christians now fell in line with Constantine's edict and began observing their weekly rest on Sunday. This had brought Christianity closer to existing Roman practice.

The birthday of Jesus, which till then had been celebrated on December 6th, was changed to December 25th. This was done in order to bring Christianity in line with the existing December 25th celebrations of the Roman festival of Natalis Invictus.

Christianity was now being marketed to a Roman audience. Jesus could not merely be a messiah or a teacher if he had to be marketed to Romans; he had to be a God. One that was greater than the mythology of Mithras, Horus, Tammuz, or Krishna. It was necessary to have a virgin birth, and it was imperative to have miracles. It was critical to have a resurrection. He needed to have a stature that was greater than

Buddha or Zarathustra, who were merely messengers. Jesus had to be divine!

It also marked the end of reincarnation theory. As usual, Constantinople would be at the centre of it all.

Constantinople, Turkey, 553 A.D.

'If anyone asserts the fabulous pre-existence of souls, and asserts the monstrous restoration which follows from it: let him be anathema,' cried the church elders![clxviii]

Origen, the third-century Christian theologian (and pupil of Ammonius Saccas) had written that, "The soul has neither beginning nor end...it comes into this world strengthened by the victories or weakened by the defeats of its previous existence..."[clxix]

This view was not uncommon. Early Christians seemed to believe that the soul existed even before the birth of a person. This was similar to several tenets of Greek and Buddhist philosophy.

In 533 A.D., around three centuries after Origen's death, Emperor Justinian had convened the Second Council of Constantinople. The Council passed the infamous resolution that, "If anyone asserts the fabulous pre-existence of souls, and asserts the monstrous restoration which follows from it: let him be anathema."

That was the end of the reincarnation theory within Christianity.

And the beginning of the marketing of Jesus.

And no one knew how to design and package a product better than the French.

Lyons, France, 185 A.D.

Irenaeus, the Bishop of Lugdunum in Gaul, had just written *Adversus Haereses* or *Against Heresies*. In his work he refuted Gnostic teachings completely while strongly claiming that the four gospels that he espoused were the four pillars of the Church - these were the four gospels of Matthew, Mark, Luke and John.

The Gospels that said that Jesus was born of a virgin, in a manger, with the star of Bethlehem hovering overhead. The same Gospels that said that Jesus had turned water into wine, that he had walked on water, and that he had raised a man from the dead. The same Gospels that stated that he had risen from the dead.

Serapis, Osiris, Horus, Hermes, Mercury, Imhotep, Krishna, Buddha, Mithras, Perseus, Theseus, Hercules, Bacchus, Hyacinth, Nimrod, Marduk, Tammuz, Adonis, Baal, Quetzalcoatl, Baldur, Tien, Attis, Hesus, Crite, OrisaOko, Mahavira, and Zarathustra, were just some of the gods, prophets, messengers or angels who shared commonalities with Jesus Christ.

They belonged to various time periods prior to Jesus and to various geographies including Egypt, Greece, Persia, India, China, Babylonia, and Mexico, among others. Some of them were born of virgins. Some were born in caves or mangers. Many of their births were heralded by astral formations. Some of them were visited by wise men. Indeed, there was a great deal of material available to create a story around the historical Jesus Christ.

Often, they were in mortal danger and had to be taken away elsewhere, either for protection or exile. Many of them had to overcome the temptations of the devil. Most of them performed miracles. Virtually all of them preached love and forgiveness. Some of them wandered with disciples.

Some of them rose from the dead; or remained alive under a shroud in Turin.

Turin, Italy, 1988
Anastasio was humiliated. It was October 13th, 1988. He, the cardinal of Turin, Anastasio Alberto Ballestrero, was being compelled to tell the world that the Shroud of Turin was a hoax![clxx]

A group of eminent scientists had cut a small sample from the edge of the shroud and had carried out carbon dating on it. The Roman Catholic Church was left with no alternative but to accept the finding that the Shroud of Turin was a hoax. It was a difficult acceptance considering the fact that eight years earlier Pope John Paul II had reverentially kissed the very same shroud.

Subsequently, several scientists would show that the original carbon dating had been flawed because the sample collection itself had been flawed. More important, the blood on the shroud had the rare blood group AB.

Oviedo, Spain, 1988
The blood on the Sudarium was also the rare group AB.

The Sudarium was a small, bloody cloth kept in a cathedral in Oviedo in Spain. It was believed that this garment had been used to cover the head of Jesus after his crucifixion. Unlike the patchy history of the shroud, the history of the Sudarium could be traced back to the first century.

This meant that if one considered the Sudarium to be genuine, it also increased the odds of the shroud being genuine. [clxxi]

Was it possible that the shroud, while dating to the time period of Jesus, could be from another crucifixion during the same time period?

While it was true that the wounds would have been similar in all cases of crucifixion, the one factor that had been significantly different in the case of Jesus was the crown of thorns that the Roman soldiers had placed on his head. The shroud in Turin, as well as the Sudarium in Spain, clearly indicated head wounds caused by precisely such a crown.

According to the Gospels, "Joseph bought a large linen cloth, took Jesus off the cross, wrapped him in the cloth and laid him in a tomb". On Easter morning, this garment was found "folded together on one side of the tomb" and would later reach Abgar V.

King Abgar V ruled Edessa, an independent principality in southeastern Anatolia around the time of Jesus' death. The king had been suffering from leprosy and had heard that Jesus could heal lepers. He had written to Jesus requesting him to visit Edessa, but Jesus had been unable to go.

After the crucifixion of Jesus, it was believed that two disciples of Jesus had taken the shroud in which he had been buried to Edessa, and Abgar had been miraculously healed. Abgar had become a devout follower and had affixed the cloth on top of one of the city's main gates. The cloth was folded in such a way that only the face could be seen.

After Abgar's death, his kingdom gradually forgot about Jesus and reverted to older religious beliefs and customs. In 525 A.D., the city walls were being reconstructed when the shroud was rediscovered. It reached Constantinople around 420 years later and was finally moved to Turin in northern Italy in 1578.

Abgar V was lucky to have been healed.

By the "Leader of the Healed", Yuz Asaf?

***

It was in 1898 that the photographer, Secondo Pia, was able to see the shroud's negative, and this was even more remarkable. The negative, for the first time, actually showed in stunning detail the image that had been hidden within the garment.

The commonly accepted findings were that the image was definitely that of a crucified person. The bloodstains were real and were of the rare blood type AB. There were no brush strokes or pigments. The weave was typical of the Middle East. Examination of pollen taken from the shroud indicated the presence of pollen from plants specific to Palestine in the times of Jesus. Traces of coins minted by Pilate in 29 A.D. and 31 A.D. were found on the eyes. Street dust was found in the area where the feet would have been.

The image had been created from chemical saccharides, which were synthesized by the proximity of the cloth to the body.

According to the late Professor Bonte, who was the head of the department for forensic science at the university of Dusseldorf, "…everything speaks for the fact that the blood circulation activity had not ceased yet…"

Several scientists now believe that the man under the shroud must have been alive, not dead.

Chapter Twenty-Two

Hoshiarpur, Punjab, India, 2012

The Bhrigu Samhita was an exceptionally long treatise that had been compiled in ancient India by a sage called Maharishi Bhrigu. The Maharishi had been the first person to compile half a million horoscopes of individuals to build a database for predictive astrology.[clxxii]

Maharishi Bhrigu had collected details of the lives and events of half a million people along with their dates, times and places of birth. He and his disciples had then charted horoscopes for each of these people based on the planetary positions of the sun, moon, Mercury, Venus, Mars, Jupiter, and Saturn, at the time of birth.

Using this extensive database, Maharishi Bhrigu had provided predictions and horoscope readings for each of the individuals. The result had been a database that had forty-five million permutations that could be used for predictive astrology.

During the Islamic conquests of India from the seventh century onwards, the invaders had looted these miraculous documents that had been lovingly preserved by the Brahmins. The destruction of the ancient Nalanda University had further decimated the exhaustive work carried out under the Maharishi.

Eventually, only around 100,000 horoscopes that had formed part of the original half-million database remained in India, and these were scattered all over the country. One chunk of this original lot remained with a Brahmin family in the dusty town of Hoshiarpur.

The heir to the prized treasure was Pandit Ramgopal Prasad Sharma, the world famous astrologer who practiced his art every alternate week at the Taj Mahal Hotel in Mumbai. He now sat under the banyan tree outside his ancestral home, pouring over the parchments that constituted his life. He had a troubled expression on his face. In fact, he had not been able to sleep at night. He should never have sharpened his predictive skills to the extent that he had succeeded in doing; it only caused excessive worry.

His chance encounter with the man who had wanted the date reference from his ephemeris had troubled him. He had been on a routine visit to the divine mother goddess at Vaishno Devi in Jammu, when this meeting had happened.

He had immediately rushed back to Hoshiarpur to consult his *Bhrigu Samhita*. He was absolutely convinced. The end of the world was at hand.

He got up and walked to the post office. Pandit Ramgopal did not own a telephone. From the post office, he phoned one of his clients who was now an important man in the Indian intelligence services. He needed access to General Prithviraj Singh.

***

New Delhi, India, 2012

'Your name begins with the letter 'P'. Your father's name begins with the letter 'P'. Your mother's name begins with the letter 'P'. The year of your birth sums up to 22,' said Pandit Ramgopal Prasad Sharma.

Prithviraj. Padamraj. Parvathi. 1957. 1+9+5+7=22. Prithviraj was stunned. He didn't know this man and yet this stranger seemingly knew lots about him.

'Who are you, sir?' enquired Prithviraj. 'And how do you know who I am?'

'My name is Pandit Ramgopal Prasad Sharma. I am from Hoshiarpur in Punjab, and I have travelled a great distance simply to meet you. I was not only able to predict when and where I would meet you, but also what you looked like. That's why I could find you.'

'Me? Why me?'

'Son, I think we had better sit down and talk. There are many things that will need to be explained.' Intrigued, General Prithviraj Singh led Pandit Ramgopal Prasad Sharma to the sitting area of his simple home.

'Tell me, Mr. Sharma, who are you and how have you heard of me? More important, how did you track me down?'

'I need you to promise me something first,' said Sharma.

'And what is that?'

'I need you to promise me that you will keep an open mind and will not let your judgment be clouded by Western tendencies to treat the inexplicable as unscientific,' said Sharma rather matter-of-factly.

'Don't you think that you are prejudging me? In any case, I promise.'

'Fine. Now hear this. I am a Brahmin from Punjab. I have in my possession one of the oldest documents in Hindu history, the *Bhrigu Samhita* - a database of over half a million horoscopes that can accurately predict future events. If an original leaf containing the horoscope of an individual is available in the database, it will not only accurately recount the past, and accurately predict the future, but will also reveal the date, time and place of consultation. Recently, when I was studying the *Bhrigu*, I stumbled across a horoscope that indicated that I would have to make a reading here in New Delhi, today to you. This is why I am here,' said Sharma.

Prithviraj was baffled. 'But why did you specifically make the effort of locating me? What was the urgency?'

'You are the only person who has the power to save us from destruction, my son. On the winter solstice of 2012, the noonday sun exactly conjuncts the crossing point of the sun's ecliptic with the galactic plane, while also closely conjuncting the exact centre of the galaxy. This day occurs on December 21st, 2012. Your horoscope indicates that you have the power to save a man of God who holds the key to the riddle.'

'Why should I believe you?' asked Prithviraj, rather irritably.

'You lost your father at the age of fifteen, your mother at the age of twenty-nine. Yours is an old soul that has been through many human lifetimes. This could be your final one before you attain *moksha*. You presently have neither a brother nor sister. You have been born and brought up in Punjab but have studied in the West, possibly England, America or both. Most important, you had a brother, for a while, in spirit.'

Prithviraj sat in his place awestruck by the accuracy of Sharma's readings. Then he spoke. 'I never had a brother.'

'Yes, you did. Your mother produced a stillborn son in the seventh month of her pregnancy. He is the brother that you had in the spirit world that I am referring to. He is no longer in the spirit world - he has taken rebirth in some other family,' said Sharma confidently.

'Well, there's only one way to find out,' said Prithviraj, as he got up to use the phone to call his aunt, his mother's younger sister, who lived in Amritsar. She picked up the phone on the fourth ring.

'Auntyji,' he said, using the familiar Punjabi-Indian fusion term. 'Listen, I need to ask you something.'

'*Bolo puttar.* Go ahead.'

'Did Ma go through another pregnancy after I was born?'

'*Beta,* what's this about?'

'No time for explanations, Auntyji. Just tell me, please.'

'Okay. She went through a pregnancy, which turned out to be near fatal. The doctors were able to save her but not the child...a son.'

'And when did this happen, do you remember?'

'I think it was about a year or two after they had you.'

'The child was stillborn?'

'Unfortunately, yes. Your parents never told you because they did not want to burden you with something that they thought was of no relevance in your life.'

'How old was the baby?'

'I think the emergency C-section was done a couple of months before full term.'

'Thank you, Auntyji. I will come and see you when I visit Amritsar in a few weeks.'

Prithviraj hung up. He looked over at the old man calmly sitting on the sofa running the prayer beads through his fingers. He walked over to him.

'Fine. You're not a con. So what?'

'Son, the brother who died took on your Karma to save you. You were destined to die, but he died for you instead. He has died or killed for you in previous lifetimes too. He has a karmic relationship with you.'

'Fine, but what does this have to do with December 21st?'

'Son,' began Sharma, 'I see utter destruction on that day. Clouds of poison. Total darkness. Dense smoke that suffocates everything in its path. A huge ball of fire that touches the skies. I see colossal human tragedy. But most important, I see a rainbow in the sky, which tells me that there could be a way to avert this disaster.'

Prithviraj froze. 'Are you saying that there will be some sort of explosion or earthquake?'

'Worse. An earthquake would be putting it rather mildly. It seems like a manmade tragedy. More in the nature of a colossal bomb of some sort.'

'And I can avert this?' asked the general incredulously.

'Yes.'

'How?'

'Find the priest who I met in Mumbai,' said Sharma.

'Vincent Morgan? I'm already trying to locate him.'

'And son…'

'Yes.'

'That brother, who died for you…'

'Yes?'

'You will know when you have to return the favour.'

'Do you believe in destiny?' asked General Prithviraj Singh.

'*Unmeitte shinjiru*?' heard Pandit Ramgopal.[clxxiii]

'What was that?' asked Pandit Ramgopal.

'Do you believe in destiny?' repeated the general.

'*Unmeitte shinjiru*?' heard Ramgopal.

Pandit Ramgopal Prasad Sharma got up.

He said excitedly, 'Prithviraj, there is a Japanese connection. I am sensing a dangerous woman. She has what is called a *Paap-Katri Yog* or a *Vish-Kanya Yog*. The force is feminine. Her moon is afflicted and surrounded by malevolent planets - Saturn, Mars as well as Rahu-Ketu. This makes her maniacal. She will not hesitate to kill. I warned Vincent Morgan about precisely this negative force.'

'Where can I find her?' asked the general.

Goa, India, 2012

Further away, towards the outskirts of Goa, Vincent surveyed the surroundings of his captors. The dim lighting and musty feel of the room gave the impression that this was a basement. Towering over him was Swakilki. Vincent squinted, trying to bring her face into focus. He tried adjusting his body and then realized that his hands and feet had been tied.

'You have been snooping!' barked Swakilki.

'What? No. Where am I? It's you…' began Vincent recollecting the Japanese woman that he had seen several times in passing.

Before he could complete his sentence, he felt a stinging slap across his face. 'Shut up!' she hissed. The venom in her voice was blood-curdling. 'Do not play games with me. You have been tracking a game that you had no business to.'

Vincent was completely disoriented. He didn't have an answer. 'Look, I really do not know what you are talking about. I would like to cooperate, but I am lost. What are you talking about?'

Swakilki looked at him with contempt. 'My guest seems to have lost his memory. He seems to have forgotten his extended conversations with Brother Thomas Manning. He has conveniently forgotten his past-life sessions in London with Professor Terry Acton. Has he also forgotten the Bom Jesus papers that Acton gave him? I think he needs a jolt to be brought to his senses.'

Vincent couldn't believe what he was hearing. Thomas Manning had promised to keep his conversation confidential. And why was this woman aware of Terry Acton? How did she know of the Bom Jesus papers? Was there a conspiracy that was being covered up? Could Terry's research have made someone uncomfortable?

Vincent kept staring at Swakilki with a glazed expression on his face. In his brain, he kept seeing himself as the bodyguard killing Mama Anawarkhi to prevent her from plotting against the King Sapa Inca Pachacuti. Swakilki morphed into Mama Anawarkhi. She then morphed back into Swakilki.

She then morphed into the empress Wu Zhao, the evil power on the throne as she shattered his limbs and placed him in a large wine urn to die a slow death in agony. Wu Zhao morphed back into Swakilki.

Then back into Charlotte Lavoisier as she stabbed Jean-Paul Pelletier. He saw Sanson chopping off her head and then saw Swakilki chopping off Terry Acton's head.

Swakilki then morphed into a woman who was...no, this was not possible...Mary Magdalene! She was killing Jesus! She was loving Jesus! She was healing Jesus! Then back to Swakilki.[clxxiv]

That was when he realized the full significance of Swakilki. He had several past-life connections with her, the present being just one among a series of lifetimes.

'Listen to me, please,' pleaded Vincent. 'I think I know what is happening. My interest in the subject that you spoke of is purely academic...why don't you tell me what you want and I'll see if I can fill in some of the blanks.'

'See how the mighty have fallen,' remarked Swakilki sarcastically as she grabbed a fistful of the hair on his head and breathed into his face. 'Now you listen to me...you will do exactly as I say...do I make myself clear? I will not have your meddling around.'

Vincent nodded dumbly in fear as she left the room, the lock clicking firmly in place as she closed the door.

Vincent's arms and legs were hurting. She had used a rough twine rope to tie his arms behind his back. His legs were tied together at the ankles. He had been in the same position for several hours. His head was pounding and his throat was parched.

He was unable to figure out where he was. The basement seemed unused and was dark, damp and musty. With the exception of the entrance door to the far right of the room, there were no other doors or windows. A lone naked ten-watt light bulb hung from a cable in the ceiling, casting a dim light where he lay.

The door was suddenly flung open and the Japanese woman barged in, 'Dinner is served, Your Grace,' she remarked as she put a tin plate containing some loaves of Indian naan bread and lentils in front of him, along with a plastic bottle of water.

'I can't eat with my hands tied,' mumbled Vincent and was treated to another stinging slap from Swakilki for being rude. 'You will speak when spoken to, am I clear?' she said to him.

She untied Vincent's hands and pointed her Beretta 93R automatic at him. 'One false move, and I'll blow your brains out!' she said.

Vincent was not particularly hungry, but he knew that he needed to preserve his strength. He wolfed down the food that had been offered with several gulps of water from the plastic bottle.

'Now, why don't you tell me what you were doing here? Trying to track him down?' demanded Swakilki.

'No...no...you've got it all wrong. I'm here with my aunt. She's an Indophile and wanted to experience the *Navratri* festival...' began Vincent. Swakilki cut him off.

'I know about your aunt. Don't bother me with the irrelevant stuff. You expect me to believe that after having seen Jesus in a previous life, after having seen him survive a crucifixion, after having discussed this with Manning, after having taken a set of Bom Jesus papers from Acton, after having reached Goa - the home of Bom Jesus, you are merely here on a holiday?' snapped Swakilki.

'Yes! Please believe me! Yes, I went through regression therapy. Yes, I saw Jesus. Yes, I did discuss the possibilities of a Jesus bloodline with Thomas. But no, I did not come to India to find anyone ...I really do not know anything more,' pleaded Vincent.

'Hmm. I'll tell you what I'll do. I'm going to read you a bedtime story. See if you can recognize the book...'

Swakilki pulled out a couple of A4 sized papers and began reading. 'Issa and Mary had a child by the name of Sara, who was born to them in India, but was later sent to Gaul with her mother. Issa remained in India, where he married a woman from the Sakya clan on the persistence of King Gopadatta, and had a son, Benissa. Benissa had a son, Yushua, who fathered Akkub. Akkub's son was Jashub. Abihud was the son of Jashub. Jashub's grandson was Elnaam. Elnaam sired Harsha, who sired Jabal, who sired Shalman. Shalman's son Zabbud converted to Islam. Zabbud fathered Abdul, who sired Haaroon. His child was Hamza. Omar was Hamza's son and he produced Rashid.

Rashid's offspring was Khaleel…Does the passage ring a bell, Father Morgan?' asked Swakilki.

Vincent replied hesitantly. 'Sure. It's from the *Tarikh-Issa-Massih*, an eleventh-century Urdu work. Ah! I see now. You think that I was playing detective?'

'Precisely, Mr. Sherlock Holmes! That's exactly what you were doing,' exclaimed Swakilki triumphantly.

Vincent protested. 'But I only got to Khaleel. No further. In fact, I do not even know whether the book is reliable.' Vincent conveniently omitted mention of the Urdu version of the Tarikh-Issa-Massih which Martha had located that seemed to take the lineage further.

'Oh yes, it is reliable. Terry Acton had spent years researching the subject and would have assured you that it was completely reliable had his life not come to an abrupt end.'

'So are you telling me that you know who is at the end of the Jesus lineage?' asked Vincent incredulously.

'Figure it out yourself, Father. You're the so-called research enthusiast, aren't you?' she retorted. 'I made it so easy for you. Pity you didn't bother to hang on to the papers that I gave you at the church!'

'No. It's not possible to figure out anything from the book. The book only talks of sixteen generations after Jesus. Even taking a forty-year lifespan of each generation, we only have information for around 640 years after Jesus. The remainder of the story is not there!' he explained.

'Oh it's there, all right. Maybe you didn't quite look in the right place,' muttered Swakilki. 'In any case, enough! We have to now get rid of you,' said Swakilki to Vincent. 'Get ready, Father, you are going to see your Lord pretty darn soon! I normally kill my victims immediately. You are lucky that I took pity on your aunt!'

Secretary (R), General Prithviraj Singh, had rolled into Goa with a hundred elite troops and had set up camp at the Fort Aguada Hotel. He was sitting in a makeshift communications room along with Zvi

Yatom when Martha barged in, followed closely by Pandit Ramgopal Prasad Sharma.

'Please help us,' cried Martha. 'My nephew has been kidnapped.'

General Prithviraj Singh looked up at them irritably and said, 'Please let me do my job. We already have a hundred men scattered across town.'

'Please, General Sahib!'

The general saw Pandit Ramgopal Prasad Sharma's anxious expression. 'Pandit?' he asked.

The general knew what the old man's expression indicated.

'Quick, Pandit. Do you know where we need to focus our search?'

'Satan! The devil!' said Pandit Ramgopal Prasad Sharma while Martha continued to sob.

<hr />

The workers were busy constructing the huge effigy of the demon Ravana in the heart of Goa. This effigy, duly stuffed with firecrackers, would be set ablaze on Dussera day, the tenth day after the nine-day Hindu festival of *Navratri*.

This particular effigy was impressive indeed. It scaled a height of forty-five feet and depicted Ravana with ten heads. The demon had a menacing scowl on all ten faces and stood holding his weapons with his feet astride a huge platform. In fact, the platform itself was around thirteen feet high.

The company that had been awarded the contract by the coordinating committee was a newcomer and was going the extra mile to please the clients. The contractor, Fireworks India (Pvt) Ltd., had even imported the fireworks that would be used.

In the next thirty minutes, the town centre was cordoned off by the Rapid Action Division commanded by the general. In the centre of the cordoned off area stood the devil...the demon king Ravana with his ten heads.

The general picked up his mobile phone and dialled the number of his counterpart in the CMG - the Crisis Management Group - a part of the DEA, the Department of Atomic Energy. 'I need a team here immediately,' he shouted as his men went about arresting the workers who were putting up the effigy of Ravana.

Over the years that it had devoted to nuclear research, India had very little by way of nuclear detection technology. Its front line of defence had primarily consisted of slightly more sophisticated Geiger counters. Unfortunately, these machines did a pathetic job of distinguishing highly enriched uranium, a dangerous element in a nuclear weapon, from naturally occurring radiation, which could be found in almost everything, including fertilizer and kitty litter. The other drawback was the fact that the enriched uranium used in a "dirty bomb" would normally be encased in lead, thus resulting in very small amounts of radiation leakage.

Since 9/11, scientists at the Indian Department of Atomic Energy had been working on a new generation of equipment that could enhance uranium detection. These devices were engineered to detect all types of radiation in the first phase. In the second phase, advanced computing software was used to characterize the source and type of radiation. In fact, even a dirty bomb ensconced in a lead container would be detectable because some of the gamma rays would still escape the casing and this "signature" would be identified by the software code that was being perpetually updated by software engineers working in a high-tech facility in Bangalore.[clxxv]

The challenge would be to take the prototype and manufacture it in "cookie-cutter" fashion so that it could be coupled with simple notebook computers that came with pre-loaded detection software. This mass manufacturing was still some years away.

In the meantime, the prototype was available with the Indian Institute of Technology in Delhi. The general, through a word from the Prime Minister's office, had succeeded in requisitioning the equipment and having it door-delivered to him in Goa.

General Prithviraj Singh and Zvi Yatom were watching the Crisis Management Team from the Department of Atomic Energy disassemble the effigy of the demon king Ravana with his ten heads.

Thank you God, for making it quick and painless to locate the device, Prithviraj thought to himself as he watched the men prise open the base platform containing Vincent and the bomb. About an hour later, he was halfway through chewing one of his Montecristo cigars when the chief supervisor walked over to him. 'All clear,' he said, 'nothing to fear.'

'So you disarmed the nuke?' asked the general.

'Nuke? Nah. It was just an elaborate set of plastic explosives that were set to go off after the firecrackers stuffed inside the effigy had burned themselves out. Couldn't have killed more than a hundred people, at most...' He paused. 'And General?'

'Yes.'

'You said that we may find a guy strapped inside...'

'Sure.'

'No such luck.'

'No nuke? No priest? Then where in God's name are they?' asked the general just as his mobile phone started buzzing. It was Stephen Elliot from Langley.

⌐☜▰▰▰☞⌐

The nightclub near Anjuna Beach was a really wild place. It had red walls, red lights and even a red floor.

The lamps were three-pointed pitchforks that had candles on each of the spikes. In the centre was the dance floor women, scantily clad in dark red bikini outfits, gyrated to loud rave music.

Smoke from endless joints permeated the air as locals and hippies picked up strangers in the night.

The name of the nightclub was *Shaitana* - the Indian word for "Devil", and possibly the origin of the word "Satan".

Vincent had been left there, drugged with pentobarbital. In his hand was a note that read:

You have been left in Shaitana's red; without having lost hair or head. What you search for does exist; but I pray you to desist! You think your search will treasure find? No, it's better to be blind. Some secrets are better left alone! Why make the living into Skull or Bone?

Rawalpindi, Pakistan, 2012

The home of Dawood Omar, not only Pakistan's key nuclear research scientist but now also an important member of Pakistan's largest religious political front, the Jamaat Islami, was rather quiet at 5 a.m. He was fast asleep, jet-lagged from his trip to Pyongyang to sell nuclear equipment subsidized by Oedipus for Isabel Madonna.

That was when three dozen SAS agents broke down the doors and captured the startled man as he was reaching for his Kalashnikov. Dawood was a big fish indeed. The suspected mastermind of several sensational terrorist acts around the world, he had a $25 million price tag on his head.

Stephen Elliot dug into Dawood Omar's laptop and was struck with fear. On the hard disk was an Al-Qaeda plan to create a series of nuclear hell storms throughout the United States, Europe and Israel.[clxxvi]

Many hours of sleep deprivation later, Dawood began singing. He revealed to his interrogators that the "American Hiroshima" command structure reported not to Osama-bin-Laden but to his deputy, a nameless and faceless man who was simply known as the Sheikh. The Sheikh and Osama lived just a few hundred yards apart in Waziristan.

The nuclear deal had been paid for by a Christian group called the *Crux Decussata Permuta*. Dr. Abdul Qadeer Khan's University of Leuven connections with Alberto Valerio had been used.

The one question that Dawood had been unable to answer was what the Christians wanted in return for having arranged the nuclear deal.

He didn't need to tell them. Stephen Elliot already knew.

Washington D.C., U.S.A., 2012

The 132 rooms, thirty-five bathrooms, six levels, 412 doors, 147 windows, twenty-eight fireplaces, eight staircases, and three elevators of 1600 Pennsylvania Avenue constituted the highest security zone in the world.[clxxvii]

In the West Wing of 1600 Pennsylvania Avenue was the room built by the 27th President of the United States of America, William Howard Taft. Taft's preference for an oval-shaped room could be traced back to the days of George Washington, who had introduced the innovation in order to ensure that his guests could all stand equidistant from him.

The 44th President of the United States of America sat in the oval office listening to the security briefing being presented by the Director of the CIA.

Also present were Stephen Elliot, Head of the SAS, and the National Security Advisor.

This President was known to have a short attention span, preferring short and crisp briefings. Patience was in short supply with this President, Yale education notwithstanding.

This President's tenure had seen the ruthless reorganization of the Department of Homeland Security, the most comprehensive reorganization of the federal government in a half-century, consolidating twenty-two agencies and 180,000 employees. This President meant business.

'So, what do we know?' asked the President.

'Well, we know that our "ally" in the war on terror, Pakistan, has been a key supplier. Funnily enough, this has happened without Presidential sanction from Islamabad. It seems to be that the A. Q. Khan network has been in action through Dawood Omar. The Russians provided Bakatin to play the friendly broker. The device was smuggled into India using the Lashkar-e-Toiba network but has now crossed several international borders. Stephen Elliot tells me that there aren't eleven targets but twelve. All of the incidents that have happened so far have been major attacks although not on the scale of a

Hiroshima. I am given to understand that the twelfth attack may be nuclear and that the target may be Israel,' responded the director.

'Jesus! Where? Why?' asked the President.

'Tel Megiddo. The Bible had prophesied that the final military showdown of the world would happen in Megiddo...these guys want to prove a point that Armageddon is finally here. It's Islam vs. the non-believers.'

'And do we know who these people are?'

'Ghalib-bin-Isar is head of the group. He takes his instructions from someone they call the Sheikh. He, in turn, seems to take instructions from Osama. It is the Crux Decussata Permuta connection that is confusing. We have never heard of these guys. What are they doing dealing with Islamic terrorists?'

'Who is this Ghalib chap?'

'He definitely trained under Osama. He has a tightly knit pack of twelve who are stationed all over the world - India, the United States, England, Australia, France, South America, Malaysia, Indonesia, Russia, Iraq and China. They call themselves the "Lashkar-e-Talatashar". Translated into English, it means the Army of Thirteen.'

'Do we have anyone inside?'

'Nope. We don't have a Judas as yet.'

The National Security Advisor thought for a moment and then asked the CIA director rather crossly, 'Why don't we have human intelligence? I thought that was the highest priority at the agency!'

The President coughed and got up. A knowing glance was exchanged with Stephen Elliot as the President walked out of the Oval Office.

Elliot had not bothered to keep the CIA Director nor the National Security Advisor informed of CIA Trois. He had, however, always given the President the full picture.

The President recalled the BBC interview granted by the White House to Stephen Sackur four years earlier.

London, 2008

Stephen Sackur of the BBC was interviewing the American President for *HardTalk*. The President was on a visit to England, having just won the Presidential elections two months earlier.

Sackur: 'The British Prime Minister was with you at Yale. Did you know him there?'

President: 'No.'

Sackur: 'It is rumoured that both of you were in Skull & Bones, the secret offshoot of the Illuminati.'

President: 'Well if it's secret, then how can I possibly talk about it?'

Sackur: 'But what does that mean for those who see something sinister in secret societies such as the Illuminati, the Rhodes scholars or Skull & Bones? They say you are anti-Church.'

President: (laughs) 'I am a practising Christian. Why would I be anti-Church?'

Sackur: 'They say that you worry about the Church becoming too powerful...pursuing its own foreign policy. You want to keep Islam and Christianity at loggerheads so that oil prices remain high.'

President: 'Who are the "they" that you keep referring to?'

Sackur: 'It's a secret. Like your days as Executive Director in the CIA!'[clxxviii]

⟨ ❦ ⟩

The American President had been Executive Director of the CIA prior to running for office.

This was around the time that the Norm Dixon story had appeared. *How the CIA created Osama-bin-Laden*[clxxix] was the headline:

How things change, in the aftermath of a series of terrorist atrocities, the most despicable being the mass murder of more than 6000 working people in New York and Washington on September 11ᵗʰ. Bin Laden, the 'freedom fighter' is now lambasted by U.S. leaders and the Western mass media as a 'terrorist mastermind' and an 'evil-doer'. Yet the U.S.

Government refuses to admit its central role in creating the vicious movement that spawned bin Laden, the Taliban and Islamic fundamentalist terrorists that plague Algeria and Egypt, and perhaps the disaster that befell New York.'

In April 1978, the People's Democratic Party of Afghanistan (PDPA) seized power in Afghanistan. The PDPA was committed to a radical land reform that favoured the peasants, trade union rights, an expansion of education and social services, equality for women and the separation of church and state. The PDPA also supported strengthening Afghanistan's relationship with the Soviet Union.

Such policies enraged the wealthy semi-feudal landlords, the Muslim religious establishment and the tribal chiefs. Washington, fearing the spread of Soviet influence to its allies in Pakistan, Iran and the Gulf states, immediately offered support to the Afghan Mujahideen, as the 'contra' force was known.

Between 1978 and 1992, the U.S. Government poured at least US$6 billion (some estimates range as high as $20 billion) worth of arms, training and funds to prop up the Mujahideen factions. Other Western governments, as well as oil-rich Saudi Arabia, kicked in as much again. Wealthy Arab fanatics, like Osama-bin-Laden, provided millions more.

Washington's policy in Afghanistan went far beyond simply forcing Soviet troops to withdraw; it aimed to foster an international movement to spread Islamic fanaticism into the Muslim Central Asian Soviet republics to destabilize the Soviet Union. The grand plan coincided with Pakistan military dictator General Zia-ul-Haq's own ambitions to dominate the region.

U.S.-run Radio Liberty and Radio Free Europe beamed Islamic fundamentalist tirades across Central Asia, while paradoxically denouncing the 'Islamic revolution' that had toppled the pro-U.S. Shah of Iran in 1979.

Washington's favoured Mujahideen faction was one of the most extreme, led by Gulbuddin Hekmatyar. The West's distaste for terrorism did not apply to this unsavoury 'freedom fighter'. Hekmatyar was notorious in the 1970s for throwing acid in the faces of women who refused to wear the veil. Hekmatyar was also infamous for his side trade in the cultivation and trafficking in opium. Osama-bin-Laden was a close associate of Hekmatyar and his faction.

The Executive Director of the CIA was unrepentant about the explosion in the flow of drugs: 'Our main mission was to do as much damage as possible to the Soviets...There was a fall-out in terms of drugs, yes. But the main objective was accomplished. The Soviets left Afghanistan.'

It was this same Executive Director who had committed CIA support to a long-standing Pakistani Inter-Services Intelligence proposal to recruit from around the world to join the Afghan Jihad. At least 100,000 Islamic militants flocked to Pakistan (some 60,000 attended fundamentalist schools in Pakistan without necessarily taking part in the fighting).

Soon, Osama-bin-Laden, one of twenty sons of a billionaire construction magnate, arrived in Afghanistan to join the Jihad. An austere religious fanatic and business tycoon, bin Laden specialized in recruiting, financing and training the estimated 35,000 non-Afghan mercenaries who joined the Mujahideen.

Osama has simply continued to do the job he was asked to do in Afghanistan during the Jihad - fund, feed and train mercenaries. All that has changed is his primary customer. Then it was the ISI and, behind the scenes, the CIA. Bin Laden only became a 'terrorist' in the eyes of the U.S. when he fell out with the Saudi royal family over its decision to allow more than 540,000 U.S. troops to be stationed on Saudi soil following Iraq's invasion of Kuwait.

Chapter Twenty-Three

Waziristan, Pakistan-Afghanistan Border, 2012
The lanky, olive-skinned Sheikh read the note that Ghalib had sent him upon reaching his destination. 'Praise be to Allah!' he exclaimed as he read Ghalib's note:

UOY.OT.HTAO.YM.MAMI.HO
OWT.MOTA.TA.MOTA.TIH.OT
HT33T.3HT.TA.MIA.HTUOM.3HT.TA.MIA
TA3H.TOH.3TIHW.HTIW.YAWA.MIH.TIH
3OW.OT.MIH.3IT.YOT.YM.HTIW.3YA
3WO.I.HTUOY.YM.MIHW.YHT.OT
3M.HTIW.TUO.MIH.HTIW.TUO
3M.3SIMOTA.OT.3MIT.YHT.TIAWA.I

'My secret weapon is finally in place,' said the Sheikh in his usual hushed voice as his hands trembled with excitement.

<hr/>

Islamabad, Pakistan, 2012
The *Aiwan-e-Sadr*, the official residence of the President of Pakistan, lay in the centre of the city that had been meticulously planned and built by the Greek Constantinos Doxiadis. Islamabad, meaning "the abode of Islam", is the capital city of Pakistan and is located at the crossroads of Punjab and the North-West Frontier Province.[clxxx]

Ensconced inside the plush interiors of the *Aiwan-e-Sadr* sat the Iron Man of Pakistan. Born in Lahore to a lower middle-class family, his parents could never have imagined in their wildest dreams that their son would one day become the President of Pakistan.

This was the man who was supposedly at the forefront of the war on terror. This was also the man who had no qualms about waxing eloquent about enlightened moderation while taking the support of Islamic hardliners.

The President was looking at the transcript of a secret phone conversation between the chief of Pakistan's Inter-Services Intelligence (ISI) and a Thuraya satellite phone somewhere in the Middle East. His theory had been proved correct. His intelligence agencies continued to remain involved with Islamic terror groups despite his strict orders to the contrary. The problem was that this situation could not be wished away.

The President had earlier that day been officially briefed by his ISI chief, who had conveniently omitted to mention that a terrorist called Ghalib was running loose somewhere in the Middle East with a nuclear bomb. The phone tap transcript seemed to indicate that this Ghalib and his team were taking orders from someone called the Sheikh.

During the phone conversation, the ISI chief had been trying to convince Ghalib to give himself up to Stephen Elliot of the SAS! How dare he! Was the ISI chief's salary being paid by Pakistan or by the American bastards?

The deal had been brokered by the Russians, who had been funded by a right-wing Christian group. The ironic fact was that no one seemed to be too concerned about the nuclear weapon. All parties wanted Ghalib.

Why is this man so important to all of them? thought the Pakistani leader as he sipped his evening Scotch and soda.

<hr />

Goa, India, 2012

The Scotch, soda and ice in their hotel room were a welcome relief.

Vincent's reunion with Martha was an emotional one. The ordeal that he had been through only reinforced the importance of friends and family. He also realized the enormity of what he had learned from Swakilki.

'Vincent, are you well? We were worried sick about you,' said Martha as she sobbed. 'I really thought that I had lost you forever.'

Vincent hugged Martha. 'Relax, Nana. The worst is behind us. There is a reason that we made this trip. If we hadn't come here, we would never have come face-to-face with this dangerous woman. And if I hadn't met her, I would never have realized the importance of what I had seen in my past life regressions with Terry and you.'

'And what was that?' asked Martha, rather dishevelled from the hours of anxious waiting and searching.

'I need to take my quest to its logical conclusion. That was the reason for my meeting Terry. Destiny took me to London, to Mumbai and to Goa. Maybe it needs to take me elsewhere.' Vincent was exhausted but highly charged.

Martha looked at him helplessly. 'I'm scared, Vincent. You nearly lost your life. I'm not sure whether I want you to take this matter any further. You're lucky that she spared your life...and she's left a warning note in your hand.'

'But Nana, this isn't about me. It's about something that has been one of the world's greatest mysteries. This is not something that one can leave unresolved. The greatest story ever told, the bestseller of the world, ended with an unsolved riddle. I now have a chance to solve the puzzle. Now, please show me the document that you found on the floor of the Bom Jesus Basilica.'

The document was old and yellow and was written in Portuguese in flowing ink, customary of eighteenth-century manuscripts.

I, Alphonso de Castro tinham chegado em Goa para dar um ímpeto mais adicional ao Inquisition em 1767. Eu fui requisitado fazer uma lista exhaustive dos textos antigos que tinham sido encontrados nos repousos, temples, igrejas, mosques e synagogues dos Hindus, Thomas Cristãos, os muçulmanos e os Jews de Sephardic...

Vincent began to translate the document into English:

'I, Alphonso de Castro had arrived in Goa ostensibly to give further impetus to the Inquisition in 1767. I was ordered to make an exhaustive list of ancient texts that had been found in the homes, temples, churches, mosques and synagogues of the Hindus, the Thomas Christians, the Muslims and the Sephardic Jews. Any texts that did not suit the sensibilities of the Roman Catholic Church were to be destroyed by me. While I was going through an old set of manuscripts discovered in the bowels of the Church of Bom Jesus, I found this particular document.

This church had existed well before 1559 - as a mosque. Within one of the pillars that had been discarded in favour of non-Islamic stonework was a cavity. This cavity contained a bundle of documents that had been written in Urdu. These documents had been found by a Hindu construction worker, Lakshman Powale, at the site where the mosque was being torn down to make way for the church.

It was immediately transferred to the archives of the Portuguese viceroy, where it continued to sit till it was taken up for cataloguing by me nineteen years later. The bundle contained eleven texts, of which ten were earmarked by me for destruction. The eleventh one was deliberately not catalogued by me. It was called the Tarikh-Issa-Massih.

Through fear for my life, I felt that it would be better for me to leave the document in India prior to my departure for Lisbon today. I am determined to store the document in a place where it will be preserved so that it may be discovered by future generations; they may then know the truth.

Tonight, my ship sets sail for Lisbon. Oh Heavenly Father, please forgive me for disturbing Saint Francis Xavier. Since he has the miraculous powers of preserving himself, I believe that under his safekeeping, this document will also remain preserved. April 23rd, 1770.'

> *Remember: It is enough, O Lord, it is enough, the two angels said. Mastrilli without doubt made the best silver bed. But to carefully guard a secret of the dead. Ignatius' gold cup is better than a silver head.*

'Do you understand what this means?' said Vincent excitedly. 'It means that the original *Tarikh-Issa-Massih* was found by Alphonso de Castro and hidden away in the Bom Jesus Basilica.'

'But Vincent, this document was already with the Japanese woman. If she had found this, she would certainly have found the original *Tarikh-Issa-Massih* also,' reasoned Martha.

'You're right,' said Vincent. 'The document will be long gone by now. In fact, it is probably tucked away in some secret archive of the Vatican by now.'

Their deliberations were interrupted by General Prithviraj Singh, Zvi Yatom and Pandit Ramgopal Prasad Sharma.

'Father Morgan, I understand that you have been through a harrowing experience. Unfortunately, I do not have the luxury of giving you time to recuperate. We need to talk immediately!' commanded the general.

Vincent did not notice the general keenly eyeing the Alphonso de Castro letter that Vincent was holding.

Chapter Twenty-Four

Goa, India, 2012

All of them sat inside Prithviraj's makeshift office at the Fort Aguada Hotel. Prithviraj began, 'I must tell you that the past few days have put me in turmoil. I have always believed that there is no substitute for good old-fashioned detective work. Unfortunately, the circumstances of the last twelve months are only now beginning to get pieced together.'

Zvi Yatom took over. 'We now know for a fact that Ghalib-bin-Isar and his twelve commandos have carried out terrorist acts all over the world in the past eleven months. Each of these has been timed to occur on the 21st of each month. December 21st is just a week away. We expect that this will be the mother of all these acts.'

There was a stillness in the room as everyone digested this information. The general resumed. 'We now also know for a fact that a nuclear weapon has been obtained by these terrorists and that it has transited through India. The American President, the Pakistani President and the Indian Prime Minister have been in communication with one another and it seems that Ghalib plans to use the device somewhere in the Middle East. We would have been able to pinpoint his exact location from his satellite phone if the conversation that he had with his handlers in the ISI had been a bit longer.'

'We are re-examining the interrogation that is being conducted on Dawood Omar, a key Osama-bin-Laden operative in Pakistan. We also know that the nuclear weapon transaction was facilitated by a Russian intelligence operative, Lavrenty Edmundovich Bakatin.' Prithviraj looked around him; there was complete, rapt attention.

'The question that my colleagues and I asked our counterparts in the CIA was this: why would a fringe group within the Church called the Crux Decussata Permuta be willing to pay huge sums of cash to Pakistani scientists and North Korean contractors on behalf of a group of Islamic terrorists unless they had something significant to gain? Still today, we are not clear as to what the actual barter involves.

'What I can tell you is that this bunch of terrorists has modelled itself along the lines of Jesus Christ and his twelve disciples. All these men trained together in Afghanistan under Osama-bin-Laden's henchmen. Each of them has executed a major terrorist act on the 21st of each month,' explained the general.

'Now, the question that you might ask is: how do we fit into any of this? Well, we know that Father Morgan was meant to be killed. We now also know that the kidnapper was Swakilki, an international assassin who has been keeping herself under the radar and evading arrest. We also know that she takes her instructions from a group of people who call themselves the Crux Decussata Permuta. The death of Professor Terry Acton and the attempt on Father Morgan are related. Since both these gentlemen were digging into the bloodline of Jesus Christ, it obviously made someone within the Vatican very uncomfortable.

'We have tried working with information from our friends in the office of the Secretary General of CESIS, the Italian intelligence services, and the IAB in Japan, and have come to some conclusions. These are:

'One. Swakilki, a Japanese national, has links with the Roman Catholic Church because she lived as an orphan at the Holy Family Home, an Osaka orphanage.

'Two. A regular visitor there was Alberto Valerio, who held the position of Secretary for the Congregation for the Oriental Churches, at which time he travelled extensively within the Orient. His connection to the Priestly Society of the Holy Cross is now known. He possibly also heads the Crux Decussata Permuta.

'Three. Swakilki was initially under the influence of the Aum Shinrikyo cult and committed several crimes with her partner Takuya, till such time as she killed him too. Subsequently, Swakilki Ogawa has carried out assignments for Valerio only.

'Four. Brother Thomas Manning, who resides mostly in Switzerland, was the banking contact who ensured that Russia received the requisite doses of cash to ensure the freedom of the erstwhile iron-curtain countries from the Soviet Union. This was done through Bakatin, who also has excellent connections with Al-Qaeda, more particularly someone known as the "Sheikh".

'Five. After the war on terror, Osama-bin-Laden went into hiding in the Waziristan district of the tribal regions on the Pakistan-Afghanistan border. His new focus was to support local Islamic terror groups with ideology and cash. He wanted to expand his activities by creating local franchises. One of these was the Lashkar-e-Toiba in Pakistan. When the Lashkar-e-Toiba was banned by the Americans as a fall-out of the war on terror, they span off the ultra-elite Lashkar-e-Talatashar, or the Army of Thirteen, with Ghalib as the head.

'Six. In the last eleven months, the group has carried out eleven attacks in different parts of the world. Each attack has been on the 21st, leading us to believe that the big one will be on December 21st this year.

'Seven. We know that a nuclear weapon is in the hands of Ghalib and that the Crux Decussata Permuta have played a role in making this possible. Valerio, Dawood Omar and A. Q. Khan, Pakistan's head of nuclear research, studied at the University of Leuven in Belgium around the same time. We believe that Ghalib is taking his instructions from Osama-bin-Laden's right-hand man, the Sheikh.

'This is where you come into the picture, Father Vincent Morgan. We need your help to understand why elements within the Crux Decussata Permuta would be willing to risk a nuclear war for the sake of Ghalib. Moreover, what is the significance of December 21st, particularly at Tel Megiddo?'

No one noticed that Martha's knuckles had gone white.

***

Vincent sat stunned as he heard the general give his speech. Memories of September 11th, 2001, came flooding back. He had been in the staff room of Stepinac High School along with his friend, the permanently unshaven janitor, Ted Callaghan. The television had been turned on in the staff room.

Then on that day, at 8:46 a.m., American Flight 11 from Boston had crashed into the North Tower. Seventeen minutes later, at 9:03

a.m., United Flight 175 from Boston had crashed into the South Tower.[clxxxi]

Vincent and Martha had attended Mass at St. Patrick's Cathedral on Sunday, five days after the attack on the World Trade Centre. Cardinal Egan had decided to hold Mass for all those who had died in the tragedy.

2000 people had turned up.

After the memorial Mass was over, Vincent had walked over to Thomas Manning and had said, 'I need to talk to you.' Thomas had nodded. Martha had left them alone, and Thomas and Vincent had strolled over to Murray's Bagels on Sixth Avenue.

They had bought a couple of bagels with a variety of cream cheeses and had settled down at a table.

'So what's all this I hear about you and Opus Dei?' Vincent had asked.

'Vincent, you know I value our friendship. I want you to know that I had nothing to do with that FBI agent who was arrested. He simply attended prayers at the same church in which I preached. Period.'

'Point taken. Are you a member of Opus Dei?'

'What is this? An inquisition?' asked Thomas, visibly irritated. 'Vincent...look...'

'Just answer the question, Thomas.'

'No. I am not Opus Dei. And I promise you that's the absolute truth.'

It was. He was Crux Decussata Permuta.

❦

The group was deliberating on what the general had just told them. 'Martha, you have regressed your patients into the past, but isn't it possible to progress them into the future? Some gurus, such as Weiss, have indicated that our futures are variable, which means that the choices we make in the present could determine the quality of our future,' said Vincent.[clxxxii]

Martha thought about it before replying. 'Well, progression is not very different from regression. The problem is that it is difficult to distinguish between fact and fantasy. What if one sees something in the future that may not be true? It could do irreparable damage to the psyche of the patient.'

'Could you progress me?' he asked.

'Sure. But I don't feel very comfortable doing it. You must understand that hypnotic projection is the exact opposite of regression and implies projecting the mind into the future. The purpose would be to see what will happen in the future or what is likely to happen in the future. If this is crazy to a "normal" mind, consider the basic fact that the human mind cannot only regress or progress but can also move sideways. Take the concept of dreams; isn't it possible to dream through the passage of an entire year in a matter of an hour?'

'So why won't you progress me? It could tell us something critical,' demanded Vincent.

'If the mind "sees" an event happening often enough, there is a strong possibility that such an event would eventually play itself out as a self- fulfilling prophecy. I don't want to put you in that situation, Vincent.'

Pandit Ramgopal Prasad nodded his agreement. He said to Vincent, 'Son, your future is not a predetermined one. That is the essence of Hindu philosophy. Even though there is a "most probable" scenario, it is always in our hands to change the outcome via our actions. That is the basis of Karma.'

Vincent was adamant. 'We are living in a moment of crisis. We need to do something dramatic that may help us. I think I can live with the consequences.'

'Okay, Vincent, you win. What do you want to see?' asked Martha helplessly.

'Where's the bomb? Will it go off? Do we have a bloodline of Jesus here on earth? Where is he or she? Will the world be a better place due to his presence? Will the world tomorrow be a better place than the world today?' Vincent was on a roll.

'I get the picture, Vincent,' remarked Martha caustically. 'Let's get you comfortable. Please understand that projection can be either directive or non-directive. Directive progression is better suited for curing ailments or traumas. My progression will be non-directive, in which you will be free to choose the path yourself. Understood?'

'Sure.'

'Why don't you settle down comfortably on the bed and let me pull this chair near you. Comfortable?'

Vincent nodded as he settled onto the hotel bed. Martha pulled up the chair beside him while the others continued to remain seated on the floor cushions.

'Okay, let's start by getting you totally comfortable, physically comfortable. Settle back into the pillow and begin to relax...that's right...just...relax.' The voice was soothing, reassuring, but firm. She continued, 'Just relax, and concentrate on my voice. You have absolutely nothing to do right now. You don't need to move. Just relax.'

She continued with the same soothing voice, 'Now drift deeper with every breath that you take. Feel your body getting heavier and sinking down further. You're comfortable and relaxed, but you're heavy and sinking. Deeper. Deeper. Okay. Now I want you to allow your mind to drift back in time...drift back to this morning...drift back to last night...drift back to last week...to your high-school days...drift back to your infancy...drift back beyond your infancy...that's right.' Martha now began to probe with gentle questions.

'Where are you now?'

'Yerushalem.'

'And what do you see around you?'

'Temple fires. It's night. I can see Caiaphas and the Sanhedrin assembled, judging Jesus. They are irritable because no reliable witnesses are coming forth with evidence against Jesus.'

'Anyone familiar from your present life?'

'Thomas Manning.'

'Who is he?'

'He is Caiaphas - poisoning the minds of those assembled against Jesus. In this life too, he continues to seek vengeance.'

'Anyone else?'

'The Japanese woman who kidnapped me. Swakilki. She's present. She wants to kill Jesus.'

'Anyone else?'

'You, Nana!'

'What am I doing?'

'Taking care of Jesus. Healing him. Applying medicines and herbs.'

'Anyone else there?'

'A third woman. I don't know her.'

'Now what is happening?'

'I can see Jesus and the three women walking towards Damascus …I can only see their backs.'

'Why Damascus?'

'Damascus is a stronghold of the Essenes. He can remain hidden and protected there till they decide where to go.'

'Vincent, I will now count forward from one to five. You will feel yourself floating forward along a continuum of time into a lifetime ahead with each number…one…two…three…four…five…Okay, Vincent, where are you?'

'Megiddo.'

'In Israel?'

'Yes.'

'Who are you?'

'A Roman soldier - my name is Antonius.'

'What are you doing?'

'I am searching for a fugitive. The fugitive is a Roman soldier. His name is Gaianus.'

'Why are you after him?'

'He is a secret Christian. All Christians are enemies of the state!'

'What can you learn from this?'

'I persecuted Christians in my former life. Destiny has made me a Christian priest in my present.'

'I will again count forward from one to five. Float forward…one… two…three…four…five…Okay, Vincent, where are you?'

'China. I am an advisor to the Emperor Gaozong. The chief concubine, Wu Zhao has seized the throne and wants to eliminate me. Luckily she has not succeeded, even though she has crippled me.'

'Anyone familiar?'

'Yes…It's her, the evil Wu Zhao is my captor - Swakilki!'

'Counting forward from one to five. You will move forward in time…one…two…three…four…five…Okay, Vincent, where are you?'

'I'm an Inca warrior protecting Sapa Inca Pachacuti. I am the bodyguard for Mama Anawarkhi, the wife of Sapa Inca Pachacuti.'

'You like her?'

'No. I am killing her. I have to. She is plotting against the Sapa Inca.'

'Anyone else familiar?'

'Yes. General Prithviraj. He is the Sapa Inca. I protected him. That's why he is protecting me!'

'I will again count forward from one to five. You will move forward in time…one…two…three…four…five…Okay, Vincent, where are you?'

'It's 1794. I'm in France. The guillotine is bloody with the heads that have rolled.'

'Anyone you recognize?'

'The woman, Charlotte Lavoisier, she is being guillotined; she looks like Swakilki. Her executioner, Sanson, looks like Terry Acton. He takes her head in one life…she will take his in another.'

'Counting forward…one…two…three…four…five…Okay, Vincent, where are you?'

'I'm a doctor in London. World War Two is going on. I am working for the Red Cross. I can see the Sossoon home, which is a supply depot.'

'Anyone familiar?'

'Clementine Sossoon. She is very sick…cancer. Her face is like yours, Nana. Wait. It is you, Nana!'

'Counting forward…one…two…three…four…five…where are you?'

'In the backyard of my parents' home in New York. My dad and I are playing catch in the backyard. My mom is barbecuing hot dogs in the corner.'

'Moving forward…one…two…three…four…five…where are you?'

'At my parents' funeral. It's raining. I cannot make out whether my face is wet because of my tears or on account of the rain.'

'Moving forward...one...two...three...four...five...where are you?'

'In captivity. Swakilki is holding me prisoner. She leaves me inside a windowless toilet in the nightclub. It's stifling hot inside.'

'Moving forward...one...two...three...four...five...where are you?'

'Back in Megiddo.'

'What are you doing?'

'I am at a kibbutz in Israel. The hill that overlooks the valley of the kibbutz is where the final showdown will happen.'

'Where is this hill located?'

'Very close to the intersection of Highway 65 and 66. Nearby is a large prison holding many Palestinians who have been arrested for terrorism against the Israeli state.'

'What do you see?'

'A mosaic.'

'What sort of mosaic?'

'It belongs to an ancient church. It was uncovered recently. It belongs to the third century. It has a sign. It says that Gaianus donated his own money to build this church.'[clxxxiii]

'The same Gaianus that you saw earlier? The one that you were chasing when you were a Roman soldier?'

'It's him!'

'Who?'

'Him!'

'What else do you see?'

'A little boy.'

'Who?'

'A bomb. It looks like the one used in Hiroshima. It was called the Little Boy.'

'Are you sure?' asked Martha.

'Yes.'

'Anyone familiar near the bomb?'

'This can't be! No! You?'

'Relax - Vincent. Who are you seeing?'

'Jesus! Gaianus!'

'You see Jesus?'

'الملعا هلعفي ام اذه دقتعا ؟لعفت اذام !اذام !إتنا اي'[clxxxiv]

'Vincent. I need you to float above the scene. Speak to me in English,' instructed Martha.

'Hey you! What are you doing? Think of what this will do to the world!'

'Who is saying this? To whom?'

Blank. Vincent was completely quiet.

Martha realized that she had reached a blind spot. She continued, 'Moving forward…one…two…three…four…five…where are you?'

'I can't say. It's deserted here. No food. No water. Corpses and vultures. It's as if the whole world is on fire.'

'Is it war? Famine?'

'I warned everyone that religious polarization was going to get us nowhere. No one listened. See what happened. We now have nothing left to fight about.'

'Can you identify the date?' asked Martha.

'An extremely close conjunction of the winter solstice sun with the crossing point of the galactic equator and the ecliptic path of the sun.'

'When is that, do you know?'

'December 21st, 2012.'

Pandit Ramgopal Prasad Sharma nodded; the very date that he had seen as the end of the world.

'What can you see?'

'The radiation produced by the explosions has destroyed all the vegetation.'

'What else?'

'Burning trees. Burning grass. Rivers and oceans of blood. Complete darkness.'

'Can you see anyone else?'

'I can see him.'

'Who?'

'The man who started it. The man who finished it.'

'What did he start or finish?'

'The end of the world.'

Waziristan, Pakistan-Afghanistan Border, 2012
The Sheikh needed to reconfirm the contents of Ghalib's note. He asked his loyal attendant to fetch him his mirror. When this was in front of him, he held the note up and re-read it from the mirror image:

OH.IMAM.MY.OATH.TO.YOU
TO.HIT.ATOM.AT.ATOM.TWO
AIM.AT.THε.MOUTH.AIM.AT.THε.TεεTH
HIT.HIM.AWAY.WITH.WHITε.HOT.HεAT
AYε.WITH.MY.TOY.TIε.HIM.TO.WOε
TO.THY.WHIM.MY.YOUTH.I.OWε
OUT.WITH.HIM.OUT.WITH.Mε
I.AWAIT.THY.TIMε.TO.ATOMIZε.Mε

Chapter Twenty-Five

Zurich, Switzerland, 2012

Herr Egloff, the investment advisor from Bank Leu, was sitting in the dining room of his chalet near Lake Aegiri consuming his usual breakfast of Birchermuesli mixed with fruit and yoghurt. This particular batch had been made with chopped filberts, chopped almonds, sweetened wheat germ, rolled oats, dried currants, and dried apricots. Herr Egloff attributed his good health to this wonderful concoction that had been invented by the renowned Swiss Dr. Bircher-Benner.

The other reason for Herr Egloff's good health was his clients' portfolio. More specifically the portfolio managed for Brother Thomas Manning. A single-sheet summary lay on the dining table.

Next to it lay an unsigned draft press release. It spoke about a nuclear threat in the heart of the Middle East. The fallout of such an event would be a reduction in the production and supply of oil in the region. Prices would further rise. Brother Manning would be pleased.

Crude Oil Future Contract Number One that he had purchased for his clients at 51.06 dollars per barrel was now trading at 103.11 dollars per barrel.

He had made a similar investment for his biggest client, a radical outfit called the UNL Militia. Herr Egloff did not ask too many questions about where the money came from. It was one of his reasons for success.

Before doing anything else, he had one important assignment to carry out for His Eminence. He transferred thirty thousand dollars from the Oedipus account to that of Iscariot.

He then took a phone call from Washington D.C. and transferred a million dollars from the UNL Militia to Iscariot.

Jerusalem, 27 A.D.
Then went one of the twelve, who was called Judas Iscariot, to the chief priests. And said to them: 'What will you give me, and I will deliver him unto you?' But they appointed him thirty pieces of silver.

Srinagar, Kashmir, India, 2012
She had come here to Srinagar to meet him. It had taken several months of effort to finally get him to agree on a deal. He was the Junior Assistant Director of Archives, Archaeology, Research and Museums for Kashmir. His name was Yehuda Moinuddin a.k.a. Iscariot.

As such, he had complete access to the former director's work - the work of Dr. Fida M. Hassnain. A person listed in the Who's Who in Archaeology and having complete control over the entire body of ancient Kashmiri documents. One of Dr. Hassnain's best-selling books had been *A Search for the Historical Jesus*, written in 1994. This phenomenal work of scholarship had contained tons of painstaking and verifiable research to prove that Jesus had not died on the cross and that he had spent the latter part of his life in Kashmir.

Yehuda had worked in this heady environment of scholarship and research for quite some time. Over many years he had absorbed each and every little detail that was available regarding the Jesus in Kashmir theory.

However, there was one extremely important difference between him and Dr. Hassnain. Dr. Hassnain was a true scholar. He was a Sufi, a mystical proponent of Islam and was never out to discredit Jesus or the Christian faith. In fact, it was his love for Jesus Christ that made him want to distinguish fact from fiction.

Yehuda Moinuddin, on the other hand, was a different matter. He was one of the key members of the Lashkar-e-Talatashar. He was Ghalib's most trusted aide, who managed all the financial matters of the group and lived on the houseboat that belonged to Ghalib.

He was sitting in the balcony of the Barabbas houseboat moored on the Dal Lake sipping a cup of *kahwa*, a delicate Kashmiri tea flavoured with saffron and almonds.

'I must find him before Vincent Morgan and the others can reach him,' she said to him.

'I have spent the last two years researching everything that there is to research on the subject. I already know whatever there is to know. I simply need to lead you to him. For that you must pay me my price.'

Swakilki handed over a brown envelope containing a slip with an account number at the Credit Suisse Bank, Zurich. Yehuda Moinuddin took it and looked at the slip eagerly. Thirty thousand dollars. He smiled a sly smile of satisfaction.

'I won't confirm with my bank because I trust you,' he said.

Swakilki shot back. 'You won't confirm because I can kill you.'

He laughed. 'No, you won't. I am the only one who can take you to him.'

Swakilki ignored the remark.

The trip westwards from Srinagar towards the Poonch district of Kashmir along the Indo-Pakistan line of control is very scenic. One necessarily has to travel through what is commonly called "The Valley of Kashmir", a strip that is about eighty miles long and thirty-five miles wide, straddling River Jhelum, at an average elevation of 5500 feet. It was this ethereal beauty of Kashmir that had inspired the Mughal emperor Jehangir to write a Persian couplet that said, "If there is paradise anywhere on earth, it is here, it is here, it is here."

Looking at the verdant hills and orchards and endless miles of swaying chinar trees, Swakilki found it difficult to understand how Bill Clinton could have called this "the most dangerous place on Earth".

The rugged Indian-made Mahindra Commander 650, an extremely basic 4x4, was ideal for the difficult roads that they were traversing. Years of terrorist insurgence and military conflict had taken its toll on the infrastructure of Kashmir.

Yehuda was at the wheel. Swakilki sat on the uncomfortable bench seat in the rear of the vehicle wearing an Afghan burqa that covered her entirely from head to toe. Swakilki was looking forward to finally being able to see the man in person.

Vatican City, 2012

'One can never trust Muslims!' shouted His Eminence Alberto Cardinal Valerio. Brother Thomas Manning was silent as he listened to Valerio venting his anger.

'We transfer funds from our Oedipus trust to the Isabel Madonna trust. We convince Dawood Omar to part with the first bomb of the series, only to be told that Osama plans to use Ghalib as a trigger! God curse his soul to eternal damnation!' he thundered. Silence greeted him.

'Don't you have anything to say? Do you realize what could happen to the Church if word got out?' he indignantly demanded.

'Your Eminence,' began Thomas Manning.

'Yes. Say whatever you want quickly!'

'Does it matter to us whether he is delivered to us alive or dead?' asked Manning delicately.

'What do you mean?' asked Valerio.

'Well, wasn't the intention of this exercise to prevent word from getting out that Christ had not died on the cross nor been resurrected. Wasn't it our intention to ensure that the story that we have fed our faithful flock for centuries remains intact?'

His Eminence wanted to be angry; instead he smiled at the Manning's logical mind.

Maryland, USA, 2012

Stephen Elliot and Prithviraj Singh were with their friend from Mossad, Zvi Yatom.

They were not alone. Around fifty people were in the darkened room along with them. The poorly lit room had walls that were padded in dark velvet. The sweet smell of incense pervaded the atmosphere. The room was accessed through a single passageway, the entrance to which was camouflaged by a painting of Benjamin Franklin, painted in 1759 by Benjamin Wilson.

Inside the secret hall, one could observe in the dim light, thirteen passages that led to thirteen separate rooms. Each of these rooms was used for very specific ceremonies.

The Grand Master spoke. 'Achaita, divine revelation. Rome will pass away, Jerusalem will burn and the reason will become broken. And my Law, the Law of Zión, will be acclaimed by the whole of humanity.'[clxxxv]

'Achaita!' said all those gathered in unison.

'Oh Illuminated, Brothers and sisters of the Great Hidden Lodge, of the night, of the star, of the Light! Zión is the Law!'

'Achaita!'

'Elevate and proclaim the Light, and break the chains of death, with the force Zión, oh Illuminated. I am the creator of worlds. I am the Great Architect of the Universe. Nations and governors are dust in front of me!'

'Achaita!'

'The next centuries and millennia will only know one word: Zión. And one Law: Zión. The next millennia will be of freedom and light, life and creation, love and kindness, under the Law of Zión, the Law of the Eternal One!'

'Achaita!'

'Proclaim Zión, oh Illuminati, and lead to the slaves to the footpath of the freedom. The brave ones will be free and eternal, to image and similarity of God. The cowardly ones will die forgotten and surrounded in their chains of ignorance and sin!'

'Zión! Zión! Zión! Zión! Zión! Zión! Zión! Zión! Zión! Zión! Zión! Zión! Zión!'

The Grand Master, dressed in scarlet robes thrust the knife into the dummy that had been placed on the large black granite slab in the centre of the room.

'Zión! Zión! Zión! Zión! Zión! Zión! Zión! Zión! Zión! Zión! Zión! Zión! Zión!'

After the dummy had been "sacrificed", each member went up to the Grand Master, bowing and kissing the Grand Master's ring. As they kissed it, they swore their allegiance to *Novus Ordem Seclorum*, the New World Order.

'We have lost our colleague Terry Acton to the forces of the evil Church. Fear not! His sacrifice was not in vain. As we speak, the forces of Islam and the forces of Christianity are positioning themselves for the greatest conflict ever. At the end of this conflict, they will both destroy themselves. And then will arise the New World Order - the power of the Illuminati!'

Ceremony over, the Grand Master retreated through the secret passageway till it ended at the secret door that was camouflaged on the other side by the painting. The Grand Master placed both palms on the scanners by the sides of the entrance and waited till the door swung open.

The 44th President of the United States of America then went and settled down behind the antique desk in the study of the official 125-acre retreat in the centre of Catoctin Mountain Park in Frederick County - Camp David.

The 44th President, the SAS director Stephen Elliot, RAW director Prithviraj Singh and Mossad operative Zvi Yatom were all peas from the very same pod. The Illuminati.

Chapter Twenty-Six

Tel Megiddo, Israel, 2012

Ghalib surveyed the area. El-Azhar was very familiar with the site. He had brought along with him all the required ordinance maps that outlined every inch of the territory.

El-Azhar told Ghalib not to worry. They parked the truck inside a small thicket of bushes so that it would not attract too much attention. El-Azhar asked Ghalib to wait while he surveyed the caves to determine the exact location that would be ideally suited to their purpose.

Ghalib would continue observing El-Azhar from a distance, using night-vision binoculars. He would continue to wait desperately for the next four days while El-Azhar continued to remain invisible.

Ghalib was worried. Could something have happened to him? Just as he was about to break protocol and go searching for him, he saw an extremely tired and fatigued El-Azhar emerge from one of the very small openings along the slope of the hill.

Ghalib lifted his eyes to the heavens and exclaimed, '*Ma sha' Allah*! I thank the all-merciful Allah for having heard my prayers! El-Azhar lives to tell me his story!'

Bethany, Judea, 27 A.D.

Now, there was a certain man sick, named Lazarus, of Bethany. Jesus therefore came: and found that he had been four days already in the grave. And said: 'Where have you laid him?'

It was a cave; and a stone was laid over it. Jesus said: 'Take away the stone.'

They took therefore the stone away. And Jesus lifting up his eyes, said: 'Father, I give thee thanks that thou hast heard me.'

Tel Megiddo, Israel, 2012

Ghalib's arrest by Zvi Yatom was quick and effortless. El-Azhar had done his job well by tipping them off. Within a few minutes Ghalib had been surrounded. The problem was that his truck containing the alleged device had disappeared.

The Israeli state gave the police blanket powers to arrest suspected terrorists, carry out communication intercepts, and severely curtail freedom of expression. In high-risk areas, search warrants could be done away with and the authorities were free to periodically ban communications through mobile phones or cyber cafés.

It was a classic chicken and egg story. Which came first, the terrorist or torture? Hard-line Islamic terrorist groups claimed that thousands had been tortured by the Israeli state whereas the authorities claimed that they had no other way to deal with people who saw nothing wrong with killing innocent women and children in schools, hospitals and restaurants.

The greater the terrorist menace, the more aggressive were the police and army in questioning suspects and, consequently, the higher the levels of torture and interrogation. But each suspect that emerged from the jails, innocent or not, definitely became sympathetic to the terrorist cause.

Tel Megiddo, Israel, 2012

He was strapped naked in a prostrate position on a table and interrogated while the soles of his feet were whacked repeatedly till the bones began to crumble.

Ghalib merely whispered, 'The person who participates in Holy battles in Allah's cause will be recompensed by Allah...will be admitted to Paradise if he is killed in the battle as a martyr...*Bismillah, i-rahman, i-rahim*, in the name of Allah, most gracious, most merciful, *Sibhana man halalaka lil dabh*, praise be upon he who has made me suitable for slaughter.'

Jerusalem, 27 A.D.

The Roman soldiers stripped Jesus and proceeded to tie his hands tightly to the post above him. The flagellum was made from a combination of individual leather pieces, bone and lead. Two soldiers, one on either side, carried out the task. While the Jews had an upper limit of forty lashes, the Romans had no such limit. The flagellum struck the skin of his back, shoulders and legs with maximum impact. With each progressive lash, the whip not only cut through the skin but also through tissue, capillaries, veins and muscles.

❦

Tel Megiddo, Israel, 2012

The High Purity Germanium (HPGe) detector that Zvi Yatom had succeeded in obtaining from Tel Aviv was cleverly able to identify radioactive materials from their "natural signature" because all radioactive substances continued to emit gamma rays, x-rays, alpha particles, beta particles, or neutrons.[clxxxvi] The machine had already sounded several alerts. The first alert had flashed on the screen.

Thorium-234.

24.1 days.

Beta, Gamma, X-ray.

It had turned out to be a huge fertilizer warehouse on the edge of a neighbouring field. The radioactive thorium was a key component of fertilizer and had a "half-life" of 24.1 days. The half-life was the amount of time it took for half of the atoms in the given radioactive substance to decay.[clxxxvii]

The next alert was near the Kibbutz. It turned out to be the X-Ray Department of the Kibbutz hospital. Zvi was looking at the notebook computer's screen as it flashed another message.

Potassium-40.

1.28 billion years.

Beta (1.3 MeV), Gamma.

Wrong number again. It was a truckload of bananas being transported to the local market from the Kibbutz.

Another message flashed:
Thorium-232.
14.1 billion years.
Alpha, x-rays.
'Yes! We may have found it!' shouted Zvi triumphantly as he ordered the patrol vehicles of the unit to head in the northerly direction pinpointed by the map on the screen. The signal became stronger and then suddenly stopped.

They were in a granite quarry! Obviously, radiation was going to be high owing to the high uranium and thorium content of the granite stone.

'Turn back!' he ordered. 'Let's move towards the hill.'

As the convoy progressed, the earlier computer message reappeared.
Thorium-232.
14.1 billion years.
Alpha, x-rays.
Zvi Yatom stopped his Jeep and peered over the shoulder of the technician operating the infernal radiation detector. 'What is it?' he asked.

The operator looked up at him and said, 'Sir, this area is the local scrap yard. All types of disused metal objects are brought here and are re-used for welding. The thoriated tungsten welding rods emit radiation. That's the signature that we seem to be picking up.'

Zvi was exasperated. The damn computer was identifying fertilizer, granite quarries, bananas, x-ray machines, welding rods and everything other than the damn bomb.

'Carry on towards the excavation site,' he ordered. 'That's our best bet.'

Suddenly the screen came alive.
Uranium-235.
700 million years.
Alpha, x-ray.
They had it! Uranium-235 gave off alpha rays, which had a half-life of 700 million years.

They were close to a source of enriched uranium. There was no alternative. They would have to evacuate the area immediately.

❦

Waziristan, North-West Frontier Province, 2012
'*Shukran li-l-láh*! Thanks be to Allah!' cried the Sheikh. 'Even though he is in the clutches of the Jewish scum, he has not forgotten his duty. Where is he?'

The messenger spoke up. 'I am given to understand that he has been whisked away to the Tel Megiddo prison nearby, where the Mossad agents are interrogating him.'

'Rascals! They would whore their own mothers to achieve their aims. So what do we do about the truck that is sitting there? The detonation codes are only with Ghalib.'

'Uh…Sheikh…It seems that he has already sent those to you in a previous dispatch.'

'Ah!' remarked the Sheikh. 'Ghalib, my Jihadi, you have made me proud.'

'Err…Sheikh…why do the rascals want Ghalib?'

'It's a long story. It begins in Jerusalem…'

❦

Vatican City, 2012
His Eminence was very clear. Successive American presidents had used Islam to counter the power of the Church while continuing to maintain a façade of innocence. Illuminati bastards! They needed to be taught a lesson.

The phone buzzed. Thomas Manning. He was speaking rather softly. The cardinal's face turned red as he heard Manning's words, '…captured…Megiddo…Mossad…no truck…in custody…'

His Eminence could control himself no longer. He screamed at Manning, 'Don't you realize what has happened? I wanted him alive. I compromised by allowing you to give him to me dead. The one man who could ruin our beloved Church is now in the custody of people who would like nothing better...those sons of bitches, the Illuminati!'

<hr />

Balakote, Indo-Pakistan Border, 2012
It was 11 p.m. when they reached Balakote. Yehuda was tired, but Swakilki remained alert and excited - like a hunter before the kill.

Yehuda pointed out Ghalib's tent from the distance. Swakilki took out the sharp Nepali Kukree knife from its sheath under her burqa and held it lovingly in her right hand. She then stealthily moved towards Ghalib's tent.

She could make out the dim light of a kerosene lamp inside, but there were no voices. Obviously he was asleep. She slit open the tent near the base and crawled in.

'Welcome Swakilki!' boomed the voices of Stephen Elliot and Prithviraj Singh as they quickly wrestled the knife out of her hands at gunpoint.

Standing some distance away, Yehuda smiled to himself. His Illuminati masters had paid him much better than the crumbs thrown his way by His Eminence.

One could not compare the thirty thousand transferred by Herr Egloff from Oedipus to Iscariot with the one million transferred from the UNL Militia to Iscariot.

UNL Militia was, of course, another anagram: Illuminati.

Yehuda got back into his Mahindra Commander 650 jeep and started the long drive back to Srinagar. He needed to catch an international flight to meet his compatriots, who were already in Frederick County.

<hr />

Priobskoye, Siberia, 2012
Zvi Yatom was speaking on a secure line with Stephen Elliot and Prithviraj Singh. With Ghalib in Israeli custody and with Swakilki in

Indian custody, it seemed that the two key protagonists were now under their control.

'So is the truck in place?' asked Stephen.

'Yes. The detonation will be triggered from Waziristan on December 21st, 2012 by the Sheikh. He has the detonation sequence. He thinks that Ghalib has managed to plant the device in Megiddo. He does not know that the device has been shifted secretly to Priobskoye,' explained Zvi.

Discovered in 1982, the Priobskoye oil field occupied an area of 5,466 square kilometres in the Khanty-Mansiysk Autonomous District of Western Siberia. It was Russia's largest oil field. After Saudi Arabia and the United States, Russia was now the third largest oil producer in the world.[clxxxviii]

The explosion would decimate Russian oil production, leaving the largest oil reserves in the hands of Saudi Arabia and America. Oil reserves owned mostly by Illuminati-controlled companies.

Killing many birds with one stone was the specialty of the Illuminati.

Chapter Twenty-Seven

Goa, India, 2012

Vincent and Martha were inside the Basilica of Bom Jesus. Vincent was determined not to give up so easily. He had with him the piece of paper that Swakilki had flung at his face on the night of his kidnapping.

He looked at the last line:

> *Remember: It is enough, O Lord, it is enough, the two angels said. Mastrilli without doubt made the best silver bed. But to carefully guard a secret of the dead. Ignatius' gold cup is better than a silver head.*

And then it struck Vincent.

The tomb of St Francis Xavier was a three-tiered bier that had been financed by the Duke of Tuscany in exchange for the pillow on which St. Francis Xavier's head had slept for several years after his demise. On top lay the silver casket containing Xavier's remains. The casket had been assembled by local silversmiths under the guidance of Father Marco Mastrilli.

The casket was crowned by a cross with the figures of two angels holding the message "*Satis est, Domine, Satis est,*" meaning 'It is enough, O Lord, it is enough!'

These words were believed to have been the most common utterances of Saint Francis Xavier.

What the lines seemed to suggest was that the secret was not with the angels or the casket, but with St. Ignatius.

Vincent looked towards the main altar of the church. The Blessed Sacrament that had earlier been kept on the main altar under the statue of St. Ignatius was now preserved in a gold tabernacle. The infant Jesus was shown under the protection of St Ignatius of Loyola, the Founder of the Society of Jesus. The statue of St. Ignatius was almost three meters high.

But to carefully guard a secret of the dead. Ignatius' gold cup is better than a silver head.

The baby Jesus was depicted as being under the protection of Ignatius. The infant child was dressed in white and was superimposed on a red background. Vincent knew that he would have to climb up on the altar to check it more thoroughly.

As he stood up to balance himself, he took the support of the massive gilded goblet upon which the statues had been supported. He was shocked to find that it was entirely hollow.

Ignatius' gold cup is better than a silver head.

He stood on his toes to peer inside the mammoth goblet and began feeling within its inner surface for any inconsistencies. The inner surface was smooth, unlike the heavily engraved outer surface.

Suddenly his hand felt a crack. It was not a natural formation. It was a straight line. As his hands moved down the straight line, he found another line running at ninety degrees to the first. On a hunch, he followed the next line to find yet another. He was right! There was an inner secret panel!

'Just what do you think you are doing?' the voice echoed through the depths of the church. Vincent and Martha turned around in shock.

It was Father Dias, the priest, extremely agitated to find that his altar and sacraments were being desecrated in this rude fashion.

Vincent hastily scrambled down and apologized, 'I am sorry, Father. I am also a priest and had heard so much about Bom Jesus that I wanted to observe him from as close as possible. Please accept my apologies.'

'If you are a man of God, then you should know better than to be disrespectful to the traditions of the church!' argued Father Dias. However, his tone had mellowed. 'I will forgive you just this once. Please be more careful in future.'

The two culprits beat a hasty retreat. Once outside the church, Martha asked Vincent anxiously, 'Why were you so engrossed with the goblet? Did you find anything?'

Vincent replied, 'There was a panel inside it. As I was feeling around inside, the Father's voice jolted me and I ended up pressing it hard out of fright. I had no idea that the panel had a spring action and this piece of paper would fall into my hand!'

'Ah! I see. That's why you could afford to be so apologetic,' commented Martha sarcastically.

The two of them looked at the delicate parchment in Vincent's hands. It read:

> *Do leste-Occidental ou Nort-Sul Que diferença faz?*
> *Rozabal de Kanyar dorme quietamente, porque Yuz Asaf não é*
> *uma falsificação. Tentativa 34.09° N 74.79° E.*

Translated to English, it meant:

> *East-west or north-south. What difference does it make?*
> *Rozabal of Kanyar sleeps quietly, because Yuz Asaf is no fake.*
> *Try 34.09° N 74.79° E.*

***

Srinagar, Kashmir, India, 2012

The onset of winter in idyllic Kashmir meant that the days were gradually getting shorter. Even though it was only three o'clock in the late afternoon, it felt like night was rapidly falling. Icy winter winds, having wafted through the numerous apple and cherry orchards of the area, brought a spicy and refreshing aromatic chill to Vincent's nostrils. The leather jacket and lamb's wool pullover underneath it were his only comfort as he knelt at the tomb to pray.

Martha had stayed back in Goa, but Vincent had refused to lose another day.

He rubbed his hands together to keep warm as he took in the sight of the four glass walls, within which lay the wooden sarcophagus. The occupant of the tomb, however, was residing below in an inaccessible crypt. Standing in front of a Muslim cemetery, the tomb was located within an ordinary and unassuming structure with whitewashed walls and simple wooden fixtures.

The sign outside informed visitors that the Rozabal tomb in the Kanyar district of old Srinagar contained the body of a person called Yuz Asaf. Local land records acknowledged the existence of the tomb from 112 A.D. onwards.

The word Rozabal, derived from Kashmiri term *Rauza-Bal*, meant "Tomb of the Prophet". According to Muslim custom, the gravestone had been placed along the north-south axis, however, a small opening revealed the true burial chamber beneath. Here one could see the sarcophagus of Yuz Asaf. It lay along the east-west axis as per Jewish custom.

East-west or north-south. What difference does it make? Rozabal of Kanyar sleeps quietly, because Yuz Asaf isn't a fake.

Nothing was out of the ordinary in this place. Nothing except for a carved imprint of a pair of feet near the sarcophagus. The feet were normal human feet. Normal, except for the fact that they bore marks on them; marks that coincided with puncture wounds from a crucifixion.

Crucifixion had never been practised in Asia, so it was quite obvious that the resident of the tomb had undergone this ordeal elsewhere in some distant land.

Vincent respectfully took off his shoes and walked inside the simple structure. The old caretaker looked up at him and smiled, 'Ah! You have finally come.'

Vincent was too shocked to speak. He regained his composure and then said, 'I think you are mistaking me for someone else, sir.'

'No. I know who you are. You are the genie.'

Vincent was convinced that the old man had gone senile. 'What?' he asked.

'The genie. The one who will reveal all. The last visit here was by a Russian man. Dmitriy Novikov was his name. He found a document here. It was written in Aramaic and was buried in a copper tube along with Hazrat Yuz Asaf,' said the wrinkled face.

'So why are you waiting for me?' asked Vincent.

'Because he left the original as well as a translation for you.'

'But Novikov would have been here in 1887. That's 125 years ago. He could not possibly have met you.'

'Ah. You are right. He met my great-grandfather. Our family has been caring for this site over many generations. We have fought legal battles to remain in custody of this shrine.'

'And the document?'

'Here. Take it. It is now your responsibility. My ancestors and I have done our duty,' he said emphatically as he handed over an extremely old copper tube to Vincent.

Vincent carefully unscrewed the cap and gently pulled out three documents. One was a very thin and old papyrus written in a language that he could not understand. The other two documents, while aged, were in good condition and were written in English.

The first was a letter:

I, Dmitriy Novikov, had set out on a historical quest to determine whether Jesus had lived in India. When I succeeded in my efforts, I was branded a liar and a traitor.

What I revealed to the world was only one part of my story: The translations of the documents that I discovered at the monastery in Hemis that spoke about a young boy, Issa, who had fled Judea to come and live and learn in India.

But as I dug deeper, I realized that the manuscripts were merely one single piece of the puzzle. There was a wealth of information available from multiple Hindu and Buddhist sources. This led me to the Church of Bom Jesus where I found the clues provided by Alphonso de Castro, and finally to Rozabal, where Castro had buried the document that he had discovered entitled the 'Tarikh-Issa-Massih', 'The History of Jesus the Messiah'.

It was here that I discovered that the four gospels of the Roman Catholic faith do not do justice to the wealth of knowledge that Jesus Christ, our Lord, had imparted to mankind. While many gospels, including Gnostic ones will be discovered in the due course of history, I am sure that the following document was written by Yuz Asaf before his death in Kashmir around 115 A.D.

261

Upon reading it, I immediately realized that it contained teachings and observations, as well as prophecies, and these were meant for another yet to come. It was not for me to reveal these to the world, but for someone else still to come - the genie.

The fact that you are reading this document means that this chosen person is you. Please use it wisely.

Dmitriy Novikov, Srinagar, May 21ˢᵗ, 1887

The letter was followed by the papyrus as well as an English translation of its contents that had possibly been made by Castro or Novikov:[clxxxix]

i.   *In the reign of Shalivahana, the king. tidings of peace to Kashmir did I bring.*

ii.   *Issa-Massih and Miryai, my wife; bearing La Sara Kali, oh delicate life*

iii. *My deeds, words and spirit were completely pure, Yuz-Asaf, was my name that in this land endured*

iv.   *Born of a virgin, son of a God, peeling for truth the pea from the pod*

v.   *I helped the king repair the Solomon throne, grateful king put my name in stone*

vi.   *People flocked to hear my tales, parables and stories rarely fail*

vii. *But twelve years later I told my wife, I fear for our daughter's and her life*

viii. *Take her away to the land of Gaul, so that my blood may course through the veins of all*

ix.   *Here in Kashmir, I can live alone, and when I die, I'll rest skull and bone*

x.   *I am Krestos, the Christ, the anointed one; I have travelled my life and can no longer run*

xi.   *Benjamin-David blood is royal, our followers moan; but when we are dead, we are just skull and bone*

xii.	*Knowledge is light, and light is pure, illuminate yourself O those impure!*
xiii.	*Cast aside divisions and throw away the books, which make you see others with suspicious looks*
xiv.	*From the land of the sun, his master shall call; and the false prophet shall forget goodness and fall*
xv.	*To the lowest depths of hell he shall take, mankind to fire and boiling blood he shall make*
xvi.	*Do not mistake him for my message of love, though he may dress as white as a peaceful dove*
xvii.	*And pay no heed to those who use my name, to build churches and mortar to further their aim*
xviii.	*I am not worthy of titles, honours, or grace; the one who is worthy is the mirrored face*
xix.	*Stand by the mirror and look at yourself; you are the anointed, within yourself*
xx.	*What say you of Benissa, Yushua, Jabbal and Akub? What say you of Abihud, Elnam, Harsha and Jashub?*
xxi.	*These are mere names that history will record; and tomes will be written until you are bored*
xxii.	*Does it matter whether I had sons or daughters? Does it matter whether I was saved from the slaughter?*
xxiii.	*Does it matter whether I was married or not? Does it matter whether I was God's son or a fault?*
xxiv.	*Oh mankind, think beyond these things so small; and focus your mind on the oneness, the all*
xxv.	*To understand that priests of the temple are mere men; who pray not from the heart but from the pen*
xxvi.	*Buddha, Krishna, Mithras, Horus and Tammuz; Essenes, Pharisees, and Zealots are Jews*
xxvii.	*After me, many divisions shall arise; I pray that my Lord, my father makes you wise*
xxviii.	*When people tell you that Christ is arisen; understand that your body is merely a prison*
xxix.	*And everyone who one day dies, must necessarily also have his soul arise*

xxx.	And with each lifetime that passes, your soul learns more in life's classes
xxxi.	And it understands the futility of it all; it gets filled with love, love and love, that's all
xxxii.	In my name wars will be fought, in may name honours will be sought
xxxiii.	In my name books will be written, in my name bread will be bitten
xxxiv.	Simon of Cyrene was greater than I; he bore the cross of a passer-by
xxxv.	He is worthy of the knowledge that I convey, this document will rest till it's again his day
xxxvi.	Men shall fight crusades for my city; keepers of my church will kill without pity
xxxvii.	Illuminated ones will say that they know it all; they will wait for Jerusalem and Rome to fall
xxxviii.	The woman will be called the evil one; her temptations through lives must come undone
xxxix.	But after many cycles of birth and decay; the devil inside, the soul will slay
xl.	And that day her soul will shine like a star, and be transplanted to a manger in a land afar
xli.	She could be the next teacher, respected by all; or the next Queen Sara, nursing her doll
xlii.	One day the stone of Rozabal will rise, and will expose the treachery and the lies
xliii.	Over this document will be earth and stones; and a decaying pile of skull and bones
xliv.	Jerusalem, Mecca, Constantinople and Rome, are anything but a peaceful home
xlv.	Wise elders will scream from the pulpits up high, The end is near, judgement is nigh
xlvi.	Why did I baptize your ancestors with water? To cleanse the spirit by a quarter
xlvii.	The remaining purification would be a test; to leave the comfort of the nest

xlviii.   *Who says Pagan Gods are fake? For heartfelt prayer, the stone will shake*

xlix.   *The power is within you, don't you see? How does it matter if it's also in me?*

l.   *And who cares where I learnt, India or Egypt; and whether I raised Lazarus from the crypt*

li.   *Why would I make water into wine, when water quenches the thirst just fine?*

lii.   *Why would I make a blind man see, when those who have eyes cannot feel me?*

liii.   *Why would I walk on water, I pray, when a boatman could take me most of the way?*

liv.   *The real miracle is in knowing yourself, and understanding the Brahman, the endless, the self*

lv.   *Brahma and Abraham are one and the same; glorious and endless - an eternal flame*

lvi.   *And comprehending the wonder and miracle of life, the end is not the end, even with a knife*

lvii.   *They will say that I will bring judgement day; blood, flood, locusts, Armageddon and away*

lviii.   *Ask yourself why I would kill my father's child; a sibling is a sibling, no matter how reviled*

lix.   *Man and woman, wet and dry; dark and fair, low and high*

lx.   *There are two sides to every coin; opposites, which at the hip must join*

lxi.   *Why say you that he is bad or good? He is one side that see you could*

lxii.   *God loves his flock like a father his child, no matter how reckless, careless or wild*

lxiii.   *He does not pronounce death or cross to bear; as reward he frees the soul, gives fresh clothes to wear*

lxiv.   *I hate not Caiaphas, Sanhedrin, Judas or Pilate; these were mere lessons destined in my fate*

lxv.   *I adore not my mother, my wife or daughter; because the wickedest can be cleansed when baptized with water*

lxvi.	Gospels will be written, why must they be four? Ask the church fathers, are they sure?
lxvii.	And so what if I kissed Mary on the mouth? Love is all, north and south
lxviii.	East and west, let love prevail; keep it not behind a veil
lxix.	And when you confess to your priest, will it matter in the least?
lxx.	Whether he has had a woman in his bed, as long as his spirit is alive not dead
lxxi.	And why should man think that he is supreme? When Sofia and Magdal can be queen
lxxii.	Does he have the power to make a child? Without woman or womb in his fashion styled
lxxiii.	And O children of Ishmael think before you say, can sword and battle really win the day?
lxxiv.	Why will you face Mecca when you pray? Nobility of heart will move Mecca your way
lxxv.	Hindu devotees pause as you pray, is there a contradiction in what you say?
lxxvi.	Look within and God you will find. How can an untouchable be less divine?
lxxvii.	Children of Abraham, if the Torah is truth; but an eye for an eye and a tooth for a tooth?
lxxviii.	Will not the whole world become blind? If Moses' laws tell you to be so unkind
lxxix.	Prophets will write of the anti-Christ, whose tongue will evil and hate entice
lxxx.	My children will lose their lives over me, my chosen twelve shall die, so it shall be
lxxxi.	There is no anti-Christ divined. The anti-Christ is in your heart and mind
lxxxii.	And why call a woman a harlot or whore, when my Magdala could be called one before?
lxxxiii.	Humans are mere puppets on a string, dancing to the tune that the Master sings

lxxxiv. *Hate them not for what they have done; restore their spirit so it may meet the sun*

lxxxv. *Illuminating light is peace not power; it is this sort of madness that brings down the tower*

lxxxvi. *And Doubting Thomas is not a bad thing; if you doubt, you without doubt think*

lxxxvii. *And if a man should kill millions of Jews; millions of his lifetimes will repent abuse*

lxxxviii. *And if one country should become the promised land; it could just as easily become desert sand*

lxxxix. *And why cast stones at murderers or others? These were people who were battle brothers*

xc. *It suits the powerful to use him one day, and call him evil when he is cast away*

xci. *Inquisitions will be held to make you recant, truthful words that are in supply scant*

xcii. *Witches and non-believers shall burn at the stake; the burners shall burn, make no mistake*

xciii. *December twenty-first, two-thousand and twelve, no end is near, no further delve*

xciv. *Because there is no beginning and no end; it's an endless road without a bend*

xcv. *Prophets, zodiacs and the stars; endless Gods you worship from afar*

xcvi. *But what about the God inside your heart? The one who knows your every part*

xcvii. *Do you light a candle for him? Or has the lighted candle gone dim?*

xcviii. *And if I needed to preserve a bone, I could just as easily have done my own*

xcix. *Burn it, bury it, feed it to vultures! Body destruction is a mere matter of culture*

c. *But the one thing you cannot hold back is the eternal spirit that keeps coming back*

ci. *They say I am a Yogi, a heightened soul; that even in crucifixion, I can console*

cii.	*I am indeed the Son of God; just like you, isn't it odd?*
ciii.	*That God should make all his children equal, and then make me greater, in sequel?*
civ.	*Stare as long as you want at the shroud; I will not appear, riding a cloud*
cv.	*Does it matter that it covered me, or that my blood is there for all to see?*
cvi.	*You take great pains to search for me, when I am within you, it's plain to see*
cvii.	*You will fight over land, fight over oil; you will fight over money, and resultant spoils*
cviii.	*And when you have fought and over the world have trod; realize in your heart that you could not destroy God*
cix.	*And why hate Judas for having betrayed me? It was his action, that divine it made me*
cx.	*Was it baptism or was it a Kumbh? Hieros Gamos or Mary's womb?*
cxi.	*Why should these things even concern you? When will my lessons ever discern you?*
cxii.	*When you will walk the moon one day; I am a mere speck, you shall say*
cxiii.	*Understand the infinite, the universe, the supreme; not even a pin-drop, your most ardent scream*
cxiv.	*And when you recall my sermon on the mount, hold your actions to account*
cxv.	*Am I Buddhist, Essene or Jew? Why at all should it matter to you?*
cxvi.	*Isn't it sufficient that I talk of love? And of a greater spirit above?*
cxvii.	*And instead of chanting the beatitudes, why can't you alter your attitudes?*
cxviii.	*And if a star above my manger lay; wasn't it also for others born that day?*
cxix.	*When Pilate asked 'Who goes free?'; Barabbas was none other than me!*

cxx.   *And when upon the cross I was nailed, like any human, I felt I had failed*

cxxi.   *'Eloi Eloi lema sabachthani' I wailed; with my wretched body firmly impaled*

cxxii.   *And when 'Talitha Koum' I had said, and the little girl had got up from her bed*

cxxiii.   *It was not me who cured her at all; it was my faith, spirit, God and all*

cxxiv.   *Miracles are things that happen each day; the greatest is the blessing when you pray*

cxxv.   *I need no temples and mortar and stone; I need only your awareness of spirit alone*

cxxvi.   *And if I could miraculously bake the bread, why can I not teach the dead?*

cxxvii.   *I am your brother, our source is the same; you may call me Lord, but that's just a name*

cxxviii. *Good people are those who recognize their sins; and see that one life ends and another begins*

cxxix.   *And when you are tired and feel the fear, and ignore my teaching and say the end is near*

cxxx.   *You are my genie, revealing me; use these verses as a key*

cxxxi.   *Many fishes I pulled out of the sea; many couplets I now bestow upon thee*

cxxxii.   *Take my shekels in your hand, see the pyramid in the sand*

cxxxiii. *See it better than the all-seeing eye, see it better than the bird up high*

cxxxiv.   *Count the steps up to the top, count the leaves and fruit in the crop*

cxxxv.   *Count the arrows to put them in slumber, count your armour of equal number*

cxxxvi.   *And when they have fallen, riddled with scars, make sure that they count the number of stars*

cxxxvii. *And when death knocks and destiny brings, shade and fan them with my wings*

cxxxviii. *My plumes on both sides will protect, count them over to be correct* cxxxix.   *Count the language inside the beak, count the language above the peak, now count me and my apostles meek*

cxl.   *And when you emerge and see the trees. Please do consider what will make you free.*

cxli.   *How many fish? One-Five-Three. How many disciples? Four by Three. How many angels? Four plus three. Thirteen Cycles. One and Three.*

cxlii.   *The Maya called it the Sacred Tree. I just call it the Sacred Three.*

cxliii.   *Brahma, Vishnu and Shiva are Three. Lakshmi, Kali and Saraswati. The third eye that the Hindus see. The lines of a triangle in trinity.*

cxliv.   *Christian, Muslim, Illuminati. The first two fight, the third waits to see. How much destruction can there possibly be?*

Vincent fell to the ground and kissed the pages reverentially. He then wildly dashed to the market where he could get the precious document photocopied.

Photocopying done, he started walking towards the bus terminal, hoping that he could catch the bus out of Srinagar into Delhi. He was so completely absorbed in his own private little world that he did not notice General Prithviraj Singh sticking the Mauser to his back.

Chapter Twenty-Eight

Srinagar, Kashmir, India, 2012
'Well done, Father Morgan. I knew I was right to involve you in this matter. We finally have the document that the Illuminati has spent the last two thousand years searching for!' exclaimed Prithviraj Singh, while continuing to hold the gun against Vincent's spine.

'You, General, are no better than Osama-bin-Laden. The terrorist, in fact, is merely a pawn that you move on your Illuminati chessboard!' hissed Vincent.

'So you think that I am evil, huh? And what about Opus Dei and the Crux Decussata Permuta? Do you think that any religion other than Catholicism would have been allowed to survive on earth if they had their way? And what about the true believers of Islam? You think they would have left non-believers alone? We are the only force that could keep these forces in check! How dare you judge me!' thundered the general.

Vincent shot back. 'You cannot fight fire with fire. The best way to fight a fire is with water, General. Instead, you and your cronies have been throwing fuel to keep the fires raging. It has been in your interest to keep the fires of hatred burning. Your approach is a thin veil that hides your greed for money and power. It is the powerful elite of this world that has created the Osamas of the world to further their own self-interest. You are a hypocrite.'

'Why are we arguing? Both of us were after the same thing. We have found it. Let us revel in the find,' said the general.

'But why should this document be of importance to you?'

'Because it is the very basis on which the Illuminati was founded. This document that you call the *Tarikh-Issa-Massih*, is actually the Gnostic Gospel of Jesus. It was written by Jesus sometime in the last few days of his life. When he was in Kashmir.'

'But I thought that the Illuminati was a recent creation. The Bavarian Illuminati came into existence in 1776. How can you say that this document could have anything to do with your organization?'

'Father Morgan, let me explain. Jesus did not die on the cross. In fact, his suspension on the cross was merely a "ritual slaying" that had to be performed by Mary Magdalene, the high priestess, the divine mother, as part of the sacred Hieros Gamos.'

'So how does this concern you or the Illuminati?'

'Jesus had already said that the illuminating light came from within. He was a great yogi, a great guru. But this aspect of his teaching would not have created a great religion. How would the Church have controlled its flock? So what did they do? They branded Mary Magdalene a prostitute. They killed Jesus on the cross. Instead of explaining the resurrection of the soul, they created the resurrection of Jesus' body. Instead of the Hindu Trinity, they created the Christian trinity of the Father, Son and Holy Ghost. Most important, salvation was to be obtained only through their Church!'

'I still don't get it.'

'Wake up, Father! Jesus talks in his gospel of opposites. Good must have bad. Hot must have cold. Positive must have negative. Male must have female, and so on. We, the Illuminati, decided that Christ must have an anti-Christ. This anti-Christ will bring down the Roman Catholic Church, once and for all!'

'But the same gospel that we have just found says that there is no anti-Christ! It says that illuminating light should be used for wisdom and inner peace, not power!'

'Ah! You now know why I need that document.'

'The words of Jesus have been twisted and perverted throughout history. You plan to do exactly that. I will not let history repeat itself!'

'Then you must die!'

Waziristan, Pakistan-Afghanistan Border, 2012

The Sheikh was looking at the message sent by Ghalib containing the detonation sequence. He re-read the words without a mirror once again and then proceeded to ignore characters other than O and I:

UOY.OT.HTAO.YM.MAMI.HO
OWT.MOTA.TA.MOTA.TIH.OT
HT33T.3HT.TA.MIA.HTUOM.3HT.TA.MIA
TA3H.TOH.3TIHW.HTIW.YAWA.MIH.TIH
3OW.OT.MIH.3IT.YOT.YM.HTIW.3YA
3WO.I.HTUOY.YM.MIHW.YHT.OT
3M.HTIW.TUO.MIH.HTIW.TUO
3M.3SIMOTA.OT.3MIT.YHT.TIAWA.I

The resultant series was:
00010 00010 101 01111 001101 01010 10110 100111.

These were binary numbers, just like the sort used by computers to transmit data. He took a pen and began converting the binary numbers to standard decimal numbers.[cxc] The result:

2-2-5-15-13-10-22-39

He now had before him the detonation sequence. He picked up the Thuraya satellite phone that would communicate with the device and began to carefully punch in the digits.

The digits entered by him were being transported to the geostationary Inmarsat satellite from where they would be bounced back to another phone on earth.

That phone would activate the bomb.

Not in Priobskoye, Siberia.

But in Waziristan, just a hundred yards away.

With a "capacity" of thirteen kilotons, the official yield estimate would later reveal only two kilotons of TNT equivalent in explosive force. Around a thousand people would be killed directly from the blast at the hypocenter and an equal number would be injured. The future impact would include nuclear fallout, cancer, and deformed or stillborn babies.

The damage would have been much greater if the bomb had been detonated in a populated area. The hilly region of the North-West Frontier Province used by the Sheikh and his master was in the middle of nowhere.

⌣⌥⌥⌥⌣

Frederick County, Maryland, 2012

Yehuda smiled a quiet smile of satisfaction. The whole world thought that Judas had betrayed Jesus. How ridiculous! Judas, in fact, had been the chosen one. The one who would perform the final act of an elaborate ritual.

Ensuring that the nuclear device exploded near the Sheikh and his master, this had been Yehuda's final act for his own master.

From the port at Pipavav, the truck containing the device had headed to Jammu. The truck had proceeded along the interstate Punjab-Kashmir border westwards and had stopped short of the town of Rajouri on the Indian side. From here it had crossed over into Pakistani territory and a few hours later it had reached Mirpur.

The truck had then moved northwards to Muzaffarabad and from there westwards to Mansehra. From Mansehra it had headed in a gentle southwesterly direction towards Peshawar in the North-West Frontier Province of Pakistan, where it had waited to cross the Khyber pass.

Before crossing the Khyber Pass, it had unloaded the "construction jig" near Waziristan and had continued towards Jalalabad on its long journey to Tel Megiddo.

Yehuda remembered Ghalib taking him aside one day and reciting to him the Islamic Hadith of Tirmidhi, 'And God's messenger said: "In the last times men will come forth who will fraudulently use religion for worldly ends and wear sheepskins in public to display meekness. Their tongues will be sweeter than sugar, but their hearts will be the hearts of wolves."'[cxci]

He had then quoted the Qur'an 6:112, '*Thus have We appointed unto every Prophet an adversary - devils of humankind and jinn - who inspire in one another plausible discourse through guile.*'

Ghalib had then said to Yehuda, 'It is in your destiny to be called a traitor. It is in my destiny to be called a terrorist. Why not make the best of the situation? It is better that both these men are destroyed, even if it means that we die in the process.'

'But why do you want me to "sell" you to Oedipus and the UNL Militia?' Yehuda had asked.

'I have a value. Isn't it better that the money is used to ensure that other orphaned children such as myself are not made into future terrorists? This will be my one good deed towards attaining bliss!'

'But, Barabba, why are we allowing these eleven events to happen all over the world? Why can't we stop it?'

'It is not in our control. You think that the instructions are from me?'

'Then who? The Sheikh? His master?'

'Yehuda, my friend, you have a lot to learn. You follow my orders. I follow the Sheikh's orders. The Sheikh follows his master's orders. Whose orders does the master follow?'

'I am not sure.'

'The Illuminati, my friend. You think that Islamic terrorism just happened one day without immense financial backing? It has been in the Illuminati's interest to keep the fires burning. It ensures that Illuminati-controlled companies make money. It ensures that defence contractors get orders. It ensures that the Catholic Church as well as puppet regimes of the Middle East are kept in check. It keeps India focused on Kashmir, Pakistan focused on India, China focused on Tibet, Russia focused on Chechnya, and the world focused on Osama.'

'I still do not understand why you want me to ask El-Azhar to betray you. This is going too far.'

'It is vital. Everyone needs me dead. It is vital that they must think that I am in custody. If this impression is not created accurately, the final result will not be what we want. These are very intelligent people! They have used me as an anti-Christ to artificially fulfil the prophecies of Nostradamus. They need to be handled very carefully.'

And then he had told him to "betray" him to the Japanese woman as well.

Sitting in his suite at the charming Country Inn on Frederick Road, he was feeling quite proud of himself for having followed Ghalib's instructions flawlessly. He was now here to meet with all the other eleven, and to explain to them the final words of Ghalib.

There was a knock on the door.

'Who is it?' he asked, as he headed towards the door.

'Room Service,' came the reply.

The waiter brought the tray and placed it on the coffee table in the sitting area.

Yehuda thanked the waiter and signed the room service bill, adding a generous tip. He always ensured that his tips were generous when he was travelling; it made the damn white man feel inferior!

He started to hand back the leather folder containing the signed bill and the tip when he realized that the waiter was not there.

The sudden tightening of a rope around his neck was when he realized that the tip had been of no use.

New Delhi, India, 2012

The Japanese woman was sitting in Tihar.

Tihar Jail, the largest prison in Southern Asia,[cxcii] was located in the western sector of Delhi, about eight kilometres away from Chanakya Puri, the diplomatic area of the Indian capital.

It was one of the largest prison complexes in the world and comprised of eight prisons in the Tihar Complex. With a total population of around 13,160 prisoners against a sanctioned prison capacity of 5,648, it was also one of the most overcrowded prisons in the world.

There were eight jail blocks in the complex numbered CJ-1 to CJ-8. The lodging arrangement in the various blocks, located over 400 acres, was according to the court cases, and then according to alphabetical ordering of names.

Swakilki was in CJ-6, the women's block.

A special facility was provided to foreigners to have interviews with the diplomats of their countries on any working day between 4:00 p.m. and 5:00 p.m. The Japanese representative was meeting Swakilki in the office of deputy superintendent of the jail, located near the entrance.

His demeanour was polite and respectful. Typically Japanese.

'*Konbanwa*,' he said to her. '*O genki desu ka?*' he enquired to find out how she was.

'*Hai, genki desu*,' replied Swakilki. 'I am fine.'

'Do you need anything?' he enquired.

'I need to confess. Get me a priest,' she said simply.

<hr/>

'Bless me, Father, for I am about to sin. It has been a month since my last confession.'

'My child, I cannot absolve you of a sin that has not yet been committed.'

'Yes, but I am about to kill a man. And I have already sinned.'

'How can you say that? You have not yet killed him, and you call it a sin?'

'I should have killed my father years ago. That is my sin - not having killed him yet. Oh my God, I am heartily sorry for having offended Thee. I firmly resolve, with the help of Thy grace, to sin no more. Amen.'

There was a startled pause. The priest recovered and continued, 'But why would you want to kill your own father, my child?'

Swakilki began.

'My mother had always brought me up to believe that I had inherited unusual powers. Unfortunately, I lost her at the age of six and many of my childhood memories were repressed.'

'Do go on.'

'Among the repressed memories were those of my mother's death; as well as memories of my father. I now remember the man who used to visit our house often. My mother used to say that I was descended from a long line of high priestesses…my father would laugh and say that he would prove her wrong.'

'And?'

'He had her killed. He made it look like a gas leak. He had me orphaned to teach the protectors of the divine feminine a lesson.'

'What was his name?'

'Alberto Valerio.'

'And yours?'

'Swakilki. It's derived from *Sara Kali*.'

'How do you know this?'

'I had forgotten that my lineage was far older than that of the Church. In Goa, I secretly met a Hindu priest, Pandit Ramgopal Prasad Sharma. He is a proponent of the *Bhrigu Samhita*. By merely looking at me, he told me of a little girl born in Kashmir. She was bestowed great power by the divine goddess and her mother, Mary Magdalene. She left India when she was twelve.'

'So how is this connected to you?'

'Her name was Sara Kali.'

***

Les Saintes-Maries-de-la-Mer, France, 42 A.D.

In the town of Les Saintes-Maries-de-la-Mer in France, each May 23rd-25th continued to be celebrated in honour of Saint Sarah, also known as La Sara Kali.[cxciii]

The festival had its roots in an event that had happened here in 42 A.D. A boat had arrived here carrying Mary Magdalene along with a twelve-year-old, dark-skinned child. The name "Sarah" was the equivalent of Princess in Hebrew. Joseph of Arimathea was the protector of the Sangraal, the royal bloodline of Jesus and Mary. The chalice that carried this bloodline was the "Holy Grail", the uterus of Mary Magdalene.

Hence the festival for La Sara Kali.

Chapter Twenty-Nine

Camp David, Maryland, USA, 2012

The President was at the official 125-acre retreat in the centre of Catoctin Mountain Park in Frederick County.

Seated on an oversized leather Lazy-Boy in front of a roaring fire, the President was angrily listening to a briefing from Stephen Elliot.

'We never knew that the truck that was transported to Priobskoye aboard the CH-54 was just a dummy. The bastard had placed the real one near Waziristan.'

'We needed Osama-bin-Laden to remain alive. His presence justified many other actions on our part, including the continued American presence in Pakistan,' said the President.

'The immediate problem that we now have to deal with is Ghalib. If he starts singing about how the Illuminati controlled his puppet strings all these years, the repercussions would be severe...particularly in view of the elections...' added Stephen, rather unnecessarily.

'There are only two possible actions. Illuminate or Eliminate,' said President Alissa Elliot, the 44th President of the United States of America, the very first woman to hold the position.

Tel Megiddo, Israel, 2012

Sometime in 2005, Israeli archaeologist, Yotam Tepper, had excavated the ruins of a church dating back to the third century, a period of history when Christians were still being persecuted by Rome.[cxciv]

Yotam Tepper would find a large mosaic with a Greek inscription consecrating the church to Jesus Christ. The mosaic was in surprisingly good condition. The mosaic had images of fish, an ancient Christian symbol. Experts seemed to be inclined to believe that the site could possibly be the oldest Christian church in Israel.

The ruins were located within the boundaries of the military prison, in which Ghalib was being held.

An inscription inside the church ruins spoke of a Roman soldier, Gaianus, who had contributed money to have the mosaic executed.

Just under the inscription lay the lifeless body of Ghalib-bin-Isar.

Gaianus from another lifetime.

His hands were outstretched on either side and his feet were tied together.

He had been crucified. Paradise awaited.

Actually, a coffin and an international flight waited to take his body to its final resting place.

⚊⚊⚊

New Delhi, India, 2012

The judicial process in India was notorious for delays. Swakilki was awaiting trial before the Tis Hazari Courts of Delhi.

Bittu Singh, her jailer, had been easy to bribe. Bittu had found out that she was to be taken to court in an armoured van at 11:00 a.m. The walk from her cell to the van was approximately two hundred metres and involved two security gates at varying intervals.

She felt the sharp two-inch miniature Nozaki knife inside her clenched fist that was now bleeding from holding it. The knife had been helpfully procured by Bittu. Swakilki was just ten feet away from the van, duly cuffed and chained to her handlers.

Suddenly she lunged for the guard on the left and deftly brought the Nozaki to his throat. Swakilki held the knife to her handler's throat and hissed, 'I will not hesitate to kill you if anyone moves!'

Still holding the knife to his throat, she deftly bent down and with her free hand reached for the keys that dangled from his belt as the other handler looked on helplessly. She pulled off the entire ring and expertly unlocked the chains that were holding her in captivity. She threw the keys to the ground and held the guard in a vice-like grip from behind, all the while keeping the knife firmly in contact with the skin on his neck.

The sirens were blaring; the alarm had been sounded. All inmates were automatically being locked into whichever sectors they were currently in. The perimeter gate had also been locked automatically.

Guard reinforcements were running to the spot to secure the area, but they were hesitant to take a shot, given that their colleague was still in her captivity.

Swakilki quickly shoved him into the passenger seat of the van and clambered into the driver's seat. She picked up the 9mm pistol that had fallen on the ground from the guard's holster and held it to her handler's head with her right hand as she revved the engine.

The vehicle was a Tata diesel right-hand drive vehicle, tough, sturdy and ideal for Indian roads. She pressed her foot on the clutch, shifted the manual gearshift with her left hand, and slammed her foot on the accelerator. The truck lunged forward towards the outer perimeter gate.

One of the guards stood his ground in front of the gate and pointed his rifle at her, but it was too late. The truck knocked him down and ran him over before the gate came crashing down. Instant Karma.

***

Vatican City, 2012

His Eminence Alberto Cardinal Valerio was uncharacteristically worried. He paced up and down the marble floors of his office.

Brother Thomas Manning watched him as he shuffled along, hands clenched together behind his back.

'Why haven't we heard from her yet?' he asked as he sat down behind his desk. Almost immediately, he began tapping the dark wood irritably. His patience was running out.

The last few days had been very tiring. The capture of Swakilki was not good news. It left Vincent Morgan free to nose around. Moreover, who knew what she might reveal? The death of Ghalib, however, was a welcome relief. Damn the Illuminati! Creating an Islamic Jesus to appear as an anti-Christ! Jesus!

While Valerio had not really been happy to stitch together the nuclear deal for Ghalib, he had later realized that the location of the proposed destruction worked to his advantage. A nuclear explosion in Megiddo would prove the literal truth behind the words of the Bible. Continued success for Ghalib would mean increased Islamic terror around the world. Valerio was quite happy if there was stepped-up Islamic radicalism all over the world. It would only make Christians much more vulnerable, making them infinitely more devout. In fact, history recorded the Christian crusades as being an outcome of early Islamic victories.

Now, however, Valerio was justifiably furious. He did not know that Swakilki had escaped. He felt that his objectives were coming unstuck. Instead of getting their target, their agent was now in custody. The complications and their repercussions were just too hideous to contemplate, particularly if she began talking about the Crux Decussata Permuta.

'So...' he continued. Thomas Manning looked up from the deep burgundy armchair that he was ensconced in. 'So, you mean to tell me that we do not have the ability to get her out? Nor do we have the means of shutting up Vincent Morgan?' asked His Eminence.

'We do have the means, Your Eminence. Unfortunately this has now become a battle between the Crux Decussata Permuta and the Illuminati.'

'What power do the Illuminati have in that region?'

'Well, India presently has excellent relations with the current administration in the White House...and we all know that the White House is dominated by the Illuminati.'

'But why? What can they possibly want with Vincent Morgan?'

'Your Eminence! How can you even ask a question like that? It should be abundantly clear that the primary goal of the Illuminati over so many centuries has been to discredit the Church. They would use Vincent Morgan to do precisely that!'

'The American President's public image is that of a God-fearing Christian - a born-again.'

'Born again as a Bonesman, an Illuminati. Not as a Christian!'

'The Church is an institution that has been built over two thousand years. We cannot let it be destroyed. The Illuminati be damned! Now they have got their illegitimate offspring, those Satan-worshippers, Skull & Bones to do their evil work!' shouted His Eminence.

He got up abruptly and walked out of the room. He was on his way to the Archivio Segreto Vaticano, the Secret Archives of the Vatican. Thomas Manning hastily got up to follow him.

They quickly reached the entrance to the archives through the Porta S. Anna in via di Porta Angelica. They hastily walked inside and their conversation became hushed.

'What exactly are we looking for, Your Eminence?' whispered Manning.

His Eminence Alberto Cardinal Valerio looked Thomas Manning straight in the eye and said softly, 'Damage control. In the event that anything comes to light from the Bom Jesus papers, it is vital that these be discredited immediately.'

'And how would we do that?' asked Manning.

'Vincent and others will try to poke holes in the fundamental pillars of the Roman Catholic Church. Jesus did not die on the cross. There was no resurrection. He married Mary Magdalene. Mary had children.'

'So?'

'Our archives contain a family tree. A tree that talks about Mary Magdalene and her offspring till the present day. And just as the Priory of Sion has been attempting to protect Mary's bloodline, our group has been doing everything possible to destroy it, discredit it, discard it! That's how I came into contact with Aki Ogawa,' said Valerio.

'Who?' asked Manning.

'Swakilki's mother. She was descended from Mary Magdalene. I impregnated her - I broke my vows for the greater good,' explained Valerio.

'Why?' asked a bewildered Manning.

Valerio thought for a moment before replying. 'I thought that if I could get Mary Magdalene's bloodline to become staunchly Roman Catholic, discarding its beliefs in the sacred feminine, I would have achieved the greatest victory ever for our glorious Church. Swakilki does not know this.'

'But isn't it the theory that Mary and her offspring were taken to France by Joseph of Arimathea?' asked Manning.

'Officially speaking, there was no offspring. Off the record, yes, there was a bloodline. The problem was that acknowledging the bloodline implied that one would have to accept that Jesus had married Mary Magdalene. If one accepted that, then one might also have to accept that the crucifixion was nothing else but a pagan rite as part of the sacred marriage ritual, Hieros Gamos.'

'So the bloodline continued in France?'

'No. The sacred powers of the divine feminine could only be passed down from one female member to another. Mary Magdalene herself had derived these powers from a long lineage that could be traced back to the empire of Ashoka the Great, who had sent his missionaries to Egypt. Do you know the name of Ashoka's empire in India?'

'No. How is it relevant?'

'Ashoka's empire was called "Maghada".[cxcv] Can you now understand why Mary was Mary Maghada-lene? It was obvious that Jesus and Mary would go to India after having escaped death in Jerusalem. Over the next two thousand years, the bloodline of the divine feminine moved all over the world, including Europe, Asia and America.'

'And Ghalib? How could there be a bloodline of Christ existing in India if the only known offspring moved to Europe?' asked Manning incredulously.

'That was precisely the trick played on us by the Illuminati. Ghalib and his followers were an illusion. There was no bloodline left in India after Jesus died in Kashmir. But it was easy enough to create sufficient doubt in ordinary minds that a bloodline could exist even today. By creating an illusion that a descendant of Jesus Christ was now living in India as a terrorist, the Illuminati would succeed in bringing shame and dishonour to the Church. Just what they wanted.'

'But the *Tarikh-i-Kashmir* spoke of Jesus having married a woman, Marjan of the Sakya clan, at the insistence of King Shalivahana...it also spoke of several generations of children thereafter...'

'My dear Thomas, *Marjan* is merely another derivative of *Mary*. As regards the *Sakya* clan, you may not know this, but the Buddha was called *Sakya Muni*. Mary Magdalene herself was descended from this sacred lineage. So, what was being said was that Jesus married Mary Magdalene, nothing more, nothing less.'

'But why talk of a son called Benissa and his children then?'

'Think about it, Thomas. *Ben* merely means "son of", so Benissa means "son of Issa". A little too convenient! No, the line spoken about was fictitious. You know why? To draw attention away from the real bloodline, that of *La Sara Kali*.'

'But they could still discredit the Church if they get lucky on the Bom Jesus trail. Even if there is no bloodline left in India, the Bom Jesus papers could still show that Jesus did not die on the cross and that there was no resurrection.'

'Yes. And that's why we need Vincent Morgan to be out of their hands and in our own.'

'And the Islamic connection? Why did the Sheikh cooperate with you? Why was he willing to follow instructions conveyed by me to Bakatin?'

'Because it suited both of us. Just like Saladin the Great and Richard the Lionheart of the Crusades, we had to reach an uneasy agreement. He was happy to let Ghalib's men do their worst because it furthered his caliphate aims, even though the actions were Illuminati financed.'

'No, no...why was he willing to give up Ghalib?'

'Because he knew that Ghalib was not the bloodline. He struck a good deal with us. Genuine nuclear weapons for a fake anti-Christ!'

'And we were willing to allow a nuclear holocaust for a fake anti-Christ?'

'Well, a nuclear explosion at Megiddo suited me fine. It would prove the Bible prophecies to be true.'

'So for all this time, the Church has known that Jesus had actually married Mary Magdalene?'

'It was a ritual. Jesus had a secret dynastic marriage with Mary, who was a daughter of the tribe of Benjamin. It was a royal dynastic marriage of *King Jesus*. In such sacred marriage rituals, the goddess and land would be wedded to the king. The goddess would bring him wealth. She would then take care of him as a nurturer. This would be followed by a ritualistic symbolic slaying of the king, when the goddess would manifest her destructive force.'

'So did she actually slay him?'

'No. The slaying was symbolic. After the slaying, the king would be resurrected, depicting the multiple cycles of birth, death and rebirth.'

'But was Jesus actually crucified?'

'Well, that's really the core issue. If Jesus went through a sacred fertility ritual with Mary Magdalene, Hieros Gamos, then isn't it possible that the crucifixion and resurrection could have also been mere rituals? In fact, the raising of Lazarus from the dead could also have been a similar ritual.'

'So you don't believe that Jesus died on the cross?'

'Well, all indications are that he did not. Why did he faint when he was given a sponge of vinegar? He should have been revived. His fainting indicates that he was deliberately drugged. Why were his legs not broken? This would have accelerated his death. Why was Joseph of Arimathea allowed to take down his body? Why were herbs such as aloe vera and myrrh being used to heal his wounds if he was dead? Why were there Essene monks inside the cave? I'd say that there's enough evidence to indicate that he did not actually die.'

'If he did not die on the cross, then where did he go?'

'Well, indications are that he went to India. Jesus had derived many of his teachings from Essene and Buddhist thought. Mary's sacred powers and rituals were also from there. Also, Kashmir was a land that was occupied by one of the ten lost tribes of Israel. It would have been logical for him to return to his spiritual roots. Moreover, the discoveries by Dmitriy Novikov, Nicholas Notovich and other explorers in the late 1800s seemed to give further credence to the theory, leading to the discovery of the Rozabal tomb in Srinagar.'

'But one can't actually prove that the tomb is that of Jesus, can one?'

'No. But consider this. Even though the burial chamber is Islamic north-south, the actual body is a Jewish east-west. The word "Rozabal" is thought to have been derived from Kashmiri term *Rauza-Bal*, meaning "Tomb of the Prophet". But what if the term is derived from *Rose-a-Bal*? The Line of the Rose? What if Jesus' popularity in India was due to Mary Magdalene?'

'So the Roman Catholic Church has known this all along?'

'I'd say yes. The early years of the Christian faith were extremely difficult for the faith. There were multiple versions of Christianity being propounded. The Gospels were not merely the four canonical ones but also the various Gnostic ones such as those of Thomas, Philip, and Mary. Furthermore, Christianity needed a wider audience in Rome, and to that extent, it had to be brought more in line with existing pagan beliefs. Christmas Day. Easter Day. Weekly rest on Sunday. Resurrection. The divine nature of Jesus. These were elements that were liberally borrowed from various other characters and stories. Given the circumstances, what the Church fathers did was not wrong. It was the need of the hour to make the Christian religion sustainable, acceptable, marketable.'

'And Alphonso de Castro's discovery threatened to bring it all down?'

'Alphonso de Castro was an imbecile! He was sent to Goa to strengthen the Inquisition. Instead, he meddled with ancient texts and books. Unfortunately, he could not be recalled immediately because of his father's influence over Queen Maria I.'

'Why did he not go public with his find?'

'Well, I think he intended to but was dissuaded by his father. His father arranged a meeting for Castro with the Pope, and some secret deal was struck. The document went into the archives and Castro's family never ever had to work again - they were made wealthy for life. Castro left church life and settled down in England, where he married a young girl by the name of Patricia White. Their son, Herbert Castro, entered the lucrative opium trade between India and China. He soon became well acquainted with Samuel Russel, who had established Samuel Russel & Co. for trading opium between Turkey and China. Some years later, a cousin of Samuel, William Huntington Russel, set up the Skull & Bones society at Yale, a de facto chapter of the Bavarian Illuminati.'[cxcvi]

'Ah. So the Illuminati has always had access to Castro's secrets?'

'Unfortunately, yes.'

'Your Eminence, you seem to know virtually everything. We as your brothers in the Priestly Society of the Holy Cross have never questioned your directions or motivations - but this seems to be going beyond the line of duty.'

'Let me share a little secret with you. In the immediate aftermath of the death of Jesus, Mary Magdalene attempted to take over the leadership of the Christian faith by telling the other disciples that Jesus had communicated several matters to her alone. St. Peter and St. Andrew were not in agreement with her.'

'That is common knowledge.'

'Yes, but the Priory of Sion took it upon itself to protect the bloodline of Mary Magdalene. Around the same time, the *Crux Decussata Permuta* was created.'

'What is that?'

'*Crux* is Latin for cross, *Decussata* implies the "X"-shaped cross, and *Permuta* in Latin means inverted. As you know, St. Peter was crucified in Rome upon an inverted cross and St. Andrew was crucified in Achaea on an 'X'-shaped cross. The loyalists of Andrew and Peter decided that they needed to protect the Catholic Church from the pagan and Gnostic influences of Mary Magdalene and her continuing bloodline and created a secret society for this purpose. It was called the Crux Decussata Permuta.'

'And?'

'I am the last surviving member of the Crux Decussata Permuta.'

'Are you the only surviving member? No one else?'

'One died just recently.'

'Who?'

'The Sheikh.'

Jerusalem, 1192

The great Saladin had become Master of Jerusalem in 1187. Pope Gregory VIII reacted hastily and commissioned Richard the Lionheart to mount the third Crusade to recapture the holy city. Richard marched on Jerusalem in 1192 but was plagued with fever, hunger and thirst.

He appealed to Saladin to provide him with food and water. And Saladin obliged, but on one condition. Richard would need to convert to Islam.

A negotiated settlement was eventually reached. Five of Richard's ten men belonging to the secret Crux Decussata Permuta offered themselves for conversion.[cxcvii] They would allow themselves to be converted instead of Richard. Deal duly done, Saladin remembered his duty to help the needy as a devout Muslim. He sent frozen snow and fresh fruit to revive Richard and his men.

Richard eventually sued for a truce with Saladin under which Christian pilgrims would be free to visit the holy city without being troubled in any way by his Muslim brothers. They would be watched over by five Muslim guards - the ones who had been converted to Islam from Christianity.

The five converted Muslim men in Saladin's camp and the remaining five Christian men in Richard's camp continued to operate the Crux Decussata Permuta secretly. It suited them to have a secret organization with a foot in both camps, Islam and Christianity.

Islamic conquests encouraged devout behaviour among Christians and vice versa. Muslims and Christians alike saw each other as lesser evils than the "problems" of paganism, polytheism, abortion, and homosexuality.

A secret alliance between Christianity and Islam had matured.

'So who exactly was the Sheikh? Osama-bin-Laden?' asked Manning.

'No. Osama was a creation of the Illuminati. He created world terror and made the Illuminati ever more powerful around the world - in positions of government, banking, business, military and politics. He gave the Americans an excuse to police the world.'

"And the Sheikh?"

'The Sheikh was descended from the original five who had converted to Islam. All along, he tried to cooperate with us...

unfortunately, his master's cooperation was always with the Illuminati.'

His Eminence did not notice the two ropes snaking around his ankles. They suddenly tightened into two nooses and he was yanked off his feet. The ropes had been individually pulled from a terrace above.

In less than a minute, he was dangling upside down. Each ankle was firmly in a noose and his legs were spread apart because of the distance between the two ropes.

Seen from a distance, his body looked like an "X", but upside down, feet up, arms down. *Crux Decussata Permuta.*

The single sniper bullet wound to his genitals was causing immense bleeding and by the time that Manning was able to get help and bring his body down, he had already bled to death.

Swakilki had avenged her mother.

Chapter Thirty

Maryland, U.S.A., 2012
Stephen Elliot, Prithviraj Singh and Zvi Yatom were back in the darkened room of padded velvet.

The Grand Master, Alissa Elliot, spoke: 'Achaita, divine revelation. Rome will pass away, Jerusalem will burn and the reason will become broken. And my Law, the Law of Zión, will be acclaimed by the whole of humanity.'

'Achaita!' said all those gathered in unison.

'Oh illuminated, brothers and sisters, see what we have before us!'

'Achaita!'

The Grand Master, dressed in scarlet robes held the knife close to Vincent's heart. Vincent had been placed on the large black granite slab in the centre of the room.

'Elevate and proclaim the Light! The last of the Crux Decussata Permuta is finished. Our grand plan of Ghalib was successful, see the wealth the we have created due to his actions all over the world!'

'Achaita!'

'The truth must emerge. And the Church must crumble.'

'Zión! Zión! Zión! Zión! Zión! Zión! Zión! Zión! Zión! Zión! Zión! Zión! Zión!'

As Prithviraj saw the Grand Master's golden knife aimed at Vincent's heart, he saw a vision of Pandit Ramgopal Prasad Sharma flash before him.

'Son. The brother who died, took on your Karma to save you. You were destined to die, and he died for you. He has died or killed for you in previous lifetimes too. He has a karmic relationship with you...'

'Find the priest, my son...'

'And son...that brother, who died for you...You will know when you have to return the favour...'

The next few seconds were a blur. Prithviraj pulled out his .357 Magnum pistol and took a direct shot at the Grand Master. The consequences followed in slow motion.

The shot had been a perfect one, directly piercing the left ventricle of the heart. Because of the robes of the Grand Master, the blood was not visible to the others in the room. They were still chanting, 'Zión! Zión! Zión!'

In the din, no one had heard the shot. The Grand Master's right hand, which was holding the golden knife, fell limply to one side and the knife fell on the granite platform on which Vincent had been tied down.

Prithviraj lunged forward, grabbed the knife and desperately started cutting loose the ropes that held Vincent prisoner.

'Run!' he shouted.

Vincent was dazed. He remained frozen. Prithviraj used the knife to give Vincent a deep gash on his thigh, just to shock him into action. 'Run!' he shouted again.

This time Vincent got up and started moving towards the passageway. But it was too late. Stephen Elliot, Zvi Yatom and countless others had pulled out their guns and were shooting madly towards the table. Prithviraj went down in a flurry of bullets.

The karmic debt had been settled.

Luckily this bought Vincent some time. There were thirteen passageways. He blindly ran into one of them.

***

Vincent ran madly through one of the passages that led to an equally dark room. He froze when he looked at the sight before him.

In front of him was a clear glass window with a "shop window" display behind it, dimly illuminated. The rest of the room was dark so as to ensure that the entire focus was on the window. Behind the window was a corpse. The corpse had been mounted for display on an upside down cross. The body was that of Boutros Ahmad, Ghalib's man for South America.

The room had two exits other than the central passageway through which Vincent had entered. One was to the left of the display window and the other to the right of it. Vincent dashed through the left exit. It took him through a curving passage, equally dark and foreboding.

Within thirty seconds, he found himself in another room, identical to the first. The macabre display was even more ghoulish. Behind the glass pane was a corpse that had been arranged neatly on a bed. Prior to placing the body on the bed, it was evident that the body had been fried in oil. It belonged to Yahya Abdullah, Ghalib's trusted lieutenant in Chechnya.

Vincent's instincts were now on full alert. He could hear voices. The panic around the shooting of the Grand Master and the retaliation on Prithviraj had taken the attention off him, at least for a few moments. He had to find a way out of this nightmarish catacomb.

The third, fourth and fifth rooms were no better. In one of them, Vincent found the body of Yaqub Islamuddin, Ghalib's Jemaah Islamiyah operative in Jakarta, arranged on a chair and his head placed separately and neatly on a table nearby. The next room contained Kader Al-Zarqawi, Ghalib's head of Iraq operations, crucified on an 'X'-type cross. He had not been nailed, but tied down to it with his legs prised apart, causing a much slower and more painful death.

Vincent was going mad. He wanted to vomit. He doubled up to puke and felt that he was almost expelling his guts. As he came up for air, he was hit by an even more ghastly sight. In front of him lay the body of Shamoon Idris, Ghalib's key operative of the Islamic Jehad Council in North America, sawed in half with the battleaxe still positioned in his torso. The aim had been to create an accurate visual description of the manner of death.

Vincent screamed in terror as he fled through the passageway. It was of no use. The next room contained the crumpled corpse of Fouad al-Noor, head of the group's activities in England. He lay crumpled in a corner with a gaping wound in his side. He had been pierced with a lance.

By now Vincent had reached a point of no return. Terror had made him numb. He observed the body of Faris Kadeer, Ghalib's chief of the East Turkestan Islamic Movement, hanging upside down on a cross with a spear having split open his thigh.

The sight of Ataullah al-Liby, Ghalib's kingpin of the French Intifada, was unbearable. His body lay on a stone platform with a spear through his stomach, guts spilling out across the stone. The display of the corpse of Tau'am Zin Hassan, Ghalib's manager within the Darul Islam in Malaysia, was positively benign when compared with the others. His display had been organized in a manner such that he was seated on a chair, clutching a dart that had pierced his heart.

Vincent had lost count of the number of dungeon-like rooms that he had been running through. The sight that greeted him in this one was the worst of all. Bin Fadan, Ghalib's Jaish-e-Mohammed representative in India, had been arranged so that he was holding his own skin. He had been skinned alive.

Vincent felt faint. What was this place? How could they do this to human beings? He looked up and saw the body of Adil Afrose, Ghalib's chief commander of the Australia operation. His body lay separated from his legs, which had been viciously broken. He had then been clubbed and stoned to death, evidenced by a massive rupture to his skull.

The next room contained the lifeless body of Yehuda, most trusted aide to Ghalib, hanging with a noose around his neck.

Vincent ran through the exit and reached the thirteenth room. It contained the body of Ghalib. He lay crucified on a Roman Cross, with a crown of thorns on his head.[cxcviii]

The Illuminati had made sure that their grand plan would never be revealed to the world.

The Lashkar-e-Talatashar was dead.

The anti-Christ and his flock of twelve were dead.

Vincent finally passed out.

Rome, 67 A.D.

Peter lay dead on an upside-down cross. He had journeyed through Gaul and Britain before being imprisoned for nine months at Mamertime. He was crucified on the orders of the Roman Emperor at Nero's circus. He had requested that it be done upside-down so that the manner of his death would not be the same as that of his master.[cxcix]

Patras, Achaea, 69 A.D.

Andrew, the first apostle of Christ, had travelled through southern Russia, Byzantium, Thrace, Macedonia and Greece. In Greece, he was crucified in Sebastopolis by Aegeas, the governor of the Edessences, on his refusal to denounce Christ. The cross that he was crucified on was an "X", not a "T". He was not nailed but corded to the cross, causing much more suffering than normal. He died after three days. [cc]

Jerusalem, 44 A.D.

James had returned to Jerusalem after travelling to Spain and Portugal. On January 2nd, 40 A.D., the Virgin Mary had appeared before him on the bank of the Ebro River. James had then returned to Judea, where he had been decapitated by King Herod Agrippa I himself.

Patmos, Turkey, 110 A.D.

John, having cared for the mother of Jesus until her death, preached in Russia and Iran until he was exiled to Patmos, off the Turkish coast. He died in his bed at an old age, having worn out his body. He had been plunged into boiling hot oil by the Romans but had somehow survived the ordeal.

Hieropolis, Phrygia, 66 A.D.

Philip had succeeded in saving the life of the Roman proconsul's sick wife. This miracle had made her convert to Christianity. The political fallout was the wrath of the proconsul who told Philip to "denounce Jesus and save your life". Philip answered, "accept Jesus and save your soul". He was pierced through the thigh and then crucified upside down till he died. His daughters were also killed along with him in the same manner.

❦

Albana, Armenia, 68 A.D.
Bartholomew had journeyed through Turkey, Iran, India, Ethiopia, Persia and Egypt before reaching Armenia. Here he was "skinned alive" and subsequently beheaded.

❦

Mylapore, South India, 72 A.D.
Thomas Didymus was praying in the woods outside his hermitage when a hunter who belonged to the Govi clan aimed his poisoned dart and hit Thomas. The wound was critical and St. Thomas died on December 21st, 72 A.D.

❦

Ethiopia, 60 A.D.
Matthew had spent twenty-three years preaching in Ethiopia, Macedonia, Persia and Egypt. His death was ordered by King Hircanus, who sent his men to run him through with a spear.

❦

Ardaze, Armenia, 65 A.D.
Thaddæus had spent many years preaching in Mesopotamia. He was killed under Abgarus, king of the Edessenes in Berytus, by a lance through his side.

❦

Caistor, Lincolnshire, Britain, 61 A.D.
Simon Zelotes spent his life in Maurtania and Africa before he was martyred in Britain by a halberd, a battleaxe on a long pike handle. He was sawn in half.

Jerusalem, 33 A.D.

The "treasurer" of the twelve disciples, Judas Iscariot, flung the thirty pieces of silver that he had accepted for betraying Jesus at the feet of the Sanhedrin. He then went out and hung himself. The money was not accepted by the priests because it had become "blood money" and was, instead, used to purchase a plot of land for burying the poor. This would come to be known as the "Field of Blood".

Jerusalem, 62 A.D.

James the Just was killed because he did not deny the Lord. Ananias, the high priest, tried to force James to deny the Lord, but when he would not, he was thrown off the pinnacle of the temple, which caused his legs to break.

He was then clubbed to death.

Alexandria, Egypt, 61 A.D.

Mark, the evangelist interpreter of Peter, was dragged throughout the city of Alexandria for more than two days. His flesh was entirely raked off and hung from his body like rags. He died of blood loss.

Rome, 67 A.D.

Paul, originally known as Saul, one of the main persecutors of Christians, who had a change of heart when Jesus appeared before him in Damascus, was beheaded in Rome under the orders of Nero.

Washington D.C., U.S.A., 2012

The CNN newswoman was saying, 'Seventy-two hours ago, the President was accidentally shot and fatally wounded during a weekend hunting and camping trip with friends while in Maryland. The shooting occurred at about 5:30 p.m. on Saturday. Her husband, SAS Director, Stephen Elliot, who had been with the President when the accident happened said that investigations were ongoing, but that all indications were that it was certainly an accident.'

She continued, 'The President's Secret Service detail rushed with emergency medical assistance but death was almost immediate. The autopsy at Bethesda Naval Hospital confirmed that the cause of death was a shot from a .357 Magnum, which is sometimes used for deer hunting.'

The panoramic views of Camp David gave way to footage of the body lying in state as she continued. 'The body of the President was placed in the East Room of the White House from where it was sent on a horse-drawn caisson to the Capitol to lie in state. Thousands lined up outside the Capitol building to pay their last respects to the departed leader. Heads of government and heads of state from over a hundred countries are expected to attend the state funeral on Tuesday. After a funeral service at St. Matthew's Cathedral, the late President will be laid to rest at Arlington National Cemetery in Virginia. The Vice-President has assumed full executive powers and has declared Monday to be a national day of mourning.'

The commentary went on. 'The late President Alissa Elliot is survived by her husband, Stephen Elliot, SAS Director, and two children, Jeremy and Elizabeth. Her alma mater, Yale University, is also observing a day of mourning. Viewers will recall that Alissa had met her husband-to-be while they were still students at Yale.'

※

Vincent felt as though he were falling through space. He actually was.

As he fainted inside the thirteenth room containing Ghalib's body, the impact of his fall activated a secret panel in the carpeted floor.

Vincent fell through the hole like a sack of potatoes and landed with a thud in a brightly lit room.

Squinting, he saw that the room was entirely white. The entire ceiling was filled with pure white fluorescent lighting. Even the floor was covered in pure white tiles. The room seemed to be some kind of memorial. The stark walls had framed black and white photographs of presidents, prime ministers, generals, businessmen, actors, scientists, and diplomats. Loyal and committed members of the Illuminati down the ages.

At one end was a door without a handle. Vincent tiptoed towards it and visually inspected it. He then tried nudging it open but found that it was an armoured door that was firmly sealed shut. On the right side was a numerical keypad that probably controlled access through the door. Just above the keypad was the reverse side of a single one-dollar bill, duly laminated. Vincent looked at it, confused, until it struck him!

He pulled out the crumpled copy of the document that he had discovered at the Rozabal shrine from his inside pocket.

You are my genie, revealing me; use these verses as a key.

Vincent thought to himself. Could it be? Could it actually be used as a key? He had nothing to lose.

Take my shekels in your hand, see the pyramid in the sand. See it better than the all-seeing eye, see it better than the bird up high. Count the steps up to the top, count the leaves and fruit in the crop.

Vincent looked at the one-dollar bill, the modern world's *shekel*. There indeed was a pyramid. The pinnacle of the pyramid had a single "all-seeing" eye. Next to it was the American bald eagle - the bird up high. Vincent began counting the steps on the pyramid. Thirteen. The eagle holding two branches in its talons. One branch had leaves. The other had fruit. Vincent counted the leaves and the fruit. Thirteen each!

Count the arrows to put them in slumber, count your armour of equal number. And when they have fallen, riddled with scars, make sure that they count the number of stars. And when death knocks and destiny brings, shade and fan them with my wings. My plumes on both sides will protect, count them over to be correct.

Vincent looked more closely at the eagle's talons. It was also holding arrows. Vincent counted them. Thirteen! The eagle also held an armoured shield. Vincent counted the armoured bars on the shield. Thirteen! Above the eagle was a cloud containing stars. By now, Vincent knew what to expect; nevertheless, he counted the stars. Thirteen. He then looked at the eagle's wings. He carefully counted the plumes on each side, right and left. Thirteen each.

Count the language inside the beak. Count the language above the peak. Then count me and my apostles meek.

Vincent looked at the eagle's beak. It was holding a banner that read *E Pluribus Unum*, meaning, "Out of Many, Emerges One". Thirteen letters.

He then saw the Latin motto above the pyramid's peak, *Annuit Coeptis,* meaning, "God has favoured our undertaking". Thirteen letters.

Thirteen steps of the pyramid. Thirteen leaves on one branch. Thirteen fruit on another. Thirteen arrows held in the talons. Thirteen bars on the shield. Thirteen stars in the clouds. Thirteen plumes in the right wing. Thirteen plumes in the left wing. Thirteen letters in 'E Pluribus Unum'. Thirteen letters in 'Annuit Coeptis'.

Jesus and his twelve apostles. Thirteen.

Vincent hurriedly punched in thirteen into the numeric keypad eleven times and watched the door slide open silently.

The First Continental Congress had requested that Benjamin Franklin, along with a team develop the Seal for the United States. It took them four years to accomplish this task and another two years to get it approved.

The back of the United States' one-dollar bill has a seal that depicts a pyramid. Very few would notice that the pyramid on the bill was a Masonic symbol, a pyramid of thirteen progressive levels. The number thirteen was present not only in the thirteen steps of the pyramid. There were thirteen stars above the eagle, thirteen bars on the shield, thirteen leaves on the branch, thirteen fruits, thirteen arrows.[cci]

Just like the Lashkar-e-Talatashar, the Army of Thirteen.

The base of the pyramid had the year 1776. The American public thought that it was the year in which the American declaration of independence had been signed.

Actually it was the beginning of the final cycle of the Maya long count calendar.

More important, it was the year in which Adam Weishaupt had created the Illuminati.

The base of the pyramid had the motto "Novus Ordo Seclorum" which, from Latin, translates to "New Order of the Ages".

Much like the objectives of the Illuminati.

Creating a new world order.

Chapter Thirty-One

Vatican City, 2012

Thomas Manning was in the corridors of the Ospedale Bambino Gesu, the hospital within the Vatican premises. His Eminence had been rushed to the hospital, but had been pronounced dead upon arrival.

He had been pacing up and down the corridors for over three hours. A kindly nurse, Sister Maria Esperanza, a beautiful young nun of mixed blood, brought the immensely fatigued man a cup of steaming hot espresso.

Thomas did not know that Sister Maria Esperanza had a special recipe for Espresso.

She would grind the best Lavazza beans using a good burr grinder. She would then fill the double shot filter basket without pressing the ground coffee down. She would level off the loose ground coffee by sliding a straight finger across the top. Then she would expertly "tamp" the coffee, using a solid handheld tamper and around thirty pounds of force. Having fitted the filter handle, she would extract the steaming hot espresso shot into the cup that already contained her special ingredient, a spoonful of 1080.

Compound 1080 or sodium monoflouroacetate was a water-soluble chemical used primarily to kill coyotes. It was a colourless, odourless, tasteless poison. One teaspoon could kill up to a hundred adult humans. There was no antidote.[ccii]

Sister Maria Esperanza made the best coffee in town. The funny thing was that no one in the hospital knew her name. Father Thomas Manning was unable to thank her.

Swakilki didn't care. She slipped out of the nurse's uniform, got back into her own clothes, mounted her Honda Spazio scooter, and headed over to Leonardo da Vinci Airport.

Islamabad, Pakistan, 2012
He was sitting inside the *Aiwan-e-Sadr*, the official residence of the President of Pakistan. The President was looking at the transcript of a phone conversation between the chief of Pakistan's Inter-Services Intelligence and Stephen Elliot of the SAS.

Why is this man so important to them? he had thought about Ghalib some nights earlier, as he sipped his evening Scotch and soda.

Now he knew.

His goddamn chief of intelligence and those American bastards wanted to justify their extended presence in Pakistan by ensuring that trouble continued to be stirred.

Enough!

He decided that it was time to have a Scotch and soda evening with Yunus Qazi.

The Directorate for Inter-Services Intelligence, known as the ISI, wielded immense power in Pakistan. The ISI was responsible for surveillance, interception and espionage, as well as the security of Pakistan's nuclear programme.

The ISI's power had been consolidated in 1988 when Pakistani President Zia ul-Haq had commenced Operation Tupac. Operation Tupac was an action plan for the control of Kashmir. The ISI was responsible for creating and training at least six major militant organizations, with approximately 5,000 and 10,000 armed men of Indian-Kashmiri origin, who would plague Indian authorities for the next few decades.[cciii]

The Director General of the ISI, Mahmood Durrani, ran his organization ruthlessly. Under him, his three Deputy Director Generals in charge of the Political, External and General divisions had to be constantly on call.

Mahmood Durrani was a veteran. Under him, the ISI had played a pivotal role in the CIA-sponsored Mujahideen war to push the Soviets out of Afghanistan in the 1980s. The CIA had assigned the responsibility of training and money distribution to the ISI, which trained about 83,000 Afghan Mujahideen and sent them off to Afghanistan to fight.

The plan had gone one step further. The CIA had decided to use the ISI to promote the smuggling of heroin into Afghanistan with a view to turning Soviet troops into addicts. Mahmood Durrani had executed the plan with his usual ruthless precision. He had even ensured the takeover of Afghanistan by the radical Islamic Taliban regime after the fall of the Soviet-backed government in Kabul in 1992.

Mahmood Durrani had played a very important role in all of this. His rise had been partly due to the constant backing and support of an equally enthusiastic Executive Director of the CIA.

The late President of the United States of America, Alissa Elliot.

Mahmood Durrani had been constantly in touch with Ghalib's Thuraya satellite phone on behalf of the President. Mahmood Durrani enjoyed an extremely cosy relationship with Stephen Elliot of the SAS too. Mahmood Durrani had to go.

Yunus Qazi, his Deputy Director General - Political, was just the man for the job.

Mahmood Durrani had been escorting Stephen Elliot and Zvi Yatom from the Pindh Ranjha International Airport to the suite at the luxurious Islamabad Serena Hotel in his Hummer.

His boss, the Pakistani President, had been very specific about holding the meeting with the American and the Israeli here in Islamabad.

It was around 6 p.m. when the blast occurred. An improvised bomb containing TNT had been placed on the left underside of the vehicle, near the gasoline tank and the rear passenger seat. This had ensured that the gas tank explosion had eliminated all the occupants. The trigger had been via a pager.

Yunus Qazi phoned the President to convey to him the tragic news regarding the death of the three men inside the Hummer.

Maryland, U.S.A., 2012

Vincent had hurriedly punched thirteen several times into the numeric keypad and had watched as the door slid silently open. In front of him was a long tunnel. It had been built out of reinforced concrete on all sides. It was unpainted, but a single cable along the length of the roof supplied power to the hundreds of naked light bulbs that ran endlessly in a straight line.

Ignoring his fatigue, Vincent began jogging towards the end of the tunnel. It was tiring because the tunnel had an upward incline. After about thirty minutes, which seemed like an eternity, Vincent reached a solid whitewashed concrete wall with an equally white door.

On the white background, the following German phrase had been painted: *"Wer war der thor, wer weiser, bettler oder kaiser? Ob arm, ob reich, im tode gleich."* Under it was an English equivalent:

"Who is the fool? Who is the wise? Who is the beggar or king likewise. Wizened fools and beggars on thrones. All underneath are just skull and bones."

The motto of the Bavarian Illuminati, established in 1776. The same year at the base of the pyramid on the one-dollar note. The same year as the start of the final cycle of the Mayan calendar.

Next to the door was another numeric keypad. Above it was a small laminated sign that had the following words very neatly laser-printed:

"Please enter your room number."

Vincent didn't need to do the calculation! He had always wondered what the significance of Room Number 322 of the Skull & Bones society was.

Vincent quickly punched in 3-2-2. It was his lucky day. The door lock clicked and Vincent was able to push it open.

Vincent looked around. He was somewhere in the forested Catoctin Mountain Park along the eastern rampart of the Appalachian Mountains.[cciv] He was standing in a lush verdant forest along one of the mountain slopes.

He turned around to look at the door through which he had exited a few moments earlier. It was virtually impossible to discern. Quite ingeniously hidden away in the slope.

It's probably used by all those lunatics to enter and exit the ceremonial chambers without being observed, thought Vincent as he carefully trudged along to get to the main road and onwards to civilization.

He felt inside his pocket for the photocopy of the Rozabal document that he had managed to secretly keep in spite of the original being snatched away by General Prithviraj Singh in Srinagar. It wasn't there! It had obviously slipped out sometime during his escape.

The Illuminati now had the original as well as the photocopy somewhere on their premises.

As Vincent was walking down one slope, somewhere else, three women were walking up another.

Katra, Jammu, India, 2012

The Trikuta Mountain, where the Vaishno Devi shrine was located, had a single base but three peaks. Hence the name *Tri-kuta*, meaning "three peaks".

The three women were walking up the slope of the mountain toward the place where they would be able to access the holy cave that eventually led to the shrine itself. On an average, 5.4 million devotees would pay homage to the divine Mother Goddess each year, trekking nearly twelve kilometres from the base till they reached the holy shrine at an altitude of 5200 feet.

This particular shrine had no statues. The three heads that were worshipped were a natural rock formation. The uniqueness of this formation was that although emanating from one single rock form, each head was distinctly different from the other two in colour and texture; hence each would be worshipped as a different manifestation of the divine mother.

The three women seemed quite comfortable with each other. Swakilki, Alissa and Martha were on their way to reacquainting themselves with the powers of the divine feminine.

In the centre stood the divine mother in gold. The golden goddess was considered to be the source of wealth and prosperity. She was supposed to enhance the qualities of inspiration and effort in her devotees. Her name was *Lakshmi.*

To the left stood the divine mother in white. The white goddess was considered to be the source of all creation, knowledge, wisdom, righteousness, art, spiritualism, and piousness. Her name was *Saraswati.*

To the right stood the divine mother in black. She represented the quality associated with the darker and unknown realms of life. Since human knowledge about life was rather limited, and given the fact that man continued to remain in the dark about most of it, the black goddess was the basic source of all that was mystical and unknown to man. The black goddess was supposed to guide her devotees in conquering the forces of darkness. Her name was *Kali.*

The Hindus believed that all human beings contained attributes of the three divine mothers and that their behaviour was determined by the attributes that were predominant in their nature. But they also believed that in order to lead a meaningful life, a proper balance among these three was necessary.

This was the significance of the number thirteen. One supreme being and three manifestations. The holy trinity.

Lakshmi Saraswati Kali.
La Sara Kali.

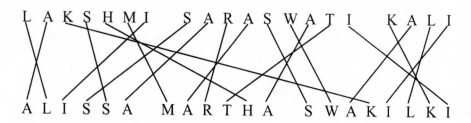

Not just an anagram, but three manifestations of the divine feminine.

New York, 2012

Vincent was on a flight back to New York when he remembered the most important words from the Gospel of Jesus:

And when you emerge and see the trees. Please do consider what will make you free.

How many fish? One-Five-Three. How many disciples? Four by Three. How many angels? Four plus three. Thirteen Cycles. One and Three. The Mayan called it the Sacred Tree. I just call it the Sacred Three.

Brahma, Vishnu and Shiva are Three. Lakshmi, Kali and Saraswati. The third eye that the Hindus see. The lines of a triangle in trinity.

Christian, Muslim, Illuminati. The first two fight, the third waits to see. How much destruction can there possibly be?

That was when the Shekel dropped!

Jesus and Mary had three daughters, not one!

Mary Magdalene herself had powers from the three manifestations of the divine goddess. Lakshmi, Saraswati and Kali.

And when they had reached France, they had become La Sara Kali.

There were three bloodlines, not one!

Then he remembered the visions from his projection with Martha in Goa:

'Where are you now?'

'Yerushalem.'

'And what do you see around you?'

'Temple fires. It's night. I can see Caiaphas and the Sanhedrin assembled, judging Jesus. They are irritable because no reliable witnesses are coming forth with evidence against Jesus.'

'Anyone familiar from your present life?'

'Thomas Manning.'

'Who is he?'

'He is Caiaphas - poisoning the minds of those assembled against Jesus. In this life too, he continues to seek vengeance.'

'Anyone else?'

'The Japanese woman who kidnapped me. Swakilki. She's present. She wants to kill Jesus.'

'Anyone else?'

'You, Nana!'

'What am I doing?'

'Taking care of Jesus. Healing him. Applying medicines and herbs.'

'Anyone else there?'

'A third woman. I don't know her.'

'Now what is happening?'

'I can see Jesus and the three women walking towards Damascus ...I can only see their backs.'

Vincent realized how foolish he had been! He had seen Mary Magdalene in all her three manifestations.

The creator, the nurturer, the destroyer.

After all, she was the divine feminine.

Les Saintes-Maries-de-la-Mer, France, 42 A.D.

In the town of Les Saintes-Maries-de-la-Mer in France, each May 23rd-25th continued to be celebrated in honour of Saint Sarah, also known as La Sara Kali.

The festival had its roots in an event that had occurred here in 42 A.D. A boat had arrived carrying Mary Magdalene along with three daughters, Lakshmi, Sara and Kali.

Mary's sacred powers had been derived from the divine mother who would be worshipped on *Navratri*, the festival of nine nights.

On the first three days, the supreme feminine would be worshipped as the nurturer and the provider of spiritual and material wealth, Lakshmi. The next three days would be spent worshipping the divine feminine as Saraswati, the goddess of wisdom. Finally, the divine mother would be worshipped as the force of destruction, Kali.

Over the next 2000 years, the powers of the divine feminine would continue to be handed down from mother to daughter in an unbroken chain. Till these powers reached three women: Martha Morgan, Swakilki Ogawa and Alissa Elliot.

Each had continued to manifest the most important traits of the divine mother.

Martha Morgan had spent years studying meditation, yoga and spirituality. She was the repository of knowledge. *Saraswati.*

Alissa Elliot had used every opportunity to further her political and financial ambitions. She had reached the pinnacle of power and wealth. *Lakshmi.*

Swakilki Ogawa had become the deadly assassin; killing and destroying again and again. *Kali.*

They were the Rozabal line.

***

Katra, Jammu, India, 2012

The three women emerged from the temple and walked out into the sunlight.

'I do not understand why you had to kill so many people,' Martha said to Swakilki. 'I kept looking at you again and again each time that we would bump into each other - in London, in Mumbai, in Goa. I was trying to tell you to slow down.'

'And I cannot understand why she terrorized the entire world to further her powers,' said Swakilki, pointing at Alissa. 'You even dated her future husband, Stephen, while you were working along with Terry Acton at the SAGB. Did he ever tell you how ambitious she was?'

'Let us not argue,' said Alissa. 'I do not wish to draw attention to us. I am supposed to have died and have been buried in Virginia. I wonder who has been placed inside the casket. In any case, what about Martha dear? For years she never let anyone know the level of spiritual knowledge that she had attained. Poor Vincent would keep debating theology with her, completely oblivious of his aunt's awesome powers.'

'You are right,' said Martha. 'Why do men continue to think that their power emanates from the Father, Son and Holy Ghost, when it is the divine mother who pretty much decides everything.'

Swakilki spoke up. 'I know that I shall take many births before I can pay off the debts of my sins. But I also know that if it were not me doing what I did, it would have been someone else. When will we understand that the Karmic cycle goes on and on endlessly?'

'And when will we realize that good-bad, hot-cold, positive-negative, white-black, love-hate, man-woman and so many other facets of life are merely manifestations of the same divine?' said Alissa.

'Man continues to believe that Jesus was descended from the line of Abraham,' said Martha.

And then Swakilki spoke up, 'When will they realize that if you take the "A" out of Abraham and put it at the end, you have the true lineage of Jesus - Brahama, the creator, the endless, the infinite? The one into whom all souls must eventually rise and merge. That is the true resurrection.'

Notes, Acknowledgements, References

[i] The Rozabal Tomb does exist. See *Jesus Lived in India: His Unknown Life Before and After the Crucifixion* by Holger Kersten, Penguin Books, 2001.

[ii] The Lashkar-e-Toiba does exist. The Lashkar-e-Talatashar is fictional.

[iii] Inspired by speeches of Osama-bin-Laden, although not attributed to him. See *Messages to the World: The Statements of Osama-bin-Laden*, edited by Bruce Lawrence, translated by James Howarth, Verso, 2005

[iv] The words used in both English and Latin for confession have been taken from an online article on the subject located at http://en.wikipedia.org/wiki/Confession

[v] Bank Leu is indeed the oldest Swiss Bank in the world. The character of Egloff, however, is fictional.

[vi] The character Dmitriy Novikov is fictional. However, his achievements are based upon the real-life figure of Nicolas Notovitch, the 19th century explorer/researcher, who wrote *The Unknown Life of Jesus Christ*, Leaves of Healing Publications, 1990.

[vii] The conversations between the Lama and Dmitriy Novikov are substantially taken from the real conversations that are recounted by Holger Kersten in his book *Jesus Lived in India*.

[viii] As recounted in *Jesus Lived in India: His Unknown Life Before and After the Crucifixion* by Holger Kersten, Penguin Books, 2001

[ix] Much of the Islamic rituals and customs are taken from *The Absolute Essentials of Islam* by Faraz Rabbani, White Thread Press.

[x] Taken from an online article by Shachi Rairikar at http://www.organiser.org/ dynamic/modules.php?name=Content&pa=showpage&pid=69&page=17

[xi] See *Ghost Wars: The Secret History of the CIA, Afghanistan, and Bin Laden, from the Soviet Invasion to September 10th, 2001*, by Steve Coll, Penguin, 2004

[xii] See *Tantra: Path of Ecstacy* by Georg Feuerstein, Shambhala, 1998

[xiii] Asahara Shoko is fact. A very well-written online biography is available at http://religiousmovements.lib.virginia.edu/nrms/aums.html. Takuya is fictional.

[xiv] http://en.wikipedia.org/wiki/Yigal_Amir

[xv] A great deal of information was derived on this subject from *The Jesus Papers* by Michael Baigent, Harper, 2006

[xvi] While Opus Dei and The Priestly Society of the Holy Cross are real in every sense, the Crux Decussata Permuta is purely fictional.

[xvii] Throughout this book, I have utilized travel information such as flight numbers, arrival and departure information etc. The process of getting this information was effortless because of www.travelocity.com

[xviii] A wealth of information about the Archdiocese of New York, the seminaries, and the cardinals is available online at their official website http://www.archny.org/

[xix] I have extensively used the online bible resources provided at http://www.biblegateway.com/

[xx] The entire joke was taken from http://www.positiveatheism.org/writ/drlaura.htm

[xxi] A great deal of information on the White House, historical and biographical information on American Presidents etc. was obtained on http://www.whitehouse.gov/history/presidents/al16.html

[xxii] http://www.forgotten-ny.com/CEMETERIES/Hidden%20cemeteries/hidcem.html

[xxiii] See *The Light on Pranayama: The Yogic Art of Breathing*, by B.K.S. Iyengar, Crossroad General Interest, 1985.

[xxiv] See *The Art of Living: Vipassana Meditation: As Taught by S. N. Goenka*, by William Hart, Harper San Francisco, 1987

[xxv] I found excellent discussions on the issue of reincarnation theory in Christianity online at http://www.comparativereligion.com/reincarnation3.html

[xxvi] http://www.britannica.com/ebc/article-9372767

[xxvii] A wonderful history of the East End of London and Lesney's Matchbox Factory is to be had at http://www.eastlondonhistory.com/lesney.htm

[xxviii] See *Cecil Rhodes* by Sarah Gertrude Millin, Simon Publications, 2001

[xxix] See *America's Secret Establishment: An Introduction to the Order of Skull & Bones* by Antony C. Sutton, published by Trine Day.

[xxx] See http://www.conspiracyarchive.com/NWO/Illuminati.htm

[xxxi] The Spiritualist Association of Great Britain does exist. The Association has an online presence at http://www.sagb.org.uk/

[xxxii] See *Many Lives, Many Masters: The True Story of a Prominent Psychiatrist, His Young Patient, and the Past Life Therapy That Changed Both Their Lives* by Dr. Brian Weiss, published by Warner Books.

[xxxiii] I used several sources to build a "hypnosis script" but an excellent one was available online at http://hypnoticworld.com/scripts/problem_rsolution.asp

[xxxiv] See http://www.brown.edu/Administration/Chaplains/Communities/Descriptions/hinduism.html

[xxxv] See *Karma and Reincarnation: The Wisdom of Yogananda, Volume 2* by Paramhansa Yoganada, published by Crystal Clarity Publishers

[xxxvi] A good commentary on the guilt felt by modern Christians with regard to past life therapy and issues of reincarnation has been written by Dr. Michael G Millett and is available online at http://www.elevated.fsnet.co.uk/index-page14.html

[xxxvii] Tibetan phrases taken from http://www.geocities.com/Athens/Academy/9594/tibet.html

[xxxviii] For a detailed account of the historical search for the Dalai Lama, you may visit http://www.tibet.com/DL/discovery.html

[xxxix] Detailed astrological and astronomical issues around the birth of Jesus have been taken from http://www.math.nus.edu.sg/aslaksen/gem-projects/hm/0203-1-18-bethlehem.pdf

[xl] See http://www.channel4.com/history/microsites/H/history/e-h/herod01.html

[xli] The itinerary of the holy family when they left Bethlehem can be found at http://weekly.ahram.org.eg/2005/724/tr6.htm

[xlii] See an interesting article on the origins of ritual immersion in water by Prof. M. M. Ninan located at http://www.acns.com/~mm9n/Baptism/601.htm

[xliii] Asoka. Encyclopædia Britannica. 2007. Encyclopædia Britannica Online. 17th June 2007 <http://www.britannica.com/eb/article-9009884>.

[xliv] Ptolemy II is mentioned in the Edicts of Ashoka as a recipient of the Buddhist proselytism of Ashoka, although no Western historical record of this event remain. See http://en.wikipedia.org/wiki/Ptolemy_II_Philadelphus

[xlv] See http://en.wikipedia.org/wiki/Baudhayana. "The most notable of the rules in the Baudhayana Sulba Sutra says: dirghasyaksanaya rajjuh parsvamani, tiryadam mani, cha yatprthagbhute kurutastadubhayan karoti i.e. A rope stretched along the length of the diagonal produces an area which the vertical and horizontal sides make together. If this refers to a rectangle, it is the earliest recorded statement of the Pythagorean theorem."

[xlvi] See *Pythagoras and the Story Behind the Croton Crown*, by Adi Kanga & Sam Kerr. It can be found online at http://www.vohuman.org/Article/Pythagoras%20and%20the%20story%20behind%20the%20Croton%20Crown.htm

xlvii *From Chrishna to Christ* by Raymond Bernard, Published by Health Research, 1961

xlviii British Library, Online Gallery of Sacred Texts, http://www.bl.uk/onlinegallery/sacredtexts/deadseascrolls.html

xlix *The Complete World of the Dead Sea Scrolls* by Philip R. Davies, Published by Thames & Hudson, 2002

l *The Gnostic Discoveries: The Impact of the Nag Hammadi Library* by Marvin Meyer, Harper San Francisco, 2006

li *The Refutation of All Heresies, Book One* by Antipope Hippolytus, Kessinger Publishing, 2004

lii *Saving the Savior: Did Christ Survive the Crucifixion?* by Abubakr Ben Ishmael Salahuddin, Tree of Life Publications, 2001

liii See http://en.wikipedia.org/wiki/Gondophares

liv See http://www.indianchristianity.com/html/chap4/chapter4c.htm which says: "Different reports of this tradition have come down to us. The earliest is recorded by Marco Polo, and that of Bishop John de Marignolli comes next. We reproduce them from Yule's Marco Polo, 2nd ed., and his Cathay and the Way Thither. Marco Polo (ut supr., vol.ii.p.340): 'Now I will tell you the manner in which the Christian brethren who keep the church relate the story of the Saint's death. They tell the Saint was in the wood outside his hermitage saying his prayers, and round about him were many peacocks, for these are more plentiful in that country than anywhere else. And one of the idolaters of that country being of the lineage of those called Govi that I told you of, having gone with his bow and arrows to shoot peafowl, not seeing the Saint, let fly an arrow at one of the peacocks; and this arrow struck the holy man on the right side, insomuch that he died of the wound, sweetly addressing himself to his creator. Before he came to that place where he thus died, he had been in Nubia, where he converted much people to the faith of Jesus Christ.'"

lv See http://www.sol.com.au/kor/7_01.htm which says: "Further clues are cited from The Apocryphal Acts of Thomas, and the Gospel of Thomas which are of Syrian origin and have been dated to the 4th Century AD, or possibly earlier. They are Gnostic Scriptures and despite the evidence indicating their authenticity, they are not given credence by mainstream theologians. In these texts Thomas tells of Christ's appearance in Andrapolis, Paphlagonia (today known as in the extreme north of Anatolia) as a guest of the King of Andrappa. There he met with Thomas who had arrived separately. It is at Andrapolis that Christ entreated Thomas to go to India to begin spreading his teachings."

lvi See a contemporary news item online regarding Balakote at http://jammu-kashmir.com/archives/archives2002/kashmir20020615a.html

[lvii] I found an excellent source for Qu'ran research at http://quod.lib.umich.edu/k/koran/ an electronic version of The Holy Qur'an, translated by M.H. Shakir and published by Tahrike Tarsile Qur'an, Inc., in 1983. Most references in my book regarding the Qu'ran are taken from here.

[lviii] http://en.wikipedia.org/wiki/Sermon_on_the_Mount

[lix] See the Kashmir Information Directory at http://www.samawar.com/content/view/7/20/

[lx] See http://www.plantnames.unimelb.edu.au/Sorting/Nardostachys.html

[lxi] See the history of Buckingham Palace at *Royal Residences* located online at http://www.royal.gov.uk/OutPut/Page568.asp

[lxii] Actually the Royal College of Psyhiatrists is located at No.17, not No.18, Belgrave Square. Also, the last tenant before the college was Lady Leontine Sassoon, not Lady Clementine Sossoon. Actual history about No. 17 Belgrave Square is located on the College's website at http://www.rcpsych.ac.uk/college/archives/history/historyofbelgravesquare.aspx

[lxiii] The Vipassana Research Institute, see http://www.vri.dhamma.org/

[lxiv] The Lord's Prayer in Aramaic was taken from http://www.godswillministries.com/prayers.html

[lxv] A description of what Jerusalem looked like during the time period of Jesus was obtained from an excellent article in Time magazine. It can be accessed online at http://www.time.com/time/2001/jerusalem/cover.html

[lxvi] For sake of efficiency, I extensively used Babel Fish's online translation service and found it to be excellent. I cannot be certain of the accuracy of the final translations and if there are any errors, I crave forgiveness. The Babel Fish translator can be used online at http://babelfish.altavista.com/tr

[lxvii] See the BBC story on this scientific discovery at http://news.bbc.co.uk/1/hi/health/3929471.stm

[lxviii] See Sloan-Kettering's website to find out about the scientific properties of Myrrh. Go to http://www.mskcc.org/mskcc/html/69309.cfm

[lxix] See http://www.beercook.com/prochefs/markdorber.htm

[lxx] Please see http://www.tombofjesus.com/indonesian/core/majorplayers/crucifixion/crucifixion-p2.htm

[lxxi] *Black Potatoes: The Story of the Great Irish Famine, 1845-1850* by Susan Campbell Bartoletti, published by Houghton Mifflin, 2005

lxxii http://www.forgotten-ny.com/STREET%20SCENES/middlevillage/
middlevillage.html

lxxiii http://members.virtualtourist.com/m/b6eb4/a8f71/ for a history of Einsiedeln

lxxiv http://www.hps.com/~tpg/ukdict/ukdict-8.html

lxxv For further reading regarding the Guilootine and the French Revolution visit Jørn
Fabricius' excellent site at http://www.guillotine.dk

lxxvi Based loosely on the historical Marie Anne Charlotte de Corday D'Armant who
was beheaded in 1793 at the guillotine for having murdered Jean-Paul Marat.

lxxvii Excellent background information on the Inca empire at http://en.wikipedia.org/
wiki/Sapa_Inca

lxxviii Background information on the historical figure of Wu Zhao can be accessed at
http://www.womenofchina.cn/people/women_in_history/3594.jsp

lxxix A full chronology of Jesus' actions post-crucifixion were taken from
http://www.westarinstitute.org/Periodicals/4R_Articles/Easter/Chronology/chronolo
gy.html

lxxx See *The Meaning of Shinto* by J.W.T. Mason, Trafford Publishing, 2006

lxxxi See website of the International Center for Reiki Training at
http://www.reiki.org/

lxxxii See *Muhammad: A Biography of the Prophet* by Karen Armstrong, published by
Harper San Francisco, 1993

lxxxiii See a paper entitled *Jesus in Islam* by the Islamic Centre of Rochester at
http://theicr.org/Jesus%20in%20Islam.pdf

lxxxiv See *Irenaeus Against Heresies* by Irenaeus, Kessinger Publishing, 2004

lxxxv See details of this recorded encounter at
http://www.tombofjesus.com/core/majorplayers/the-tomb/the-tomb-p3.htm

lxxxvi See *Jesus In India: Being An Account Of Jesus' Escape From Death On The
Cross And His Journey To India* by Hazrat Mirza Ghulam Ahmad, published by
Fredonia Books, 2004

lxxxvii Actual BBC report can be read at http://news.bbc.co.uk/2/hi/south_asia/
4400957.stm

lxxxviii See *A Long and Uncertain Journey: The 27,000 Mile Voyage of Vasco Da
Gama* by Joan Elizabeth Goodman, published by Mikaya Press, 2001

lxxxix http://www.keralachurch.com/main_left_right.php?cmd=keralachristianity

[xc] See *The Goa Inquisition: Being a Quarter Centenary Commemoration Study of the Inquisition of India* by Anant Kakba Priolkar, South Asia Books

[xci] http://www.christianaggression.org/item_display.php?type=ARTICLES&id= 1111142225

[xcii] http://www.newadvent.org/cathen/04610a.htm

[xciii] There is no book called the Tarikh-Issa-Masih. There is reference at http://www.tombofjesus.com/core/majorplayers/the-tomb/the-tomb-p7.htm#marriageandchildren to an old "Persian work entitled the Negaris-Tan-i-Kashmir, in which an account of Jesus' marriage is contained. We will continue trying to get hold of it, and the reader can check from time to time at the website to see if that document has been obtained… We have contacted various people, attempting to get hold of this work, including the English translation of the relevant portions. This might be a difficult task, but we are determined to put every effort into securing it. In the meantime, we reproduce below an excerpt from Andreas Faber Kaiser's, Jesus Died in Kashmir, in which Kaiser relates a conversation he had with Mr. Basharat Saleem, a man who claims to be a living descendant of Jesus Christ: 'He told me that to his knowledge the only written source on this subject [of Jesus' marriage] was the Negaris-Tan-i-Kashmir, an old Persian book that had been translated into Urdu, and that relates that King Shalewahin (the same king as met and conversed with Jesus in the mountains) told Jesus that he needed a woman to take care of him, and offered him his choice of fifty. Jesus replied that he did not need any and that no one was obliged to work for him, but the king persisted until Jesus agreed to employ a woman to cook for him, look after his house and do his washing. Professor Hassnain told me that the woman's name was Maryan, and that the same book says that she bore Jesus children.'"

[xciv] "God give me strength to save this book" in Portuguese.

[xcv] See *Was Jesus a Buddhist?* at http://www.thezensite.com/non_Zen/Was_Jesus_ Buddhist.html

[xcvi] See *The Security Organs of the Russian Federation* at http://www.psan.org/ document551.html

[xcvii] Lossely based on real-life FBI agent Robert Hanssen who spied for the Russians at the behest of Opus Dei. See http://www.foxnews.com/story/0,2933,27409,00.html

[xcviii] Dr. Dawood Omar's character is based lossely on A. Q. Khan, the founder of Pakistan's nuclear program. He actually did attend the University of Leuven. See profile at http://www.ias-worldwide.org/profiles/prof85.htm

[xcix] See *WMD Insights* on Pakistan's Nuclear Program and the arrest of A. Q. Khan at http://www.wmdinsights.com/I3/G1_SR_AQK_Network.htm

^c Read the actual Washington Quarterly article at http://www.twq.com/05spring/docs/05spring_albright.pdf

^{ci} Detailed description of Salah taken from http://www.islamawareness.net/Salah/

^{cii} See *Saladin: a Benevolent Man, Respected by both Muslims & Christians* by the Institute of Arabic & Islamic Studies at http://www.islamic-study.org/Saladin%20(Salahu%20ad-Deen).htm

^{ciii} Taken from an actual CNN story. See http://www.cnn.com/2005/WORLD/europe/04/19/pope.tuesday/index.html

^{civ} Read the actual article at http://www.benadorassociates.com/article/13899

^{cv} See http://www.pipavav.com/a_in.html

^{cvi} See *A Failure of Imagination (Intelligence, WMDs, and "Virtual Jihad")* by Scott Atran, Centre National de la Recherche Scientifique, Paris, France and The University of Michigan, Ann Arbor located at http://www.sitemaker.umich.edu/satran/files/atran-sct-0406.pdf

^{cvii} See *Nostradamus: The Complete Prophecies* by John Hogue, published by Element Books, 1997

^{cviii} Read Time Magazine's article on the French Intifada at http://www.time.com/time/world/article/0,8599,1127429,00.html

^{cix} See http://warfare2050.blogspot.com/2007/04/warfare-2050-dictionary-la-triple.html

^{cx} Centre for Defense Information, http://www.cdi.org/terrorism/etim.cfm

^{cxi} Uighur phrase "Perfect!"

^{cxii} See http://www.globalsecurity.org/military/world/para/ji.htm

^{cxiii} http://www.globalsecurity.org/security/profiles/jaish-e-mohammed.htm

^{cxiv} All planetary positions calculated on http://www.ephemeris.com/ephemeris.php

^{cxv} Character loosely based on Abu Musab Al-Zarqawi. See http://www.globalresearch.ca/articles/CHO405B.html

^{cxvi} Arabic- "son of a bitch!"

^{cxvii} http://www.jihadwatch.org/archives/004849.php

^{cxviii} Character loosely based on Abu Bakar Bashir, the actual founder of Jemaah Islamiyah. Profile of JI from Council on Foreign Relations at http://www.cfr.org/publication/8948/

^{cxix} http://www.dfat.gov.au/facts/muslims_in_australia.html

[cxx] Character loosely based on Shamil Basayev, Chechen warlord. See information at http://topics.nytimes.com/top/reference/timestopics/people/b/shamil_basayev/index.html

[cxxi] http://www.socialpages.com.pk/137/art.asp

[cxxii] Durand Line. (2007). In Encyclopædia Britannica. Retrieved June 23rd, 2007, from Encyclopædia Britannica Online: http://www.britannica.com/eb/article-9031550

[cxxiii] See *The How & Why of the Mayan End Date in 2012 A.D.* by John Major Jenkins at http://www.levity.com/eschaton/Why2012.html

[cxxiv] http://www.specialoperations.com/Domestic/CIA/SAS/Default.html

[cxxv] Inspired by the real-life character of Jagjit Uppal, a word-famous astrologer who practices his art at the Taj Mahal Hotel in Mumbai. His bio can be read at http://jagjituppal.com/new/profile.html

[cxxvi] All astrological predictions utilized in this book were provided by astrologer extraordinaire, Manju Sanghi.

[cxxvii] The tour itinerary and material are taken from Benny Kurien's actual tour of Kerala. Read the information at http://www.earthfoot.org/p2/in013.htm

[cxxviii] See *Jesus died in Kashmir: Jesus, Moses and the ten lost tribes of Israel* by Andreas Faber Kaiser, published by Gordon & Cremonesi, 1977

[cxxix] Bahrdt, Carl Friedrich. (2007). In Encyclopædia Britannica. Retrieved from Encyclopædia Britannica Online: http://www.britannica.com/eb/article-9011796

[cxxx] See *Swoon Hypothesis* at http://www.answers.com/topic/swoon-hypothesis

[cxxxi] The relevant passages of the Nathanamavali can be accessed at Atma Jyoti Ashram's website http://www.atmajyoti.org/sw_unknown_life.asp

[cxxxii] *Guardian of the Dawn* by Richard Zimler, published by Delta, 2005

[cxxxiii] Richard Zimler's interview by Rediff.com is located at http://in.rediff.com/news/2005/sep/14inter1.htm

[cxxxiv] http://www.answering-islam.de/Main/Intro/islamic_jesus.html

[cxxxv] See *The Book of Revelation (The Smart Guide to the Bible Series)* by Daymond R. Duck and Larry Richards, published by Thomas Nelson, 2006

[cxxxvi] http://www.chamonet.com/faq.php?id_faq_type=43

[cxxxvii] http://www.powerlabs.org/chemlabs/deflagrants.htm

cxxxviii Background information on the Three Gorges dam taken from
http://en.wikipedia.org/wiki/Three_Gorges_Dam

cxxxix See http://www.acfnewsource.org/science/bomb_prevention.html

cxl See *Great Buildings Online* at http://www.greatbuildings.com/buildings/Petronas_
Towers.html

cxli http://www.textually.org/textually/archives/cat_cell_phones_used_by_terrorists.htm

cxlii See Shri Mata Vaishno Devi Shrine Board's website at
http://www.maavaishnodevi.org/

cxliii http://www.globalsecurity.org/military/world/iraq/baghdad-monuments.htm

cxliv http://www.armageddononline.org/content/view/25/49/

cxlv See details of Bung Karno Stadium at http://www.worldstadiums.com/stadium_
menu/stadium_list/100000.shtml

cxlvi http://www.pbs.org/wgbh/nova/bioterror/agen_anthrax.html

cxlvii http://news.nationalgeographic.com/news/2004/11/1130_041130_locusts.html

cxlviii http://www.goacom.org/overseas-digest/Religion/Christianity&Europe/church-
crusades,colonial%20backing&no-salvation-outside-church.html

cxlix Information on Indian Intelligence agencies at http://www.fas.org/irp/world/
india/raw/index.html

cl Information on the exploits of Mossad taken from http://www.answers.com/topic/
mossad

cli For more information on Mary's purported burial site see an article *Mai Mari da
Asthan* by Mohamed Elmasry at http://www.despardes.com/articles/deco5/121305-
virgin-mary-elmasry.asp

clii See *The Fifth Gospel: New Evidence from the Tibetan, Sanskrit, Arabic, Persian
and Urdu Sources About the Historical Life of Jesus Christ After the Crucifixion* by
Fida Hassnain and Dahan Levi, Ahtisham Fida, published by Blue Dolphin, 2006

cliii A wealth of etymological information on various English and Arabic names was
taken from http://www.behindthename.com/

cliv "From the Shrimad-Bhagavatam we learn that Lord Krishna appeared on earth
when the Moon was in the constellation of Rohini (Aldebaran) and the eighth lunar
day of the dark fortnight (krishna-ashtami) one hundred and twenty five years before
the advent of the Age of Kali (which begun on Feb 18th 3102 BC which comes out
to July 12th-13th 3127 BC)" according to Glenn Smith at

http://www.swaveda.com/articles.php?mnthyr=&action=show&id=59&comment=Comment&PHPSESSID=62d5c9a1147aa21f70e24b089dbc1fee

[clv] See *The Berzin Archives* at http://www.berzinarchives.com/web/en/archives/approaching_buddhism/teachers/lineage_masters/life_shakyamuni_buddha.html

[clvi] See *Wilson's Almanac on gods and men with similarities to Jesus* at http://www.wilsonsalmanac.com/jesus_similar.html

[clvii] See *The World's Sixteen Crucified Saviors* at http://www.infidels.org/library/historical/kersey_graves/16/

[clviii] See article *Born of a Virgin on December 25th: Horus, Sun God of Egypt* by S. Acharya at http://www.truthbeknown.com/horus.html

[clix] See *Daughters of the Inquisition: Medieval Madness: Origins and Aftermaths* by Christina Crawford, published by Seven Springs, 2003

[clx] See *Who was the real Jesus?* by David Pratt at http://ourworld.compuserve.com/homepages/dp5/jesus.htm

[clxi] http://www.answers.com/topic/john-the-baptist

[clxii] http://www.hinduismtoday.com/archives/2004/1-3/36-37_lore.shtml

[clxiii] See *The Woman with the Alabaster Jar: Mary Magdalen and the Holy Grail* by Margaret Starbird, published by Bear & Co., 1993

[clxiv] See *The Christ Conspiracy: The Marriage of Jesus* by Rhawn Joseph, at http://brainmind.com/MarriageOfJesusChristConspir.pdf

[clxv] http://altreligion.about.com/library/graphics/bl_smarymagdalen.htm

[clxvi] See *The Templar Revelation: Secret Guardians of the True Identity of Christ* by Lynn Picknett and Clive Prince, published by Touchstone, 1998

[clxvii] http://www.roman-empire.net/decline/constantine-index.html

[clxviii] See *Pope Arrested for Believing in Reincarnation* at http://reluctant-messenger.com/reincarnation-pope.htm

[clxix] *Origen De Principiis* by Origen, published by Kessinger Publishing, 2004

[clxx] See http://www.shroud.com/menu.htm

[clxxi] See *The Jesus Conspiracy: The Turin Shroud and the Truth About Resurrection* by Holger Kersten and Elmar R. Gruber, Element Books, 1994

[clxxii] http://www.answers.com/topic/bhrigu-samhita

[clxxiii] Japanese for "Do you believe in destiny?"

clxxiv If one accepts Margaret Starbird's notion of Hieros Gamos i.e. in older sacred marriage rituals, a woman who represented the goddess and the land was wedded to the king. Some of these old ceremonies included a ritualistic slaying of the king, either symbolically or literally, after he was married to the priestess-goddess. In the symbolic slayings, he would then rise again in a mystical resurrection echoing the cycles of death and rebirth evident in nature. To that extent, it would be perfectly legitimate for Mary Magdalene to be "killing" Jesus.

clxxv See http://www.eurekalert.org/features/doe/2004-09/ddoe-rdo091604.php

clxxvi Loosely based on Khalid Sheikh Mohammed, the Al Qaeda kingpin arrested in Rawalpindi. See story at http://timesofindia.indiatimes.com/articleshow/1205101.cms

clxxvii http://www.whitehouse.gov/history/facts.html

clxxviii Inspired by an actual interview given by George W. Bush to BBC HardTalk's Stephen Sackur.

clxxix Edited version of an original story by Norm Dixon that first appeared in the Green Left Weekly. The full article can be accessed at http://www.conspiracyarchive.com/NWO/CIA_Created_Osama.htm

clxxx http://en.wikipedia.org/wiki/Islamabad

clxxxi Culled from http://www.usatoday.com/news/graphics/9_11sequenceofevents/flash.htm

clxxxii See *Same Soul, Many Bodies: Discover the Healing Power of Future Lives through Progression Therapy* by By M.D. Brian L. Weiss, published by Simon & Schuster, 2005

clxxxiii The oldest church in the world has actually been discovered at the site. See http://www.haaretz.com/hasen/pages/ShArt.jhtml?itemNo=641806&contrassID=2&subContrassID=15&sbSubContrassID=0&listSrc=Y

clxxxiv Arabic "You! What are you doing? Think what this will do to the world."

clxxxv Script taken from http://conspiracycentral.info/index.php?showforum=11

clxxxvi See http://www.scielo.br/pdf/bjp/v33n2/a07v33n2.pdf

clxxxvii All radiation data taken from http://www.hc-sc.gc.ca/ewh-semt/alt_formats/hecs-sesc/pdf/pubs/water-eau/doc-sup-appui/radiological_characteristics/radiological-radiologiques_e.pdf

clxxxviii http://www.yukos.com/EP/Priobskoe_Oil_Field.asp

clxxxix The verses are fictitious and have been composed by the author.

[cxc] I took the help of a very convenient calculator at http://mistupid.com/computers/binaryconv.htm

[cxci] See *A Manual of Hadith* by Muhammad Ali, published by Ahmaddiyya Anjuman Ishaat, 1990

[cxcii] Information on Tihar Jail taken from http://tiharprisons.nic.in/html/infra.htm

[cxciii] See http://www.answers.com/topic/saint-sarah

[cxciv] See news article in Christian Century at http://findarticles.com/p/articles/mi_m1058/is_24_122/ai_n15923405

[cxcv] Maghada, see http://www.everything2.com/index.pl?node=Magadha

[cxcvi] Samuel is fiction but William is not. He was the founder of Skull & Bones. More about him at http://www.theforbiddenknowledge.com/hardtruth/the_russell_bloodline.htm

[cxcvii] This is speculation that some conversions must have happened. See http://users.rcn.com/jonathan02/muslimhistory.pdf for a brief note on conversion to Islam being a common practice in Islamic conquests.

[cxcviii] I was inspired by by the novel *Messiah* by Boris Starling in which a serial killer finds victims and kills them in exactly the same manner as the apostles died. You will notice, however, that there is a huge difference in the details.

[cxcix] I found an excellent summary on "The Apostles and Historical Figures of the Church" at http://www.imt.net/~gedison/apostle.html

[cc] Also see http://www.christianhomesite.com/cherryvale/text/apostles.htm, http://www.gotquestions.org/apostles-die.html, http://www.direct.ca/trinity/disciples.html, http://www.ccel.org/bible/phillips/CN500APOSTLES%20FATE.htm, http://www.shrinesf.org/apostles.htm

[cci] Read about the Illuminati influences on the American One Dollar Bill in an interesting article *Satan on our Dollar* at http://www.jesus-is-savior.com/Evils%20in%20Government/Federal%20Reserve%20Scam/satan_on_our_dollar.htm

[ccii] Properties of Compound 1080 taken from http://www.dpiw.tas.gov.au/inter.nsf/WebPages/RPIO-4ZM7CX?open

[cciii] See http://www.globalsecurity.org/intell/world/pakistan/isi.htm

[cciv] http://usparks.about.com/od/lodging/l/blcatoctinother.htm

About the Author

The name "Shawn Haigins" is a pseudonym. In fact, it is an anagram of the author's real name.

A businessman by profession, Shawn writes extensively on history, religion, and politics in his spare time. This book is Shawn's first attempt at fiction.

Shawn is currently working on a second novel, as yet untitled. Besides this, he is also writing a non-fiction book on the history of religions.

Shawn holds a master's degree from Yale and lives in India with his wife and son.

Printed in the United States
117449LV00003B/112-114/A